GREAT STORIES
Remembered
III

FOCUS ON THE FAMILY
presents

GREAT STORIES
Remembered
III

compiled and edited by
JOE L. WHEELER

TYNDALE
Tyndale House Publishers, Wheaton, Illinois

GREAT STORIES REMEMBERED III

Copyright © 2000 by Joe L. Wheeler
All rights reserved. International copyright secured.

ISBN: 1-56179-835-5

A Focus on the Family book published by Tyndale House Publishers, Wheaton, Illinois.

No part of this publication may be reproduced, stored in a retrieval system, or transmitted in any form or by any means—electronic, mechanical, photocopy, recording, or otherwise—without prior permission of the publisher.

Woodcut illustrations from the library of Joe L. Wheeler

Joe Wheeler is represented by the literary agency of Alive Communications, 7680 Goddard Street, Suite 200, Colorado Springs, Colorado 80920.

Editor: Michele A. Kendall
Cover Illustration: Christi Baughman
Cover Design: Brad Lind and Candi Park D'Agnese

Printed in the United States of America

00 01 02 03 04 05/10 9 8 7 6 5 4 3 2 1

Table of Contents

Introduction

The Dream Machine
Joseph Leininger Wheeler

Each of us longs to be creative—to be a celebrated artist, a renowned novelist, a world-famous scientist or inventor. The list goes on and on. That is what we *wish*—but what many of us *do* is entirely different. Few of us are willing to put in the time and effort needed for creative people to become successful. Two words more and more describe our time: *instant gratification.* We want it *all*, and we want it *now.* Worst of all, we are less and less a creative people: We can only clone someone else's ideas and insights. Where did we go wrong? To find the answers, we will have to take a few side-trips, along the way reevaluating this thing we call "creativity." What follows would not have been possible had I not spent thirty years of my life studying the impact of television on our lives, the result being my book *Remote Controlled* (Hagerstown, Md.: Review and Herald Publishing Association, 1993). Much of what I say in the following pages is based on the prodigious research that made that book a reality.

For our first side-trip, I'd like to share a revealing anecdote with you. Shortly after *Remote Controlled* was published, a lady came up to me and said, "Dr. Wheeler, I just *have* to share an experience with you!"

The story had to do with a civic activity for which her family orchestra (two parents and five children) had been asked to provide background music. They performed for five hours without repeating a piece.

Afterward, someone came up to the woman and said, "You don't have a television set in your home, do you?"

Flabbergasted, she replied, "Well, as a matter of fact, we don't. But how did you know?"

The answer floored her. "Because if you did, your children wouldn't be able to play like this."

The Road to the Truth

What possible connection is there between truth and creativity and personal growth? Let's find out.

Misplaced priorities—that is America at the dawn of the new millennium. As a people, we have become masters of trivia and ignoramuses of substance. Listen to most quiz shows and you will note that rarely are the questions about meaningful subjects, such as history, literature, art, architecture, biography, science, philosophy, or religion; instead of focusing on the cultural pillars undergirding our civilization, emphasis is placed on popular culture. Aldous Huxley's *Brave New World* has finally arrived. His World Controller would gloat over a society that substitutes the false for the real, the veneer for the trusses. In the book, the World Controller declares that when he can get people to bypass truth for hype, then democracy will cease to exist. If the average citizen accepts movie "reality" for historical truth, studying no history to compare celluloid with hard facts, then historical truth dies; the false has replaced the genuine. For, as Machiavelli put it five centuries ago, the *perception* of truth is more powerful than truth itself.

All this is a roundabout way of getting to my basic premise, which is this: Parents ought to be the ultimate guardians of truth, of the avenues to truth, for their children. To guard well the avenues to our children's souls is a divinely ordained responsibility, a responsibility that can sometimes be terrifying, for as America's greatest poet, Emily Dickinson, put it many years ago:

Truth must dazzle gradually
Or every man be blind.

Our media does not dazzle gradually. The tender minds, hearts, and souls of small children can be so seared, so charred, so shriveled up, by media-generated lightning strikes of evil, degeneracy, and taboos that their highly strung nervous systems are short-circuited. This can happen in mere seconds. As though that weren't enough, a child's once razor-sharp imagination is likely to be blunted and dulled as well, passivity being the usual result.

All this was graphically brought home to me recently when I was reading a story to children during a church service. Children were sitting around me in a circle and listening with various degrees of attentiveness. Some appeared bored, others appeared fairly interested; but there was one little girl who was fascinated—drinking in every word, every gesture, every nuance, her eyes alight with wonder. I was so struck by her responsiveness that, after the service, I asked the pastor about her. Not knowing her name made it difficult; consequently, the pastor took me over to a wall of photographs of the children in the church.

Without a moment's hesitation, she pointed to one figure and asked, "Is this the girl?"

I was so amazed at how she knew whom I was referring to that I asked her, "How did you know who she was? And what makes her so different from the others?"

Never shall I forget her answer! "Because, you see, her parents have no television in the house."

It was that simple.

A Sense of Wonder

God created each of us 100 percent creative. All you have to do to verify this is to watch a baby or a young child before television becomes a part of his or her life. The baby touches everything, tastes everything, tests everything, and takes nothing for granted. The young child asks question after question, in an unending cascade of dominoes. Words, experiences, knowledge, all are assimilated at blinding speed. Never again will that person grow at such a rate. This insatiable curiosity is God-instilled.

Now for the bad news: Studies have shown that whereas the average two-year-old is about 97 to 100 percent creative, the average eighteen-year-old is only 2 to 3 percent creative. Somewhere during those sixteen years we become zombies; we dumb down. We almost completely lose that exciting sense of wonder we were born with. We no longer possess that early excitement about the world, that early zest for continuous personal growth, that joyful rushing from moment to moment, experience to experience, answer to answer, solution to solution.

We parents will have to take part of the blame for this diminution in our children's creativity. Every time we say, "I'm too busy!" or "Don't bother me!" or "Go ask your mother!" (or father) or "Go watch TV!" we blunt our children's sense of wonder. The school system will have to take part of the blame also—especially the schools where classes are overcrowded—for all too often the individual student gets lost in the shuffle. As a teacher, I know well the sense of frustration that comes with failure to reach each student where his or her need is the greatest. And let's face it, we all tend to standardize: to measure progress, not by individual growth, but by bureaucratically imposed criteria of what is normal. As a result, all too often the creative student is viewed and treated as a square bolt in a round hole.

There is a third party that must bear a significant portion of the blame for killing creativity in our children. I am referring to the media. Permit me to explain.

If a child learns on his or her own—wandering through the woods; playing in the sand; tinkering with machinery; studying the stars at night; identifying trees, flowers, animals, birds, or insects—that process is 100 percent creative because no two children learn or internalize in the same way, or come up with the same mental imagery. The same is true when they listen to a radio drama or read a magazine or book. Each listener or reader will create inner imagery unique to himself or herself. Take the word "father." The dictionary definition will not vary, but the connotative meaning (based on what kind of father the person had) will vary greatly. Thus all three activities—actual experience, radio, and print—are 100 percent creative experiences.

Now let's take television, video, or the cinema. In these activities, all the creativity occurs at the front end, not at the receiving end. If one person views it, or 1 billion people view it, the imagery is the same. The receiver's brain has nothing to do with this pre-fab imagery; in fact, it is blasted by the brain into the mind's archives. But since the brain does not differentiate between imagery once it is archived—accepting it in the same way a bluebird does the catbird egg in her nest—once it is there, that pre-fab imagery remains for life.

Let's walk into our children's brain room and study what happens. We see in this vast library tens of thousands of videocassettes. Everything they have ever heard, seen, thought, or experienced is here: every bar of music they have performed, listened to on the radio, TV, walkman, or stereo, heard in the cinema, or seen performed live; every program, every commercial they have seen on television; every billboard they have noticed along the road; every book, magazine, or newspaper they have read; every thought, no matter how secret, how good or evil; and every dream, waking or sleeping, they have had; every church service they have gone to; every class they have attended in school; every game they have participated in or watched; every ride or trip, short or long, they have taken; every failure, every success, every sorrow, every joy they have experienced; every moment they have shared with pets; every stroll, every hike they have gone on—*everything* is there.

Now let's turn to the other side of these archives: the relationship of these experiences to their day-to-day thoughts and actions. If our children have been blessed with a serene childhood, where they are free to roam the woods, the creeks, the beaches, and the mountains, and where they are exposed to little or no television, then they probably have a favorite perch in a tree where they climb in order to dream; they probably read voraciously, both silently and out loud with the family; they probably have several hobbies, each expanding their knowledge of the world; they're probably developing their talents, pursuing activities such as music, art, sewing, woodwork, or ceramics; and they probably dream up stories and dramas of their own and then act them out.

Their thoughts tend to be original ones, uniquely their own. When they grow up, they will be the creative ones: Their brains sizzle as they conceptualize through words, imagery, and abstract print. In a nutshell, they have no limits except those that are self-imposed. This does not mean that media junkies are incapable of creativity or personal growth; merely that they are more unlikely to arrive at their own conclusions, for that part of the brain, unless used on a regular basis, tends to shrink or lose its muscle tone.

Apparently, we as a society have lost sight of the significance of early dreaming. Longfellow called it "the long thoughts of youth." As a child, adolescent, and young adult, I remember my dreams. Joseph the Dreamer was I. I dreamed of so many things: relationships, what I might do with my life, the opposite sex, God, friends, stories, responsibilities. But such dreams would not have been possible if I had not had moments of silence and serenity. In contrast to my experience, through my classroom surveys, I discovered that many college students rarely encounter silence. From the moment they get up until the moment they go to sleep, they are engulfed by sound. Most of them cannot remember the last silence they experienced. As adults we tend to forget how crucial these early dreams are, and how necessary silence and serenity are to their growth. If these dreams are never dreamed because a child isn't given solitude and peace, how can he or she ever grow, ever become? If the dream seed has never been planted, how can it ever flower into achievement?

Two Windows

Sadly, in our hectic society today, far too often we see around us children and youths who fail to take advantage of God's second book: nature. Their earliest memories are of electronic imagery. So magnetized do they become by these vivid images that they entomb themselves in their houses, surrounded by their TV sets, videocassettes, video games, and computers. As a result, they grow up overweight, flabby, and uninterested in exercise, hobbies, sports, reading, or other forms of personal growth. School bores them, church bores them, life bores them. When they are asked by a teacher to write, they panic, for they have few stylistic prototypes of good writing in their brains' archives. With only the chaotic electronic imagery to draw from, they are incapable of writing coherent sentences and paragraphs. Worse yet, virtually everything they consume is pre-fab: conceived, written, or composed by someone else. *There is hardly an original thought in their heads.* They tend to do poorly in school and college and are generally more likely to succumb to substance abuse than are their peers. They are likely to be unhappy and angry at the world for not providing them with more opportunities for success. Their window to the world is a murky one.

But then there is another group: children and youths whose parents care enough about them and the adults they will become that they spend a great deal of time with them. These parents exhibit tough love. They monitor carefully everything their children see and experience, and they limit their media viewing to programs they feel are compatible with the values they want them to live by. The electronic-media hours are kept to a minimum, for these parents encourage their children to be outside as much as possible —to exercise, to develop their muscles and stamina, to grow to know and love the great world of nature. They take their children on hikes and to museums, libraries, lectures, concerts, and films. They encourage them to develop their talents to the utmost, as God has ordained. They provide their children with periods of silence in which to dream. God and His values are made central in their lives, in their actions, in their words, and in their worship. Recognizing that we become the stories we love most, these parents encourage their children to read worthwhile books; they themselves set the pace by reading stories every day, stories that teach the kind of values they hope their children will incorporate into their own lives. As a result, these children tend to be imaginative, creative, empathetic, helpful, kind, productive, and successful. Their window to the world is a clear one.

If only more parents realized this sobering truth: that every moment we are in a state of becoming. Long before the advent of today's mass media, the American poet Walt Whitman wrote:

> There was a child went forth every day,
> And the first object he look'd upon
>   That object he became,
> And that object became part of him.

On this subject, no more powerful statement has been made than that by C. S. Lewis: "Every time you make a choice you are turning the central part of you, the part of you that chooses, into something a little different from what it was before. And taking your life as a whole, with all your innumerable choices, all your life long you are slowly turning this central thing either into a heavenly creature or into a hellish creature" (C. S. Lewis, *Mere Christianity* [New York: Macmillan Publishing Company, 1943, 1952], 86–87).

Lewis points out, in effect, that each thought we harbor, each song lyric we listen to, each sitcom we watch, each movie we see, each ad we notice, each book or magazine we read, leaves a mark on our souls. Singly, these marks don't amount to much, but over time they tend to cluster and turn into habits; these habits determine our character, and our character determines our destiny. Alfred Lord Tennyson put it more succinctly in his great poem *Ulysses:* "I am a part of all that I have met."

What all these voices agree on is this: Plateaus are rare in life; thus each day we are in a state of flux. God's supreme gift of salvation does not take us off the hook and give us free rein to become satanic. C. S. Lewis reminds us that faith and works are the two scissor-blades of our daily walk (*Mere Christianity*, 129). Therefore, each day of our children's lives, we parents must recognize the awesome responsibility we bear in helping them either to march toward God and eternity or to slide into ultimate darkness and despair.

Without silence and serenity; without the Good Book and daily communion with God; without nature, God's second book; without responsibility; without continual personal growth and development of their talents, how can our children possibly realize their full potential?

Look to This Day

The tidal wave of home-schooling that is rolling across America (growing at an astounding 20 percent a year!) is living proof that more and more parents are getting serious about their parenting. No success, no achievement, no status, no amount of money, could possibly compensate for having failed as a parent. It's a mighty tough job: the toughest one the good Lord entrusts to us. It means that we parents will have to listen with our children every second the TV or video is on so that we, as a counterforce, can explain the content or, if the subject matter or language calls for it, turn the set off. It means that we must grant our children the great gift of time, so they can dream. It means that we must introduce our children to the magic that is print, the enrichment that comes with stories. It means that we must remind our children that each precious day is a miniature lifetime—with a beginning, a middle, and an end— and that we should so live that we can joyfully surrender each day of our lives to God, saying, "Lord, You can see I tried to do my best today." It means that we must set aside our desire for instant gratification, for wanting to hear our young children and teenagers say right now, "We appreciate the tough love you're showing us and the sacrifices you're making," and be willing to wait several years or longer before we receive that acknowledgment, if we ever do.

For a millennium and a half, Kalidasa, India's greatest poet, has been speaking to men, women, and children everywhere through a poem that has stubbornly refused to be forgotten. If every one of us memorized it and hung it on a wall in our homes, what a difference these words would make in our lives!

Salutation to the Dawn

Look to this day!
For it is life, the very life of life.
In its brief course
Lie all the verities and realities of your existence:
The bliss of growth
The glory of action
The splendor of achievement,
For yesterday is already a dream
And tomorrow is only a vision,
But today well lived
Makes every yesterday a dream of happiness
And every tomorrow a vision of hope.

Look well, therefore, to this day!
Such is the salutation to the dawn.

$\mathcal{T}$his Third Collection

In 1996, the first collection of *Great Stories Remembered* was published; the second collection, *Great Stories Remembered II,* followed in 1998; here now is our third collection. From the beginning, we planned this series to be unique: It is our answer to readers who desired collections of heartfelt stories that embraced the entire calendar year, from New Year's to Christmas. We have divided the stories by season; thus, if you are looking for a Valentine's Day love story, you'll find it in the section "Winter to Spring"; a Mother's Day or Father's Day story, in "Spring to Summer"; a Fourth of July story, in "Summer to Autumn"; and a Thanksgiving or Christmas story, in "Autumn to Winter." Of course, not all of the stories are datable by season, but in general that is the format we have followed here.

We have used another criterion to select our stories: Each one has to be so memorable and so powerful that the reader will have no trouble understanding why we attached the label "Great" to this collection. We believe the stories in this volume are as strong as any we have yet fielded.

For this third collection, we brought back a number of authors you have come to cherish: Mabel McKee, Josephine DeFord Terrill, Annie Hamilton Donnell, G. E. Wallace, Arthur A. Milward, Grace S. Richmond, Arthur Gordon, and Margaret E. Sangster, Jr. We are also introducing authors we feel you will like just as much: P. J. Platz, Penny Porter, Rudyard Kipling, Earl Reed Silvers, Elizabeth Goudge, and Anton Chekhov, to name a few. Altogether, a veritable treasure chest!

The woodcut illustrations so popular with our readers have been continued here; in some cases, we have used engravings or half-tones, all of ancient vintage.

Coda

It is always a joy to hear from you. If you have any reactions or comments, positive or negative; or if you have stories you'd like us to consider for future collections, please send them—along with authorship and earliest known publication date and place—to

Joe L. Wheeler, Ph.D.
c/o Focus on the Family
Colorado Springs, CO 80920

Winter to Spring

Three Thousand Miles from Home

·

Frank R. Adams

During World War I, deadly poison-gas shells fired into the trenches by the Germans destroyed thousands of Allied lives, either by outright death or by crippling for life. This love story dates back to the waning days of that war.

The first letter was one of the great surprises of Catherine's life. Jerry was the last person she had ever expected to hear from again. That "again" indicates exactly the status quo of affairs between them. Everything had been definitely and decisively finished. She even hesitated about opening the envelope. But it bore a superscription that was scarcely to be … ignored…:

J. B. Thomas, 2nd Lt. F.A., O.R.C.
Officer's Mail
U.S.A.P.O. 711, A.E.F., France
    Mrs. Catherine Thomas,
    1742, St. Anne Place,

Lorchester,
N.Y.,
U.S.A.

O.K.
J. B. Thomas
2nd Lt. F.A., O.R.C.

And besides that, there was the censor stamp of an army post office.

Letters from overseas cannot be destroyed without reading even if they have been written by—yes, she would open it without thinking about it for another moment.

She had not even heard that he was in the army. Her affairs had been deliberately ordered during the last few years so that she would not hear of his doings. She had even moved to a different part of the country, the better to avoid the bitterness of a possible chance meeting with him.

"Dear Kate," the letter began. At least he had the decency not to address her as "Wops," which had once been his nickname for her. As soon as she got over thinking how angry she would have been if he had, she began to feel rather sorry that he had not.

Dear Kate:

I've sorted over everyone I've ever known in all my life, and you are the only one I want to talk to. Of course, you are privileged not to listen. I certainly should never blame you. But on the other hand I rather need you as a conversational ground-wire. Close the circuit, will you, old girl, and listen in once in a while. I'll know you are there even if you never say a word.

It's a bit desperate, being over here in France, with the

trenches just ahead and finding that there is only one worthwhile person in all your life. Not that I have any idea of being killed. I'm pretty sure I won't be. We all are. But at that, we're on the eve of a great adventure, and lots of the inconsequential things that have happened to us have rather faded into insignificance.

That was how I found out how big you have been in my life. Why, you dominate all my thoughts! If something funny happens, I want to run and write it to you, because I know that once you used to laugh at the same things that I did. And if some little tragedy occurs among the men of the battery, I feel that it would be a little less acute if you knew about it, because you've got such a darn fool tender heart that you would want to share some of the troubles of my boys too.

And they have some very real griefs. I'm battery censor and have to read all the mail of the enlisted men before it goes out, so I know all about their affairs…. It's a good deal like shelling peas in five-bushel lots. I did that once when I was a boy, and I never saw so many pods in all my life.

Most of the letters are just about as much alike as the vegetables just mentioned. Heaven knows they have to be if they come anywhere near conforming to the A.E.F. general orders governing overseas mail. The average man, when confronted by the list of things he must not say for fear that the German high command will plan the next western offensive on the basis of information inadvertently spilled by him, seems to suffer an acute attack of cramp colic in the imagination. Most of them do not appear to know how to put any interesting variations into the theme of their health and the weather. They do say "I love you" in one way or another, but they are very self-conscious about it. I suppose the censorship is responsible for that, too. It would be rather difficult to be as foolish as you know how to be if you were sure that somebody was going to go over it later with a magnifying glass and developing chemicals to see what you really meant.

Of course, not all the men are hampered by hobbled imaginations. We have several very accomplished liars in our outfit. We've only been in France three weeks and we're at least two hundred miles away from the sound of a gun, but the battles we have been in already, according to their reports, make the little affair which the French pulled off at the Marne look like a preliminary debate in the high school league. They mention hostile airplanes just as if they were mosquitoes, and you'd think our boys had a bomb for breakfast every morning, instead of grapefruit.

But I understand that quite the contrary is the case when troops actually do go into action. Then they never say much about it, I am told, but write home only about how nice the weather is and how is the baby?

But now I come to the real reason for writing. I know you have been wondering what it is, all the time, because you are quite sure that it was not simply to tell you about these rather trivial things. The real reason is a letter from the heart of a man which came to me for censoring this afternoon. I'm going to take the liberty of lifting a few paragraphs to send to you.

The letter began simply "Dear," which is one of the finest ways for a letter to begin if it is written by someone who really cares. The part that I particularly wanted you to know about was this:

It is not only houses which are haunted by the spirits of men. Sometimes men are haunted by the restless phantoms of once familiar homes.

By that I do not mean that we are homesick; it is only that we remember what we are coming back to. I doubt if a man who is here would be content at home so long as America's frontier is so far-flung. But many of us are stirred by [thoughts of what used to be].

It's spring in France, and I thought it would forget to come. It hardly seems possible that there can be spring anywhere that you are not. Why, they've even got violets here, heartbreaking blue ones that simply beg to be bought and given to you. No one has told them that you are thousands of miles away, and they wonder why I pass them by.

And there are peonies, too,... just like the great flaming red ones that light the way up that hill to where you are.

There, you see I couldn't bring a thing like that to anyone but you. No one else would see anything in it but sentimental mush. This fellow happens to be a real man, though; I never would have guessed that he had anything like that in his system if I had not been obliged to look over his shoulder, so to speak, while he poured his soul out of his fountain pen.

He isn't always making love to his wife, though—did I mention that the letter was addressed to Mrs. John Scarborough, Hale's Ferry, New York, and that he is Sergeant John Scarborough, doubtless of the same place?—sometimes his letters are altogether different. Here is an extract taken from an earlier letter of his:

Friend Wife:

... What do you mean in your last letter by saying that our cat, Blackberry Smith, has left home? I'll bet the old scoundrel has joined the army. He never could seem to get enough fighting around home. I don't suppose that black kittens will be nearly so stylish among the best families in our neighborhood this spring as they were last. But you may be mistaken. Blackberry may be back by now. He was a very durable cat, and I raised him to keep the faith. You remember that I especially charged him before I left not to let a single mouse annoy you while I was away. Do you suppose he got tired of waiting for me to come back and pull his tail? Maybe life got too tame for him with no one there to tease him.

Just now, while I was writing, someone outside whistled, and it sounded just like the whistle you used to call to me with in the lifetime I lived before this, the one that came to an end six months ago. It was so vivid that I got half up off my bunk at the urgent command of my heart before my reasonable but disagreeable common sense told me that it was only a coincidence. It brought you so close to me for an instant that I reached out to touch you....

There goes the bugle. It's uncomplimentary, but I must leave you for mess.

Your Husband

Jerry had not even signed his name. Catherine guessed rather shrewdly that he had not known exactly how to finish his own note and so had allowed the other man's final message to go for both....

She sighed and let the letter lie folded ... in her lap. It had opened up memories that were both pleasant and painful. He had caused her the happiest hours in her life, as well as the most miserable. Just as he had said, there had been between them a whimsical touch-and-go understanding that she had never attained with anyone else. It was because it had been so perfect a thing that she regretted so poignantly that everything else had marred their relationship.

If he had only been a little more like this man whose letters he had quoted to her! Catherine felt a sudden envy of the woman who had inspired the home-longing of John Scarborough. Why, that woman did not live so very far away.... For a moment Catherine was almost tempted to look up the other end of the skein that had come into her hands so unexpectedly and see what Mrs. John was like. But she decided against it as a foolish idea. Besides, it was none of her business. She would forget the entire affair.

But that was easier said than done. That letter from the man who had never been successfully supplanted in her life fretted the edges of her consciousness for many days. It had to be reread every once in a while to see just why it so insistently tugged at her thoughts.

And in three weeks there was another letter. It began "Dear Kate," just as the first one had, but in this "Wops" had been written first and then thoroughly scratched out. She knew because it took her about ten minutes to erase the scratches enough to make sure.... And she was not angry, not so long as he had scratched it out. He could not help it if he still thought of her by that name and his pen had slipped.

The letter:

> We've moved up a little nearer the front lines and we're doing a lot of firing on the practice range, but the whole thing is strangely unreal and in some way it's not warlike. There is more feeling of tremendous conflict in New York than there is here....
>
> We have French officers and noncommissioned officers instructing us in some of the work we are to do at the front.

They are charming and never seem to lose patience with us no matter how stupid we are. As an officer I am entitled to the salute of these battle-scarred sergeants, but I always feel like remonstrating when an old fellow with two or three wound stripes on his arm comes up smart with his right hand when we pass each other. I'd like to tell him not to mind until I, too, have at least a service badge on my own arm....

I think that's all the information and personal opinion that I can crowd in before referring to John Scarborough's letter, which is my flimsy excuse for addressing you at all. He loves that woman so much that everyone but myself would doubt that she was his wife. Probably at home he treats her like a dog, but over here he certainly has suffered a change of heart. I can't pick out anything particular to send you from his latest imitation of Abélard, so I'll transcribe all of it. As follows:

Dear:

Would you be interested to know that the little watch you gave me when I left for France has scarcely varied an instant since the day you put it on my wrist? Personally I am a little disgusted with it. In its place I should try to hasten over the hours that we have to be apart.

I received your letter with the perfumed handkerchief in it. Of course I recognized the faint fragrance of it. I had never been conscious of that perfume at all when I was with you, but when I smelled it again, I knew what it was that I had been missing all this time. It was rather a maddening trick of yours to send me so sensory a reminder of you. Don't you know that there are laws ... which punish those who induce soldiers to desert from Uncle

Sam's army? I don't know just what they would do to you as punishment, but I do know what I will do when I catch you.

By the way, that particular brand of essence of flowers is made right here in the part of France where we are stationed. I saw some in a shop window the other day and inquired about it in my crippled French. They told me that it was a local product. Fleur Elise is the name of it, is it not?

You say that you are well. Thank God for that. Keep yourself so, dear. The bugles are just beginning to sound my nightly prayer for you—Taps. It's the loneliest call for soldiers in all the world. Good night.

John

…After censoring that letter, I went out to the tiny parfumerie in the village over the line from our camp and bought a small bottle of Fleur Elise. It is exquisite, and I know that you will like it. I have placed a drop of the haunting stuff on this sheet of paper so you may judge, too, with your patrician nose, if there is not something alluring about this Mrs. Scarborough. I don't think that either she or John will mind our having eavesdropped this little bit.

If I may, I shall write you again if I can think up a plausible excuse, or even without any if my need becomes great.

Jerry

Of course, Catherine did not answer it. She could not answer without forgiving him for the things that could never be forgiven. The mere fact that he was playing on her heartstrings again after she had thought them long since out of tune was no reason for retiring her common sense to the sidelines and becoming a sentimental schoolgirl once more.

But she wavered a little when the next letter came, quite two months later. "Wops," it began without apology. Later, when she had read the letter through, she had not the heart to be offended. Evidently he was not thinking about trivial things, and it had not occurred to him that his pen had slipped.

Wops:

We're "going in" tomorrow. There is some kind of a hurry-up call for light artillery—that's us—and we're to move up sooner than we expected. I suppose it means a big offensive.... We've been within sound of the guns for a long time, but some way their rumble sounds a little more menacing tonight, a little more personal....

The thing about which I spoke in my first letter has proved itself true. I refer to the fact that the closer the men get to the battle line, the less they say about it. Scarcely a man in the outfit has suggested a thing in his letters back home—and there have been lots of letters, too, since we found out that we were going to move—that would indicate to a soul the extra tension we are under.

The only man who wrote anything at all pertinent to the situation was John Scarborough. John, apparently, has a gloomy foreboding that all is not well with the stars of his destiny. He did not say so, but I caught the undercurrent of farewell in his letter to his wife. But it was never sent. He came to me before the mail went out and asked to have his letter destroyed.

"Why, Sergeant?" I asked....

"I'm a little afraid to have her get that letter, sir. There's going to be a youngster at our house pretty soon, and I'm afraid I've said something that might make her worry. I don't even want her to know if something does happen to me up in the ditch. Not for a while, anyway. I've thought it out, sir, and I've written a couple of extra letters that I wish you would take charge of and mail about two weeks apart if I should try to stop any shrapnel or shell splinters."

So I destroyed his letter for him and told him to run along and forget his troubles…. I'm almost sorry not to be able to send you any extracts from the letter because in it he made it quite plain to that woman that he loved her. She certainly ought to have the letter herself, but John is right. If anything should happen—but we don't think of such things.

I have to go out as liaison officer tonight to go through the preliminaries of taking over the battery position. Maybe I'll have something more interesting to write next time—if you'll let me. And I hope that you will.

Jerry

He was strangely awkward and diffident about closing his letters. It would be hard for him to be formal with her and, of course, quite impossible to step back to the old informal basis. She smiled as she thought how he must have struggled with that finish and had at last given it up and put down the lamest of conclusions.

It was curious to get that word from him, written three weeks before, as she discovered by the date and the postmark, speaking about something interesting that he was going to do that night. Why, what had happened was now history. His battery had been in position for three weeks now, had probably taken part in the struggle begun by the great German drive and Foch's greater counteroffensive. Even as she read his letter, he might be living in a hell of bursting shell. Or he might be—but, as he said, people do not speak of such things….

Her indifference failed her somewhat when there was no letter the following week or the next. She found her mind constantly and unwillingly straying to that far-off battle line where the hearts of so many American women were trying to interpose themselves as shields to the breasts of those they loved. Catherine would not admit it to anyone, but she had fretted herself into a state bordering upon nervous collapse before the next letter came, thirty-seven days after the last one.

It was not in his handwriting at all and was on the stationery of a base hospital, designated only by a cryptic army-post-office number. But it was from him because it started off, "Wops dear," and she supplied to herself, quoting, "which is one of the finest ways for a letter to begin," and went on:

> Don't be surprised because this is written by someone else. I'm slightly wounded and cannot use my right arm; so I am asking one of the nurses to write this for me…. Now I know how the boys used to feel when they were writing their letters home, knowing that I was going to censor them.
>
> I would have waited until I was able to write this myself, except that I knew you would be interested in the story of John Scarborough. Briefly, John was gassed. That doesn't sound very serious, but unfortunately it is…. John got a bad case, which has caused him rather intolerable agony for some time since and has destroyed his eyesight, at least temporarily. By a lucky chance, we were both taken to the same hospital. I call it lucky because I think that otherwise, John would never be going back to his wife, who, I trust, loves him as much as he loves her. She must love him very much now, especially for the memory of what he once was, because he will never again be quite the same.
>
> I did not hear anything about him for several days after we

were brought here. I didn't even know that he was not with the battery, in fact, until a hospital orderly came through looking for any officer from the —th Regiment, Battery C. I admitted that those were my general descriptions.

"There's a bad case from your battery here, sir," the orderly reported, "and the nurse in charge had an idea that one of his officers might be able to help. The man is mighty popular with the staff, and we didn't want to let him slip if there is anything that could be done."

"Who is it?"

"A sergeant by the name of Scarborough, sir—a gas case, pretty bad. Do you think you'd be able to come and see him, sir?"

I was quite able to get around, so I trotted over to the ward. He was out of his head when I got there, so I just talked with the nurse on duty. The orderly was right. John is certainly popular with the female help around this man's hospital. The darn fool woman nearly cried when she told me about him, and that's saying a lot about a war-time nurse, who has to put her heart away in the brine of all her tears before she tackles her job.

It seems that John was fretting himself into almost incurable agitation because he hadn't received even a word from his wife. I didn't know this myself, but it seems that for some time before we went in he had not had a letter from home, and quite naturally all of our mail has been more or less messed up during the drive. As a consequence it had been something like two months since he had received word from his family. The nurses had done all they could by writing to regimental headquarters for his mail, but they

hadn't got any action out of that and probably they won't until after the present disturbance is over and the mail clerk can do his work without keeping a bayonet in his left hand.

And in the meantime, John was getting worse, not doing a blessed thing to help himself but spending all his energy that he needed so badly in worrying about that fool letter. The nurse put it up to me strong to do something. And I wanted to help, too. You know how much I think of John. But I couldn't see just exactly what good it would do for me to talk to him. He didn't want any good advice; what he needed was a letter from his wife.

That nurse and I talked for some time about the problem, and I told her about the baby that John was hoping for back home, and we agreed that we couldn't blame John for worrying. "We've got to get that letter somehow," she said.

I agreed with her, and being an imaginative sort of a rabbit, I thought out the way to do it. You can guess how we managed. It was only a short note; a mother would not be apt to write much the first time. It said:

Dear:

We two are waiting for you to bring us back our hearts from across the sea.

That was nice and indefinite, but it conveyed the idea in a sentimental sort of way. The signature bothered me most…. Every wife has some little pet name that her husband has given her and that no one else ever uses, just as—you know how it is—and it was a cinch that she would sign that name to that letter if to no other. You'll never guess how I got around it. I admit it was pretty good. I put a big dauby cross at the end of the letter and labeled it "His Mark."

I kept away from John entirely. He doesn't know yet that I am anywhere near the hospital. But I was where I could watch when they brought him the letter. Of course he couldn't see it, but he held it in his hands in the envelope, unopened. He wanted to believe it was from her, but he was afraid it wasn't. Finally he put it to the supreme test—raised it to his nose and *smelled of it.*

Fortunately, I had guessed that he would do just that, so the letter passed the test. I had that small bottle of Fleur Elise in my baggage, which had been sent on from the regiment, and I had put just the faintest suspicion of the scent on the paper. The way all of John Scarborough's doubts passed away before that almost indistinguishable breath of springtime was enough to make me a believer in magic.

The rest of the letter went across like a shot. The part

about having the baby's signature made a tremendous hit, and I was almost as proud as he was. He laughed until all the nurses and I cried. There is something some way affecting about watching a six-footer like John, with bandaged eyes that may never see again, sitting up in bed and laughing as if all the world were going to be one continuous springtime of comedy for him from then on.

But it worked. The boy is getting well. He can go home sometime not so very far off, and that is helping, too. A letter did come from his wife finally, but we haven't given it to him. Why? None of the rest of us has any right to open it first, and it might contradict part of our manufactured story. We know she's all right, though, or else she could not have written at the date the letter is postmarked. And we have written her all the facts of the case so he need never know until he is back home and perfectly safe from any further harm that this world can do him.

This, then, is all that I shall ever know of the story of John Scarborough. I am afraid that I shall never again find so good an excuse for writing to you. For that reason and for others, dear, which I cannot explain, I take the thread of communication between you and the man who was once your husband, here in my two hands, and break it—thus.

Jerry

The signature was not even Jerry's own, and yet some way the entire letter was his. It was strange that the man could project his personality to her through someone else, that someone else another woman. And that totally unexpected shock at the end about never writing to her again. Just what did he mean by that? Why?

She read the letter through once more to see if there were something she had missed the first time. There was nothing unless you counted an occasional slight stain on the paper, stains that looked as if something had been dropped on it. There were two or three on each sheet. At first she thought maybe he had put a few drops of Fleur Elise on her letter, too, but the faint stains were odorless. Catherine cudgeled her brain for hours over the matter, and because she really had a brain, it finally brought forth some slight results.

One of them was that she packed up a suitcase and went to the railroad station. The ticket agent not only knew where Hale's Ferry was but also was able to sell her a ticket to it. When she arrived, she went to the post office as the most likely place to get the information she desired. "Does Mrs. John Scarborough get her mail here?" Catherine asked of the lady postmistress politely.

"She does not," the latter replied with some politeness and more firmness.

"I didn't think that she did," Catherine confessed blandly. "Does anyone by that name live here, or has she lived here recently?"

"No, and … I've been here a long time." …

That was all Catherine needed to know. In fact, it was information that she had already sensed…. There had never been any Mrs. John Scarborough, nor any Sergeant John Scarborough, nor any baby. It had all been just a trick that Jerry had played…. All those love letters he had pretended to quote were simply the ones he had written to her himself but dared not send over his own name.

Catherine's eyes swam a little as she read back over his letters. For, of course, she carried them with her. And that last one. Those stains on each page. Suddenly she knew what they were. They were the tears of the nurse who was taking down what he dictated. For, of course, he must be pretty badly hurt himself, although he had said that he was not. He was doubtless the one who had been gassed, and blinded, too, perhaps permanently…. That, then, was why he had said that he would write no more. Before, he had been hoping, but now, he was afraid that the trail of ink might lead them together again. For her sake he had broken the thread without letting her pity him.

It did not require much deep thinking to reason out … the undeniable fact that out of the rather nebulous and uncertain personality that had once been her husband, the war had fashioned and tempered something very real: a man. And because he had turned out so and because it was a nice day and because—well, because of everything—Catherine cried about it…. But weeping was not all that she did that day. She knew when she had got her cue to enter, and she proceeded to take a hand in affairs as soon as she could get to a telegraph office that would accept cablegrams for overseas.

They say that the result of her activity did more good to one of the gas patients in an American base hospital in France than all the efforts of the nurses, who were very fond of that particular gas case, and of the chief surgeon, who spent time when he should have been sleeping in bending over the patient's bed, trying with drugs, lances, and prayer to make him stay on this side of the great frontier. When Jerry heard his cablegram read to him, he decided that he could not afford not to get well. So he got at it right away.

Here's the cablegram. Judge for yourself:

2nd Lt. Jerry Thomas, F.A., O.R.C.
Base Hospital No. ____
A.E.F., France.

Dear: This is the first of a series of communications for you to censor daily until you come back to the home we never had. Mr. and Mrs. Scarborough, son, and cat, Blackberry Smith, all here waiting for you, but more than all the rest,

Wops, Her Mark

Nearest His Heart

Josephine DeFord Terrill

The minister spoke movingly of the needs of those overseas who knew not God. And when he asked the congregation for a gift, Benny decided he would give the thing that was "nearest his heart."

It was a long sermon, but no one minded. Benny hardly took his eyes from the missionary's face as he talked. His hands clasped together between his knees, his chest heaving, he leaned forward to catch every word.

The kind-faced minister seemed to be looking straight at Benny when he asked, "Why should the children in America have all the good things, and the children in Africa all the poor things? I want to know if there isn't some little boy or girl here who would like to give just one of his blessings to one of those children over there?"

Benny's hand went up highest of all.

"You know," the missionary went on to say, "some of us over here give the poor heathen only the things that we don't want: our old clothes, or our old broken-up toys, or maybe a nickel that is left after we have bought all the ice cream and all the candy, and all the bicycles and baseballs and balloons and kites, and everything else we want. But you know, the things that help the most, the things that Jesus appreciates the most, are the things that we *sacrifice* to give—the things that lie nearest our hearts."

He paused, and in the tense silence Benny's throat clicked in a dry sob.

When the last song, "I Gave My Life for Thee; What Hast Thou Given for Me?" was sung, Benny followed Grandfather out of the church. On the sidewalk a big German police dog sprang up to meet him, and the boy's heart stood still. Instantly he knew what it was that he must give. "The things that lie *nearest our hearts,*" the minister had said. It would be Rex; he must give him to one of those poor heathen boys.

The dog snuggled his nose into Benny's hand as they started home. Benny walked numbly, his heart filled with the sudden ecstasy of sacrifice. Inside the church his heart had been aching, for he thought that he had nothing to give. But what a glorious gift Rex would be for some little African boy. How thrilling to make such a gift!

Grandfather looked down, and his old face wrinkled into a neuralgic smile. "What ails ye, Benny boy?" he asked in his high, cracked voice. "Thinkin' 'bout them black boys over in Africa?"

Benny raised shining eyes that were filled with tears.

Grandfather saw the tears, but his eyes did not detect the light shining from Benny's soul. He ruminated consolingly, "Well, sonny, you an' me an' Mother have seen some pretty hard times, but I guess we ain't as bad off as the heathen yet. Got a heap to be thankful for in spite of it all."

They reached the edge of town, where their tiny brown house stood. Grandmother was waiting for them in the small bedroom where she had lain for several years.

"Well, we are back, Mother," called Grandfather cheerfully.

A thin, small voice answered from the bed: "Lasted longer today, didn't it?"

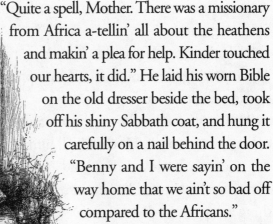

"Quite a spell, Mother. There was a missionary from Africa a-tellin' all about the heathens and makin' a plea for help. Kinder touched our hearts, it did." He laid his worn Bible on the old dresser beside the bed, took off his shiny Sabbath coat, and hung it carefully on a nail behind the door. "Benny and I were sayin' on the way home that we ain't so bad off compared to the Africans."

Benny changed his "good" clothes and went out with Rex. They sat down together in the sunshine outside the door, and Benny felt again the missionary fervor mounting in his heart. "Rex, how'd you like to belong to a little black, neckud African boy?" he asked solemnly.

Rex blinked and licked his hand, but those words were not in his vocabulary, broad though it was; so he maintained a polite silence while his master talked. The sermon was explained to him, and the wonderful dog seemed almost to understand what Benny said.

"So you see," Benny concluded, "you are nearest my heart: *so you must go to Africa!*"

They went into the house in answer to Grandfather's call to dinner. But Benny was not hungry for the first time in his nine years. He passed his corn bread down to Rex, who eagerly swallowed each piece and waited for more. Grandfather's nearly blind eyes did not notice the boy's lack of appetite. A kind woman from the church came in with a little Sabbath delicacy for Grandmother, which she ate in bed.

Benny interrupted Grandfather's silent thinking: "Would the Africans like a dog, Gramp?"

"What! A dog? No, child. They have more dogs than they need now." Then, peering at the boy's face, he emphasized his remark: "No, Ben, you can't give Rex to 'em."

But Rex was *nearest* Benny's heart, and somehow he *must* go. The answer came almost at once. He could sell him and send the money. The surly old dog trainer who loved dogs and hated everything else had once asked Benny for how much he would sell his beautiful dog. There was no such thing as a price for Rex—not *then*. But now he would sell him for $1,000 maybe, or $100. That much money ought to buy a lot of things for the black children who had only poor things.

Grandfather did not seem to notice the little boy's unusual quietness as he helped wash their few dishes. As soon as the work was finished, Benny asked permission to go for a walk and took his cap and hurried away, Rex trotting beside him.

They had gone but a few blocks when Benny began to realize what it would mean to give up his pal. He recalled how he had become the happy owner of this beautiful dog. A lady had stopped at their humble little home two years ago, lifted a little puppy out of the backseat of her car, and asked Benny if she might let it run about a bit on his grass. She was, she explained, taking it to her mother, who lived in another town, but the motion of the car had made the puppy sick. When she saw how tenderly Benny followed it with his eyes, she decided to leave it with him for a few days, promising to pay him for the care of it. When she returned, Benny gave the little fellow into her hands with such touching reluctance that she suddenly thrust it back into his arms and told him to keep it for his own. He had not seen her since, but her generous gift had filled his two years with an unbelievably happy companionship.

At first Grandfather couldn't see how they could keep a dog, for it was all he could do to get enough food for themselves. But one look into his orphaned grandson's eyes and Grandfather gave in. He had had a dog when he was a boy. Kindly neighbors with sympathetic hearts had occasionally helped out on the food problem for the growing boy and dog.

Benny stopped on a street crossing, the sudden complete realization of his intentions paralyzing his legs for a moment. An automobile honked loudly, and Rex gave Benny a violent shove toward the sidewalk. Nothing could happen to Benny while the dog was along. On they went, his steps lagging more and more as they neared the trainer's place.

The man who loved dogs was carrying water to the kennels when Benny walked into the yard.

"Well, hello!" he said, stopping abruptly, a bucket in each hand. "How is the dog today?" He had always been rather friendly to Benny on account of Rex. Rarely did he allow the boys of the town to visit the kennels, and then more because he wanted to show off his dogs than to be obliging. But Ben was always welcome.

The boy spoke quickly, afraid to trust himself with any delay in stating his errand. "Would you like to buy him?"

"Buy him? Sure I'll buy him. Do you want to sell him?"

Benny felt the fervor again and raised his head proudly. "Yes. I want to send the money to Africa to help the heathen boys there."

"What's that? You want to send the money to the *heathen?*" He muttered some oaths and turned to place his buckets on the ground.

Benny stood quietly, unmoved, his eyes shining in spite of the misery in his heart.

The trainer gave him a careful scrutiny and then asked, "You *really* want to sell him? I'll be glad to have him, of course, but you'll be back for him by morning."

Benny shook his head. "No, I'll not. The minister said that it didn't mean much unless we gave what was *nearest* our hearts. I love Rex almost more than I do Gramp and Gram; so I want to give *him*. You let me have the money, and I'll take it to the minister."

The dog trainer looked at the boy again closely and shrugged his shoulders in indifference. "Well," he said, "you are only a boy. I'll not argue with you. If you really want to sell your dog, I'll take him." He reached into his pocket and handed Benny a crisp bill. The dog was worth many times the amount of the bill, but the man was sure the boy would be back and did not want more money involved.

Benny put the bill into his pocket and then knelt beside his pet. *How he loved him!* Many times he had gone hungry that Rex might not miss a dinner. The big dog seemed to sense some trouble. He whined and licked Benny's face. The boy took the huge dog's head between his hands and looked into the soft brown eyes, and then with a sob he turned, ran out of the enclosure, and down the street. Rex's bark followed him till the sound no longer reached him.

Benny crept into the house. Grandfather lay back in his chair, taking his Sabbath afternoon nap. The little boy who had given his all lay down on the floor behind the old kitchen stove, where Rex had slept for the last two years. No sound came, but tears streamed down his cheeks.

Twilight came. Grandfather awoke with a start and shouted for Benny to come and help do the chores. The cow must be milked and the milk delivered. The chickens must be fed and put away for the night. It was when Benny came back to the house and saw that Grandfather had filled Rex's pan with milk that he sobbed out the story.

"Well, well, well!" the old man exclaimed slowly. "So you sold Rex to help the Africans. Well, well, well!" He sat down on the old bench outside the kitchen door. Benny crouched at his feet. The old man thought of all the martyrdoms and sacrifices of the ages while the small boy sobbed himself to sleep.

The next morning Benny was coming with slow steps from the woodshed when Rex bounded onto his shoulders. They greeted each other with sobs and barks of delight.

The dog trainer stood by the gate, waiting for Benny's attention. Finally, he asked, "Well, son, do you still want to sell your dog?"

Benny stood up and lifted his haggard face to the man. All his loneliness had been swept away. He had forgotten that Rex was no longer his. The expression in his eyes was pitiful to see. *"Oh, why did you bring him?"* He fell upon Rex's neck, crying uncontrollably.

The profane dog dealer laid his hand on the heaving shoulder. "My boy," he began, "I sat up all night beside Rex's kennel, trying to comfort him. And I got to thinking. I don't believe much in God nor in foreign missions; but any minister who can make a boy give up a dog like Rex must have something to tell the world. So I'm going to let you give that money to the heathen, and you can have your dog, too. You can't sell him, for he is a part of your family. Who knows? I may drop into your church someday and listen to your minister."

He then walked quickly away and left Benny looking entirely bewildered, one arm thrown tightly about the big police dog's neck.

Family Ties

P. J. Platz

Kathleen was a modern, career-minded woman who had no marriage, no children, and no family to worry about. All she had was John, still there after eleven fruitless years of marriage proposals. But now her father was dying, and family was coming to the hospital to say good-bye. Family she didn't want to face.

Kathleen liked the crisp, authoritative click of her heels against the cement sidewalk. She'd always liked that sound. As a child she'd stuffed fat little toes into her mother's spike-heeled pumps and clattered up and down the sidewalk in front of their house, trying to duplicate the smart click-click of her mother's step. She knew now that almost every little girl had done that at least once; that they all wanted to make the same noise. Click, click, click. The decisive, businesslike sound of the twentieth-century woman. Not a very feminine sound, maybe; but a reassuring one. Especially on this sidewalk. It was a magic sidewalk, but the magic was bad, and she wondered if all the sidewalks that led to hospital front doors all over the country were the same.

She'd been tramping this one every day for the past three weeks and had come to think of it as a great equalizer. At its end, standing in front of the glass entrance doors of the hospital, all who had walked it were remarkably the same: hushed, somber, and somehow defeated. It didn't matter how strong, how confident you were in the parking lot, or how sure of your power to control your own life; by the time you got to the end of that sidewalk and stood in front of those doors, you were a child again, facing the fear of the unknown, the unexpected, the one enemy who could be deluded for a time but never defeated.

She'd tried to pinpoint a dozen times the exact place on the sidewalk where she started to regress, but she could never mark it. All she knew was that she started in the parking lot as a rather tall, well-dressed thirty-two-year-old woman, a little too stern to be pretty; but by the time she reached the electric eye that opened the door for her in morbid welcome, she was a roly-poly kid again, with lopsided pigtails and a jelly smear on her cheek—a tiny girl-child on her way to talk to her father.

Let's talk about it, honey. Let's just talk it all out, and we'll get through it together. Just you wait. Ten years from now we'll look back and laugh.

And they had. They'd talked through the agonies of scraped knees and bully boys and puppy love and puberty, and laughed about them all ten years later. But not this time. Death didn't get better when you talked about it, and you most certainly didn't laugh about it ten years later.

"Kathleen?"

She glanced over at John on her left, wondered why he had said her name, and then realized she'd stopped in the middle of the sidewalk, halfway to the hospital entrance. She couldn't begin to guess how long she'd been standing there, saying nothing. The big white building loomed ahead, glass doors looking like a black mouth ready to swallow anyone who ventured too close.

"Sorry." She started walking again, concentrating on the click of her heels.

"Kathleen, wait." John's hand was on her elbow, pulling her back gently. "Let's not go in just yet." He nodded toward a stone bench set off the walk.

She resisted the pull of his arm. "You don't have to go in at all, John. He's not *your* father."

Quiet gray eyes flicked sideways to touch her, then flicked away again, wounded.

Kathleen sighed, regretting her words immediately. John loved her father almost as much as she did. This wasn't easy for him, either.

"I'm sorry, John. That didn't come out right. I just meant that you didn't have to come in *today*."

He smiled a little and took her hand. "Come on, Kathleen. We've got plenty of time. Let's relax for a minute."

She allowed herself to be led to the bench, then sagged onto it like a broken doll. Boy, was she going to owe John for this one! She hated the idea of him supporting her through this particular crisis, making the daily trips to the hospital with her, listening to all her tearful regrets, and waiting patiently during those times when she started to cry and couldn't seem to stop . . . always after they'd left the hospital, so her father wouldn't see. It was too big, too heavy a demand on their friendship, tipping the scales so sharply that she wasn't certain she could ever even them out again. But whenever she tried to put that into words, his response was always the same.

"Don't be silly. What are friends for?" And then he'd remind her of all the other troubles they had shared, because no one else could touch the bond of the lifetime that stretched behind them.

They'd grown up in separate apartments in the same duplex, sharing parents, playpens, schools, histories, more a part of the same large family than of two separate ones. They'd grown up and grown older together, knowing each other far too well for a simple chemical attraction to ever threaten their closeness. Thank God! John was the only one, in fact, who

understood Kathleen's conscious, modern choice not to marry, not to have children; to instead devote her life to career and causes, much as he had done.

"I feel bad, John, dragging you through this with me," she sighed, staring morosely at the bed of bright yellow marigolds in front of the bench. They shouldn't have yellow flowers in front of a building where people are dying. They should all be black.

"You're not dragging me through anything, Kathleen. We're muddling through it together, just as we did when my folks died, and your mother. As a matter of fact, we've weathered a lot of storms together. I don't know why this one is so much worse, but it is."

"Because he's the last one," she whispered.

John thought about that for a moment, then nodded. They'd both started with four parents; now Kathleen's father was the only one left.

"I couldn't get through it without you," she added, meaning it.

"Marry me, and we'll call it even," he teased, trying to break the black mood. His proposal made her smile a little, as it always did.

She glanced at her calendar watch and shook her head, making a little clicking noise with her tongue. "It's not the tenth yet, John."

John delivered his joking proposal on the tenth of each August, precisely. He'd never missed once during the last eleven years, even calling her from England once when business had taken him overseas.

He leaned back on the bench and turned his face up to the sun. "Sorry. Lost my head. Oh, the sun is grand today. Try it."

She tipped her head back obediently and saw orange on the inside of her eyelids. "I hate this place."

"Don't think about it. Think about something else."

Think about something else, indeed. What else can you think about when your father is dying?

"Do you remember the rabbits?" John asked suddenly, and a picture flew into her mind, banishing death, the hospital, and the awful sidewalk.

"Oh, yes," she said with a smile.

They'd both been nine years old then, and it was the first year John had proposed, only it hadn't been a proposal, really. More like the first verbal acknowledgment of something that seemed inevitable. The annual Easter bunnies were on sale at the pet shop, and even though little Johnny and Katy were absolutely convinced they would die, simply die, without a pet bunny to call their own, both sets of parents had vetoed the idea. Their disappointment had been mutual and furious.

"We'll get *our* kids bunnies if they want them, won't we, Katy?" John had said defiantly, and she had nodded with the pouting vehemence only a nine-year-old can muster.

After all, the important point wasn't the casual mention of two gangly youngsters someday having children together; it was the prospect of having the awesome power of a Grownup, of being able to go out and buy Easter bunnies whenever you wanted. Besides, in those days it was still a given that everybody had to get married someday, and who else would she marry but Johnny? He was the only boy she knew who didn't try to shove night crawlers down the back of her blouse.

The world was different by the time they'd finished college. All of a sudden the stigma of being single was gone, the pressure to marry and have children was off, and the lure of career was strong. It was all right to be a woman alone or a man alone in this new society, and Kathleen Herold Fritz shed the Katy identity forever and stomped happily into the business world to make her mark.

"I've made a decision, Johnny," she told him on the tenth of August the year they had graduated. "I'm not going to get married. Ever. I don't have to."

"So, who asked you?"

She'd laughed at that. "No one."

"Well, then that's not a decision you made at all, is it? No one asked you to marry him, so you have no choice but to be single."

"Johnny, you're splitting hairs—"

"I am not. You've got to turn down a proposal before you can be credited with a conscious choice. Otherwise you're just another old maid. But never fear, I'm going to help you out on this. Save you from a fate worse than death. Will you marry me, Katy?"

"Of course not! Johnny, how silly—"

"There. *Now* you're single by choice."

It was their own little private joke. Every year on the tenth of August Johnny proposed dutifully, and Kathleen turned him down, and he kept a running tally so she could be the woman who had rejected one proposal, then two, then three, and this year's would make it twelve.

"So, what are you thinking about?"

She eased slowly, reluctantly, back into the present. "I was just thinking that I must be some kind of heartbreaker to have turned down twelve proposals of marriage," she said, smiling.

"Eleven."

"So far."

John smiled and straightened on the bench. "Just think. If you'd had the good sense to say yes when we were twenty, you could have had ten children by now."

The thought made her shiver, and that made John laugh.

"Sorry, kid." He put a hand on her knee. "But if you want to see your dad before the rest of them get here, we'd better go in now."

She stiffened instantly. "They shouldn't have come," she said.

"He *asked* them to come. And he wanted them here so badly that he sent plane tickets for every one of them. It must have been important to him, Kathleen. They're his family, for crying out loud. And yours."

"That's stupid. I was four when we moved away, and we haven't seen any of them since. Father's my family, and Mother was, and you. Anyone else is just another stranger."

John pulled her gently to her feet and tucked her hand in his elbow. He started to walk toward the hospital entrance, but she dug in her heels.

"Come on, Kathleen. It won't be so bad. Just think of it as a family reunion." He stopped pulling when he saw her eyes start to fill. "Kathleen? What's wrong?"

"It's *not* a reunion, John." Her voice was pitched too high, and her throat hurt. "It's a wake. . . . They're coming for a wake; only they made a mistake, because he's not dead yet." She held her eyes wide open, waiting for them to dry out before she blinked.

John's face twisted in sympathy, and he reached over to smooth a stray hair from her face, but she jerked away from him and stomped off down the sidewalk toward the hospital entrance. Her heels made hard, angry clicks on the cement as she marched off to the war that nobody wins.

* * *

"Well! There are my kids!" George Fritz was sitting up in bed, striped pajamas buttoned to his throat, the heartiness of his voice terribly out of place in the wasted body that had seemed to grow smaller and smaller with every passing day. He didn't sound like a dying man, and there was something wrong with that.

"Hi, Daddy." The little-girl voice came out of the adult mouth that brushed against a sunken cheek, then lingered there a moment.

John reached over her to clasp George's hand, marveling at the undiminished strength of a much diminished man.

"You two look like bookends today," George said, leaning back on bunched pillows, smiling at the two almost identical gray suits.

Kathleen and John glanced down, then exchanged sheepish smiles.

"We didn't notice," Kathleen murmured, speaking for them both.

"You never do, but no matter. There it is, just the same. Nice of you to come and meet the family today, John." George cocked one eyebrow and grinned. "Or should I say it was nice of you to drag Kathleen with you?"

"He didn't have to drag me," Kathleen said sharply, "but I still don't know why you wanted them all here. Half of them are Mom's relations, not yours—"

"—and they're taking some of the time we have left, when you want me all to yourself, right, honey?"

Kathleen felt her lower lip creep out a fraction of an inch and wondered if she looked as childish as she felt. "I don't even *know* these people," she mumbled.

"Know them? What's to know? They're *family*."

She lifted her hands in exasperation, then let them drop to her sides. There was no sense in arguing the point. He was from a different time, a time when life revolved around the family, a time beyond Kathleen's comprehension.

"Florence is coming, honey."

She looked at her father and frowned. "Great-Aunt Florence? But she must be in her nineties by now, and it's a 1,500-mile trip."

Her father chuckled. It was a raspy, unpleasant sound, and Kathleen winced. What could be more cruel than a disease that made laughter hurt? "She didn't jog it, Kathleen, although it is the first time she's ever been on a plane. I didn't really expect her to agree to it. The woman flatters me."

"So, how many are coming?"

"Six. Just the ones who were closest to us when your mother and I started out. And speaking of that . . . " He strained to reach an old black-and-white photo positioned next to the water glass on the bedside table. "Florence dug that out of one of her albums and mailed it to me. Thought you might get a kick out of it. That's me and your mother, of course, before we got married. I'm the pretty one in the striped suit."

Kathleen looked down at the photo and smiled at the terribly attractive, terribly young people smiling back at her. They didn't look like her parents. "Were you very much in love then?" she asked wistfully, looking up quickly when her father laughed.

"Afraid not. We weren't even married yet, and I didn't marry your mother because I loved her. That didn't come until years later. Five years, in fact. I fell in love with your mother five years after the wedding."

"That's nonsense!" she said impatiently. "Why on earth would you ever get married if you didn't love each other?"

Her father shook his head with a little smile, the way he had when she'd asked him if it hurt the pod when you scraped the peas out. "Because that's what you did, that's all. You found a suitable partner, you got married, you raised a family, and that was that. In those days, no one ever thought of doing anything else. God forbid you should be one of those single people nobody wanted. It was different then. Not like today." His grin flashed mischievously. "Good thing I wasn't born in your time, Kathleen, or you wouldn't be here now. I think I would have stayed single forever." His grin faded to a slightly off-center smile, as if he'd barely escaped something too terrible to contemplate.

"That's disgusting," she muttered, grateful she had missed being born into such an archaic time. "Having to get married just because it was something you were expected to do."

"Well now, maybe it was, and maybe it wasn't. Sometimes the choices you don't make for yourself turn out to be the best ones of all. Like with me and your mother, for instance. Of course, we were much more romantic in those days."

She chuckled at her father's naïveté and shared a raised eyebrow with John. "Romantic? Come on, Father. Marrying someone because they're 'suitable' is hardly romantic. Not like love at first sight—but I don't imagine you ever believed in that."

Her father looked almost offended. "Of *course* I believe in love at first sight. That's just what it was between me and your mother, after all."

"Now wait a minute," Kathleen interrupted. "You just said—"

"Love at first sight," he explained patiently. "That's what it was. First time I ever looked at her."

Kathleen stared at him, frustrated. "Five years after the wedding?"

"Exactly. We'd been painting the outside of your grandma Herold's house the most atrocious shade of yellow. Worst heat wave in years. We were hot and sweaty and splattered with paint, and when we finally finished, I looked over at your mother . . . " His gaze grew distant as he smiled at the memory. "And I *saw* her. For the very first time." He glanced at them both a little sheepishly. "Guess I was a slow learner."

Kathleen and John stood motionless by the bed, brows beetled in identical expressions of confusion.

"George?" The voice at the doorway was shrill, demanding, and unbelievably loud, considering its source. A tiny, stooped woman with thinning white hair and a wizened face squinted into the room, thin lips pursed in irritation. "George? Is that you?"

"Florence, you old biddy! Get in here!"

Kathleen watched in amazement as her father shot to a sitting position, knowing what the gesture had cost him in pain. Had she ever seen joy like that on his face before? If she had, she couldn't remember when.

The old woman hobbled over to the bedside, leaning heavily on a thick black cane. She brushed past Kathleen to stoop over her father and plant a dry, withered kiss on his cheek. The slight breeze of her passing was filled with the fragrance of violet water, and the scent evoked a dozen involuntary memories tumbling over one another in Kathleen's mind. Violet water, butterscotch hard candy, and white sheets billowing on a clothesline on a hill. Before she had a chance to sort them out, the old woman had turned and lifted her arms with a stern expression that commanded a hug. Kathleen bent dutifully to the embrace, almost pulling back when the violet water filled her nostrils and whisked her instantly to another place and another time.

"I can't believe it!" she whispered without thinking, stunned. "I remember you."

The old woman pushed her away by the shoulders and clicked her tongue. "Well, of *course* you do, child. What did you expect? I used to mind you a lot when you were just a youngster. For a whole week once, when your ma and pa came out here to look for a house, fools that they were. When was that, George? Little Katy was what? Three? No, four. You never should have moved so far away, George." She scolded him bitterly for a twenty-eight-year-old transgression. "I told you then and I'll tell you now. Look at this child. Grown up already, and her own flesh and blood never did get to see it happen."

But her father wasn't paying any attention to Great-Aunt Florence anymore. He was too busy getting hugs and handshakes from men and women Kathleen didn't recognize . . . except maybe, maybe that one man was just a little familiar . . . maybe she did know him from somewhere. He had gentle brown eyes that met hers suddenly, and when he grinned shyly, a name popped into her head. *Lenny.* How did she know that?

"How about me, Katy?" he asked with a hopeful smile. "Do you remember me, too?"

It was so stupid to want to cry just then, but it took every ounce of willpower she had to keep from doing it. She was all right until this Lenny person wrapped her in a big hug and smacked her loudly on the cheek, and it was the familiar sound of that kiss that stirred up the memories of a young, handsome uncle and the little girl that had idolized him.

"I do!" she whispered, astonished, then pulled away far enough to look at him. "You had a hundred old cars lined up in Grandma Herold's backyard."

Lenny laughed. "Not quite a hundred. Three. A '48 Studebaker, a '39 Ford, and the old Nash. You used to love those old things, Katy. You'd sit in them for hours."

She nodded, lips pressed tightly together. "They smelled good. Cars don't smell that way anymore."

Suddenly, she remembered the carnival. Lenny had taken her when everyone else was too busy. She'd gotten sick on the merry-go-round, and he'd put her on his lap on the way home and let her pretend to steer to make her forget her queasy stomach.

The trickle of Lenny memories was building to a flood when she was grabbed from behind, and in the instant that she turned, her mind flashed a picture of a bouncy, ponytailed teenager who had held a tiny Katy on her lap while they listened to the tinkling song of a music box from Japan. The ponytail was gone, and the music box, but all of that still lingered behind the serene gaze of an adult woman who had exchanged bounce for the mature beauty of contentment.

"Penny," Kathleen whispered; but then Aunt Isabelle moved in from the side and the word froze in her throat because she was seeing her mother as she would have looked had she lived another fifteen years. When Isabelle reached out with her arms, the tears finally began.

It wasn't the awful gut-wrenching sobbing she'd been doing so much lately. It was just a continual, harmless stream she kept brushing away while she laughed and remembered and felt her heart swell in the most painful way.

Connections. They clicked on their own high heels through the sidewalks of her mind as she listened to the endless river of tales, started by one, picked up by another, leading inevitably to another story altogether. They spoke of parents she had never known—teenagers, young adults, pre-Katy people who suddenly took on a new identity; and then the stories introduced her to herself—the colicky, wailing infant who spit up strained peas on her baptismal gown and got the hiccups whenever she was tickled; the toddler fascinated by Grandma Fritz's bunny-shaped cookie jar and Grandpa Herold's wire-rimmed glasses; the cuddly young child who had loved hugs and kisses and doled them out indiscriminately. *Her?* Kathleen Herold Fritz? No. Of course not! That had been someone else. Someone named Katy.

The afternoon became old as she listened to a roomful of strangers give her the gift of her own history. The threads tightened, drawing her close to people who only belonged in the past, not the present; but when she tried to fight against the pull, she thought of her father. Soon he would be a part of the past, too. She would lose him, and through him, the only link to her mother, and no one would know who they had been and what they had done and how empty the world would be without them—no one, except these strangers.

Finally, the watch nurse came in, took one look at George's drawn face, and shooed all but Kathleen and John from the room. The crowd went noisily, reluctantly, mollified only by the assurance that they could return the following day.

"Three minutes," the nurse told Kathleen and John sternly, "then you're out, too. For heaven's sake, look at the man! What have you people been doing in here? Aerobics?"

John and Kathleen stood next to the bed, arm-in-arm, both smiling down at the worn face smiling up.

"Well, John," George said, "what do you think of the sorry lot that just left here?"

John tipped his head until it touched Kathleen's and grinned. "What I think of them doesn't seem to be the question. More to the point is what they think of me. I've never been interrogated so thoroughly in my life!"

George chuckled. "Florence?"

"All of them. It was a gang questioning."

Kathleen cocked her head. "About what?"

John half smiled almost apologetically. "My background, my profession, my income, when precisely the wedding would be, and how many children I wanted."

Kathleen chuckled sympathetically. "Oh, dear. Sorry about that, John. We should have guessed they'd all jump to the same conclusion."

"They're all very protective of Katy, you know," her father said fondly. "Always were."

Kathleen bent to kiss her father, then hugged him as fiercely as she had dared since the pain had spread everywhere. He didn't seem to mind. "Thank you, Daddy," she whispered. "I had a wonderful time today. In a way, I'm sorry they have to go home tomorrow."

Her father's hand reached for hers and squeezed weakly. "Most of them work, you know, except Florence, and she has to get back to her garden. God forbid she should miss the bean harvest. Besides—" He fixed Kathleen with a tender look. "—they'll be back, honey."

She straightened and stood rigidly for a moment. *Of course they'd be back. For the funeral.* The successful, decisive woman's body stood straight and strong while a little girl's tears fell from a broken heart.

As if he had read her thoughts, her father said, "And any other time that you need them or want them, they'll come. Or you can go there. They're family, Kathleen. They'll always be there."

* * *

The magic sidewalk wasn't so bad heading back to the parking lot, or maybe she was too strangely content for its power to affect her just now. She walked with her right arm twined through John's, her head resting on his shoulder. He snuggled his arm closer to his body, pulling her with it.

"It wasn't really so bad, was it, Katy?"

She couldn't remember the last time he'd called her that; only that it had been a long time ago, when they were both still children. "Not for *me,*" she said with a smile. "But it must have been terrible for *you.*" She chuckled at the thought of John fielding all those embarrassing questions. "How many children did you tell them you wanted?"

He walked three full paces before he answered: "As many as I could get."

"Father John." She laughed softly, but the laugh faded quickly because it wasn't such a preposterous picture after all. John would have been such a wonderful father; could still be a wonderful father, if he wanted to be.

"That was the number one question, you know, from all of them," he said softly. "Whether or not I wanted a family. That was the important part. They'll forgive you anything else, I think, as long as you promise to continue the old family tree. As your great-aunt Florence said at least twenty times, 'What else is there?'"

Kathleen stopped dead in the middle of the magic sidewalk and, in the space of an instant, relived the first four years of her life, the few hours of this afternoon, and the peculiar void in between. *There is nothing else,* she realized suddenly. *Absolutely nothing. It's all we're born into, all that sustains us in the time we have, and the one and only thing we leave behind. Family. The gift beyond price. The last gift her father would ever give her, and the most important.*

John was pulling her gently forward, digging in his pocket for the car keys, talking just as if this were any other day, as if the world was exactly the same place it had been just a few hours before. "You know," he was saying, brows tilted just so, "Florence kept bugging me about when we were getting married, and just to keep her quiet I finally told her I was proposing on the tenth. I didn't tell her it was an annual joke, of course, so I'm afraid she has all sorts of expectations. She swore she was going to call you on the eleventh to congratulate you." He dropped her arm and bent to insert the key into the car door lock, then grinned up at her. "You're going to have to think up a terrific reason for turning down a splendid fellow like me."

Kathleen was standing next to the car, her hands clasped loosely in front of her, smiling down at the tops of her shoes.

And then, in this the twenty-eighth year of their friendship, she raised her head and looked at John. For the very first time.

The Leaf That Mother Turned

Annie Hamilton Donnell

Mother looked at herself in the mirror and sighed heavily. A Campbell New Year's tradition was at stake, and it looked as if she would fail her family. Then came the $100 check. What should she do with it? When this story was written almost a century ago, $100 would have bought much more than it would today.

Mother's soft brow was wrinkled in perplexity. She tore off a leaf of her little shopping pad and began all over on a fresh one. One hundred dollars, which had seemed so tremendous a sum to Mother when she opened Aunt-in-law Lavinia's Christmas letter a few days ago, was proving inelastic enough to be actually a worrisome $100! She was finding difficulty in stretching it to cover Victoria's music lessons, and Victor's microscope, and the new best dress Glory really needed, to keep pace with the other college girls. Besides, the minute she had unfolded that check and read, "One hundred and no/100 dollars" on its face, she had said, "Phonograph," and had seen one set up in that faraway prairie home of her married boy, dispensing sweet music to hungering and thirsting ears. Mother had *heard* that music herself.

"But I don't know . . . ," hesitated Mother thoughtfully, the wrinkles on her soft forehead deepening. "Perhaps I ought to spend it having the house done over—such a lovely lot could be done for $100. Or maybe I'd better just put it in the bank for Hughie's nest egg. Time he got to be of college age, it would have grown beautifully. Oh, Aunt-in-law Lavinia, you darling!" Mother's lips drew up, and twinkles crept into her eyes. "You don't know how puzzling it is to be suddenly rich!"

Aunt-in-law Lavinia had always been rich. She had never had to cover a shopping pad with anxious little "sums," as Mother went on covering hers. Sum after sum, and still the puzzle grew.

"If I could only think who needed it most," she sighed. "Now, that microscope for Victor—of course it looks like an extravagance, but Victor's wanted it all his fifteen years, bless him! And Victoria's piano lessons had to be interrupted when Hughie's doctor bills mounted up so; and honestly, Glory's best dress is so out of style!"

Mother's own "best" dress had been in style so long ago that it was nearly time for it to be in style again. But of course Mother's didn't much matter, since she never needed to dress up, anyway. She got up now, with her puzzle still unsolved, and prepared to go downstairs to Father and the children. Preparation with Mother meant smoothing her smooth hair a little smoother and slipping into a clean apron. Accidentally, she caught a glimpse of herself in the looking glass. It was as if she found herself confronting a stranger: a thin, tired, unattractive stranger that she did not want to be introduced to. No, not to that faded creature!

"I don't like your looks," scolded Mother. "Go away! Years ago I knew somebody you remind me of a little, but you can't make me believe you're *her!*" Grammar failed at this exasperating minute. "Why, she wouldn't be old now—just nice and middle-aged. You are *old!*"

The faded creature in the looking glass seemed to be trying to reply, perhaps to defend herself. Her lips moved as she faced Mother.

"Oh!" Mother cried. "Don't say a word—not a word! I pity you, poor thing; but don't *talk!* Just go away, and never let me see your face again."

Then Mother laughed wholesomely. Why scold and sigh? She had known all the time that the faded creature was there. Aunt-in-law Lavinia's check was much more interesting than faded creatures. She fell again to smoothing her hair between her fingers and counting the beautiful chickens the check could hatch. When had she ever had a check for "one hundred and no/100 dollars" before?

Strange of Aunt-in-law Lavinia to ask her not to tell anyone of it. But it would make the surprise chickens when they hatched all the thrillier for the family. If one only knew the best chickens!

"Mother, Mother!" Victoria, young and joyously boisterous, burst into the room. "You went and forgot what day it is, Mother. New Year's! I've put on my new silk stockings, and Victor's going to put his Christmas slippers on; he's worn all his neckties so soon. Glory is dressing up in something new. Quick, Mother, get on something new and come down. *You* ought to have reminded *us.* You're the Campbellest of us all."

It was a Campbell custom, this greeting the New Year with something symbolically fresh and new. That faded creature in the looking glass—or, rather, the young creature she reminded Mother of—had been a Campbell and had always worn something new on New Year's Day. The pretty little custom had descended to daughters and sons.

Mother was suddenly astir with interest. Of course it was New Year's; how could she have "gone and forgotten"—*she,* the "Campbellest" one in the whole family?

Father's drawer was hastily pulled out, and Mother rummaged in it. What a pity Father had already worn his new muffler—and his four-in-hand necktie, too! Here it was, all mussed where it had been twisted and tied. Well, there was no other way, then. Mother pulled out a bulky garment. At the head of the stairs, she called down.

"Victor, you there? *Victor!* Oh, well, here's a new shirt for Father to put on. Catch it! Tell him it's the only brand-new thing in his drawer. He can put it on down there in the spare room, to save his lame foot coming upstairs."

Back in her room, Mother opened her own drawer. Her face was wrinkled thoughtfully. Her Christmas had not been a *wearable* one. She could not put on Glory's book or the twins' cup and saucer. But anything new, Christmas or not, would do. She turned over the contents of her drawer consideringly.

"Nothing new there. I might put on new stockings. Poor Campbells, how they'd groan! But new's new, fripperies or stockings. And stockings would match Father's shirt."

Mother smiled; and when Mother smiled, her resemblance to the faded creature was less striking. Mother's lips were made for smiling.

But the stockings failed her, too. They were the girls' stockings mostly, neatly patched. Girls do so hate wearing patches, and mothers don't mind. It was the best way to save worth-saving stockings. There was not a new pair. Silk stockings would satisfy the Campbells, but Glory's old ones weren't new; that seemed apparent by the feet of them!

Well, then, blouses—but they were Glory's blouses, too! Too worn for college, but too good to waste. Mother looked them over carefully.

"I shall have to wear my cup and saucer," she sighed. "No, I can't! I've drunk out of it. And I've begun to read my book."

The little custom of the Campbells seemed destined to go unfollowed by this "Campbellest" one of all in the family. It was a little thing, perhaps; but suddenly to Mother it seemed a big thing. Mother sank into a chair and sobbed. She was not really pitying herself; it was the Campbells she was pitying. She had promised a long-ago dear grandmother Campbell to celebrate all her New Year's Days, and her husband's and sons' and daughters' New Year's Days, in this simple, pretty way. That dear grandmother seemed to be looking reproachfully at her now.

"Aren't you going to put on something new, my dear? This is New Year's Day."

And must she answer, "Oh, Grandmother, I can't! I haven't anything new"?

The sobbing ceased. Now Mother was ashamed. Her soft, middle-aged cheeks flushed. She could not look that long-ago dear grandmother in the face and say that humiliating thing.

"Mother, Mother! Aren't you coming down? May we put on a new tablecloth, spandy new? Please—and new napkins, Mother? We'll have new bread to eat!" Victoria's merry girl's voice came up to Mother as she sat confronting her self-shame. Tablecloths and napkins added to it.

"There aren't any new ones—tablecloths or napkins," Mother called back reluctantly. She saw inside that linen drawer downstairs, and patient darnings and patchings danced before her eyes impishly. Was there anything "spandy" new in all the world? Not in Mother's world, not there. Linen drawers had always seemed, like stockings and blouses, personal to Mother; and nothing personal to Mother was spandy new. She had denied herself napkins and tablecloths.

"Don't open that drawer!" her soul cried out to the dear grandmother of long ago.

This time she stayed before the looking glass and forced herself to gaze at the faded creature. She would not go away.

"You are to blame!" she stormed at the creature. "You—you! Don't dare to pity yourself! You've made your own bed; now lie on it! Oh, oh, how you do look! How you do look! And I tell you, you're not old—just nice and middle-aged. I won't have you old!"

With both hands, Mother clung to the youth her soul loved. Suddenly it seemed a priceless possession, and she had almost lost it. She had denied it to herself needlessly. Soon enough, oh, soon enough, she must be old—but not yet. She would not listen to the sad, slow bells that toll the old, old knell of age.

Aunt-in-law Lavinia's letter, with its precious check, had fallen to the floor. Mother caught it up and read her own name again: "Pay to Mary Campbell Rice," that "one hundred and no/100 dollars"; to her—*to her!* She slipped the precious blue slip into the bosom of her dress, put on her clean apron, and went downstairs.

"What have you got on that's new, Mother?" Victor and Victoria demanded. The twins' imperiousness was dear to Mother, and she smiled back at them.

"Something new," she said. "Spandy. But I'm not going to tell small children! Not yet awhile. Now I'll make new biscuits, and we'll open new strawberries, and begin to love each other all over new."

"There's a big patch on the clean tablecloth."

"Put the cake plate over it, and the salt shaker over the little patch!" Mother answered joyfully.

A curious new life surged within her since she had spoken her mind to the faded creature upstairs. Standing there in front of the looking glass on New Year's Day, Mother had turned over a new leaf. The rejuvenating crackle of it was in the ears of her soul now. She made her biscuits and cut her cake as if to some inward militant music.

Around the table the family gathered presently, and Mother smiled at them cheerily.

"Guess what?" she said as she poured Father's cocoa. "I'm going to run away from you folks!"

"Mother!"

"Mary!"

"To Aunt-in-law Lavinia's, for nobody knows how long. Anyway, a week. Glory won't go back to college for a week; and you'll pour the cocoa, won't you, Glory?"

Turning over new leaves was not altogether easy. The astonishment in all their dear, dismayed faces pricked Mother's heart, but she kept on smiling. She would not turn back the leaf.

"Aunt-in-law Lavinia is old. It is dreadful to be old. I shall try to comfort her. Besides, I want her advice about something."

Suddenly, Mother's smile shook on her lips. What was this thing she was doing and going to do? Only the memory of the faded creature upstairs held up Mother's hands.

She was gone six days. How life dragged to them all! They had never thought before about a motherless life, and the awakening to what it meant was almost startling. It was Victoria, the girl twin, who made the real discovery for the family, however. Quite unexpectedly she made it. Up in Mother's room, rummaging for something, she suddenly discovered it.

"Glory! Vic! Father!" she called in her clear, young treble. "Oh, come up here to Mother's room, where I am! Bring pocket handkerchiefs."

They found her surrounded with clothes, Mother's clothes, mended and faded. Glory's eye took in instantly her worn blouses. Victoria pointed to a pair of shoes.

"Mine! Mother's feet aren't but sixteen years big. I didn't want to wear those shoes after they were patched. I—I made a fuss."

Glory winced. She had "made a fuss" about those blouses. Even Mother's beautiful little mendings she had not been willing to wear. She had disdainfully discarded all the beautiful clothes at college that were thrown aside as soon as they needed mending. A strange feeling grew and grew within Glory. It had already grown within the girl twin. Victoria made a sudden gesture toward Victor, who was staring amazedly.

"Go downstairs. There's nothing of yours here. Mother doesn't wear your things, or Father's—yet. Go along down, Vic. I'm glad Father didn't come up; this is a woman's affair."

And the two "women," left alone, settled it together. They were grave-eyed and a little older when they, too, went down.

Mother came on the seventh day, early in the morning. In spite of her night on a sleeper, she was sweet and fresh. She stood before her dear

family, a vision of freshness and sweetness. They knew her because she was Mother, but it was as though they looked at her through long-ago childish eyes that had seen her when she was young. For this was a young mother smiling at them from the doorway. Her sweet lips shook as she smiled.

"Mother!"

"Mary!"

She took one step, and it was toward Father.

"Father dear, first. Oh, Father dear!" she cried.

His big arms took her in, and from the dear shelter of them she made her speech. It came brokenly.

"Oh, Twinnies—oh, Glory, love me! I'm just the same inside. It's only the clothes that are different. I decided not to grow old yet, and you *have* to have a new garment or two to keep young in. Look!" Suddenly, she broke away from Father and pirouetted before them gaily, tears on her cheeks.

"Look! This is my new suit, and there are two new blouses besides. And does anybody see anything else?"

New hat—new shoes—a new Mother! She paraded before them with her smiling, tearful face. They noticed how soft her hair was, how pink her dear cheeks were with excitement. They noticed—oh, they noticed how sweet she was!

"I had them all on, on New Year's Day!" said this new Mother, laughing. "But you never knew, now, did you? You never saw how fine I looked. Poor dears, how I'm plaguing you! It was Aunt-in-law Lavinia's Christmas check I had on, to celebrate the Campbell custom. I had it tucked in my dress. Then, because I'd decided not to be a faded old creature, I went away and grew young. Look at me just one more minute, and then come and kiss me *in a body!* I want you all at the same time! If you don't come, I'll know you think I'm a selfish mother—" But how could she finish with them all there in a body? All at the same time, kissing her.

"Now"—rather breathlessly a little after—"somebody clear the dining room table. I have three new tablecloths in my trunk. You can put them all on, or one at a time. And napkins—everything's hemmed and ready. I did it at Aunt-in-law Lavinia's, and the dear, blind stitches are hers. Oh, my dears, my dears, it's so beautiful to feel young! Only I feel so selfish, too!"

"If that isn't just like mothers," Glory cried, "to patch up even the family's selfishness and try to wear that! Oh, mothers are strange! Mothers are *dear!*"

Love on the Wing

Penny Porter

**"Dumbest birds on earth!" Bill grumbled.
Perhaps they were, but that didn't stop
eight-year-old Jaymee from wanting to
save the injured dove's life.
And that was the beginning of it all.**

One unforgettable morning, while jouncing along twisting cattle trails and dirt roads on our Arizona Hereford ranch, we came across the mourning doves. Pegged out like clothespins along miles of sagging telephone wires, their sunlit feathers reflected rainbows in the early glow of dawn, but their bead-bright eyes were riveted on our pickup load of grain.

"Dumbest birds on earth!" Bill grumbled as he pulled up beside the first of six eighteen-foot aluminum feed troughs.

"Why do you always call them dumb, Daddy?" Jaymee asked.

"Because doves are out to kill themselves before they even hatch." He struggled to light his pipe, a familiar sign he had more to say. "They fly into windowpanes and break their necks.

55

They lean over too far and drown in stock tanks." He climbed from the truck and hauled an eighty-pound sack of grain onto his shoulders. "And they build nests with such big holes in the bottom, they wouldn't hold a Ping-Pong ball, let alone an egg."

"Then how come there's so many?" Jaymee called as we watched him buck his way through the herd of milling cattle, rip open a sack, and begin to pour. He never had time to answer.

Alerted by the clatter of grain, doves suddenly darkened the sky. We heard the surge of whistling wings and the phantom rush of air as they swooped down in a frenzied quest for corn. Some lit on the cows' horns. Others blanketed their backs. But most silvered the earth like a restless sea around the stomping hooves of cattle.

Jaymee screamed, "Daddy! That cow's standing on a dove's wing!"

Bill tossed the empty feed sack into the back of the pickup and hurried toward the cow. "Dumb bird!" he muttered as he twisted the cow's tail till she shifted her weight. The dove was free, but one wing lay on the ground, severed from its body at the shoulder.

I don't know how long we watched the pathetic creature flap its remaining wing and spin in useless circles as though winding itself into the ground. At last it tipped forward, buried its beak in the dirt, and mercifully lay still.

Thank God! I thought, torn between scrambled emotions of sadness and relief. *It's dead.* After all, there was nothing we could do for a bird with only one wing.

Bill nudged the dove with the toe of his boot. Horrified, we watched it flip onto its back, wild-eyed with pain.

Jaymee's small hands flew to her lips. "Oh, no!" she cried. "It's still alive! Daddy, do something!"

Bill leaned down and wrapped the tiny, broken creature in his red handkerchief and handed it to Jaymee. "Here, honey," he said, "you'll have to hold it till we get home."

"But it's going to die!" I heard the tremor of fear in her voice.

"I don't think so," he said. "They're even—"

I caught his eye and defied him to say "too dumb to die."

"What are we going to do with it, Mama?" Jaymee's brow was creased with worry. Only eight years old, she loved small animals and was forever rescuing soft, fluffy kittens, baby rabbits, and ground squirrels. But this was different. This was a bird. Furthermore, it was grotesquely wounded.

"We'll put it in a box and give it water and grain." I stopped right there, knowing too well the rest was up to God.

Sorrow clouded Jaymee's small face. "But if it lives, it won't ever be able to fly again, and it'll have to live in a cage—forever."

"Lots of birds do," I said.

"But those are canaries and parakeets . . . and they're pretty." Then, in a whisper, she added, "And they're smart."

On our way back to the house, Jaymee sat quietly between us, holding the young dove in her lap. Deep in thoughts of her own, she stroked its tiny head with two fingers until she walked into the kitchen, where Becky, her ten-year-old sister, was eating breakfast. She showed her the bird.

"A cow chopped off its wing," she told her.

Becky wrinkled her nose. Then later, after putting the bird in a shoe box filled with dried grass and setting the box and bird near the wood-stove for warmth, Becky asked, "What are you going to name it?"

"Olive," Jaymee said.

"Olive! That's an awful name. Why Olive?"

"Because Noah's dove flew all the way back to the ark with an olive branch . . . and that wasn't so dumb."

While the girls were in school, I listened for sounds of life from the box and repeatedly peeked inside at the tiny gray, ghostlike creature hiding in the dark, head drooped, rainbows gone. In the barn I found a jar of antibiotic salve.

"For Olive," I said to Bill, wishing I could have slipped by unseen. He shrugged.

"Well, it's worth a try," I insisted, hurrying back to the house.

There I lathered the hideous wound with the medicine and asked myself, *Why am I doing this?* More to the point, I wondered why nature hadn't simply claimed the life of this pitiful creature. How could this bird live with only one wing? Poor little thing. Certain it was suffering, convinced it would die, I closed the lid. We'd done everything we could.

The next morning we heard a stirring in the box.

"Olive's eating!" Jaymee announced. Then, with absolute conviction, she added, "And she's a girl."

"How can you tell?" Becky asked.

"Boys have blue and purple feathers on their heads. Olive's just plain gray—and sometimes pink."

We kept the little bird near the stove in a large wire-mesh cage prepared with seeds, leaves, and twigs. In the sudden shock of light and space, Olive sensed freedom and again tried to fly. She flapped her one wing, repeatedly hurling herself against the wire-mesh squares, waffing her breast feathers, and falling over backward. It hurt to watch her try.

In time the wing fluttered slower and slower till finally it stopped altogether. From then on, Olive wandered around the cage sort of off-kilter, like half a bird, barely existing yet taking the time to preen and rearrange her feathers as though trying to draw a cape over the gaping hole. When evening came, she curled her pink claws around a small manzanita limb we'd wedged in the bottom of the cage in one corner. There she perched in a trancelike state, dreaming of life in the sky, I supposed, a life put on hold, until . . .

Early one morning, Jaymee was cleaning the cage. "Olive laid an egg!" she squealed. "Come look!" Resembling an elliptical, oversized pearl, the egg rolled around like a magic thing between a few twigs and leaves in Olive's favorite corner of the cage. "But why didn't she build a nest?" Jaymee asked.

"Just like in the wild," Bill said. "Too lazy to build a decent nest. They either lay their eggs in other birds' nests or slap three twigs together and call it home."

He was right. I, too, had seen doves' nests: flimsy little platforms, tossed at random among the mesquite and manzanita bushes, spanning weak boughs or remnant nests of other birds. Some were precariously balanced on knots of mistletoe. Most were within easy reach of predators: the bobcat, raccoon, and coyote. I'd walked often beneath branches to view the eggs from below, or discovered the empty, broken shells at my feet after they'd fallen through. Yet these birds kept right on laying in the same miserable nests.

Now here was Olive, caged, piteously wounded, soon laying an egg almost every day. For Jaymee, this was magic. But I had to question the little bird's efforts. Why was this happening? Without a mate, the eggs would be infertile. But Jaymee was a child, and children make plans. Instead of worrying about why, she accepted the miracle with her whole heart and began collecting the eggs in a teacup.

At first Bill didn't pay much attention to the dove. He had cattle, horses, and fields to care for. But then one Sunday, when he noticed Jaymee's cup was full, he made plans of his own. Out in his workshop he built a wooden egg box for her with a clear plastic lid revealing forty two-inch cubicles padded with black velvet inside.

"It's a treasure chest," he told her, "with a special place for each little egg." When he handed her the key to the tiny brass padlock, he added, "You can keep them safe forever."

She hugged him.

By now Olive was becoming very tame. No longer spooked by human hands, she tottered around the cage with anticipation. At the sight of

Jaymee, she cooed softly and pecked seeds or morsels of apple from her palm. And when Jaymee took her out of the cage to carry her around on her finger, the little dove no longer tried to fly. Instead she perched, seemingly content, and shared an ice cream cone till it was time to go back into the cage—and lay another egg.

Like all creatures wild and tame, Olive responded to love and care with growing trust. She looked forward to her daily dust bath in the metal cake pan filled with sand, and she especially enjoyed her shower, a gentle misting of water from a spray bottle, after which she cleaned her feathers vigorously. We liked to think she was happy. But our crippled dove's longing for her own kind and the life she'd left behind showed when we moved her cage to the glassed-in porch, where she could look out at the cobalt sky and sun-drenched fields of green alfalfa. Occasionally another dove would sail by, and Olive's wing would quiver and her little gray head would bob anxiously, begging to be noticed.

Incredibly, the egg laying continued. Sixteen! Seventeen! Eighteen! *How much longer can this go on?* I wondered.

Bill shared our concern with a gruff "The bird's gonna lay herself to death."

At least he didn't say "dumb," I thought.

Recently, I'd caught him putting small logs in the cattle troughs. "Rafts," he'd said when I inquired, "so the doves can climb out when they fall in." Was he starting to care just a little bit? Or had he always, in his own way?

When the nineteenth egg arrived, so did the first storm out of Mexico. Fearsome winds and stinging sands ripped birds' nests from the trees, dashing eggs and the newly hatched to the ground. The girls spent the morning burying dead newborns before the barn cats got them, and Jaymee gathered many different kinds of wild bird eggs, miraculously unbroken, and put them in her treasure chest. Most had tinted shells.

Rainbow colors, I thought, *displayed like precious jewels among pearls on velvet black.*

One storm often follows another in Arizona, so I wasn't surprised when the second one roared through, and Jaymee dashed into the kitchen cupping a naked-pink, open-beaked baby bird in her hands.

"It's hungry!" she cried. "Maybe Olive can be its mama."

I wasn't so sure, but Jaymee hurriedly named the newborn "Pinky." With an eyedropper, we squeezed chicken mash mixed with warm water into the orphan's yawning yellow mouth and debated bestowing such a helpless gift on our fragile dove.

What will she do? I wondered. Then I realized, *What did it matter?* We didn't know how to keep the hours-old creature the right temperature at night anyway. Only a mother bird could do that. My broody hen hatched and raised baby ducks, guinea hens, pheasants, and quail along with her own chicks. So, why couldn't a dove raise a stranger, too? Besides, if it worked, life in a cage wouldn't be so lonesome for Olive. I asked Bill what he thought.

"She'll probably think he's dinner," he said.

Jaymee's eyes widened. "Oh, Daddy!" she scolded. "Olive's smarter than that. We've got to try!"

"We'll fix up a nice nest first," I said, "a good sturdy one like a dove should make—soft and deep so the baby won't fall out."

The girls found a storm-damaged nest and lined it with horse hair and plenty

of chicken feathers for added softness. I worried the feathers might have an alien scent that Olive wouldn't appreciate, but since doves frequently feasted side by side with my chickens, I decided she wouldn't mind. Also, since Pinky was already a scented bouquet of human hands and chicken mash, and Olive was accustomed to both, we laid the newborn in the nest with one egg of her own at his side.

"Maybe that will help her think the baby is really hers," Jaymee said, and she placed the nest inside the cage.

During the night I awoke to strange sounds, living reminders that wild birds belong outdoors—not in my kitchen. Expecting the worst, I reached for my flashlight, not wanting to awaken Bill, and hurried to the scene. The nest was destroyed. At first I couldn't see any birds at all. Then, in that favorite corner where eggs were laid, one of nature's miracles unfolded like a flower bud in the beam of my light. On three small twigs, bright eyes aglow with joy, nested Olive—with Pinky cradled under her only wing.

The egg laying ceased. Pinky had a mother. Proud and protective, Olive chirped anxiously when we took him out for feeding countless times a day. When we put him back in Olive's nest, with a little dry grass tucked around and under him so he wouldn't tip over, she paced back and forth till she was certain he wasn't leaving again. Then she examined him thoroughly, picking and tweaking him as though trying to weave their lives together. It was clear to see she loved him.

Pinky thrived. Pink skin one day, milkweed down the next. Finally, feathers appeared on stubby wings, then everywhere. A delicate tapestry of silver-white and black, the fledgling soon needed a far more fitting name. When the short, hooked beak was topped by a tiny black-bandit mask, our bird book dubbed him a loggerhead shrike, lover of wetlands and rarely seen on our ranch after several years of drought. Jaymee renamed him Bandit.

Soon Bandit was perching on Jaymee's finger just like his mama did. Teetering on tiny black claws, he gobbled down spaghetti and bologna and pepperoni sliced into slender wormlike strips. As more feathers grew, his gourmet palate expanded to include moths, bugs, and any insect Jaymee could pick up with eyebrow tweezers. His passion was flies, but they had to be alive.

Flies are a part of ranch and farm life, and a door rarely opened without a herd of these miserable pests stampeding in. Unable to get out, they'd sizzle up and down windowpanes and fall on the sills, exhausted. Then Jaymee grabbed them by one leg with the tweezers and fed them, still buzzing, to Bandit, while Olive waited patiently for her serving on the bottom of the cage.

The morning we'd been dreading came when Bandit discovered he had wings. We found him clinging upside down to the top of the cage. Unable to figure out how to let go, he chatted and fluttered his wings eagerly, while Olive cringed in her corner, feathers frazzled.

"You're going to have to let him go," Bill told Jaymee. "He's scaring the heck out of the poor dove."

"But he needs to practice flying first," she argued, removing Bandit from the cage and perching him on her finger. Instantly, the young shrike took a test flight. He shot up and positioned himself on the wagon-wheel chandelier, took stock of his surroundings and shuttled awkwardly to the bullhorn hat rack, and from there to the toaster. By now Olive was chirping with alarm.

"Jaymee, you've got to put him outside," Bill said. "I don't want feathers in my coffee."

"But the cats'll get him!"

"He has to learn," he responded.

Outside we placed Bandit in a cottonwood tree so he could practice flying. We watched him flit from branch to branch and grabbed him twice when he landed on the ground. He learned fast. Too fast. The moment we tried to step inside, he zipped past us through the doorway and greeted us from the chandelier. Then he heard Olive and dived to the top of the cage, where she watched him from below, her wing vibrating with memory.

"She wants to go with him," Jaymee said sadly.

And he doesn't understand why she can't come, I thought.

Bandit remained housebound. Every time we took him outside, he'd perch for an hour on the milk separator right by the front door, mask cocked, wings ready, waiting patiently for someone to go through the door so he could sneak back in.

Night came. We knew he'd never survive with so many barn cats on the prowl. Furthermore, spring rains had lured many birds back to the lands by the White River draw. Perhaps the shrikes would return. Until he was ready to be on his own, we had to keep him safe, so we rigged up a temporary nighttime cage near Olive's. She seemed pleased.

Bandit grew increasingly adept at flying and was soon darting in and out of the front door at will, eager to remain part of the only home he knew. I warned Bill and everybody else, "Be careful when you come in for lunch. Our little shrike is going to sneak in, and he might get hurt if the door shuts too quickly."

As fate would have it, Bill was the one who forgot. Worse still, it was he who had put the heavy-duty spring on the door so it would snap shut faster and not let so many flies into the house. When he saw the little bird spiral over his head and land on the rug at his feet, his first words were, "I guess I had other things on my mind besides holding a door open for a bird." Then his voice dropped, and I could tell something was struggling within him. "I never saw the poor thing at all . . . till it was lying in front of me."

For the second time that year I watched him lean over to pick up a wounded bird. They are so delicate, and I knew he felt bad. Bandit was gasping, but the tiny needle-clawed feet gripped Bill's callused palm.

Reassured, Bill said, "Maybe he just got the wind knocked out of him." He handed the stunned creature to me to put back in his cage, right beside Olive's.

The next day, Bandit seemed cheerful enough but ruffled at being caged. We let him out. No longer the wing-testing, house-crashing maniac of previous flights, he flitted quite professionally among barn roofs, scattered trees, and barbed-wire fences. Our little shrike had grown up, and gradually he flew farther away. Easy to spot in his flashing white and black and silver, wing beats too fast to count, we watched him leave for the river. That was the last we ever saw of him.

Later in the summer, the girls were busy getting their projects ready for the Cochise County Fair only ten days away. Becky planned to show her horse, and Jaymee busied herself grooming her rabbits for the 4-H competitions. The egg chest had been set aside, perhaps for the following year, when suddenly Jaymee said, "Maybe I should show Olive and her eggs in the wildlife division, too."

"But Olive's been sick," I reminded her.

Indeed, after Bandit's departure, the little mourning dove had begun sleeping most of the day. Eyes half closed, she perched unnaturally fluffed on her manzanita limb. The only sign she showed of interest in life came with the early dawn: a plaintive "Oooh-ah-hoo-hoo-hoo," like the sorrowful cry of a lost soul in the desert, seeking comfort. Then she started molting.

Clearly unwell, she soon didn't seem to care where she roosted. Often she simply crouched uncomfortably over a few stray twigs and leaves. We tried to cheer her through her long, dark hours of sadness by adding sugar to her water and a nightlight to her cage. I played happy songs on the radio. Nothing worked. When she stopped taking dust baths altogether and dripped resentfully in a pool of water after misting, I was afraid she was going to die.

Then Bill returned from the feed store in Tucson with a truckload of cattle feed—and one small box that read "Special Diet for Indisposed Canaries."

"I just happened to walk through the small-pet section," he said, looking a little sheepish. "A bird's a bird, but I thought maybe a couple of vitamins might help Olive."

To our surprise, she seemed to perk up.

Jaymee added the cost of her daddy's purchase to her list of eggs, dates laid, and other miscellaneous dove project expenses in her 4-H journal. She even entered a paragraph about Olive's baby, Bandit, and facts she had learned from books about doves. "Unlike most birds," she wrote, "doves will keep right on laying when their eggs slip through flimsy nests or are stolen by predators." And finally, "Doves have been known to lay more than one clutch (nest of eggs) at a time and incubate a second and even a third batch while raising a lucky survivor from the first."

Meanwhile, Becky weighed Jaymee's idea about displaying her treasure chest, and she did an egg count for her sister. "You only have thirty-one, Jaymee. That leaves nine empty holes, so the project isn't complete. You'll have to wait till next year when birds start laying again."

I felt a strange sense of relief because Olive had never fully recovered from her sadness, despite the vitamins. She'd become frail, dusty-looking, almost spectral. If she were around strange animals and surroundings at the fair, I feared she would pick up an infection. At home she'd be safe. Then, the following morning, she laid another egg.

Hope lit Jaymee's eyes. She put the egg in her treasure chest—number thirty-two. "Only eight more to go," she said happily and dashed off to catch every live fly she could find for Olive.

During the short week that followed, Olive rallied with six more eggs.

Then three days before the fair, and two more eggs to go, our weary little dove huddled on her manzanita limb for the last time. We found her in the morning, motionless, like a tiny piece of driftwood washed up on desert sands.

"Do you think Olive was happy locked in a cage?" Jaymee asked her daddy as he wrapped the little one-winged dove in his red handkerchief, just as he'd done only a few short months ago.

"Why . . . of course she was," he answered awkwardly.

"How do you know for sure?"

He looked over Jaymee's head at me as though grasping for thoughts, trying to make sense out of the life of a bird. Then, in a blur of words that a man would never say except to a child, he stumbled ahead. "You took care of her. You fed her and . . . and gave her showers . . . and a baby . . . and told her how smart she was." He paused for a long moment. "And you know, she was smart . . . because out of all those things you did for her, she knew how much you loved her."

"And she gave me her eggs because she loved me too?"

"Her treasures," he said. "All that she had." He watched his youngest child gather two small handfuls of pale pink and gray feathers and fill the empty velvet nests before she turned the key.

"I'm going to show my egg collection anyway, Daddy." she murmured.

He smiled and hugged her. "I'll bet you win the blue ribbon."

And she did.

Ransom's Papers

Mary Wells

A soldier lay ill in his hospital bed, growing weaker each day. Only a miracle could save his life. Miss Eliot was determined to make one last try. It was only a letter, but who knew what it might do!

The old Southern mansion made an ideal army hospital. Standing as it did on the outskirts of Fernandina, it caught the slightest breeze from Amelia Harbor on one side of the island and from the ocean on the other. The broad windows gave a view of the white sandy beaches and the blue waters of the bay beyond.

The beauty of the scene, however, had little charm for Ransom, the gaunt soldier in the east corner room. His hollow eyes were fixed wistfully on a flitting sail, the progress of which he watched until the little craft had passed beyond his field of vision. Then he turned to the sweet-faced young nurse who was busy about the room.

"I suppose Fernandina's a pretty old town," he said with his slow New England drawl.

Miss Eliot straightened deftly the pillows with which Ransom was propped. "It was settled by the Spaniards in 1632," she said, "so it *has* had quite a history. There are some interesting places near here. Cumberland Island was the home of General Nathaniel Greene, and 'Light-Horse Harry' Lee is buried there."

A look of interest came into Ransom's face. "You don't say!" he exclaimed. "They was big men, both of 'em. Now, I ain't so surprised about General Lee, but it seems kind of funny that Nathan'el Greene would want to come off down here to live, don't it now?"

Miss Eliot's blue eyes twinkled. "Where is your home, Ransom?"

"Maine," said the soldier promptly, "and I'm proud of it, too. You ain't ever been in Maine, have you, Miss Eliot?" His tone was wistful.

"No, I never have, Ransom, but I mean to go there someday," she said pleasantly. "All of my great-great-ancestors were New Englanders, though my own family has always lived in Ohio."

"Ohio's a great state," said Ransom gallantly, "but I don't know as it quite comes up to Maine. It's a great country, all right, but Maine's a kind of long stretch from Fernandina," Ransom added with a sigh.

"Oh, not so far," said Miss Eliot cheerfully. "It takes only a few weeks for the transports to make the trip. You must hurry to get strong and well, or you won't be ready."

"That's right," said Ransom. "It won't be very long now before my discharge papers come, and just as soon as I git up among the pines, I'll begin to pick up. This here climate sort of takes the stiffenin' out of you, don't it?"

"It is enervating," acknowledged Miss Eliot. "By the way, how do you happen to be here, Ransom? I've never thought to ask you before."

"Guess you was too busy takin' care of me," said the soldier shyly. "You've been pretty good to me, Miss Eliot. I must have been an awful nuisance, 'specially when I was out of my head so long."

"An awful nuisance, Ransom," said the girl with mock seriousness. "But about your being in Fernandina?"

"Does seem kind of funny; but it come about natural enough. I was in the 42nd Maine, Army of the Potomac, and our regiment got orders to join Grant in Vicksburg. I was kind of ailin' before we set out from Fortress Monroe; got a cold doin' sentinel duty in the rain.

"It hung on and hung on, and it's hangin' on yet. So when we got to Fernandina, they dropped me off. 'Unfit for service,' they said." Ransom's voice faltered. "And here I am, a-waitin' for my discharge papers to come.

"It was hard to feel that I wasn't no more use, so to speak, when I'd just turned thirty-seven. Seems as if all the things I thought was hard before wa'n't nothin' to it. At first I thought I couldn't stand it, but land sakes, folks can stand most anything in this world! They have to."

Miss Eliot nodded in sympathetic comprehension.

"I've been doin' considerable thinkin' since I've been lyin' here," he went on. "War's a terrible thing, a cruel thing, with a lot of sufferin' for folks that ain't in any ways to blame—the women, the old folks, and the little children." His voice grew tender. "Don't seem right, somehow. Of course a man's got to do his duty. Now I could no more help enlistin' than I can help breathin', so that's no credit to me. When the call come, I just left Pa to run the farm and look after Adelaide and little Mary. Then there's them on the other side, the fellers that's goin' to be beat sure. They're such plucky fighters. I believe I'm right, and I'd fight 'em to a finish, but they don't see it that way, and it *is* kind of hard on 'em, ain't it, now?"

"That's the hard part of it," said the nurse gently. "The victory of one always means the defeat of the other." Something in Ransom's unspoken sympathy led her to open her heart. "Father's with Thomas in Tennessee. One brother's in the navy, and the youngest—" Her voice broke. "—is with Lee in Virginia. We were always great chums, Bob and I. He was Father's favorite, too. It was hard for Father."

She was silent. Then, as her eyes met Ransom's direct look of gentle compassion, she went on almost as if the words were forced from her. "And a man of whom I was very fond died at Shiloh, Ransom." Her voice lapsed into silence.

The bearded soldier reached out his thin hand and stroked the girl's sleeve. "I suspected you had an untold story, but I never dreamed it was like that. You're a brave little woman," he said tenderly, "way down here lookin' after us battered veterans."

Miss Eliot smiled through her tears. "Oh, I couldn't help it, Ransom, any more than I can help breathing; so you see it's no credit to me."

Day followed day in the cool old mansion over which fluttered the Stars and Stripes. At intervals came letters, official and unofficial, bulky documents with imposing government seals, communications for the commandant of the fort, papers galore; but among them all, Ransom's papers were not.

When the next transport sailed without him, he bade a cheerful adieu to the men going north. "I'm right down glad for you boys," he said to a soldier who had come to say good-bye. "It won't be long now before I'll be a-followin' you."

"That's right, Ransom," said the man heartily. "Good-bye, old fellow, and good luck!"

Outside the room he shook his head gravely. "That cough is pretty serious. It's too bad he isn't going up on this boat. There's so much confounded red tape in these government affairs a man could die fifty times before they get 'round to him."

The next day was Sunday, and as a special treat, Ransom was taken out on the veranda for a few hours. He was delighted.

"I'm a-pickin' up right along," he said to the nurse. "Perhaps it's just as well I couldn't go with the transport. Next time I'll be a good deal stronger." He looked out across the landscape with wistful eyes. "You ain't ever seen the pictures of my wife and little girl, have you?"

Miss Eliot shook her head, whereat Ransom reached his hand into his breast pocket and drew out a little carved wooden case, which he opened with much care, disclosing two daguerreotypes.

From one compartment looked the face of a woman with a broad brow, plain-banded hair, and a firm yet sweet mouth. The eyes had a strangely direct gaze, and the entire countenance bore the stamp of strength and sincerity. Through the almost austere reserve shone a divine tenderness. The nurse instinctively recognized one of those rare natures that are not baffled by difficulties, but which persevere through suffering, even through defeat, to final triumph.

"Adelaide was teaching in our district when I married her," said Ransom. "I never quite see how she come to take me. I was older and hadn't had her schoolin', and I ain't much to look at. But she always allowed she was satisfied, and we've been mighty happy together." There was a ring of pride in Ransom's voice.

The other picture was that of a little girl, four years old. Her parted hair hung in short curls on each side of a round, serious little face. The big eyes had a questioning look, and the lips were slightly parted. The low-cut frock and short sleeves left uncovered a beautiful neck and chubby, dimpled arms.

The nurse gave a cry of delight. "The quaint little darling!" she exclaimed. "I'd just like to give her a good hug."

"I guess maybe I'd better go in now, Miss Eliot."

"Tired, Ransom?" she said gently.

"Guess I am a little mite," he said reluctantly. "When I git up home how—" A severe fit of coughing interrupted the last sentence.

In the hall, a few minutes later, she encountered the old doctor. He was a tall man with bushy eyebrows and a pair of keen eyes.

Miss Eliot looked him squarely in the eye. "What are Ransom's chances?"

The old doctor regarded her gravely.

"Unless his papers come so that we can start him off on the next transport, Ransom's chances are practically nothing. I've written to Washington, and Commandant Haskell's written, and nothing's been heard. There you have it."

Miss Eliot's lips set themselves in firm lines. "I'm going to write," she said, "but I'm going to write to Adelaide."

"Who's Adelaide?" queried the old doctor curiously.

"Adelaide is Ransom's wife. I believe if anyone can get those papers, she can."

"There's a tug going up tomorrow," he said. "Your scheme may not work, but it's worth trying."

That night the nurse wrote the letter, and her whole heart went into it.

The days went slowly by. Ransom continued sweet-tempered and cheerful, although as he grew weaker, he became daily a little more quiet. Just when he stopped asking for his papers it would be hard to say, but that time did at last come. On those occasions when the mail was brought in he would watch wistfully, but the words did not pass his lips. Only his hollow eyes questioned. Miss Eliot grew to dread those moments. From her own letter to Adelaide, she had not heard.

So, in the process of time, came the day for the second transport to sail. That morning Miss Eliot stood on the broad porch, watching the busy scene at the dock. Her face was sad. "This afternoon," she found herself saying, "the boat will go, and Ransom's chance will go with it."

As she paused on the threshold, she noticed idly, far out in the harbor, a gunboat steaming toward the shore.

Slowly, she climbed the stairs to Ransom's room. As she entered, he greeted her with his accustomed cheerfulness. It was as if he guessed her thoughts and was trying to make it easy for her.

"It's a fine day," he said.

"Yes, Ransom."

"It's this afternoon the boat sails, ain't it, Miss Eliot?"

She nodded, not trusting herself to speak.

Then, at last, Ransom broke the reticence of weeks. "I've been sort of thinkin'," he said slowly, "and I guess it ain't goin' to be my luck to get home. It looks pretty much as if my papers was a-comin' from another world.

"Don't you feel so bad about it, Miss Eliot," he said comfortingly as he noted the expression on her face. "I'm real contented. I ain't denyin' it was kind of hard at first, when I began to realize how things was goin', but I'm feelin' more reconciled now. If I had to do it over, I wouldn't do no different. War does cost, and if I'm to be a part of the price, so to speak, I'm willin' to pay my share. Only—I just would like to see Adelaide and little Mary again." There was yearning unutterable in the soldier's voice. "If I ain't here when my papers come, Miss Eliot, I'd kind of like to have Adelaide have 'em, and there's a few things—"

"I'll see to everything, Ransom," said the girl, "but don't you give up for a moment. I can't have you give up. You see, I have set my heart on your going home."

In her agitation she had gone to the window and, with tear-filled eyes, was gazing down the shady street. At the wharf the gunboat had docked, and several uniformed pedestrians were coming toward the hospital. All this she noticed mechanically; then all at once her heart gave a convulsive leap.

Turning in at the gate was a tall lieutenant with a sun-browned face. Perched on his shoulder was a little girl. Her round hat had fallen back upon her neck so that her face, with its frame of clustering curls, was distinctly visible. She was smiling down at her tall companion in a way that betokened an established comradeship. It was the dear, quaint little girl of Ransom's daguerreotype! Miss Eliot did not need a second glance in order to recognize the tall, slender woman who followed.

Without daring to look at Ransom, Miss Eliot slipped quietly from the room and hurried down the stairs.

The lieutenant had set the child down on the porch and now stood with cap in hand. "Is this Miss Eliot?" he inquired courteously.

The nurse bowed; then she turned. "This is Mrs. Ransom, isn't it?" She held out her hand.

Then Adelaide spoke. "Am I . . . Is John—" Her white lips refused to frame the question.

"He's weak, Mrs. Ransom, but there is a good chance. And now that you have come—"

But Adelaide, overcome by the reaction, swayed suddenly, groping blindly before her. The lieutenant sprang forward, supporting her to a chair, while the nurse ran for a glass of water.

Adelaide drank the water obediently; then when she was recovered, she looked up into Miss Eliot's face. "I can see him?"

"Just as soon as I've prepared him a little. You will remember he's rather weak."

The lieutenant held out his hand. "I'm glad we found good news," he said heartily. "I'll be around again to see if I can be of any further service." He stopped to pat Mary's curly head. "Good-bye, honey," he said, and with a military salute, he strode away.

Ransom had attributed Miss Eliot's abrupt departure to the emotion that had so strongly swayed her. Now he lay in the east corner room, quietly watching a wisp of white cloud, which was drifting slowly through the blue sky. He felt that he, too, was drifting, drifting out toward the wide unknown expanse of eternity.

Miss Eliot's voice roused him. "Ransom," she said quietly, "are you strong enough to bear some good news?"

Ransom turned toward her quickly, wondering at the joy in her tone. Her cheeks were pink and her eyes like stars.

"Good news!" he stammered. "Have—have my papers come?"

"They came in a gunboat this morning, Ransom, by special messenger."

Joy so intense as to be almost dazzling overspread the worn face.

"My . . . papers . . . have . . . come . . . and I can go home this afternoon?" It was astonishing to see how the vitality flamed up in the worn frame.

"Do you feel strong enough to see the messenger, Ransom?"

"Strong enough!" Ransom's tone was sufficient answer.

The nurse left the room. A moment later, the door opened softly. On the threshold stood Adelaide and little Mary. The child had clasped in her chubby hand a long envelope with a red seal. Mindful of Miss Eliot's caution, Adelaide stood quietly. Only her eyes met her husband's with deep tenderness and passionate yearning.

"Adelaide!" whispered Ransom. "Mary!" He stretched out his arms.

The child, breaking away from her mother's restraining grasp, ran forward. "Daddy, Daddy!" she cried in her shrill, sweet voice. "We've brought your papers!" And climbing onto the bed, she threw her arms about her father's neck. "Poor, sick Daddy!" she crooned.

Bowing his head above the child's curls, Ransom broke into deep, gasping sobs. A moment later Adelaide was on her knees by the bedside, her arms stretched out across her husband, as if her love would hold him by force from that which threatened.

On the stairs outside the little nurse wept tears of joy. Here, a few moments later, the old doctor found her.

"Well, young woman," he said jovially, "where's your faith in humanity and providence? Came about like a play, didn't it? Regular climax! At critical moment, enter wife and child."

"Don't joke, Doctor!" entreated the nurse.

"Joke! Bless your soul, child, nothing was further from my thoughts." The old doctor blew his nose vigorously.

When Miss Eliot opened the door of the east corner room, she found a happy group. Adelaide sat by the bedside, her husband's hand in hers. Ransom's other hand held the long envelope with the red seal. On the bed, Mary was stroking her father's thin cheeks affectionately. There were tears in Ransom's eyes as he turned toward the nurse.

"It doesn't seem possible, Miss Eliot," he said huskily. "I never knew anyone could be so happy. I haven't any idea yet how it all come about. I guess Adelaide will have to untangle the mystery." His eyes rested tenderly on his wife's face.

"It's something of a story," said Adelaide, "so perhaps I'd better begin at the first."

"Yes," said Ransom. "I want to hear it all." And with her hand still in her husband's, Adelaide, in a simple, direct way, told her story.

"Letters have been pretty uncertain up in Maine. I hadn't heard from John in months, but I kept on hoping. I *had* to." A little quiver ran over Adelaide's face, and Ransom's grasp of her hand tightened. "Then one afternoon, along about four o'clock, Jim Fellows drove into the yard with Miss Eliot's letter."

Ransom turned toward the nurse with a little start. His eyes met hers solemnly. "So it was *you*," he said. "I had enough to thank you for before, but I guess I ain't ever going to be able to pay my debt."

"Oh, I'm more than paid," said the girl brightly. "Go on with your story, Mrs. Ransom."

"It was a long time before I tore open the envelope, and even when I did, the words just danced before my eyes. I handed the letter to Pa, and he put on his spectacles kind of slowlike. His hands trembled so he could hardly hold the paper. When he had finished, he looked at me.

"'I'm going to Washington,' I said.

"Pa never said a word, but went to the old secretary, unlocked it, and took out a big roll of bills. He handed it to me.

"'I'll go right out and hitch up,' he said. 'If we hurry, you can get the night train from Old Town.'

"He went out, and all of a sudden I felt a tug at my skirts. I looked down, and there was Mary. Quick as a flash the question came to me: What should I do with her? It seemed foolish to take her, and yet, somehow, I felt that I had to. I just couldn't leave her."

Ransom raised Mary's dimpled hand to his lips. "Father's little girl," he said.

"'You'll fetch it, Adelaide,' Pa said when the train whistled and he had to get off. 'Good-bye! God bless you!'

"Everybody was kind to Mary and me. When the conductor found I was going to Washington, he began to ask me questions, and before I knew it, I found myself telling him the whole story. He had a boy in the army, and he seemed to know just how I felt. He lived in Washington, and when we got in late at night, he made us go home with him. His wife made us welcome. I'll never forget her.

"Early the next morning we went up to the Capitol. Mr. Torrey—that was the conductor's name—went with us. As early as it was, there were a lot of people waiting, and most of them looked as if they had their share of troubles, too. Mr. Torrey seemed to know a good many men. I suppose they go up and down on his train often. He spoke to one big man who was going into the inner room. The man looked at me sort of keenlike; then he said, 'I'll tell Mr. Lincoln.' Then he went in.

"I couldn't keep my eye off that door. Sometimes it would be awfully quiet in there; then again I'd hear somebody laughing. After a time, the big man came out. He was chuckling to himself as if he had heard something mighty funny. He nearly went by us; then he seemed to remember, and he turned to me. 'The President will see you, madam,' he said; then he went up and held the door open.

"Mary held on to my hand as tight as if she never meant to let go, and I felt my own heart beating pretty fast; but I just thought of John, and how I *must* get the papers. When we went in, the president was standing, looking out of the window, with his hands in his pockets. He turned 'round, and when I saw his face, all my fear left me. It was so sort of homely and good and kind. He just made me think of our own Maine folks. He's a good deal like Pa, only I guess maybe Pa's better-looking.

"He came over and shook hands with me; then he motioned me to a chair. Mary stood looking at him doubtfully for a moment; then all at once she smiled up at him. He leaned over and lifted her onto his lap, and in a minute they were talking away as if they'd known each other all their lives. I heard her telling him about her kittens."

"He likes kittens," interrupted Mary, "the president does, and he likes little girls, too. He hasn't any, though; his little girls are all boys. He told me so, and I told him about Daddy, and then he and Mother talked."

"I told him all about your war record, John," said Adelaide, "and then I gave him Miss Eliot's letter. He read it carefully and looked sort of thoughtful. Then he rang a bell, and a young fellow with spectacles came in.

"'Look through the files,' said Mr. Lincoln, 'and see what you can find about John Ransom, 42nd Maine.' His tone was real curt.

"Pretty soon the young fellow came back with a slip of paper in his hand. 'John Ransom, 42nd Maine, Army of the Potomac; in hospital at Fernandina; made application some months ago for his discharge papers; several letters about him.' He recited it all off as if he were saying a lesson.

"'If the record's right, why hasn't the case been attended to?' said the president.

"'We haven't got 'round to it,' said the young fellow, his face getting red. 'We're just working on the J's.'

"'A man's life can't go according to the alphabet,' said Mr. Lincoln. 'Make out the papers at once, and send them this afternoon to Mrs. Ransom at—' He looked at me, and I told him where I was staying.

"All of a sudden he kind of laughed; then he looked at me over his spectacles. 'How would you like to take the papers to your husband yourself?' he said. 'There's a gunboat going down tomorrow.'

"I just looked at him. I couldn't say a word, and he smiled. 'I reckon it would be a good thing,' he said, 'and I don't know but that it would be the surest way of getting them there.'

"He wrote a few words on a piece of paper, signed his name, and gave the paper to me. Then he held out his hand. I couldn't say anything but 'God bless you!' but he seemed to understand. Mary piped up, 'Good-bye, Mr. President!' He took her up in his arms and kissed her, and she put her arms 'round his neck, just as she does 'round Pa's, and said, 'I like you, Mr. President,' and he laughed again.

"'And I like you, Mary, so I reckon it's mutual.' Then we came away.

"That afternoon a messenger brought the papers, and the next morning Lieutenant Callahan came to take us to the boat. He was the one who came up with us this morning."

"That was Jerry," said Mary gravely. "He told me to call him that."

"I can't tell you," went on Adelaide, "what a relief it was when I actually held that envelope in my hand. Then my only thought was to get to

Fernandina. We made a quick trip, they said, but it seemed long to me, for I didn't know—" She stopped, her gray eyes meeting Ransom's with ineffable tenderness.

When Ransom was carried downstairs that afternoon, all the household had gathered to bid him Godspeed. But his last words and last glance were for Miss Eliot. As he bade her good-bye, he placed in her hand the little carved wooden case. The tears were streaming down his cheeks. "I hope it will be made up to you," he said.

Mary departed, jubilantly perched on the shoulder of the helpful young lieutenant, and Adelaide's face was wonderful in its newfound happiness.

On the porch the nurse stood long, watching the boat that was bearing Ransom toward home and health. At last, with a little smile, she went slowly into the house and up into the east corner room.

The Message of the Orchid

Harriet Lummis Smith

***Manning Trent sent out two valentine gifts:
one a breathtakingly beautiful orchid;
the other a homely pair of galoshes.
Unfortunately, the delivery orders
got mixed up!***

"Come out in the hall a moment. There is something I want to ask you."

"You'll have to be quick," answered Joyce Trent. "I'm in a rush." It was hardly necessary to say it, for since entering high school Joyce was habitually out of breath in her efforts to keep up with events.

Manning Trent smiled down into her glowing face. Joyce was not exactly pretty, but she was so intensely alive that her exuberant vitality seemed to take the place of beauty. He shut the door behind him and came promptly to the point. "Is there anything Ruth needs especially?"

Joyce stood staring at him. "Needs? What do you mean? She needs a permanent wave, if you ask me."

"I want to send her something for a valentine. I thought perhaps you knew what she needed."

Joyce gave a little laugh. "That's funny. I never thought of valentines in the food and fuel class."

"You wouldn't," said Manning, laughing. "You want your food regularly, but you want something extra when it comes to valentines, don't you? Luckily Ruth is more practical."

"Her galoshes are worn out, if that's the kind of thing you mean."

"Fine!" exclaimed Manning. "Nobody needs galoshes more than Ruth does. She's out in all sorts of weather. Do you know her size?"

For a wonder Joyce did. "She wears a four-A shoe, but you might get a few sizes larger, in case I should happen to want to borrow them. And say, Manning, you know my taste in chocolates, don't you?"

The older brother laughed indulgently. "If you get any valentines this year, it'll be from some of your friends in the high school. Judging from what I see, you'll be looked out for without my putting my hand in my pockets."

As a matter of fact, he ordered Joyce's candy on the way downtown and then cut his luncheon short to buy Ruth's galoshes. He was rather particular about those galoshes, insisting on seeing all the styles. He purchased the pair that looked the most substantial, and pulling out a card, he handed it to the clerk.

"Send it to the address on the back, and please take off the price tag. I think I can give you the exact amount, and then I won't have to wait."

He left in a hurry, looking at his watch and congratulating himself on just having time to get back to the office.

He had to postpone his visit to the florist's until after five, but he was glad he had attended first to Ruth's valentine. *Ruth*, her brother told himself, *deserves the best of everything*. She was the sort of girl who always would run the risk of being overlooked because she never put herself forward. When their mother had died, she had stepped into the vacant place as though its duties belonged to her. A woman came every Monday to wash and on Friday to help with the cleaning; Ruth did the rest. *We owe her a lot,* Manning Trent said to himself whenever he thought of Ruth, and after his visit to the department store, he recalled with satisfaction those good, substantial galoshes. *Why, they'll last her for years,* he reflected.

They knew him well at the florist's, although he was not an extravagant patron. Enid Fisher much preferred violets to chocolates, and she frowned upon any suggestion of giving her more expensive gifts. Since this was a valentine remembrance, however, Manning had made up his mind that she should have an orchid along with the loved violets. She was going to a party the evening of the fourteenth, and although he did not happen to be invited, he rather liked the idea of her wearing his flowers on that occasion. He made his selection and found in his pocket the card he had written the evening before.

"The address is on the other side," he said and laid a $5 bill on the counter. It was a little extravagant, he knew, but it was a pity if a fellow could not forget about money once in a while when he had a friend like Enid.

Manning was a little late getting home to dinner the next evening. When he came into the house, Joyce called to her sister, "He's here, Ruth." She then whirled upon Manning. "High time, too. Ruth wouldn't sit down without you, and I'm going to a party this evening."

"You seem to be in a rather bad temper," said Manning judicially. "I'm afraid you didn't get any valentines."

"Oh, didn't I, though! And among others—notice that I say *among others*—was a box of my favorite chocolates." She leaned forward and kissed him lightly on the cheek.

Ruth then called, "Tell Father that dinner is ready."

Ruth was invisible when the rest of the family went out to the dining room. Manning stood behind his chair, his mind busy with some problem connected with his work, but his father looked at Ruth's vacant place with mild surprise.

"Didn't Ruth say dinner was ready?"

"Yes, she did," replied Joyce. "Oh, let's sit down! She'll be in right away." In a high-pitched voice, she then uttered an exclamation that recalled Manning's wandering attention: "Well, look who's here!"

Someone was coming in from the kitchen, but Manning had to look at her twice to be sure that it was really Ruth. Often at dinner she was flushed from bending over the stove, but the color in her cheeks tonight was different. She wore her best dress, he noticed, the dress of which she was so ludicrously careful that only the most special occasions seemed to her important enough to merit it. Pinned to her shoulder was a corsage tied with a silver ribbon, violets with an orchid in the center.

With the exception of Joyce, the observers were struck dumb. No shock ever produced that effect on Joyce.

"Ruth, what are you all dressed up for?" she asked. "And where did the scrumptious flowers come from?"

"Why, this is my valentine," said Ruth and smiled at her brother. "I know it's much too lovely to wear to dinner, especially when I'm the cook, but I'm not going out and I can't leave it in the icebox."

"You might let me wear it to the party tonight," suggested Joyce.

Ruth put up her hand to her flowers with a strange, protesting gesture. "Oh, I couldn't, Joyce," she said. "Not my valentine. Any other time I'd be glad to."

"I just thought it seemed rather a waste," explained Joyce carelessly. "But it's all right if you don't want to." She looked across the table at her brother. "Changed your mind, didn't you?"

Manning did not reply, and for a very good reason. Not until Joyce spoke did he realize that the flowers Ruth was wearing were those he himself had selected. In fact, when Ruth had emerged from the kitchen, so radiant that she was hardly recognizable, he had realized with a shock that some fellow was sending Ruth flowers for St. Valentine's Day.

Joyce's assumption that he was the sender led him to look at them more closely, and he saw at once that his sister was right. These were his flowers. He flattered himself that he would recognize that orchid among a thousand. That meant—that meant . . . As he realized his colossal blunder—that he must have exchanged the cards in his vest pocket—he almost dropped his glass of water. In that case Enid had the galoshes!

Curiously, while he had thought so highly of the galoshes when he regarded them as a valentine for Ruth, he was overwhelmed with embarrassment by the realization that they had been delivered as his valentine to Enid. The blood rushed to the roots of his hair. His ears were burning. When at last he came to himself, he was eating roast beef and mashed potatoes just as though his world had not turned completely upside down. Joyce had returned to the question of "borrowing" Ruth's corsage.

"Listen, Ruth, I think you might let me wear your flowers. You don't wear orchids when you're washing dishes."

Ruth was shocked. "Of course not. I'll take them off while I'm doing the dishes, and my dress, too. But I can put them on again later."

"But who'll see them? Probably Manning will be going somewhere, and Daddy wouldn't know if you wore wreaths of flowers the way they do in Hawaii."

"But I'll know," said Ruth. She looked really distressed.

"For pity's sake," cried her younger sister. "Why, I never knew you were so crazy about flowers. You never talked that way before."

"But I never had such flowers before," said Ruth.

Momentarily, Manning forgot the galoshes and his concern over what Enid probably was thinking. He spoke with an accent of authority that made Joyce look at him from under arched brows. "Stop teasing Ruth, infant. She can't lend you her flowers—if you want to call it lending—because she's going out with me."

"Oh!" The irrepressible Joyce recognized the finality of that.

Ruth was looking at him with an indefinable expression. "Going out, Manning? Where?"

"Mighty curious, aren't you? Suppose you wait and see." He spoke teasingly in order to gain time. He thought there was a recital worth hearing somewhere downtown, but he would have to look at the evening paper in order to be sure. . . .

His impression proved correct. Ruth slipped out of her best dress into a print frock while she washed the dishes and then back into her best dress again. When her brother joined her at the foot of the stairs, she had pinned her corsage to her coat.

"I never thought that you and Joyce looked a bit alike," Manning exclaimed. "But tonight you're as alike as peas in a pod." All at once he realized the reason. Ruth had suddenly come alive. She was glowing, vital, radiant.

The next evening he called on Enid. For the first time since he had known her, he dreaded the thought of seeing her. He had made any number of attempts during the day to formulate a satisfactory apology and finally had decided to leave it to the inspiration of the moment. Sometimes he wondered whether or not any apology would be adequate.

So great was his apprehension that he was almost sorry when Enid's younger brother, who answered his ring, said that Enid was at home, without waiting for him to inquire.

"You sit down," said George, "and I'll find her." He began shouting, "Oh, Enid, Manning Trent's here."

"Coming," a voice gaily shouted, and Enid ran lightly down the stairs. She walked into the room where Manning awaited her; then, at the sight of his crestfallen face, she dropped into an armchair and went into a paroxysm of laughter.

It was a minute before either of them spoke. Finally, Manning began haltingly, "I don't wonder you're laughing. I don't know what to say—"

Enid wiped her streaming eyes. "Oh, Manning!" she gasped. "What happened? When that box came addressed to me, I couldn't imagine what it was, and the sight of those galoshes almost petrified me. Then when I found your card—" She began laughing again, that noiseless laughter that ends by being actually painful. When at last she found breath enough to speak, her cheeks were wet with tears. "Oh, dear," she said, wiping away the traces of emotion, "I don't know anything that hurts more than to laugh that way. Now tell me how it happened."

"Just an idiotic blunder of mine: I wrote two cards at home and exchanged them at the stores. I meant the galoshes for my sister."

Enid looked at him. "You don't mean for a *valentine!*" she said incredulously.

"Why, yes, that was my idea."

"But—but—why did you make such a funny choice?"

"Ruth's a practical sort of girl," said Manning uneasily.

"Yes, I know." Enid was silent a moment. "But that isn't fair!" she exclaimed suddenly.

"What isn't fair?"

"Thinking that just because Ruth's practical, she doesn't want anything but what's necessary. She's a girl like other girls. She may need galoshes, but don't imagine for a minute that's all she needs. I don't say you ought to spend a lot of money on a valentine for her, any more than for anybody else. But if you're going to send her a valentine at all, have it be a real one."

Manning remembered Ruth's face as his sister came in from the kitchen with the corsage pinned to her best gown. As she had sat beside him at the concert, still wearing the flowers, she had worn that same uplifted look— a look that seemed to transform her plain features and make her almost beautiful. Just because Ruth spent so much of her life with pots, pans, dusters, dish towels, and vacuum cleaners, it did not mean that she was uninterested in a girl's birthright of beauty.

Manning looked up and found Enid watching him gravely. "I didn't mean to criticize you," she said. "I know you're a wonderful brother, but just the same—"

"You only told me what I ought to have had sense enough to know," he interrupted. "When I mixed up those cards, I made a silly blunder, but not nearly so silly as what I'd planned in the first place."

A Promise and a Ski Run

Author Unknown

Oh, how he wished he hadn't made that promise to Mrs. Andrews! If he hadn't, he could be attending the statewide ski competition. Well, the promise had been made several months ago. . . . Perhaps she had forgotten about it.

Sandy Fairchild was a ski fan from way back. He liked skiing—whether he was doing it himself or watching others do it—better than all the other sports put together. And yet, on Washington's Birthday, when the statewide championship was to be run on Sugarloaf Mountain, he knew he couldn't stay to watch.

As Sandy fastened on his skis, he was trying not to think about what he was going to miss. Old Mrs. Andrews had given him these beautiful skis for Christmas, and he had promised then to come and visit her on Washington's Birthday.

"Good," Mrs. Andrews had said. "When you say a thing, you mean it. I'll be looking for you."

But how could Sandy have guessed, when he made that promise

two months ago, that Sugarloaf would be chosen for the championship races? And then to have Washington's Birthday picked as the day of the big ski meet seemed too much to stand.

If only Mrs. Andrews lived closer, he could keep his promise today and still get back to Sugarloaf Mountain in time for the races. But she lived hours away from the racecourse, on the far side of Mount Redfield.

As he skied over to the south end of the village, Sandy could see men marking off the racecourse with little red flags. And farther off to the right, with its caves and dips, blue-shadowed in the gleaming snow, lay Devil's Run, an opening into the valley.

If Sandy could have skied down Devil's Run, he could have reached Mount Redfield in half an hour. But only one skier in town had ever tried to make that steep and dangerous pass, and he'd been rewarded with a broken leg.

No, the only way for Sandy to go was by the middle run—a safe snow-covered wagon road. This would take hours longer, but there was nothing he could do about it.

He was just about to push off down the road when he heard someone call his name. Turning, he saw Dr. Benton, the village doctor.

"Say, Sandy!" the doctor called. "Where are you going? Don't you know the races start in half an hour?"

"Yes, I know," Sandy said. "But I'm not staying for the races. I have to go and visit a friend."

Dr. Benton stared at Sandy as though he expected to see him break out in red spots or show other signs of sickness. "You're going away?" he asked. "You're going away on the day of the races? But people are coming from all over New England! The best skiers in the country are going to be here."

"I can't help it," Sandy said, wishing that he could start down the hill and get it over with. "I made a promise two months ago, before I knew the races were going to be held today. I can't break my promise."

Dr. Benton's kindly face looked really disturbed. "No, of course you can't," he said, patting Sandy on the shoulder. "But it's a pity it had to work out this way. Why, even Dash Martin, who was in school with me, is coming. You may never get another chance as long as you live to see him ski."

For one terrible moment, Sandy hesitated. Dr. Benton, who was a good skier himself, had often said that he thought Dash Martin was the greatest skier in the whole country.

Then all of a sudden the cheerful, weather-beaten face of Mrs. Andrews flashed into Sandy's mind. He could almost hear her saying, "Good! When you say a thing, you mean it. I'll be looking for you."

"But I can't stay," repeated Sandy, picking up his ski poles. "I just can't, Doctor."

Dr. Benton nodded understandingly and stamped away over the gleaming, crusty snow.

Sandy gave himself a push with his ski poles and started down the wagon road. It was a good fast run and just about all that Sandy could handle. While he was skiing downhill, there was no time to think about anything except the run in front of him. He was tearing, flying, over the white, unbroken snow.

But from the valley on, it was a different story. No more flying now, but just a long, hard, uphill climb.

When Sandy finally reached Mrs. Andrews' little house in the clearing, he was both hot and tired. He stood still for a minute, wiping his face while he looked at the snow-covered woodshed and the buried garden.

Slowly, it dawned on Sandy that there were no tracks or footprints in the snow, and no smoke curling from the chimney.

"Mrs. Andrews!" he called out, dashing toward the house. "Mrs. Andrews, I've come! I've kept my promise!"

He had his skis off and was up the steps before he realized that there was no answer. He hesitated for a moment. Then he pulled open the door and

CARRYING THE MAIL IN 1867.

stepped forward. The silence and cold inside the house were as threatening as a storm cloud.

"Mrs. Andrews!" Sandy called again. "Mrs. Andrews!"

Then he saw her.

The old lady was lying on the sofa before him, with a red woolen shawl pulled up close to her chin. She was so still that, for one terrible moment, he thought she might be dead.

Then her eyes opened. "So it's you," she said, her voice pitifully weak. "I knew you'd come. Can you get Dr. Benton?"

Sandy nodded, watching the old woman's face. She looked dreadfully gray, and her eyes had closed again as though she didn't have enough strength to keep them open. Sandy's knees were shaking. What should he do? What should he do?

Somehow he fought down his fright. There was no telephone. He would have to ski back to the village for help. But first he must get Mrs. Andrews warm. So he brought some blankets from the neat little bedroom, and he carefully tucked them around her on the sofa. She smiled weakly.

The wood box by the fireplace was empty except for a few small sticks. Sandy plowed through the snowdrifts to the woodshed. The door was frozen shut, and he had to pound and push and pull before he could open it. With his arms loaded with wood, he stumbled back.

After he had built a small fire on the cold ashes in the fireplace, he stood up. "I'll get Dr. Benton," he said, "as fast as I can."

Mrs. Andrews didn't answer.

Sandy hurried out of the house and fastened on his skis. It was a fast trip back, compared with the long, uphill climb he had just made. If only he could find Dr. Benton in the crowd of people who had come for the races!

Sandy had climbed all the way back up the wagon road on the last hill before he saw that the races were over. *Of course*, he thought. *I guess it's been about four hours since I started out.*

The crowd had gone home, and there was only one skier left on the hill. "Hello, there!" Sandy shouted. "Have you seen Dr. Benton? Mrs. Andrews is awfully sick!"

The man turned on his skis as smoothly as a dancer. "Benton's gone," he said. "He was called away on an accident case. Is this serious?"

"I'm not sure, but I think so. Mrs. Andrews' face is all gray and sort of cold-looking." Panting for breath after his long climb, Sandy told the stranger just what he had seen.

"I'm a doctor," the skier said. "What is the quickest way of getting to her?"

Sandy looked back over his shoulder at the long wagon road he had just climbed.

"It would take you longer by car than by skis," he said. "The Devil's Run would be the quickest of all, but nobody in town has ever gone all the way down standing up."

"After the run," the doctor said, dismissing the run as though it were as safe as the wagon road, "which way do you turn?"

"Left," said Sandy, "sharp left. But nobody in town has ever made that run."

The man pulled down his cap and gripped his poles. "Go to Dr. Benton's house," he said. "When he returns, tell him to come at once with his car."

Sandy stared. "You're going down the run?" he gasped.

But the stranger had already started.

Sandy watched breathlessly as the man flashed down a steep cliff and shot around a bend. A moment later the man reappeared and flew, bird-like, twenty feet down another drop, toward the floor of the valley.

"Wow!" Sandy breathed as the figure streaked across the snow and disappeared from sight. Then Sandy started down toward Dr. Benton's house.

The doctor was just getting out of his car as Sandy slid into the driveway. He listened to Sandy's story without speaking. Then he started backing his car out through the snow of the driveway.

"I'll stop by your house this evening," he called, "and tell you how she's getting on."

Sandy nodded and waved. As he watched the doctor's car pull out of sight, he realized for the first time that he had been skiing for hours. He was more tired than he'd ever been before in his life. He trudged wearily home.

About suppertime that evening, his friend Dick Stringer stopped in to tell him about the races. "Dash Martin won everything!" he said excitedly. "And, boy, can that man ski! Dr. Benton was right—if you haven't seen Dash Martin ski, then when it comes to skiing, you haven't seen anything!"

Before Sandy had a chance to tell Dick about all that had happened to him that day, Dr. Benton's car came up the driveway. Sandy went running out to meet him.

"Mrs. Andrews is all right," the doctor said. "She said to give you her love and tell you that keeping your promise saved her life. She wasn't very far wrong, either." Dr. Benton smiled at Sandy. "Dash Martin said that if he hadn't reached her—"

"Dash Martin!" exclaimed Sandy. "You mean the doctor I saw take the Devil's Run was Dash Martin?"

Dr. Benton nodded. "Of course. Didn't you know?"

Sandy turned and raced toward the house. "Dick!" he shouted breathlessly. "Dick, I *did* see him! I *did* see Dash Martin! I saw him go straight down Devil's Run, and that's something that nobody but me has ever seen!"

Something of Father's

C. G. Kent

Pete needed to win that contest: It would mean everything to him. Now Timmy would most likely win it, and without even breaking a sweat. But wait! Up in the attic was a trunk, and if Pete copied what was in it, no one would ever know!

The sudden hush told Pete Potter they had been talking about him. There they were, the junior gang, occupying their usual tables in the corner of the lunchroom, as rangy Pete went for his lunchtime bottle of milk.

"The scholar approaches," said Timmy Bell.

They laughed.

"Greetings, drones," said Pete affably. People usually laughed when Timmy clowned. *That*, thought Pete with just a trace of envy, *is what a reputation does for you.* But in his heart he knew that Timmy was the only one he had to fear tomorrow.

"We were just wondering what you were going to write about tomorrow," said Fatso D'Allessandro. "Timmy said—"

"That it probably would be something magnificent," interrupted Timmy with his disarming blend of irony and deference.

"And a little on the stuffed-shirt side?" asked Pete.

"What Timmy really did say," rumbled the deep voice of Pete's pal tiny Foghorn Murphy, "was that you have the type of mind, Pete, that naturally turns out prizewinning essays."

"While I," said Timmy, "fill my pen with the loftiest sentiments. And the ink curdles into comedy."

As usual, there were touches of truth in Tim's clowning. Slim and delicate, wearing his clothes with an elegance that suggested that they were made for him—as most of them were—Tim had won popularity at LaSalle High School in spite of being no athlete. He had wit, friendliness, and an unsteadied air of precocious worldliness. He did everything easily, including the job of editing the school paper.

"Perhaps, Timmy, you'll lend me a little of that ink," said Pete. *Tomorrow,* he thought, sipping from the stubby bottle of milk, *Tim probably will write the essay that will give him the John Stratford Cup.* The junior class at LaSalle traditionally competed each spring for this cup, and the individual who won it had the privilege of becoming high school reporter for the *Trowbridge Gazette* at a part-time salary of $10 a week.

Badly as Pete and his mother needed that extra $10, there were more important considerations. For the boy who won the cup frequently graduated into a full-time reporter's job on the *Gazette.* Years ago Pete's own father had entered journalism in precisely that way. He had become a world-renowned correspondent, only to be lost at sea in the early days of the war. Pete wanted to become the same kind of respected, courageous journalist his father had been. To win the same contest that his father had won might, he felt, open the same door.

"Are you going to moon over that milk bottle all day?" boomed Foghorn. "Come, lean and hungry Cassius, I would have words with thee."

Tall Pete and short Foghorn crossed over to the school baseball diamond. A couple of batters were popping out flies.

"Pete, you have to win that cup," said Foghorn. "It isn't fair."

"What isn't?"

Foghorn shrugged his shoulders. "Oh, Timmy's a nice guy, only . . . everything's so easy for him. Still," he ended on a note of hope, "this thing tomorrow is an essay. Just as Tim says, it isn't in his line."

"Softly, my figuring Foghorn! Remember the rules. You can write," Pete quoted, "'a composition in any form, prose or verse, to be judged solely upon literary merit and moral content.'"

"You could write a sonnet or a news story," said Foghorn gloomily. "A news story! Say, Pete, wouldn't it be wonderful if you could dig up something of your father's? And use that . . . "

Pete just looked at him.

"No," said Foghorn lamely, "it wouldn't. You'd never pull a trick like that. Oh, well, just forget you ever knew me."

Something of your father's. The phrase kept running through Pete's mind all afternoon. He took it home with him.

And suddenly a thrill that was almost painful shot through him. There was an old trunk . . . Pete climbed the stairs to the attic.

In the bottom of the trunk, held together by granulated elastic bands that crumbled in his trembling hands, he found three old manuscripts. The one that gripped and held him until he had read every word of it was handwritten, with many corrections, on crackly, yellowed paper. It was the title that galvanized Pete: *A Truthful Press Is Free*. And written underneath: *By Peter Potter.*

"This would win," he said softly. "This would win the contest—for me." No Timmy Bell, with his adroit gift for twisting words, could ever beat this stuff! "It isn't clever," Pete murmured. "It's bigger than that."

By the time he had softly returned the manuscript, closed the trunk, and almost tiptoed down the attic stairs, he had committed every word to memory. Tomorrow, if he chose, he could sit down and rewrite that essay, word for word—even to the addition of his own signature.

If he chose.

Well, it was a sort of legacy, wasn't it? What harm could it do anybody, Pete asked himself, if he just let his own pen race on tomorrow—and he won the cup with something his own father had left him? It certainly wouldn't be stealing. It couldn't do Timmy any real harm. Timmy was going to be a doctor, not a writer. Timmy was the popular, clever editor of the school paper. Timmy had everything, and needed nothing—certainly not the $10 a week that would be paid him for the next year's job of reporting.

At breakfast, Pete was moody. His mother knew he was worrying about the contest.

"You can win, dear," she murmured softly. "And even if you don't—"

"I can win," Pete said a little bluntly. He did not add: "if I want to cheat." For he was too straight-thinking, fundamentally, to delude himself into believing that the course he had half decided upon would be anything better than outright cheating.

Even when Pete sat down at his desk that afternoon and stared at the fresh, clean paper before him, he had not made up his mind. Around him, pens began to scratch. Pete sat.

He looked at his watch. Five minutes had passed. Two seats over and one ahead, Tim Bell was writing easily, gracefully, and with scarcely a pause. It was as though the smooth flow of ink from his fountain pen scarcely could keep up with the smooth flow of words from his facile brain.

But at least, Pete thought unwillingly, *they're his own words.*

And suddenly Pete knew he was just wasting time. He couldn't do it. He couldn't win the cup with words that weren't his own.

Then lightning struck. Pete knew what to do.

It'll lose the cup for sure, he thought, *but the cup's likely half Timmy's at this moment. So I might as well have a little fun. I'll write them a bit of fiction.*

So, at white-hot pitch, Peter Potter started to write. He wrote a little story about a young student in Paris of the Middle Ages, a student named Michel, who was going to write an essay in the hope of winning a scholarship to a famous university—and how, the night before, this student found, in an ancient chest, an old manuscript that would have won him the scholarship if he had been willing to cheat.

In short, of course, Pete wrote his own story, thinly disguised. And because now he wasn't writing for a prize but for the sheer joy of it, the words came freely. Pete was amazed at how easily that student flowed out of his pen. Michel was a nice fellow but human, with all of a boy's sauciness and little impertinences overlaid upon his fundamental honesty.

Boy, Pete said to himself, *I didn't know I could write like this!* And then suddenly Pete's student began quoting—as Pete wrote—some of the words that Pete had found the night before: quoting just a few of them, and under quotation marks, which made it quite proper and honest. Shortly after, Pete turned in his paper. He felt very happy.

It was four days later when the summons came to come to Professor Magahey's office. The professor had white hair; his blue eyes were both sharp and gentle. He had been head of LaSalle High for many years, and the English teacher there for years before that. He had taught Pete's father and been proud of his pupil.

"Peter," he said, "it was a rare legacy that your father left us."

Pete was so stunned he could hardly speak. "Legacy? How did—?"

"I'm not referring," said Professor Magahey, "to the manuscript that, ah, Michel found in an old chest. Nor to the manuscript of your father's that, I gather, you probably found in a strongbox."

"It was a trunk," Pete mumbled.

"Of course. You'd hardly be poking around in a strongbox. No, Peter, I'm referring to your father's honesty."

"Then—you know—I mean—" Poor Pete was a bit at sea.

"Of course. Your essay, to be sure, was not an essay at all but a short story. Quite unusual, but entirely within the very elastic rules. The judges were particularly pleased with the light, deft way in which you presented a fundamentally serious theme—yet without flippancy. So, this afternoon, it will be my pleasure to announce that you have won the John Stratford Cup. But, Peter, that wasn't why I sent for you."

For a moment the old man looked out of his window. Then he turned back to Pete. "Tell me about it, if you feel like it," he said.

And then Pete told him the whole thing. "But what I can't understand, Prof," he ventured at last, "is how you knew that I had found my father's manuscript?"

"It must have been a first draft," the old man murmured, half under his breath. "Eh? Then, Peter, I'll have to explain. What you found must have been the first draft of an essay that I read just twenty-one years ago this month. I've remembered parts of it so well that the little quotation which you had your character 'Michel' use immediately made me remember the essay your father wrote at that time. You see, Peter, it was the one with which your father won the same contest that you have won today."

Spring to Summer

How We April Fooled Aunt Patty

O. M. Hatch

*Tomorrow was April Fool's Day, and
did they ever have a surprise for a certain
villager! Mother knew better than to
scold them. Instead, she told them a
story—a story out of her own past.
This is a turn-of-the-twentieth-century tale.*

"Oh, Mother! Tomorrow is April Fool's Day, and Ned Turner has planned for us boys to give Uncle Rasmus the biggest April fool!" exclaimed Ted Cummings as he burst into his mother's room and tossed his schoolbooks onto the table.

"Tell me all about it, Ted." And Mrs. Cummings settled back in her chair to listen, for she and Ted had been chums ever since he could remember.

"I don't believe, Mother, you will approve of his plans. And I don't exactly myself. But you know how Ned is."

Yes, Mrs. Cummings well knew Ned's set and domineering disposition, and she sighed. "Perhaps, Ted, he is not so much to blame as others. You know his mother died when he was very young, and his father and aunt reared him in the most strict and exacting manner. Very little love and sympathy have come into his life. But I believe if the right chord could be touched, Ned would respond. We will do all we can for the motherless boy. But tell me all about Ned's plans for April-fooling old Uncle Rasmus."

After Ted had finished, Mrs. Cummings made no comment, but quietly remarked, "I have a story, Ted, to tell you—a true story, taken from my own life. I wish Ned were here. I think it would do him good."

"Why, here he is now, Mother," Ted said as Ned came sauntering up the walk.

"I was just speaking about you," said Mrs. Cummings as she gave Ned a cordial greeting. "I was intending to relate to Ted an incident in my own life, and I wished you were here."

"I am glad to be here," said Ned honestly, "and hear anything you have to say, Mrs. Cummings." Secretly Ned thought there was no one quite equal to Ted's mother.

"When I was sixteen . . . ," began Mrs. Cummings. "Why, that is just your age, isn't it, Ned?"

"Yes. I was sixteen last month."

"We thought it would be great fun to April-fool Aunt Patty. Now, to know Aunt Patty was to love her. If there was anyone sick, it was Aunt Patty who was sent for. If a death occurred, it was Aunt Patty who comforted the mourners. If one was discouraged or downhearted, it was she who gave good counsel and cheer, and substantial aid whenever she had the money. Never a poor, hungry soul ever came to her door and departed unfed. In fact, no one ever came in contact with Aunt Patty without being the better for it.

"Well do I remember when my life hung in the balance with diphtheria. Mother was exhausted, and it was Aunt Patty who came and nursed me back to health and strength. And to think, Ted and Ned, that I should so far forget even common courtesy as to consent to be the leader in fooling Aunt Patty!

"Never shall I forget that night! The moon rode high in the heavens, and the clouds were dark and swift. At the appointed time we started. There were about twenty boys and girls in the party, and they were armed with old tin cans, horns, bells, fifes, and several drums. You can imagine the frightful din when all of those nerve-racking instruments were put in operation. And to think we thought *that* would be *such fun!* Little did we dream how near a tragedy that night's work might have caused.

"I was to creep up stealthily to the house and knock, and Aunt Patty's opening the door would be the signal for pandemonium to be let loose. How little people who play such pranks realize that *they* are the *biggest fools of all!*

"Slowly and silently, I approached the door. Hearing voices, as I thought, I peeped through the window, and there on the floor, before a fireless stove, knelt Aunt Patty. The tears were streaming down her wan cheeks—strange I had never before noticed how thin they were—as she pleaded with God not to forsake her and reminded Him that her coal bin was empty and her cupboard bare. As she prayed, a shiver ran through her frame, and she drew her thin shawl closer around her. She prayed for a blessing to rest on all her friends and neighbors, and especially 'dear Muriel.' I could stand no more, but fled conscience-smitten to my companions. Great was their consternation and remorse, for they all dearly loved Aunt Patty.

"'Now, boys and girls,' I exclaimed tearfully, '*something* must be done, and done right away.'

"'Suppose we run as fast as we can to your home, Muriel, and tell Mr. and Mrs. Hilton,' spoke up Alice Williams.

"'Agreed!' we all exclaimed, and away we ran to my home. It was a very sober but excited company that burst into the sitting room, where Father and Mother were quietly reading.

"'What, back so soon?' exclaimed Mother as she looked up with a smile. Then she caught sight of our sober faces and asked, 'Is there anything the matter with Aunt Patty?'

"'No and yes, Mother,' I said and hastily explained the situation.

"'Do I understand, Muriel, that you intended to April-fool Aunt Patty by hooting, screaming, ringing bells, and beating drums?' asked Father. 'If so, you may well be thankful a kind providence prevented you from carrying out your intentions, as the joke might have proved fatal.'

"'What do you mean, Father?' I gasped, horrified.

"'Just what I have said, Muriel. Aunt Patty has a very weak heart, and any sudden shock or fear might cause her death. I trust that my daughter, or any of these dear girls and boys, will never again be guilty of such an undertaking.'

"'Never, Father!' I exclaimed tearfully.

"'Now,' continued my father cheerfully, 'we will indeed April-fool Aunt Patty, but in a far different manner from what you had planned. A joyous surprise will not harm her. We will send word to her friends and neighbors to meet here inside of an hour and a half, and then we will all march together to her home, carrying with us, not only the necessities of life, but some luxuries as well.' Then, turning to Mother, he requested her to kindly write out such articles as she thought each family could bring on such short notice.

"Within fifteen minutes, the boys and girls had been commissioned and were hurrying home with their slips of paper closely treasured. Quickly the gifts were prepared, and all assembled at our home.

"'Friends,' said my father, 'in token of the love and esteem in which the citizens of Ridgefield have ever held Aunt Patty, and to show our appreciation of her loving ministrations among us, I vote we make up a purse and will start the donation with $50.'

"At the pleased murmur that resulted, Father looked toward me and said brokenly, 'I firmly believe that Muriel would not be here tonight had Aunt Patty not nursed her so devotedly during her battle with diphtheria. And I think there is not one present who has not at some time been the recipient of Aunt Patty's generosity.'

"Then Deacon Wilson arose and said, 'I remember when we were burned out, it was Aunt Patty who gave us a home and helped us to start anew. I will give $50 now and more later.'

"A thunder of applause greeted this remark, for Deacon Wilson was not noted for overgenerosity.

"Then little Miss Paterson arose and, with trembling voice, said, 'I should have lost my home thirteen years ago had it not been for Aunt Patty. And although I have little money, I will gladly give her a home with me the remainder of her life.'

"Then everybody began to talk, and what do you think, boys? In just a few minutes, they not only raised more than $400 in money, but voted to make Aunt Patty matron of Leabright Orphanage. The orphanage had formerly belonged to her father, Dr. Leabright. It was her old home. The family had been very wealthy, but after her father's death, reverses came, and I am sorry to say, through the rascality of her only brother she was obliged to sell her beautiful home to pay the debts. It left her penniless. For a long time she struggled bravely on, teaching music, tutoring, and sewing, until her health broke down, and the doctors ordered a long rest. It was during this time that her funds were exhausted and she was reduced to the condition in which I found her that April night.

"It was just half past eight o'clock when we started for Aunt Patty's, Deacon Wilson leading the way with his double team, the wagon loaded with apples, potatoes, all kinds of vegetables, besides coal and wood. What a merry party we were as we went up the moonlit road to the little brown house on the hill!

"In answer to my knock, Aunt Patty opened the door, and to say she was astonished when she saw nearly all of Ridgefield assembled in front of her house is putting it far too mildly. She seemed incapable of moving, until my father called out in his hearty voice, 'We thought we would give you a little surprise, Aunt Patty, if you will let us in!'

"Amid laughter and tears, greetings were exchanged and gifts presented. It looked more like a county fair than anything else. The tables were piled high with bread, biscuits, butter, pies, cake, jelly, preserves, and a lot of other good things too numerous to mention. Right royally had Ridgefield responded to Father's call.

"'How shall I ever be able to eat all of these good things?' said Aunt Patty as she lovingly touched the huge collection.

"'Well,' said kind Uncle Rasmus in his slow way, 'we calculated on how you love to give, so we thought we would bring enough for you to share with others less fortunate.'"

"Do you mean *our* Uncle Rasmus?" asked Ned.

"The very same, Ned, only now he is a poor, decrepit old man, his loved ones are dead, and he is all alone in the world.

"In a hush that followed the remarks of Uncle Rasmus, my father arose, and in a few well-chosen words, he presented the purse and tendered Aunt Patty the matronship of Leabright Orphanage.

"Poor, dear Aunt Patty! First she looked at Father, then at her smiling neighbors, too overcome to say a word. Finally, she exclaimed, with tears of gratitude, 'Bless the Lord, O my soul; and all that is within me, bless His holy name. Bless the Lord, O my soul, and forget not all His benefits: . . . who redeemeth thy life from destruction; who crowneth thee with loving-kindness and tender mercies; who satisfieth thy mouth with good things.'

"Then with one accord the company burst into singing 'Blest Be the Tie That Binds.' It was an evening never to be forgotten.

"On the way home, little Tillie Winchell slipped her hand into mine and whispered in awed tones, 'Didn't Aunt Patty's face look like an angel's? It was so bright and shining!'"

"Did Aunt Patty accept the position?" asked Ted.

"Yes, dear. She proved to be just the one for the place."

"Is she still living?" asked Ned, unconsciously leaning forward in his eagerness.

"Yes, very much so."

"Oh, I am so glad, for I know her, or rather, I remember her. When I was a little fellow, my father had occasion to visit Leabright Orphanage and took me with him. A kind, motherly woman with white hair and shining eyes gave me several cookies and a rosy-cheeked apple."

"It was she without doubt, as—"

Here a peal of the bell called Mrs. Cummings from the room. As the door closed behind her, Ned said huskily, "I have decided, Ted, to call off that April-fool affair. But if your mother will let you come down this evening, we will talk over the matter of giving Uncle Rasmus something like the April fool that was given Aunt Patty."

At last the right chord had been touched, and nobly did Ned respond.

The Song of Songs

Mabel McKee

Dr. and Mrs. Dean tried to make the best of it, but it was so difficult. Neither David nor Eleanor showed any signs of coming home. Not even on Mother's Day. But Mrs. Dean had one last arrow in her quiver, and it shot to its mark "Special Delivery."

When Eleanor Dean did not come home at Christmastime, people in Libertyville began to shake their heads and say to one another, "She is going to be exactly like David. Dr. and Mrs. Dean have lost not only their son, but their daughter as well."

But Mrs. Dean, who had bravely crushed her longing for her only daughter in order that she might have an opportunity to do the work she wanted to do—as had David, who the year before had graduated from a medical college—again put away her own grief and comforted Dr. Dean. "She'll come home in the springtime," she promised, "and sing in the choir so everyone can hear how her voice has improved under this study. After all, it takes time to come from Cincinnati to western Indiana, and no doubt she has some important engagement to sing in a Christmas choir."

Spring brought another letter from Eleanor. It read: "Mother dear, I know you'll understand how grieved I am to have to tell you I cannot leave my work now, even for just a few days. But soon, very soon, I hope I'll be coming home."

Dr. Dean's face had grown grave. "It seems as if our children have no more time for us, dear," he murmured. "Our neighbors were right when they said that if we let them go too far away to be educated, they would grow away from us."

Mrs. Dean's eyes were dim with tears. But courage in her heart made her whisper, "I'm not going to let them grow away from me. I shall write and tell them both they must come home for Mother's Day. Eleanor never has been away from me on a single Mother's Day. She'll come, I'm sure."

Eleanor, though just eighteen, was "still a baby" down in Mrs. Dean's heart. When David went away to college, Eleanor was only ten, and then she wept bitter tears. "Davie won't never come home just Davie."

"Oh, yes, he will," Mrs. Dean said, trying to comfort her. "He'll graduate from college and medical school. Then when he comes home for good, he'll put up a sign on the door of Father's office with his name on it, and folks will speak of them as 'the two Drs. Dean.'"

"But he'll be different then," Eleanor had persisted. "He won't love me then as he does now."

David's arms had gone around her. "Why, little sister, do you think I ever could forget you? If ever you would call and I were in the middle of the ocean, I'd still come to you."

Eleanor, a slender little girl with masses of golden curls and big blue eyes, had slipped off her brother's knee and gone to her beloved piano. Softly touching some chords, she had sung, "Love goes on forever, I shall not forget."

David's eyes had suddenly filled with tears, though he was as tall as his father and called himself a man. When a small boy his mother had taught him the words of that beautiful Norwegian folk song "Mother Dear." He, in turn, had taught it to Eleanor.

> Mother, Mother dear! When the night is near,
> When the ruddy sun is sinking,
> Then your loving care makes a tender prayer;
> Then of me your heart is thinking.

And he had told his mother then, "Eleanor is going to be a beautiful singer someday. I have never seen a child who could carry a tune as she does."

While David was away at college, Eleanor finished the lower grades and went to high school. She played the piano for the high school orchestra; she sang in the girls' glee club, and whenever the school gave an operetta, Eleanor Dean always had the leading part. Dr. and Mrs. Dean dreamed of a time when David would be home again, his father's assistant, and Eleanor would be the soloist in the church choir and would direct cantatas and sing the leading part in community oratorios.

After Eleanor graduated from high school, she begged her parents for just a year at the conservatory. Her teachers told her that she could earn part of her expenses there by singing in church choirs and teaching a few pupils. She knew that her parents had pinched and saved to educate David; so she would take from them only enough money to transport her to Cincinnati and keep her there the first few months.

"I'll come home every few weeks, Mother dear," she had promised when she went away. "Every few weeks!"

Now it would soon be a year since she'd left, and Eleanor had made only one trip home, and that had been the third week after she had left.

It was just a week before Mother's Day when a letter came to the Dean home: "It breaks my heart to disappoint you, Mother, but again I find I can't get away. So you'll have to have Mother's Day without me. I'm going to take a vacation in June or July, and then I'll surely come. And I'll be thinking of you every minute on that day, Mother. Don't forget that."

Mrs. Dean dropped down beside her little sewing table and sobbed. Dr. Dean, who had seldom seen his wife break down like this, went over to her and put his arms around her. He had known stories like this one they were living—stories in which children forgot the parents who had sacrificed for them. But this in reality . . . oh, this seemed ten times more bitter than any of the stories he had read!

They had grown used to David's being away from home over the different holidays. College was too far away for him to come. When he was awarded his diploma from medical college, the president there explained to Dr. Dean that another year's hospital work would do much for his son. That delayed David's homecoming, but the Deans had stood it. And now it was May, and he was to come home in June to stay, according to the plans that he and his father had made years before.

But Mrs. Dean was sad. "It is Eleanor my heart is hungry for. I didn't think she would so completely fail me."

The little living room in which she had read and sung to both her children grew inexpressibly dear to her then. She wiped her eyes and looked around it. There were the photographs of Eleanor. The little cuckoo clock had been a gift from David, bought with the first money he had earned running errands.

Eleanor had hemmed the drapes for the window and made the fluffy pillows on the couch. She had re-enameled the frame of grandmother's picture to match the rich maroon tones in the paper. She had chosen the rugs and the upholstered wicker suite by taking some scraps of the wallpaper to the store.

Why, Eleanor is a little homemaker! Mrs. Dean thought. *If only she had*

not had such a rare voice she would be at home with us and doubly happy, I'm sure. I remember now how she used to tiptoe to the piano and sing.

Like a dream from the land of yesterday there came directly before her the vision of a little girl and boy standing close beside her at the piano as she played. They were singing in their childish voices, so sweetly and lovingly, that old Norwegian song:

Mother, Mother dear! When the day is here,
While you count the hours without me,
Then your tender heart thinks of me apart,
Still you dream about me.

A quick smile came to her lips. Not only had memory brought it there, but a sudden inspiration as well. She waited until Dr. Dean had started to his office, and then she began a search through the bookcases and closets for an old music book—the one that contained "The Song of Songs," as David had called it. She was going to tear that leaf from the book and send it to Eleanor.

It will bring her home, if anything can, she told herself hopefully. *I mustn't tell Father. He'll think I'm taking an unfair advantage. But he doesn't understand. He is sure of David's return in a few weeks' time. But right now I'm not sure that Eleanor even wants to come home; so I'm going to call her.*

I'd rather have her here to love than to have all the fame and fortune she might win if she stays away for years and studies. Nothing else matters in the land of happiness but love.

* * *

Up in the luxurious fraternity house near a big Chicago hospital, two young men and an older one were talking at that very minute. All three were physicians. Dr. Lieber, the older one, was from a town far north in Wisconsin, where he had a noted clinic. He had come down to Chicago to find two promising young men to train as assistants. The fame of his clinic was so great that when he had trained his assistants, he was always losing them to city surgeons for younger partners.

He suddenly placed his hand on the arm of one of the younger men. "Dean," he said persuasively, "the surgeons here say that you will do well as a specialist. I feel that I can help you, as well as that you can be of great service to me. I'm willing to increase the salary I offered you if you are interested in my proposition."

David Dean hesitated. His chum Paul Hylton, who had already accepted an offer from the physician, reached and clasped his other hand. "Of course you'll go, Dave," he coaxed. "You must not go back to that sleepy little hometown of yours and hide your talents under a bushel. You must go where you will have the best opportunity."

Still David hesitated. He seemed to hear his father say, *"The people of a small town and country district are entitled to as good doctors and teachers as those in crowded cities. Fame will come to a great man no matter where he is."*

Too, he seemed to see Mother, her face sad and tears in her eyes—homesick for him and Eleanor. At times his heart held a feeling of sorrow because Eleanor thought fame came ahead of happiness and because she was away from home.

Then, like a flash from the land of yesterday, there came into his memory Eleanor's letters, which had begun to tell of her loneliness in Cincinnati. Sometimes she hinted of going home, and always then he had written her, "Buck up, Eleanor! Success is always purchased by hard work and loneliness."

Tonight he wondered if that were true. His father was successful, according to many people, yet he had stayed among the people he loved—in a small town. He turned to Dr. Lieber. "I can't decide just yet," he said. "I must find out whether my father is really well and if he needs me. Give me a week to find out. I'll telegraph you then. If I decide to come, I'll be there at the same time Hylton is."

Back in the small bachelor apartment that he and Paul Hylton shared, the two of them talked over the surgeon's offer. David listened to his chum tell of the great opportunity ahead of the man who specialized, so long as he stayed in a big city. At the same time he thought of his father's hard life, caring for men injured in mine accidents, bringing tiny babies into the world, often acting as spiritual guide as well as body physician. Yet, with all this, his father seemed much happier than most of the men whom he knew.

While David sat thinking, Paul went to the radio he had recently bought and began tuning in on a distant station for the concert he tried to get every evening. As he worked the dials, he murmured, "I wish you liked music as I do, Dave. We'd have the radio on all the time and study to music."

David didn't even hear him. To himself he was saying, *I wish something big and vital would happen to help me decide this proposition. It is entirely too much for me.*

* * *

Mother's letter to Eleanor, bearing the little song of yesterday, had gone by special delivery. It was on the hall table in her boardinghouse when she reached home that evening. When she saw the envelope, Eleanor made a dash for it, almost breaking, in her haste, the beautiful little Wedgewood pitcher she had just bought for her mother with her savings, because she thought it was the prettiest Mother's Day gift she could find.

She opened the envelope. Mrs. Dean often sent her letters by special delivery, so Eleanor was not afraid that it was a message of sickness or trouble. She expectantly slipped in her fingers and drew out the piece of music. "Oh," she cried in a disappointed tone to her chum Elsie, "Mother is getting absentminded and forgot to put her letter in with this clipping."

Halfheartedly she unfolded the sheet of music, along the edges of which were the marks of little thumbs that had touched it when she and David were tiny. Rather curiously she glanced at the page. Listlessly she read the first line:

Mother, Mother dear! When the night is near.

She stopped short. Tears rushed to her eyes, and she began to cry softly, while Elsie, carrying the precious pitcher in her own hand, helped her up the stairway to their room.

There Eleanor told Elsie what message that song had brought to her. Her mother didn't believe she wanted to come home for Mother's Day. Her mother still thought she was a success, and that leaving the city for a few days could be managed as easily as if she were in her own town (the little song had been sent to remind her), while she, still a failure, just couldn't go home to admit her defeat. When she had found some kind of success, then she could go home with her head held high, and then they would be proud of her.

Eleanor's heart had almost broken with grief when she learned from the teachers at the conservatory that she had just a sweet voice, not strong enough for concert work. She had thought of how ashamed the people at home would be if she went home and told them that she would never bring them fame as all the newspapers had predicted at the time of her graduation.

Then she had decided to win success as a pianist. Not one word about her disappointment did she write home. And when her little supply of money was used up taking lessons, she did what hundreds of other girls at that time were doing: She went searching for work to help pay her expenses.

After days of fruitless searching for a job, she had found work at the music counter of a five-and-ten-cent store. There she met Elsie, who also had determined to climb higher, and soon the two girls were rooming together. Elsie had gotten her "on" in the chorus with which she sometimes sang at a radio broadcasting station. It added to their income, and it made possible the little Wedgewood pitcher and other gifts Eleanor was sending home.

"I don't see how I can sing tonight," Eleanor sobbed. "When I think of Mother alone at home, with her heart aching, I just can't sing a note."

Elsie patted her on the shoulder, at the same time imploring her to hurry. "Nan goes on at seven," she coaxed. "If she hadn't been sick, they never would have given you a chance to sing a solo. It's your chance to get home, honey. Can't you see that? It will not be regarded as a failure in your town to be a soloist at a broadcasting station."

Eleanor laughed shakily through her tears. "I'm soloist for just one night as a substitute," she reminded her.

By the time they left the house for the broadcasting station, Eleanor was laughing. She was going to sing three popular numbers that Nan had sent her.

Folded in Eleanor's purse when she entered the room was the envelope that had brought grief to her earlier in the evening. She had quite forgotten it, however, until the announcer, glancing through the music she had placed on the piano, said, "I wish Nan had given you 'Mother Machree' or something like it. Several of our listeners have already asked for mother songs because Mother's Day is so near."

Eleanor took the song from her purse and unfolded it. "Why, I have a mother's song here!" she said. "If you like it, I'll sing it. And please announce that it is being sung especially for Dr. and Mrs. Dean of Libertyville, Indiana, by their daughter."

When the time came, the little Norwegian folk song she had always loved so dearly rang out its message on the air:

Then your loving care makes a tender prayer.

* * *

When Paul Hylton tuned in on a dinner-hour concert, David Dean rather impatiently said, "Can't endure those Italian songs any longer. Guess I'll take a walk while you listen to that."

He had just got his hat when Paul ran out of the door after him. "There's a song being sung to Dr. and Mrs. Dean of Libertyville," he said excitedly. "That's your father and mother, isn't it?"

Almost immediately a sweet, girlish voice came singing through the air:

Mother, Mother dear! When the night is near . . .

David dropped down in front of the radio set, his head resting in his hand while he listened:

Mother, Mother dear! Whether far or near,
Well I know you'll never fail me.
Mother love will be ever near to me.
When the bitter days assail me;
Love goes on forever, I shall not forget.

He jumped up when it was done. "That is my sister singing," he said. "I could hear her crying in that song. Something is wrong. She is more home-sick than her letters indicated. Paul, I am going after her tonight, and I don't think I'll go to Dr. Lieber's clinic with you. I know I won't until I have been home to see if Father needs me."

* * *

Mother's Day found Mrs. Dean without a gift except Dr. Dean's flowers. Of course it was only seven o'clock when they sat down at the breakfast table together, and a special delivery boy could come at any time, but still he had a feeling that her children had forgotten this day of days of hers.

Mrs. Dean tried to be very cheerful, so her husband wouldn't notice the absence of gifts from their children. She gaily reminded him that there was maple syrup to eat with the waffles, but it required a good deal of courage to keep the tears out of her voice. It would have been much easier if she could have cried out her grief on his shoulder.

As she began to butter her first waffle, there was a sound of footsteps on the back porch, just as there had been in the old days when her children came home from school together. With a quick jerk, the outside door was opened, and David and Eleanor rushed into the room. Together they laughed and cried, "Mother dear! Dad, you darling!"

For a few minutes, Mrs. Dean held them in her arms, murmuring foolish nothings, all the while trying to listen as they explained they were late because Eleanor had to pack her things to bring home. She had come to stay. And if Dr. Dad wanted him, David was ready to enter his office and take old Mrs. Lankford and some of the rest of his chronic patients off his hands. Mrs. Dean laughed and cried over them while she asked herself in her heart, *What was wrong with my faith as I prayed for them to come?*

Now that they were here, Mrs. Dean fairly flew to the kitchen for some more waffles and to breathe a prayer of thankfulness to God for bringing them back even while she had doubted. When she returned to the table, the bouquet of sweetheart roses that David had bought at the florist's shop down the street and the little Wedgewood pitcher were beside her plate, and on them was a card with the message she never, never would forget:

Love goes on forever, I shall not forget.

The Marshaling of the Maples

G. E. Wallace

How tough it was, Edward Blair sighed, that schooling alone wouldn't land him the job he wanted: You had to have experience. How in the world did one gain experience without a job!

Edward Blair moved down the street toward Mrs. Morton's rooming house, walking under the maples. It was a strange world. A fellow didn't get what he wanted.

"The city council says that they haven't the money; so we'll have to play ball in the street or not play at all," Billy Jones had said. Billy was fifteen years old and full of life; he lived a few houses up the street from Mrs. Morton's rooming house.

"That's hard," Edward had said and then added, "on me."

Billy's eyes had twinkled. He caught the point of the remark. Edward worked in the mills, and he liked to sleep when he came home from working on the night shift. If the boys played ball on the street, sleep would be out of the question.

127

"And I guess it is hard on *you*, too," Edward had sighed.

Since he had moved to the city, Edward had come to like the boys who lived on the block. They were a jolly lot, if somewhat noisy. But then boys fourteen, fifteen, and sixteen years old just had to play!

As he walked on down the street past the gray houses to Mrs. Morton's, he thought, *It's a strange world. A fellow doesn't ever seem to get just what he wants!* For he had taken a course at a well-known business college and was qualified to enter an office and work up into an executive position. *When I get through this business course*, he had dreamed, *I'll get a position with a future.*

"We are very sorry, but seeing that you have had no practical experience, there is no place where we can use you just now in our organization," Wilbur and Company, wholesale grocers, had written in answer to his application. And that was only *one* of the discouraging letters he had received. The Northern Bus Company had stated that its policy was to take no men for office work who had had no experience in that line. G. Whipple and Company had the same policy.

And so—well, Ed had gone into a mill, and he watched a machine. Hour after hour he stood beside it, doing the one thing he had been told to do. As he repeated the motion, it became automatic, and his brain had time to think. *I'll be doing this four years from today. . . . I'll be doing this ten years from today. . . . I'll be doing this forever!*

Unless, of course, he could get into the office work he wanted. But how could he if he didn't have experience? And if you had to have experience before you could get such a job, how could you get that experience?

"Yes, it is a nice evening," he said, smiling, as he acknowledged Mrs. Morton's greeting. "Yes, the wind surely is cold for this time of year." For it was getting along toward spring.

Without knowing why he did it, Ed looked up at the trees. Out in the country, where he had been reared, you noticed the trees. They told you whether the season was advanced or backward. The bud of the shade trees had not started to swell. The sap had not started to run.

Say! Edward stood there, looking at the street lined with shade trees, his eyes fixed on the treetops he could see over on the next block and the next. Say, the city was full of shade trees! And most of those shade trees were maples. Why, there must be thousands of them! And Mr. Adams, who owned that big sugarbush on South Hill, had thought he had a real sugarbush when he had 500 trees to tap. If those maples could be tapped—but then it couldn't be done!

Yet that evening Edward walked up and down the streets. Boys, fifteen and sixteen years of age, stood on the corners or lounged in front of stores the owners of which wished they would move away. But there wasn't anything boys of fifteen and sixteen could do in the town, save "hang around" here and there. Even later, when the weather warmed up, it would be the same. If they played ball in the streets, the police would arrest them. And the city council had no money for a playground and a ball park. The members of the city council had said so.

* * *

Ed faced the group of young fellows in front of him. He had written to the city council, and later he had gone down to one of their meetings when they had said they would be glad to listen to him. But even as he made his speech, he knew that they thought he was making statements he could not possibly carry out. Get an equipped playground for the boys and girls at no cost! They surely would be glad to let him try! And if all he wanted was someone to take charge of the money he turned in, they would be glad to see to that. But how was he going to do the impossible?

Edward had the facts and figures down in black and white. There were so many sugar maples lining the streets. If they tapped those trees, and if they had a good season, they could make so much syrup. One or two of the council members admitted that it was news to them that you get maple sugar that way. They seemed to think it was manufactured in a factory. Even those who knew enough about country things to see what he was getting at asked, "But what about collecting the sap and boiling it down?"

Well, there were the boys. If they wanted the playground and the ball diamond as much as he thought they did, they would help. And he had asked and received permission to boil the sap in an old abandoned building that once had been a shop. Most of the windowpanes in that building were broken, and the floor sagged so much that it was going to be condemned, but it would do for this project.

Assisted by Bill, to whom he had confided his plans, Ed had built an evaporator. And Bill had scouted around and gathered pails in which to

catch the sap. At least he had *some* pails. "If I can get twenty pails," Bill had said, "the other fellows can get some, too."

And as the boys sat listening to Ed as he laid the plan before the council, they said, "We can do it! We can do it!"

So it came about that they all set to work under Ed's leadership. There was no doubt that they had set themselves to a task. Out in the open country, a sugarbush is a sugarbush! Here in the city, the trees were planted in rows along miles and miles of streets. They would have to organize.

Then there were pails, or utensils that could be used as pails, to be gathered. And wood or coal would have to be solicited for the boiling. And there was the problem of sap collection. No boy could carry a pail of sap from Twentieth and Ash to the evaporator pan in that dilapidated shop at Second and Myrtle. The distance was three miles!

But they got pails. They got wood. They got helpers. They made it a citywide affair, for they had to tap as many trees as they could. And besides, the ball diamond would be for all the boys of the city.

Ed began to build up his organization. He picked the leading boy in a four-block area and gave him specific work to do. He was to see that the other fellows tapped the trees and had the sap at a designated corner at a designated time.

They had a truck, and it was all their own. "It's worth ten bucks," a garageman said, "and I was going to junk it. But you boys can have it." And on the truck the boys had rigged up a container of sorts. A metal shop had a piece of galvanized tin that was not in use, and the manager let Ed have it. He really did more than that. He had one of his men make a tank—crude to be sure, but a tank—into which the sap could be poured.

And so the work started.

If Ed had not pointed out the fact that it was a moneymaking proposition in which they were engaged, the boys would have eaten all of the first syrup and maple-sugar cakes. "It's for the playground, you know," Ed reminded them.

Some of the others expressed it more forcibly to those few who wanted to eat the sugar and lap up the syrup:

"What do you want to do, eat up the ball diamond?"

"You can be arrested! Can't he be arrested, Ed? It's the city council's money!"

One batch of sap puzzled Ed. It boiled, but it didn't make syrup.

Ed got into his car and went out to the district beyond the railroad tracks. He had thought that district, being partly vacant lots, would produce well. Instead—well, it was sending in sap, but the sap was not right. He found that, overanxious, the boys there had tapped every kind of tree in the neighborhood: sycamores, oaks, cherry trees, and elms! It took time to explain. It took more time to point out the difference between a maple and an elm. But those living there learned the difference finally. And the maple syrup and the maple sugar mounted up.

Ed was busy after his hours in the mill. Still, he would not be doing anything worthwhile if he was not doing this. And this way he was helping the youngsters. He had an office, if you could call a kitchen table a desk and a packing box a filing cabinet.

He hammered away on a typewriter, too. "Dear Sir: I have 100 gallons of first-class maple syrup for sale," or, "Your order for maple-sugar cakes to retail at five cents each has been received. At present we have none, but we will try to send some out by Friday of next week." Letters went to firms here and there, in the city and outside of it. Soon he was selling maple sugar and maple syrup to farming communities, where you would think maple sugar would be produced.

And he was having a hard time accomplishing the hundred and one things that had to be done. One truck had not been able to do the work. They had secured two more of the same type—they ran, and that was about all that could be said for them. But the boys tinkered with them so that they kept on running.

And one lad had got hold of some paint left over from a gas-station job. The station owner had said, "Sure, you can have it." Color? There were several colors, which mixed, made a bluish-lavender shade. And this was very striking when applied to the old trucks. You could not mistake the trucks for anything except "those trucks that gather the sap."

And the money came in. Down at the city office, someone said, "Say, this *is* getting something for nothing!"

Ed smiled. For nothing! "Listen," he said, "that money means work, hard work, by boys. You're not going to spend it for anything else, are you?" For there had been a rumor that some members of the council thought that there were other things more needed than a playground for boys and girls.

"You'd break faith with our junior citizens if you did," Ed told them.

They wouldn't break faith, they promised. "How can we, when you got their fathers to write us?" one of the councilmen asked.

Ed smiled.

"But what are *you* going to get out of it?" another councilman asked him.

For it was work, and that called for ability: organizing ability, marketing ability.

* * *

It was spring. And it was hot. The maple trees along the streets were in leaf. The ball diamond on the city playground was in use.

Ed Blair walked away from the mill and headed toward Mrs. Morton's rooming house. There was no danger now that the boys would play ball in the streets. He could sleep when he was tired. And he *was* tired! *I might tell the council I got* that *out of it*, he thought.

He turned the corner of Elm, and a policeman waved a greeting, then walked to meet him. "Thanks to you," he said, "I don't dread the spring months."

"You used to?"

"I did that! Many and many a time I've gone home sick in my heart after having to run some boys in just for ball-playing. I had to, for the street is no place for a ball game. Yet I felt mean about it. But this year it's different. My work's easier."

Ed started on.

"It's too bad you didn't get anything out of it, seeing you did so much of the work," the policeman remarked. "I was telling Malcolm of the *Times*— he's the one who wrote up the account of what was done—it was too bad that young fellow, Ed Blair, didn't get one thing out of all this work for himself."

"Don't worry," Ed said. "It was fun."

"And work."

"And work," Ed agreed.

And then he was at the rooming house and up in his room. Tomorrow he'd go back to his job at the mill, and the next day, too. There was little chance of advancement there. But he'd have to go on, because if one didn't have experience in the line of work he wanted and was qualified to do, he didn't stand a chance to obtain that experience—or so it seemed. So he'd go on, and on, and . . .

He noticed the letter on his table. Mrs. Morton must have brought it up. He opened it. And his weariness fell away. He hadn't expected a reward. In all his imaginations, he couldn't have dreamed of *this* reward!

"Our firm," the letter written on the stationery of White and Company, a wholesale grocery firm, ran, "is looking for a young man who can build up and take care of deliveries to the small towns and villages within a radius of fifty miles. The position has possibilities. It calls for a young man who is skillful in organizing and who is able to handle men under him. According to the newspaper account of the work you have done for the city council, you possess those qualifications. A certain amount of business education is, of course, necessary, but it—"

Ed was smiling. His business training would be sufficient to meet their demands. It always had been. It was the practical experience he had lacked!

Dawn Comes to Dr. Faris

Archie Joscelyn

Though this story is old, it's as relevant today as it was when it was written, for the war between the forces of Light and the forces of Darkness continues.

"I'm putting it up to you," said redheaded Cass O'Neill sharply. "You're a junior in college and therefore old enough to think for yourself. You're majoring in science, so no one should need to tell you that there is no God. That old myth was exploded long ago for thinking people. And I tell you this, Lynton—" The red head was thrust forward impressively. "You are the only Christian left at Blair College. Every other one, students and faculty alike, are professed atheists."

Howard Lynton stared in amazement. "Surely you don't mean that?"

"I do mean it," declared O'Neill. "Maybe you haven't noticed it, but you are the only churchgoer left. Some of us got the idea, a few years ago, of making Blair an atheistic college. We've worked quietly along those lines for a long time. Christians have been dropping out, going elsewhere; atheists have heard of us and come in from other places. You're the last Christian, and it is our ambition to have Blair 100 percent godless."

"And you mean that I've got to go?" Lynton smiled rather crookedly.

"Just that," agreed O'Neill bluntly. "We're asking you to leave—or else to be sensible and join us. We'd greatly prefer the latter, because you're a person of unusual ability."

"What you say sounds incredible," protested Lynton. "Of course, I've heard of atheistic movements in this country, read of them in the papers, and so on. But I've never taken them seriously."

"Most people don't—that is why we're able to grow. Though, of course, all thinking people know that there is no God."

"I consider that I'm a thinking person," objected Lynton. "And I know there *is* a God."

O'Neill smiled tolerantly. "You're out of date. You'll get over it. But I've told you our ambition for Blair. How about it?"

"I'm a Christian." Lynton straightened. "And I'm staying."

"I'm sorry that you take that attitude," O'Neill said, shrugging. "We will find ways of making it so unpleasant for you that you'll soon be glad to go." He stood up and left the room.

Lynton, still bewildered, stared after the retreating figure. He could not believe this sort of thing could have happened here. A militant atheism in America! The threat to make college so unpleasant that he would leave was incredible. That was not sportsmanship at all; but only among those of high Christian ideals does sportsmanship prevail. Those who fight against the good in the world would naturally fight without scruple.

In the following days, the reality of the situation was brought home to Lynton. His classmates were striving to drive him out because he hindered their plan for Blair. He was determined to remain. He believed in a militant

Christianity if necessary, and this seemed to be the time. Too many others had weakly departed or yielded, else this situation could never have come about.

Young Lynton chanced to overhear, as he passed along a darkened hall one evening, a conversation between O'Neill and one of the popular faculty members.

"Let him stay if he's bound to," the faculty member was saying. "And when it comes time for him to graduate next year, we'll frame him and expel him. That will be a warning to others, if such a situation arises again."

Lynton knew from other remarks that they were talking about him. He went on to his own room, deeply troubled. He realized he was facing hostility and persecution—unless he would accept their demands. That had seemed a dream. He had thought that such conditions had passed with the Dark Ages, were confined to less-cultured lands or remote corners of the earth.

That he was helpless, Lynton knew. The others could expel him, for they had the power. He was determined to stay on, nevertheless. He would show them that one Christian still had the courage of his convictions. He decided he would take whatever came to him, smiling.

Another week passed. Lynton prepared to go down into a mine with the other members of a science class and Dr. Faris, the instructor, as a part of the course. The big mine lay on the outskirts of the city, a couple of miles from the college. A miner, Mr. Watson, was assigned to act as a guide, and the party, twenty in all, entered a cage and dropped into the depths of the earth. They left the cage and followed the long, timbered tunnels.

Dr. Faris knew his subject and commented as they went along. Everyone, including Lynton, was keenly interested, and for the moment he forgot the hostility that had been so apparent on the campus.

In the midst of their tour, the rocking thunder of a cave-in came from the passage close at hand. The electric lights in the mine went out in a twinkling, plunging everything into an inky darkness. Now closer at hand came the sound of falling rock and breaking timbers, followed by a groan; then heavy, awful silence. It was broken by the sharp command of the guide.

"Stand perfectly still, everybody, till we get our lamps lit." A moment later his own candle, worn for such emergencies, flickered in the all-encompassing darkness.

A measure of calm was restored by the light, and with steady fingers Lynton lit his candle. Presently, all were glowing, and the students were able to look around. Someone cried out at the sight of Dr. Faris, who lay, a silent, broken figure, half-buried beneath some fallen rocks and timbers.

Quickly, the others set to work and soon had him freed; but though he was still alive, it was plain that he was badly injured. O'Neill, who was studying to be a doctor, rendered the verdict, his face strangely white under his red hair. "He's got to have a doctor soon, or he'll die."

A short, penetrating glance back the way they had come was not encouraging. The cave-in had blocked them off completely from the rest of the mine. Their guide estimated that the whole shaft had caved for a long distance.

"The men may be able to dig us out," he said huskily, "if the air lasts. It's liable to go bad on us almost anytime."

"How long should it take them to reach us?" Lynton asked.

"They might reach us in twenty-four hours—with luck," was the response.

Lynton said nothing. The chances that the air, deep in the mine and following the cave-in, would remain fit to breathe for that long were slim, he knew. He was certain that, good air or not, Dr. Faris could not live half that long without skilled attention for his injuries.

"Is there no other way out?" demanded O'Neill frantically. "Isn't there something we can do?"

"No other way that I know of," was the gloomy reply. "We were exploring an old, unused shaft, and it leads only to other old shafts that have been closed for years. We haven't any tools to dig with, even."

Surprisingly, through the gloom, Dr. Faris spoke. He had recovered consciousness, and though suffering intense pain, he smiled gamely. "That means the end, then, for me," he said. "I hope it won't be so bad—for the rest of you." Stark silence followed his words, until he spoke again. "I never thought . . . that this would be the end . . . or that it would be like this."

"This isn't the end, Dr. Faris," said Lynton quietly. "Death is not the destiny or the end of man. It is only a door."

"You are a Christian, Lynton." Dr. Faris smiled wearily. "And for you, at least, this will not be quite so bad, because of your hope." He sighed. "I wish that I, too, might have hope. But I have never found God. So can there be a God?"

"There *is* a God," replied Lynton convincingly. "You have conducted many experiments, Dr. Faris. But there are many more, as I have heard you say, yet untouched on by yourself or any man. If there is anything that you do not know, how can you say there is no God? For God might be there."

"I'd like to believe," agreed Dr. Faris, "for to die this way is hard."

Excited exclamations came from a short distance ahead where some of the others had been exploring.

"Here's a barricade of old planks that has fallen down," Alfred Harrison called.

The guide jumped up. "Careful there," he warned. "There's a shaft running straight down a little way beyond. Don't fall into it."

Heeding the warning, the others stopped at the brink and peered down. One of them gave an excited exclamation. "It looks like a faint light way down there," he said.

The guide hurried forward, Lynton by his side. Sure enough, perhaps fifty feet down, a dim streak of light could be seen.

The guide exclaimed excitedly, "This old shaft has been closed for years. I can see what's happened. The jar of the cave-in, or something, has broken through a thin wall of shaft into another old, abandoned shaft close to it down there."

"And that other one must lead out to open air," O'Neill cried. "Or there wouldn't be any light there."

"That'd be about it," agreed Mr. Watson, but without enthusiasm.

"Then can't we descend into this? See, there's an old ladder still leading down here. Possibly we can get through and out to help," the redhead demanded eagerly. "Here, let me start now."

"Not too fast, boy," was the response. "That shaft will probably be full of foul air—and if so, it's death to go down. We'll lower a lamp to see. I've some cord."

The light sank slowly, steadily. Two-thirds down, it went out abruptly.

"When the air's so bad that a light won't burn, it's death to venture," said the guide simply. "A man goes out just like a candle in such air."

O'Neill shrank back, appalled.

Lynton stepped forward. "It's practically certain death, in any case, to wait here," he summed up. "And sure death for Dr. Faris, if he doesn't have help. I'm a good underwater swimmer and can hold my breath for quite a while. I'm going to try it. If I can get through, the men can get gas masks from the armory and come back through to take you all out safely."

"You can never make it," protested O'Neill. "And it's a terrible place to die—alone."

"I won't be alone," answered Lynton.

He turned then and began climbing down the ancient ladder on the side of the shaft. It was fairly solid, however. So long as his light burned steadily, he breathed normally. When it commenced to flicker and dim, he took a deep breath, then descended swiftly, holding his breath. His light went out as though blown by a strong breath, though no air stirred. A prayer was on his lips as he continued.

Soon his feet touched the bottom. More or less debris was in the bottom of the old shaft, which was black as night. Lynton had to scramble over this as best he could. Always he moved toward that opening where light shone faintly. His lungs choked, and he felt he could not go farther without breathing. To breathe in this foul air was to die. He came to the opening, barely large enough for him to scramble through, moved a few feet, and then the light was suddenly stronger.

Here was another old shaft, as Mr. Watson had said, which ran clear to the top of the ground, nearly 100 feet up. Some old debris had fallen in, filling it up about to a level with the bottom of the other abandoned shaft. The top, which had been covered with planks, was partly opened to the air.

Lynton saw that another old ladder led up the side for perhaps forty feet. Beyond that, it too had fallen away. He made his way up it as fast as he could. He had covered some thirty feet before his tortured lungs compelled him to breathe again. The open air above had helped here.

Lynton stopped, for the ladder was too rotten to climb any farther. Above him, he heard dim voices—men of the rescue party, apparently, getting ready to descend into the mine. Lynton shouted again and again.

Suddenly, all was quiet. The men had heard him, and then someone was peering over the brink above.

"I'll get a rope," he shouted.

"Wait!" commanded Lynton, and he gave swift instructions regarding the gas masks from the armory and the way in. Quickly, a rope was dropped down and he was pulled up. Less than an hour later, the others had been rescued as well.

The next morning, in the hospital, Lynton was beside the bed of Dr. Faris, as were the others who had descended into the shaft with him.

Dr. Faris smiled wanly. "Thanks to you, Lynton," he said, "I'll live. And I want to tell you: I found God down there, when you told me where He might be. I knew then that He was there—with us."

"And your words, that you wouldn't be alone down in that shaft of death—they set me to thinking," O'Neill added. "You did the impossible from the purely human standpoint—though such things do happen, today as always. God was with you and gave you the strength to do it."

Lynton smiled. "That's it," he agreed simply. "I could never have done it alone. And now it's Sunday morning and time for church. You'll have to excuse me now."

As one man, the others of the class stood up.

O'Neill spoke. "We're going with you, if you don't mind, Lynton. We . . . we all saw a light, I guess, down there in the darkness, and we want greater things for Blair—and for ourselves."

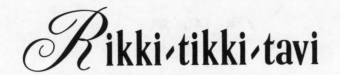

Rikki·tikki·tavi

Rudyard Kipling

At the hole where he went in
    Red-Eye called to Wrinkle-Skin.
Hear what little Red-Eye saith:
    "Nag, come up and dance with death!"

Eye to eye and head to head,
    (Keep the measure, Nag.)
This shall end when one is dead;
    (At thy pleasure, Nag.)
Turn for turn and twist for twist—
    (Run and hide thee, Nag.)
Hah! The hooded Death has missed!
    (Woe betide thee, Nag!)

Death lurked in the grass—death in the shape of Nag and Nagaina, cobras determined to regain the bungalow compound for themselves. The only thing standing in their way . . . a little mongoose named Rikki-tikki-tavi. This story is one of the most memorable tales to come out of Rudyard Kipling's classic* The Jungle Books, *popular now for more than a century.

This is the story of the great war that Rikki-tikki-tavi fought single-handed through the bathrooms of the big bungalow in Segowlee cantonment. Darzee, the tailorbird, helped him, and Chuchundra, the muskrat, who never comes out into the middle of the floor, but always creeps around by the wall, gave him advice; but Rikki-tikki did the real fighting.

He was a mongoose, rather like a little cat in his fur and his tail, but quite like a weasel in his head and his habits. His eyes and the end of his restless nose were pink; he could scratch himself anywhere he pleased, with any leg, front or back, that he chose to use; he could fluff up his tail till it looked like a bottlebrush, and his war cry, as he scuttled through the long grass, was "Rikk-tikk-tikki-tikki-tchk!"

One day, a high summer flood washed him out of the burrow where he lived with his father and mother and carried him, kicking and clucking, down a roadside ditch. He found a little wisp of grass floating there and clung to it till he lost his senses. When he revived, he was lying in the hot sun on the middle of the garden path, very draggled indeed, and a small boy was saying, "Here's a dead mongoose. Let's have a funeral."

"No," said his mother. "Let's take him in and dry him. Perhaps he isn't really dead."

They took him into the house, and a big man picked him up between his finger and thumb and said he was not dead but half choked; so they wrapped him in cotton wool and warmed him, and he opened his eyes and sneezed.

"Now," said the big man (he was an Englishman who had just moved into the bungalow), "don't frighten him, and we'll see what he'll do."

It is the hardest thing in the world to frighten a mongoose, because he is eaten up from nose to tail with curiosity. The motto of all the mongoose family is, "Run and Find Out"; and Rikki-tikki was a true mongoose. He looked at the cotton wool, decided that it was not good to eat, ran all around the table, sat up and put his fur in order, scratched himself, and jumped on the small boy's shoulder.

"Don't be frightened, Teddy," said his father. "That's his way of making friends."

"Ouch! He's tickling under my chin," said Teddy.

Rikki-tikki looked down between the boy's collar and neck, snuffed at his ear, and climbed down to the floor, where he sat rubbing his nose.

"Good gracious," said Teddy's mother, "and that's a wild creature! I suppose he's so tame because we've been kind to him."

"All mongooses are like that," said her husband. "If Teddy doesn't pick him up by the tail or try to put him in a cage, he'll run in and out of the house all day long. Let's give him something to eat."

They gave him a little piece of raw meat. Rikki-tikki liked it immensely, and when it was finished he went out into the veranda and sat in the sunshine and fluffed up his fur to make it dry to the roots. Then he felt better.

There are more things to find out about in this house, he said to himself, *than all my family could find out in all their lives. I shall certainly stay and find out.*

He spent all that day roaming over the house. He nearly drowned himself in the bathtubs, put his nose into the ink on a writing table, and burned it on the end of the big man's cigar, for he climbed up in the big man's lap to see how writing was done. At nightfall he ran into Teddy's nursery to watch how kerosene lamps were lit, and when Teddy went to bed, Rikki-tikki climbed up, too; but he was a restless companion, because he had to get up and attend to every noise all through the night and find out what made it. Teddy's mother and father came in, the last thing, to look at their boy, and Rikki-tikki was awake on the pillow.

"I don't like that," said Teddy's mother. "He may bite the child."

"He'll do no such thing," said the father. "Teddy's safer with that little beast than if he had a bloodhound to watch him. If a snake came into the nursery now—"

But Teddy's mother wouldn't think of anything so awful.

Early in the morning Rikki-tikki came to breakfast in the veranda, riding on Teddy's shoulder. They gave him a banana and some boiled egg; and he sat on all their laps one after the other, because every well-brought-up mongoose always hopes to be a house mongoose someday and have rooms to run about in, and Rikki-tikki's mother (she used to live in the general's house at Segowlee) had carefully told Rikki what to do if ever he came across white men.

Then Rikki-tikki went out into the garden to see what was to be seen. It was a large garden, only half cultivated, with bushes, as big as summer-houses, of Marshal Niel roses; lime and orange trees; clumps of bamboos, and thickets of high grass. Rikki-tikki licked his lips. "This is a splendid hunting ground," he said, and his tail grew bottlebrushy at the thought of it, and he scuttled up and down the garden, snuffing here and there till he heard very sorrowful voices in a thornbush.

It was Darzee, a tailorbird, and his wife. They had made a beautiful nest by pulling two big leaves together and stitching them up the edges with fibers, and had filled the hollow with cotton and downy fluff. The nest swayed to and fro as they sat on the rim and cried.

"What is the matter?" asked Rikki-tikki.

"We are very miserable," said Darzee. "One of our babies fell out of the nest yesterday, and Nag ate him."

"Hmm!" said Rikki-tikki. "That is very sad. But I am a stranger here. Who is Nag?"

Darzee and his wife only cowered down in the nest without answering, for from the thick grass at the foot of the bush there came a low hiss—a horrid, cold sound that made Rikki-tikki jump back two clear feet. Then inch by inch out of the grass rose up the head and spread hood of Nag, the big black cobra, and he was five feet long from tongue to tail. When he had lifted one-third of himself clear of the ground, he stayed balancing to and fro exactly as a dandelion tuft balances in the wind, and he looked at Rikki-tikki with the wicked snake's eyes that never change their expression, whatever the snake may be thinking.

"Who is Nag?" said he. "*I* am Nag. The great god Brahm put his mark upon all our people when the first cobra spread his hood to keep the sun off Brahm as he slept. Look and be afraid!"

He spread out his hood more than ever, and Rikki-tikki saw the spectacle mark on the back of it that looks exactly like the eye part of a hook-and-eye fastening. He was afraid for the minute; but it is impossible for a mongoose to stay frightened for any length of time, and though Rikki-tikki had never met a live cobra before, his mother had fed him on dead ones, and he knew that a grown mongoose's business in life was to fight and eat snakes. Nag knew that too, and at the bottom of his cold heart he was afraid.

"Well," said Rikki-tikki, and his tail began to fluff up again, "marks or no marks, do you think it is right for you to eat fledglings out of a nest?"

Nag was thinking to himself and watching the least little movement in the grass behind Rikki-tikki. He knew that mongooses in the garden meant death sooner or later for him and his family, but he wanted to get Rikki-tikki off his guard. So he dropped his head a little and put it on one side.

"Let's talk," he said. "You eat eggs. Why should not I eat birds?"

"Behind you! Look behind you!" sang Darzee.

Rikki-tikki knew better than to waste time in staring. He jumped up in the air as high as he could go, and just under him whizzed by the head of Nagaina, Nag's wicked wife. She had crept up behind him as he was talking, to make an end of him; and he heard her savage hiss as the stroke missed. He came down almost across her back, and if he had been an old mongoose he would have known that then was the time to break her back with one bite; but he was afraid of the terrible, lashing return stroke of the cobra. He bit, indeed, but did not bite long enough, and he jumped clear of the whisking tail, leaving Nagaina torn and angry.

"Wicked, wicked Darzee!" said Nag, lashing up as high as he could reach toward the nest in the thornbush; but Darzee had built it out of reach of snakes, and it only swayed to and fro.

Rikki-tikki felt his eyes growing red and hot (when a mongoose's eyes grow red, he is angry), and he sat back on his tail and hind legs like a little kangaroo, looked all around him, and chattered with rage. But Nag and Nagaina had disappeared into the grass. When a snake misses his stroke, he never says anything or gives any sign of what he means to do next. Rikki-tikki did not care to follow them, for he did not feel sure that he could manage two snakes at once. So he trotted off to the gravel path near the house and sat down to think. It was a serious matter for him.

If you read the old books of natural history, you will find they say that when a mongoose fights a snake and happens to get bitten, he runs off and eats some herb that cures him. That is not true. The victory is only a matter of quickness of eye and quickness of foot—snake's blow against mongoose's jump—and as no eye can follow the motion of a snake's head when he strikes, that makes things much more wonderful than any magic herb. Rikki-tikki knew he was a young mongoose, and it made him all the more pleased to think that he had managed to escape a blow from behind. It gave him confidence in himself, and when Teddy came running down the path, Rikki-tikki was ready to be petted.

But just as Teddy was stooping, something flinched a little in the dust, and a tiny voice said, "Be careful. I am death!" It was Karait, the dusty brown snakeling that lies by choice on the dusty earth; and his bite is as dangerous as the cobra's. But he is so small that nobody thinks of him, and so he does the more harm to people.

Rikki-tikki's eyes grew red again, and he danced up to Karait with the peculiar rocking, swaying motion that he had inherited from his family. It looks very funny, but it is so perfectly balanced a gait that you can fly off from it at any angle you please; and in dealing with snakes this is an advantage. If Rikki-tikki had only known, he was doing a much more dangerous thing than fighting Nag, for Karait is so small, and can turn so quickly, that unless Rikki bit him close to the back of the head, he would get the return stroke in his eye or lip. But Rikki did not know. His eyes were all red, and he rocked back and forth, looking for a good place to hold. Karait struck out. Rikki jumped sideways and tried to run in, but the wicked little dusty gray head lashed within a fraction of his shoulder, and he had to jump over the body, and the head followed his heels close.

Teddy shouted to the house, "Oh, look here! Our mongoose is killing a snake!" And Rikki-tikki heard a scream from Teddy's mother. His father ran out with a stick, but by the time he came up, Karait had lunged out once too far, and Rikki-tikki had sprung, jumped on the snake's back, dropped his head far between his forelegs, bitten as high up the back as he could get hold, and rolled away. That bite paralyzed Karait, and Rikki-tikki was just going to eat him up from the tail, after the custom of his family at dinner, when he remembered that a full meal makes a slow mongoose, and if he wanted all his strength and quickness ready, he must keep himself thin.

He went away for a dust bath under the castor-oil bushes while Teddy's father beat the dead Karait.

What's the use of that? thought Rikki-tikki. *I've settled it all.*

Then Teddy's mother picked him up from the dust and hugged him, crying that he had saved Teddy from death; and Teddy's father said that he was a providence, and Teddy looked on with big, scared eyes. Rikki-tikki was rather amused at all the fuss, which, of course, he did not understand. Teddy's mother might just as well have petted Teddy for playing in the dust. Rikki was thoroughly enjoying himself.

That night, at dinner, walking to and fro among the wineglasses on the table, he could have stuffed himself three times over with nice things; but he remembered Nag and Nagaina, and though it was very pleasant to be patted and petted by Teddy's mother and to sit on Teddy's shoulder, his eyes would get red from time to time, and he would go off into his long war cry of "Rikk-tikk-tikki-tikki-tchk!"

Teddy carried him off to bed and insisted on Rikki-tikki sleeping under his chin. Rikki-tikki was too well bred to bite or scratch, but as soon as Teddy was asleep he went off for his nightly walk around the house, and in the dark he ran up against Chuchundra, the muskrat, creeping around by the wall. Chuchundra is a brokenhearted little beast. He whimpers and cheeps all the night, trying to make up his mind to run into the middle of the room, but he never gets there.

"Don't kill me," said Chuchundra, almost weeping. "Rikki-tikki, don't kill me."

"Do you think a snake-killer kills muskrats?" said Rikki-tikki scornfully.

"Those who kill snakes get killed by snakes," said Chuchundra more sorrowfully than ever. "And how am I to be sure that Nag won't mistake me for you some dark night?"

"There's not the least danger," said Rikki-tikki. "But Nag is in the garden, and I know you don't go there."

"My cousin Chua, the rat, told me—" said Chuchundra, and then he stopped.

"Told you what?"

"H'sh! Nag is everywhere, Rikki-tikki. You should have talked to Chua in the garden."

"I didn't, so you must tell me. Quick, Chuchundra, or I'll bite you!"

Chuchundra sat down and cried till the tears rolled off his whiskers. "I am a very poor man," he sobbed. "I never had spirit enough to run out into the middle of the room. H'sh! I mustn't tell you anything. Can't you *hear*, Rikki-tikki?"

Rikki-tikki listened. The house was as still as still, but he thought he could just catch the faintest *scratch-scratch* in the world—a noise as faint as that of a wasp walking on a windowpane: the dry scratch of a snake's scales on brickwork.

That's Nag or Nagaina, he said to himself, *and he is crawling into the bathroom sluice. You're right, Chuchundra; I should have talked to Chua.*

He stole off to Teddy's bathroom, but there was nothing there, and then to Teddy's mother's bathroom. At the bottom of the smooth plaster wall there was a brick pulled out to make a sluice for the bathwater, and as Rikki-tikki stole in by the masonry curb where the bath is put, he heard Nag and Nagaina whispering together outside in the moonlight.

"When the house is emptied of people," said Nagaina to her husband, "*he* will have to go away, and then the garden will be our own again. Go in quietly, and remember that the big man who killed Karait is the first one to bite. Then come out and tell me, and we will hunt for Rikki-tikki together."

"But are you sure that there is anything to be gained by killing the people?" said Nag.

"Everything. When there were no people in the bungalow, did we have any mongoose in the garden? So long as the bungalow is empty, we are king and queen of the garden. And remember that as soon as our eggs in the melon bed hatch (as they may tomorrow), our children will need room and quiet."

"I had not thought of that," said Nag. "I will go, but there is no need that we should hunt for Rikki-tikki afterward. I will kill the big man and his wife, and the child if I can, and come away quietly. Then the bungalow will be empty, and Rikki-tikki will go."

Rikki-tikki tingled all over with rage and hatred at this, and then Nag's head came through the sluice, and his five feet of cold body followed it. Angry as he was, Rikki-tikki was very frightened as he saw the size of the big cobra. Nag coiled himself up, raised his head, and looked into the bathroom in the dark, and Rikki could see his eyes glitter.

"Now, if I kill him here, Nagaina will know; and if I fight him on the open floor, the odds are in his favor. What am I to do?" said Rikki-tikki-tavi.

Nag waved to and fro, and then Rikki-tikki heard him drinking from the biggest water jar that was used to fill the bath. "That is good," said the snake. "Now, when Karait was killed, the big man had a stick. He may have that stick still, but when he comes in to bathe in the morning, he will not have a stick. I shall wait here till he comes. Nagaina—do you hear me? I shall wait here in the cool till daytime."

There was no answer from outside, so Rikki-tikki knew Nagaina had gone away. Nag coiled himself down, coil by coil, around the bulge at the bottom of the water jar, and Rikki-tikki stayed still as death. After an hour he began to move, muscle by muscle, toward the jar. Nag was asleep, and Rikki-tikki looked at his big back, wondering where would be the best place for a good hold.

If I don't break his back at the first jump, thought Rikki, *he can still fight; and if he fights . . . Oh, Rikki!*

He looked at the thickness of the neck below the hood, but that was too much for him; and a bite near the tail would only make Nag savage.

"It must be the head," he said at last. "The head above the hood. And when I am once there, I must not let go."

Then he jumped. The head was lying a little clear of the water jar, under the curve of it; and, as his teeth met, Rikki braced his back against the bulge of the red earthenware to hold down the head. This gave him just one second's purchase, and he made the most of it. Then he was battered to and fro as a rat is shaken by a dog—to and fro on the floor, up and down, and around in great circles; but his eyes were red, and he held on as the body cart-whipped over the floor, upsetting the tin dipper and the soap dish and the flesh brush, and banged against the tin side of the bath.

As he held, Rikki closed his jaws tighter and tighter, for he was sure he would be banged to death, and, for the honor of his family, he preferred to be found with his teeth locked. He was dizzy, aching, and felt shaken to pieces when something went off like a thunderclap just behind him; a hot wind knocked him senseless, and red fire singed his fur. The big man had been wakened by the noise and had fired both barrels of a shotgun into Nag just behind the hood.

Rikki-tikki held on with his eyes shut, for now he was quite sure he was dead; but the head did not move, and the big man picked him up and said, "It's the mongoose again, Alice. The little chap has saved *our* lives now."

Then Teddy's mother came in with a very white face and saw what was left of Nag. Rikki-tikki dragged himself to Teddy's bedroom and spent half the rest of the night shaking himself tenderly to find out whether he really was broken into forty pieces, as he fancied.

When morning came he was very stiff but well pleased with his doings. "Now I have Nagaina to settle with, and she will be worse than five Nags, and there's no knowing when the eggs she spoke of will hatch. Goodness! I must go and see Darzee," he said.

Without waiting for breakfast, Rikki-tikki ran to the thornbush, where Darzee was singing a song of triumph at the top of his voice. The news of Nag's death was all over the garden, for the sweeper had thrown the body on the rubbish heap.

"Oh, you stupid tuft of feathers!" said Rikki-tikki angrily. "Is this the time to sing?"

"Nag is dead—is dead—is dead!" sang Darzee. "The valiant Rikki-tikki caught him by the head and held fast. The big man brought the bang-stick, and Nag fell in two pieces! He will never eat my babies again."

"All that's true enough; but where's Nagaina?" said Rikki-tikki, looking carefully around him.

"Nagaina came to the bathroom sluice and called for Nag," Darzee went on, "and Nag came out on the end of a stick. The sweeper picked him up on the end of a stick and threw him upon the rubbish heap. Let us sing about the great red-eyed Rikki-tikki!" And Darzee filled his throat and sang.

"If I could get up to your nest, I'd roll all your babies out!" said Rikki-tikki. "You don't know when to do the right thing at the right time. You're safe enough in your nest there, but it's war for me down here. Stop singing a minute, Darzee."

"For the great, the beautiful Rikki-tikki's sake, I will stop," said Darzee. "What is it, O killer of the terrible Nag?"

"Where is Nagaina, for the third time?"

"On the rubbish heap by the stables, mourning for Nag. Great is Rikki-tikki with the white teeth."

"Bother my white teeth! Have you ever heard where she keeps her eggs?"

"In the melon bed, on the end nearest the wall, where the sun strikes nearly all day. She hid them there weeks ago."

"And you never thought it worthwhile to tell me? The end nearest the wall, you said?"

"Rikki-tikki, you're not going to eat her eggs?"

"Not eat exactly, no. Darzee, if you have a grain of sense, you'll fly off to the stables and pretend that your wing is broken and let Nagaina chase you away to this bush. I must get to the melon bed, and if I went there now, she'd see me."

Darzee was a featherbrained little fellow who could never hold more than one idea at a time in his head; and because he knew that Nagaina's children were born in eggs like his own, he didn't think at first that it was fair to kill them. But his wife was a sensible bird, and she knew that cobra's eggs meant young cobras later on; so she flew off from the nest and left

Darzee to keep the babies warm and continue his song about the death of Nag. Darzee was very like a man in some ways.

She fluttered in front of Nagaina by the rubbish heap and cried out, "Oh, my wing is broken! The boy in the house threw a stone at me and broke it." Then she fluttered more desperately than ever.

Nagaina lifted up her head and hissed, "You warned Rikki-tikki when I would have killed him. Indeed and truly, you have chosen a bad place to be lame in." And she moved toward Darzee's wife, slipping along over the dust.

"The boy broke it with a stone!" shrieked Darzee's wife.

"Well! It may be some consolation to you when you're dead to know that I shall settle accounts with the boy. My husband lies on the rubbish heap this morning, but before night the boy in the house will lie very still. What is the use of running away? I am sure to catch you. Little fool, look at me!"

Darzee's wife knew better than to do *that*, for a bird who looks at a snake's eyes gets so frightened that she cannot move. Darzee's wife fluttered on, piping sorrowfully and never leaving the ground, and Nagaina quickened her pace.

Rikki-tikki heard them going up the path from the stables, and he raced for the end of the melon patch near the wall. There, in the warm litter about the melons, very cunningly hidden, he found twenty-five eggs, about the size of bantam's eggs, but with whitish skin instead of shell.

"I was not a day too soon," he said, for he could see the baby cobras curled up inside the skin, and he knew that the minute they were hatched, they could each kill a man or a mongoose. He bit off the tops of the eggs as fast as he could, taking care to crush the young cobras, and turned over the litter from time to time to see whether he had missed any. At last there were only three eggs left, and Rikki-tikki began to chuckle to himself when he heard Darzee's wife screaming, "Rikki-tikki, I led Nagaina toward the house, and she has gone into the veranda, and—oh, come quickly—she means killing!"

Rikki-tikki smashed two eggs and tumbled backward down the melon bed with the third egg in his mouth; then he scuttled to the veranda as hard as he could put foot to the ground. Teddy and his mother and father were there at early breakfast; but Rikki-tikki saw that they were not eating anything. They sat stone-still, and their faces were white. Nagaina was coiled up on the matting by Teddy's chair, within easy striking distance of Teddy's bare leg, and she was swaying to and fro, singing a song of triumph.

"Son of the big man that killed Nag," she hissed, "stay still. I am not ready yet. Wait a little. Keep very still, all you three. If you move I strike, and if you do not move I strike. Oh, foolish people who killed my Nag!"

Teddy's eyes were fixed on his father, and all his father could do was to whisper, "Sit still, Teddy. You mustn't move. Teddy, keep still."

Then Rikki-tikki came up and cried, "Turn around, Nagaina. Turn and fight!"

"All in good time," said she without moving her eyes. "I will settle my account with *you* presently. Look at your friends, Rikki-tikki. They are still and white; they are afraid. They dare not move, and if you come a step nearer, I strike."

"Look at your eggs," said Rikki-tikki, "in the melon bed near the wall. Go and look, Nagaina."

The big snake turned half around and saw the egg on the veranda floor. "Ah-h! Give it to me," she said.

Rikki-tikki put his paws one on each side of the egg, and his eyes were blood-red. "What price for a snake's egg? For a young cobra? For a young king cobra? For the last—the very last of the brood? The ants are eating all the others down by the melon bed."

Nagaina spun clear around, forgetting everything for the sake of the one egg; and Rikki-tikki saw Teddy's father shoot out a big hand, catch Teddy by the shoulder, and drag him across the little table with the teacups, safe and out of reach of Nagaina.

"Tricked! Tricked! Tricked! Rikk-tck-tck!" chuckled Rikki-tikki. "The boy is safe, and it was I—I that caught Nag by the hood last night in the bathroom." Then he began to jump up and down, all four feet together, his head close to the floor. "He threw me to and fro, but he could not shake me off. He was dead before the big man blew him in two. I did it. Rikki-tikki-tck-tck! Come then, Nagaina. Come and fight with me. You shall not be a widow long."

Nagaina saw that she had lost her chance of killing Teddy, and the egg lay between Rikki-tikki's paws. "Give me the egg, Rikki-tikki. Give me the last of my eggs, and I will go away and never come back," she said, lowering her hood.

"Yes, you will go away, and you will never come back; for you will go to the rubbish heap with Nag. Fight, widow! The big man has gone for his gun! Fight!"

Rikki-tikki was bounding all around Nagaina, keeping just out of reach of her stroke, his little eyes like hot coals. Nagaina gathered herself together and flung out at him. Rikki-tikki jumped up and backward. Again and again and again she struck, and each time her head came with a whack on the matting of the veranda, and she gathered herself together like a watch spring. Then Rikki-tikki danced in a circle to get behind her, and Nagaina spun around to keep her head to his head, so that the rustle of her tail on the matting sounded like dry leaves blown along by the wind.

He had forgotten the egg. It still lay on the veranda floor, and Nagaina came nearer and nearer to it, till at last, while Rikki-tikki was drawing breath, she caught it in her mouth, turned to the veranda steps, and flew like an arrow down the path, with Rikki-tikki behind her. When the cobra runs for her life, she goes like a whiplash flicked across a horse's neck.

Rikki-tikki knew that he must catch her, or all the trouble would begin again. She headed straight for the long grass by the thornbush, and as he was running, Rikki-tikki heard Darzee still singing his foolish little song of triumph. But Darzee's wife was wiser. She flew off her nest as Nagaina came along and flapped her wings about Nagaina's head. If Darzee had helped they might have turned her; but Nagaina only lowered her hood and went on. Still, the instant's delay brought Rikki-tikki up to her, and as she plunged into the rat hole where she and Nag used to live, his little white teeth were clinched on her tail, and he went down with her—and very few mongooses, however wise and old they may be, care to follow a cobra into her hole. It was dark in the hole; and Rikki-tikki never knew when it might open out and give Nagaina room to turn and strike at him. He held on savagely and struck out his feet to act as brakes on the dark slope of the hot, moist earth.

Then the grass by the mouth of the hole stopped waving, and Darzee said, "It is all over with Rikki-tikki! We must sing his death song. Valiant Rikki-tikki is dead! For Nagaina will surely kill him underground."

So he sang a very mournful song that he made up on the spur of the moment, and just as he got to the most touching part, the grass quivered again and Rikki-tikki, covered with dirt, dragged himself out of the hole leg by leg, licking his whiskers. Darzee stopped with a little shout.

Rikki-tikki shook some of the dust out of his fur and sneezed. "It is all over," he said. "The widow will never come out again."

And the red ants that live between the grass stems heard him and began to troop down one after another to see if he had spoken the truth.

Rikki-tikki curled himself up in the grass and slept where he was—slept and slept till it was late in the afternoon, for he had done a hard day's work.

"Now," he said when he awoke, "I will go back to the house. Tell the Coppersmith, Darzee, and he will tell the garden that Nagaina is dead."

The Coppersmith is a bird who makes a noise exactly like the beating of a little hammer on a copper pot; and the reason he is always making it is because he is the town crier to every Indian garden and tells all the news to everybody who cares to listen. As Rikki-tikki went up the path, he heard his "attention" notes, like a tiny dinner gong, and then the steady "Ding-dong-tock! Nag is dead! Dong! Nagaina is dead! Ding-dong-tock!" That set all the birds in the garden singing and the frogs croaking; for Nag and Nagaina used to eat frogs as well as little birds.

When Rikki got to the house, Teddy and Teddy's mother (she still looked very white, for she had fainted) and Teddy's father came out and almost cried over him. That night he ate all that was given to him till he could eat no more, and he went to bed on Teddy's shoulder, where Teddy's mother saw him when she came to look late at night.

"He saved our lives and Teddy's life," she said to her husband. "Just think, he saved all our lives!"

Rikki-tikki woke up with a jump, for all mongooses are light sleepers. "Oh, it's you," said he. "What are you bothering for? All the cobras are dead; and if they weren't, I'm here."

Rikki-tikki had a right to be proud of himself; but he did not grow too proud, and he kept that garden as a mongoose should keep it, with tooth and jump and spring and bite, till never a cobra dared show his head inside the walls.

Darzee's Chant

(sung in honor of Rikki-tikki-tavi)

Singer and tailor am I—
Doubled the joys that I know—
Proud of my lilt through the sky,
Proud of the house that I sew.
Over and under, so weave I my music—
So weave I the house that I sew.

Sing to your fledglings again,
Mother, oh lift up your head!
Evil that plagued us is slain,
Death in the garden lies dead.
Terror that hid in the roses is impotent—
Flung on the dunghill and dead!

Who hath delivered us, who?
Tell me his nest and his name.
Rikki, the valiant, the true,
Tikki, with eyeballs of flame,
Rikk-tikki, the ivory-fanged—
The hunter with eyeballs of flame.

Give him the thanks of the birds,
Bowing with tail feathers spread!
Praise him with nightingale words—
Nay, I will praise him instead.
Hear! I will sing you the praise
Of the bottle-tailed Rikki with eyeballs of red!

(Here Rikki-tikki interrupted, so the rest of the song is lost.)

The Frivolous Gold Digger

Delia Morris Stephenson

This story is set during the Great Depression of the 1930s, when thousands of banks and businesses failed and millions of Americans, unemployed and homeless, roamed the country as vagrants, searching for food and shelter. The entire period can be summed up in one line: "Brother, can you spare a dime?"

Cynthia Shannon's head, with its mop of unruly, smoky hair and Irish blue eyes, was bent over a letter. Cynthia herself was curled up on a window seat overlooking Puget Sound. The waves, blue as delphiniums and tipped with silver, claimed but little of her attention today.

Such a letter from her Donald! She had not heard from him since he had gone down to a tiny village in the Willamette Valley where his father, John Derringer, lay dying on the little farm where Donald had been born some twenty-five years before. "Father was buried yesterday," she read.

I think the dear old man was glad to go. Nobody has been harder hit in this depression than the farmers.

163

Granary full of wheat he couldn't sell for enough to pay for raising it; place all run-down and no money to keep it up, though he had managed to pay the taxes. Things have never gone right here since Mother went, but he held on to the land. Now it is on my hands, a perfect white elephant. I can't sell it. I can't borrow money on it, or even find a tenant who can pay me anything for a lease.

Nor is that all. I had a letter this morning from my boss. The firm is on the rocks, and he has to let us all go. What money I had is all tied up in company stock, and I can't get a dollar on it. In other words, I am just one of the 7 million unemployed. I'll see if I can sell the stock here for enough to go somewhere and look for work.

Under the circumstances, Cynthia darling, the only thing I can do is to set you free. I can't feature you here slopping pigs and feeding chickens, and I'd die of loneliness by myself. Perhaps I can find a few odd jobs wiring houses for extra outlets while I look about or until times are better; but only a cad would hold you to what little future I can see for us together. You are better off alone.

Cynthia, beloved daughter of a well-to-do father and great-granddaughter of a woman who, although the daughter of a Kentucky governor, had counted it all glory to accompany her husband and baby son across the weary miles of the Oregon Trail in an oxcart, lifted her head and went in search of her father and mother. She handed them the letter. When they had read it, she announced, "I want to get married. I want to get married right away."

"Why, Cynthia honey, how can you? Donald is right."

"He's not right! He thinks I have no grit at all. He makes me mad clear through. I am going straight down there and throw myself at him."

In vain her parents told her that this was no time to think of marrying; to wait until Donald was on his feet again, was established in a business.

"He is established right now in a business that brought him up and sent him to college."

"Cynthia, you don't mean that you want to settle on that old farm, do you? You don't know the first thing about a farm!"

"Neither did my great-grandmother Anne, and she made a go of it. It's her legacy, bless her, that will help to tide us through. I don't care if the interest is only $25 a month. That will be wealth where I am going. The only way out of this thing is the way back."

In the end she went.

"I'd have done as much for you, John," said her mother. "I glory in her spunk. Let her go. She has a right to live her life as she sees fit."

About one o'clock the next day, Cynthia was toiling up a little hill to Donald's boyhood home, carrying a heavy suitcase packed with a very unusual sort of trousseau. She had collected it in about an hour in a ready-to-wear shop. Taking her bundles home, she had added to their contents a little pile of lingerie and one silk print. "You can send the rest down with my piano if Donald doesn't send me home," Cynthia had said.

She could have telephoned from the station, but decided not to. That which she had to say had best be said face-to-face. If Donald sent her home, she wanted no witnesses to her humiliation; but he was going to have a hard time doing it!

A sky of April's own blue, flecked with fleecy bits of cloud, arched overhead. Fruit trees were white with bloom, and the sun was almost too warm. All about her, pure and clear, rose the songs of the meadowlarks.

"They said it was only a mile. These Oregonians have strange ideas of how far a mile is," complained Cynthia. "What name is that on the mailbox there? John H. Derringer! I must be here." She set down her suitcase and looked about her.

In front of her was a gate opening into a lane, the fence on either side festooned with blackberry vines. At the end of the lane was an orchard, all cascades of bloom, with a story-and-a-half house sadly in need of paint in the midst of it. She opened the heavy gate and closed it after her carefully. It behooved farmers' wives to be careful about gates, some ancestral memory told her. She could hear a sound of hammering. Donald was despondently tinkering at a broken panel of fence. It looked as though he might continue such tinkering indefinitely with great benefit to the fence. He did not see her.

Quietly, Cynthia put down her suitcase and asked demurely, "Pardon me, but are you the gentleman who was looking for a housekeeper?"

The next few minutes were chaotic—a mixture of tears, laughter, and embraces.

"How did you get here?" demanded Donald, holding her off as though to assure himself that it was really she.

"The trains still run, my dear! Show me this place, every inch of it—every cow, pig, and chicken!" The big collie had already claimed her for his own.

"Why? Why do you want to see it?"

"Because I am curious about my new home." Cynthia swung her bag onto the porch. "I am dreading the results of your housekeeping, so we will see the outside first."

"Your new home?" repeated Donald stupidly.

"Certainly! I have moved in."

"Cynthia, you can't. We can't live here."

"I'd like to know why not. I'd also like to know where else we could live. You must know a little about farming. You were eighteen when you left here. You must have helped a little."

"I helped a lot, but I didn't like it. I can't let you, with your fine musical training, bury yourself here."

Cynthia was headed for the barn lot. "Are those our cows and horses?" she asked calmly. "Such a dear little calf!"

"I promised to sell them to a neighbor. He is coming for them tomorrow," said Donald.

Cynthia was stooping to pat the little Jersey calf. "You are the cutest thing I ever saw," she told it. To Donald she said, "I believe you cannot sell community property, unless both husband and wife consent. I am not consenting."

Donald looked at her helplessly. "Cynthia, it's not right to tempt me so. There is no money to be made in farming. I love this place. It is like tearing a bone out of me to see it go into strange hands, but I can't see you sacrifice yourself for me and bury yourself alive."

Cynthia pushed the little inquisitive Jersey nose aside and tried to count the hens in the orchard. She walked up and down the rows of fruit trees, with Donald muttering that she could not stay there. If she didn't hurry she'd miss the last train north for the day, and there was no suitable hotel for her to stay in.

"Give me your knife," said Cynthia, on her knees in the old asparagus bed. "There's plenty of this just ready to be cut for our supper. I wish you'd stop talking nonsense, Donald. What do I want with a hotel? I'm staying at home tonight. But first you go to the county seat—it is only ten miles away, for I asked—and get a marriage license. Do I have to go along? I don't like to spare the time, but if I must, I will."

Donald pointed bitterly at an ancient automobile. "Will you go in that? It is the only vehicle on the place."

"And quite good enough," said Cynthia, who drove a luxurious cabriolet at home. "Now, let's talk sense awhile, Donald. Just where do you know you could find work enough to even pay board and room if you leave here?"

"Well, I ought to find something after a while."

"That's what a few million other heartsick men are saying. You are not sure of earning even enough to feed yourself away from here."

"But farmers are not able to make their salt now," Donald protested.

Cynthia rose, her hands full of asparagus. "Maybe not, but they can make their own milk, butter, eggs, fruit, vegetables, and meat. Your granary is full of wheat, and wheat, my dear, can be ground into flour in yonder grist mill."

"Yes, of course, there's no danger of starving. But farmers are not making any money."

"Suppose we don't make any money! Suppose we do produce more than we can sell! There are hungry city mouths that can use it, and we shall be doing our bit. We can 'have peace here in the bee-loud glade,'" she quoted, looking at the beehives under the apple trees. "Remember your Yeats?

Donald, it is time we spoiled American people came back to the real things: the land, the miracle of dawn and sunset over these hills; to learn to work with the rich earth and take again our strength from it."

Donald had her in his arms now and was saying in a choked voice, "Darling, darling, it was girls like you who stood beside their men and wrested this country from the wilderness. I really wanted to stay here, but could not ask you to do it. I believe you have enough pioneer in you to really want to do this, and I take you at your word. But this wedding? Where shall we have it?"

"Let me see my house," said Cynthia, and she walked into it. The shabby old rooms were clean. The old-fashioned furniture, the hair wreaths in their frames, the rag carpets on the floors, all were much as Donald's mother had left them ten years ago.

"President Coolidge took the oath of office in such a room as this, by the light of a flickering oil lamp. It would do nicely for our wedding, but I think we had better get our license and be married down in the little village church just before prayer meeting. That gives me time in between to plan our supper and straighten up a bit. You get ready now while I hang up my trousseau." She hung half a dozen bright print dresses and some khaki outdoor clothes in the closet and laid a little pile of lingerie in the dresser drawer. The silk print needed pressing, so she laid it across the bed. "Why don't you go and dress, Don, or do you plan on being married in overalls?"

"Just wondering why we should be married before prayer meeting here? Why not find a minister at the county seat?"

Cynthia went to him and put her hands on his shoulders. "Because I want to stay for prayer meeting, and I want us both to join this little church. I want to join in the worship. Maybe, if I sing my best, they'll invite me to join the choir. I want to meet the women whose advice I am going to need so terribly these coming days. I want them to know that I am one of them and that I want to fit into the life of the community."

"And yet," said Donald with a smile, "some folks say the modern girl is only a 'frivolous gold digger'!"

"We are pretty much like our great-grandmothers, you put us to the test," said Cynthia, gathering up her dress. "I was prepared to press this with an old-fashioned flat iron, but I see you have electricity. Not even enough hardship here to make it really romantic, but I'll do my best to play up to my great-grandmother Anne. Donald, I don't like to begin nagging this soon, but I do wish you'd hurry. It's half past three o'clock, and we have a busy afternoon ahead of us."

The Unmousing of Jean

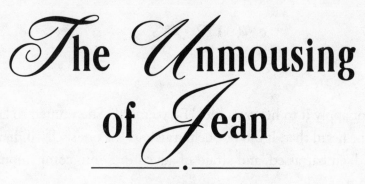

Edna Geister

Jean was a mouse. Because she felt like one, she acted like one and looked like one. But deep down she really wished she wasn't one—so she went to see confident and dynamic Mrs. Bryant, hoping that she might be able to help her out of her mousehood.

Jean Derby sat curled up on the davenport, reading: "A happy man or woman is a better thing to find than a five-pound note. He or she is a radiating focus of goodwill, and their entrance into a room is as though another candle had been lit."

She loved Stevenson and studied his writing zealously, but how easy it was to talk about happiness and how hard it was to find it! She reviewed her own life. She had a pleasant, comfortable home, parents who were her friends as well as her father and mother, a good standing at the college that was in her hometown—and what else? Very little! She was too self-conscious to make friends, however much she wanted to. She had read and heard much about the development of personality, but the advice given was so general that she could not apply it to her own life. "Be yourself!" She wanted to laugh every time she heard that. It did not help much to "be one's self" if that self was awkward, embarrassed, and afraid of adventures into companionship and friendship.

That night Jean went to hear a speaker at the Young People's Society of the church. Mrs. Bryant, speaking on character development, was everything Jean wanted to be: dynamic, magnetic, radiant. At the end of her lecture, she offered an opportunity for conferences the next day. Jean, fighting down her shyness, made an appointment. At eleven o'clock the following morning, she went into Mrs. Bryant's office, shaking with nervousness.

Mrs. Bryant greeted her quietly and instantly put her at ease by saying, "What a beautiful old ring you are wearing! Do you mind telling me if it is a family heirloom?"

That particular ring was the one thing about which Jean always waxed enthusiastic. Completely forgetting the problem about which she had come, she told the story of a great-grandmother's bravery, which had been rewarded by the general in charge of the fort where she lived.

When she had finished her story, Mrs. Bryant said smilingly, "It's wonderful to have inherited that symbol for bravery and the bravery as well, isn't it, Jean?"

Jean's face fell. "Oh, but I'm not brave! That's just what I came to see you about. I want to have friends, and I try to make friends. But when I'm with the girls, I'm so afraid they'll snub me or think I'm silly that I close up like a clam."

Mrs. Bryant leaned forward. "May I say something that sounds harsh but really isn't meant to be? Did you mean to tell me just now that you want the rewards of friendship but that you shirk the risks?"

Jean gasped. After a moment, she said slowly, "I never thought of it that way, but I guess you're right. But you see, Mrs. Bryant, I haven't the kind of personality that attracts people."

"Oh, my dear! That word *personality* has been so overworked in establishing alibis! So many young people seem to think that attractive personalities are handed to certain persons on a silver platter at birth. On the contrary, your personality is what you have made of yourself; it is the outward expression of what you really are, what you really think. If you are a timid little mouse and think like a timid little mouse, your personality will be that of a timid little mouse. If you are arrogant, selfish, or malicious in your thoughts, no politeness, suavity, or effort to please can cover it up. Personality isn't just what we do and say. It's what we *are*, Jean!"

Jean laughed ruefully. "Then because I am like a timid little mouse, that's the only kind of personality I can ever hope for?"

"Don't you ever believe it! You have a brave adventure ahead of you, and you've won the first skirmish by coming to see me. It was hard, wasn't it? And now the next step is to find out what the real Jean Derby is like. You'll find things that will have to be trained and developed, and other things that will have to be suppressed. Shall I help you in discovering some of these things?"

"Oh, please!" answered Jean eagerly.

"All right, but before we begin, I want to make sure that you see this thing in a proper light. It's perfectly natural that you want people to like you. But to be likable to people is a far greater thing than just being liked."

"But I don't see the difference between being likable to people and being liked," said the bewildered Jean.

"Then I'll put it in a nutshell. Jean, did you ever see a girl try to be graceful in the way she walked? She didn't succeed very well, did she? She was self-conscious, and that is always fatal. Now, if she had concentrated on the principles of good posture—in correcting the stoop of her shoulders and in pointing her feet straight ahead—she would gradually have acquired a graceful carriage. As it was, she merely looked silly, because she gave all her conscious thought to trying to be graceful instead of centering her attention on the things that made her awkward. Need I tell you why I told you this?"

Jean laughed quietly. "No, I haven't much of a personality, but I have a fairly good head, and I know what you mean. You don't want me to go at this thing self-consciously, always thinking, *Is she going to like me?* but rather to—" She stopped a moment and then said thoughtfully, "That Bible verse, 'He that loseth his life . . . shall find it.' Does that explain it?"

"Jean, you are a joy! It applies exactly, and the next time I come here I want you to tell me how you have worked out that application. Now I'm going to ask a favor of you. Would your mother let me come home to lunch with you? You remember I promised to help you in discovering the real Jean Derby, and I can't think of a better way than to be with you for a little while in your own home."

Mrs. Derby was so pleased and surprised at the new note in Jean's voice when she telephoned that she answered at once, "Why, of course, Jean. Bring her right along."

On the way home, Mrs. Bryant skillfully drew out Jean, finding out her major interests and a great many other things. After lunch there was an opportunity for talking with her mother. Finally, when she had to leave for her train, she called Jean aside and said to her warmly, "Jean, whatever else you do, don't try to be a carbon copy of me or anyone else in this new venture. These words 'Be yourself!' which have been such a stumbling block to you, have a real meaning behind them. As soon as I get back to the office, I'm going to write you a long letter that I hope will help you to find new and rich possibilities in that self of yours."

The letter that came the following week was read and reread so many times that Jean could have repeated it from memory. One sentence made a particularly deep impression. "The girl whom people like is the girl who likes people. You like people, Jean, but you like yourself better! You are not vain and selfish, but you have been afraid of hurting yourself, so you chose security, all the while wishing for the joy of friendships but not willing to take the risks involved. Now let's stop thinking about Jean Derby and start thinking about other people, and start right now!"

The next morning on the way to classes, Jean passed a group of girls whom she knew very well because they were juniors as she was. Ordinarily she ventured a shy "Good morning," and walked past them. This morning she forced herself to go up to Marie Kirkland and say to her, "Marie, my father said that he never heard a more clear-cut argument than the one you put up at the debate last night. He is a lawyer, and he said that you had a lawyer's brain and a mighty keen one."

The last few words were uttered with a gasp because of the effort they demanded. Marie was one of the outstanding girls in college, and Jean had never voluntarily spoken to her before. She had gone through a struggle before speaking, arguing, *She'll just think I'm silly and trying to get into her good graces. Now, why should I tell her what Father said?* The answer came from the deeply hidden Jean Derby who really liked people. *Because I know that she wants to take up law when she finishes college and is so keen on making good at it.*

An instant of silence followed Jean's remark to Marie; then Marie pounced on Jean. "Is your father Judge Derby? And do you suppose he'd let me talk with him in his office sometime?"

Jean answered quietly, "I know he would. If you'd like to come home to dinner with me some night, you can talk to Father afterward."

The girls looked at her curiously while Marie whooped in her excitement. Jean walked on with them quietly, but all morning she felt a glow of happiness.

At the close of her chemistry class that afternoon, she took her courage in her hands and went up to forbidding Professor Young, saying, "Mother and I heard that Mrs. Young was seriously ill and that you could get no help in caring for Tommy. We have plenty of room at our house, and if it would help any to have him stay with us, we'll take awfully good care of him, for we love children and would enjoy having him."

To her immense surprise, his face broke into a rare smile. "That is one of the nicest things that has happened to us since my wife became ill. It will make her feel better just to hear it. But her sister arrived last night and she is much better this morning, so we think everything is going to be all right. You and your mother have done a beautiful thing, and I do appreciate your wanting to do this for us."

Jean answered regretfully, "We weren't trying to do a beautiful thing. We love Tommy, and it would have been a joy to have had him with us. So you see, we weren't trying to do you good. We wanted Tommy!"

Professor Young shouted with laughter. "That makes it all the nicer! I detest having people feeling sorry for me and trying to do me good. But for you to really want our strenuous four-year-old whom most people consider an awful trial to have around—I can't wait to take that message home to his mother!"

A party was on for that night, and Jean dreaded it. Parties always meant an agony of trying to look as though she were having a good time. Remembering Mrs. Bryant's words, however, to "forget Jean Derby!" she determinedly forgot Jean Derby and kept her mind on other people.

Usually she sat on the sidelines and watched the games, but this time she forced herself to join the grand march. In the wild scramble for partners in the finale, she was appalled to discover that she had snatched the arm of Jim Richards, the class president.

She would have withdrawn if she could, but he looked down at her and said laughingly, "Hello! Where did you come from? Come on, let's go after the prize in the treasure hunt. Don't let me down. I'm an awful dub, and I'll probably be the last one in if you don't help me!"

Utterly unconscious of the fact that her flushed face and laughing eyes were most attractive, Jean rose to the challenge and did her best. She did it so well, in fact, that they interpreted their clues more quickly than the others and found the treasure hidden behind the gas stove in the kitchen just a second before Marie Kirkland and her partner arrived at that spot.

Jim was triumphant. "I tell you, it pays to have a smart partner. I always pick them smart!" he said, grinning.

Jean slipped away in the confusion of the discovery of the treasure, leaving the spoils to Jim, but taking with her the triumph of having again forgotten Jean Derby.

The months that followed would not have seemed particularly exciting to the average person; but to Jean each day was complete in itself, and her happiness came, not from things or events, but from her contacts with people. There was just as much honest satisfaction in talking with Tony, the Italian flagman at the railroad crossing, as there was in going to dinner at Professor Young's; in taking care of the cleaning woman's five children so that she could go to a church supper as there was in having Jim Richards ask her to go to a party with him. She had no thought of patronage when she helped Tony's wife get their oldest girl ready for graduation, nor did she feel any false humility when she went to the Youngs' house for dinner. She had, rather, a genuine interest in the lives of both groups.

Jean met setbacks, of course. It was still hard for her to approach strangers, even though they looked lonely; it was hard for her to chat easily with the members of her class until she found some common interest; it was hard for her to meet with a chilly response or a vague stare. Her deeply interested study of the people about her, however, soon showed her how often a so-called hard-boiled, flippant, or ungracious exterior is merely a protective covering for imagined shortcomings or hidden difficulties. She did not take her rebuffs as personal affronts, nor did she take her new friends as personal triumphs. She looked upon them with wonder and thanksgiving in her heart for this new beauty that had come into her life.

After a number of months, Mrs. Bryant came again. She met Jean in the

halls one day, made an appointment to go to the Derbys' for dinner the next night, and then asked with a smile, "Well, Jean, how are things going? Are you besieged with telephone calls, and are the men battling for your attention, and do all the girls want to be your one best friend? In short, are you popular?"

Jean laughed. "I must answer 'No' to all those questions!" she said gaily.

Mrs. Bryant affected disappointment. "Oh, Jean! After all the trouble I took with you! What's the matter? Did you give up?"

Jean laughed again and then became serious. "No, I didn't give up. I'm just opening up, Mrs. Bryant, thanks to you. I'll tell you about it tomorrow!"

In the meantime, Mrs. Bryant had an opportunity to talk with Professor Young, and she learned much that she never would have learned from Jean.

"I've never seen anyone change the way Jean Derby has!" he told her. "She was always good enough in her work, but she was so self-effacing that no one ever gave her a second thought. But something seems to have happened, for she has fairly bloomed in the past six months. No, she doesn't go out for the limelight, and I'm pretty sure she doesn't want it. But I don't believe there is a member of the junior class who is more genuinely liked than Jean is. She doesn't ballyhoo; she doesn't wisecrack; she is never the life of the party—but somehow she makes herself felt wherever she is. I've got it!" he cried triumphantly. "She's interesting because she's so interested!"

"In other words," said Mrs. Bryant with happy satisfaction written on her face, "'He that loseth his life . . . shall find it.'"

The Jonah Pie

Ruby Holmes Martyn

Reuben Thorpe was not known for overexerting himself—at anything. Thus, when he chose the Jonah pie, many wondered if he would try to shirk his responsibility.

It was Lorena, setting the table in the dining room, who saw him first and called out, "Here comes Reuben Thorpe!"

Agnes was standing by the range, frying pies in a kettle of boiling grease. The cooked ones were on a platter on the large shelf, and she had just begun to turn the last batch. "Oh, Mother!" she cried. "Which is the Jonah pie?"

The girls heard their mother laugh merrily somewhere in the depths of the pantry. "Put an extra plate on the table between your place and mine, Rena. You know quite well I myself couldn't tell which is the Jonah pie now that they have risen in the grease, Agnes. Frying changes all the personal marks of a pie completely."

Agnes's answering voice was tragic. "What if Cousin Reuben

181

Thorpe Johnston should happen to get the Jonah this noontime? I shall try the bottom of every pie with a fork."

"No such thing!" declared her mother. "Wearing overalls for an hour would do Reuben Thorpe a sight of—"

The mother broke off her sentence abruptly as a quick step sounded on the back doorstep. The next minute Reuben Thorpe Johnston was in the kitchen. He was tall and ruddy-faced; good nature shone in every line of his handsome features, and he gave an impartial greeting to his aunt and cousins.

"Hello, Aunt Martha! I see you've got the extra plate on already, Rena. I tell you, Aggie, those pies look good enough to eat."

Just then another young man came into the kitchen by the doorway that the first had entered, and he was a fellow so similar in features to Reuben Thorpe that they might have been taken for brothers. But the newcomer was heavier limbed; he wore a blue shirt loose at the neck, the sleeves of which were rolled snugly above his elbows, showing a pair of work-trained arms; his blue, patched overalls were splotched with the good red earth of a forenoon's following of the plow, and his hands were hardened with years of gripping plow handle, hoe, and scythe.

"I was pretty sure that was you I saw coming up the road five minutes ago, Thorpie," he said, welcoming him with an outstretched hand.

"Heard you geeing-up the horses, Reub," was the laughing answer.

Both of these handsome cousins had been named Reuben from their paternal grandfather, and the middle "Thorpe" of the city-bred cousin was habitually used by the family to distinguish the one from the other. The paternal Johnston acres had passed from father to son to grandson, and Reuben was glad to find his lifework on them, living in the big farmhouse with his widowed mother, two sisters, and Jimmy, the youngest of the Johnstons.

While they were talking, Agnes made a surreptitious attempt to hunt for the Jonah pie with her long-tined frying fork, but Jimmy's bright eyes spied her.

"Mother said Reuben Thorpe was to fare like the rest of us, Aggie," he protested openly.

"I hope so," declared Reuben Thorpe as he followed Agnes and the platter of hot brown pies into the dining room. "What's the doings I'm to share particularly?" he added.

Reuben, in his father's place at the head of the table, explained. "It's a kind of drawing-lots proposition that's always run in the Johnston blood, Thorpie. We have a Jonah pie made up in the batch of fried ones when there is some particular piece of work to be done that no one is hankering for."

"Or when it is so desirable we all want to do it," added Lorena.

"I'm in the game today," cried Jimmy.

"What's a Jonah pie?" asked Reuben Thorpe.

"A Jonah pie is filled with sawdust instead of edible filling. Mother makes them, but one of the girls does the frying, which so changes the appearance of the raw pies that Mother herself has lost track of the Jonah, so the game's perfectly fair for all of us."

Reuben lifted the platter of pies, and they went from one pair of hands to another around the table amid a babble of jolly talk. Each one chose a pie, and at a signal from Reuben, each one took a bite. Apple and mince and cranberry were found, but no sawdust Jonah for which forfeit must be paid.

"Escape one," said Lorena with a laugh.

"I wouldn't mind getting it," declared Jimmy bravely.

"Make you feel like a grown-up to do the little stunt at the end, eh?" questioned Reuben Thorpe.

And Jimmy nodded.

"I'll help you on the job if you get it," he volunteered.

"Same here. Is the forfeit picked out?"

"Yes."

"Office work slack with you, Thorpie?" asked Reuben.

"Sure not. But this morning looked so fine, I telephoned to Uncle Dan for a day off. The office gets to be a grind sometimes."

Reuben Thorpe dismissed the subject of his absence from their uncle's office nonchalantly. He really *did* consider the office work a grind to be shifted to other fellows' shoulders as much as possible, and he knew that this morning a particularly disagreeable piece of work was to be done. He felt that his relationship to the head of the firm gave him the privilege of perquisites that he was not slow in claiming. To be sure, he had always to make his peace with Uncle Daniel after one of those careless escapades, but from continued successes he had grown confident of his powers in that line. Old folks were so apt to be fogyish in their demands on a fellow.

"Your uncle Daniel is coming out to the farm someday soon," said Mrs. Johnston.

"I didn't tell him I had a notion to come today," said Reuben Thorpe with a laugh.

"Is everybody ready for another fried pie?" asked Jimmy.

"I am."

"And I."

Again the platter made the round of the table until another pie had been chosen for every plate.

"One! Two! Three! Bite!" said Reuben.

Jimmy, half hoping for the honor of a grown-up duty, found red cranberry inside the crust; Mrs. Johnston's was cranberry, too. Lorena bit into apple, and Reuben's was mince. Agnes, sitting opposite Reuben Thorpe and fearing the Jonah pie for her fastidious cousin, saw his face change as his white teeth bit through the crust; there was revealed to her his momentary disgust at the taste and then a rallying of good humor as he realized the joke was on him.

"I'm the Jonah," he said.

Lorena laughed merrily. "I'm so glad you came, Reuben Thorpe. It's such a messy job to clean the cupola," she cried.

"What about cleaning the cupola?" questioned Reuben Thorpe.

A degree of soberness had settled over the Johnstons, and it was the mother who undertook to answer him.

"That is the duty of the one who got the sawdust pie today. Once each spring one of us goes up in the barn cupola and cleans out the year's accumulation of cobwebs and flies and wasps, which has gathered there. It has to be broomed out and the windows washed."

"And it's up to me to clean the cupola?" jested Reuben Thorpe, trying to keep any distaste he might feel for the job out of his voice. "I'm game," he said as he accepted another edible pie in place of the sawdust Jonah.

After the meal was eaten, Reuben Thorpe went up to his cousin's room and changed his own faultless clothes for an outfit of farmer apparel. He rolled the coarse shirtsleeves over arms that struck him suddenly as disgustingly pale for a strong man. The blue overalls were patched even more than those his cousin wore, and they hung loosely on his more slender frame.

As he dressed, he asked himself an honest question: *Had Agnes expected him to take up her offer of declining to play the Jonah game to its finish? Had his quick-witted cousin marked him for a quitter?*

Going downstairs, he found that Aunt Martha had a broom ready for him to use.

"Kill all the blue flies and drive out the wasps, and broom the place clean of webs," she directed. "Then come down for cloths and a bucket of hot soapsuds to wash the windows."

"I'm going, too," said Jimmy, who was carrying a hand brush.

"Come on," said Reuben Thorpe with a laugh as they went out into the yard.

In the barn there was a ladder by which they climbed to the level of the haymow. Then, by a pair of rude stairs, they mounted to a higher loft that had been loaded with hay earlier in the season. From that loft another rude stairway led to the cupola above the tiptop of the barn roof. It was a tiny room some four feet square, with windows on every side. It was messy with a year's accumulation of dust and insects. A network of cobwebs was festooned from the dark rafters overhead. A dozen blue flies buzzed with an angry sound against the dirty window glass, with a score of noisy wasps in their company. And the smell was a stuffy, warm, cowy odor.

Jimmy, who had gone up ahead, was already busy catching the flies. Reuben Thorpe set to work at another window with disastrous results. The wasps were warm and lively and resented unskilled human interference. Reuben Thorpe did not succeed in evading them as he hunted flies. There were angry stabs at two fingers, and a bolder wasp ran a big stinger into the stranger's forehead.

"The wasps are an awful nuisance," said Jimmy sympathetically.

And Reuben Thorpe agreed with him right heartily as to that. He felt again that flush of a new determination that had swept over him at Agnes's words half an hour before. Discomforts were not to oust him from a game he had undertaken with good faith to play.

By the time they had opened the windows and cleared the cupola of its undesirable tenants and swept down the cobwebs, Reuben Thorpe's appearance was grotesque. There were grimy streaks running in all directions on his handsome face; dark, broken bits of cobwebs ornamented his blond hair; and his moist arms had gathered a coating of blackness.

"Soap and water takes all this off, I suppose," he said dryly to Jimmy, whose physical appearance was like his own.

"Sure," said Jimmy, undisturbed.

Reuben Thorpe saw Lorena titter over the dishpan when he went into the kitchen for the bucket of hot water.

"Didn't you think I could clean the cupola, Rena?" he asked.

"I didn't think you'd like to," she answered truthfully.

Reuben Thorpe did not answer as he took up the heavy bucket of steaming suds and an armful of soft cloths and went out. For the third time within an hour he was roused from his habitual easygoingness: Agnes had gone so far as to suggest that he be let off from fulfilling his luck at the lot drawing; the wasps had given him physical pain; Lorena had told him quite frankly that she did not think he would do a thing he disliked to do.

Up in the cupola, he and Jimmy washed and wiped and polished. The windows on one side after another took on a brilliance that did credit to the workers. Sitting on the broad sills, they managed the outside without a tremor at their height from the ground.

"You 'most wouldn't know the glass was there at all!" cried Jimmy, standing back to admire the result. "See that automobile coming way down at Will's Corner?"

Reuben Thorpe could see the motorcar Jimmy meant, coming rapidly along the turnpike toward the Johnston farm. It had a familiar look to him, but he dismissed that with the mental explanation of coincidence. But when the gray roadster turned in at the farmyard gateway, he admitted its identity.

"That's Uncle Dan," he said.

"Hurry up and finish this last window so we can go down and see him," cried Jimmy.

Reuben Thorpe twisted his mouth into a grim smile. "I'm not in the least bit of a hurry to see Uncle Dan," he said under his breath.

They washed and polished the last window as well as any they had done before. When it was finished, Jimmy slid off down the narrow stairs, fireman fashion, without a parting word.

Reuben Thorpe did not follow him. Instead he leaned against a window jamb and looked over the hills to where the green of the pines met the sap-colored patches of the leafless trees. Nearer, he could see the field where his cousin Reuben was following the plow as it turned under furrow after furrow of brown sod. And everywhere the sunshine was chasing the shadows toward the east.

Reuben Thorpe was physically tired. Unaccustomed to such bodily exertion as the last hour had held, his muscles ached; and the pain of the wasp stings was still sharp. His hands were painfully blistered, too, and he was alertly conscious that his personal appearance would not stand critical inspection. He tried to figure out by what detour he could reach the house and his own clothes, unobserved by Uncle Daniel.

"What a mess I got into playing that Jonah pie game!" he groaned.

There were voices in the barn below, Jimmy's and a man's heavy bass—the heavy bass was undoubtedly Uncle Daniel Johnston's. They seemed to come nearer, and Reuben Thorpe caught words that made him groan again.

"The windows shine so I can see through them?" queried the bass.

"Yes, sir," answered the triumphant treble of Jimmy. "I tell you, Reuben Thorpe polished them fine. He's got the muscle when he gets in practice."

Reuben Thorpe was filled with a momentary panic. Uncle Daniel and

Jimmy were coming up the last ladder to the cupola. The only means of escape he could think of was to crawl from one of the open windows and hang to the ridgepole by his fingers. But there was not time to put any such preposterous scheme into operation. Turning, he faced Uncle Daniel's twinkling eyes as nonchalantly as he could.

"Hello!"

"Hello, Thorpie," said Uncle Daniel, laughing. He had grown so portly with sixty years of living that he had to pause and catch his breath from the unaccustomed exertion of the climb. "I like the way Jimmy and you have done your sky-parlor job."

Reuben Thorpe grinned as sheepishly as a youngster caught at mischief. "I got the Jonah pie, and this was the job," he explained.

Uncle Daniel laughed again. "That Jonah pie is part and parcel of the old home place. Your grandmother used to put in a Jonah sometimes when we were boys, and I've had to do some strange stunts on that proposition before now," Uncle Daniel said with a chuckle.

"It really wasn't so bad as you might think," said Reuben Thorpe, on the defensive for what he had done.

His uncle drummed on a shining windowpane.

"See here, Thorpie," he said abruptly. "I've put another man in your place at the office. Couldn't stand your shirking when you took the fancy. And now I'm trying to think whether to give you a chance at that shipping-room job Fred's promotion will leave vacant."

Reuben Thorpe's jaw dropped. His job had *really* been taken from him! He knew there was to be some such vacancy in the shipping room, but he wasn't hankering after *that* job.

"It would be a sort of Jonah pie drawing to you, I know, but I need someone of about the caliber of you at your best in that place just now, and there'd be a chance to develop your muscle." Uncle Daniel paused an appreciable instant. "Will you try it?"

Reuben Thorpe watched the sunshine chase the cloud shadows across the Johnston fields. For almost the first time in his life he had finished a piece of work that looked distasteful to him at the outset; and there had proved to be a keen satisfaction in the doing of it well. Would this shipping-room job be another such as to rouse his mettle? If loyalty to a game compelled him to rise to an emergency, what must not a task of life accomplish? A glimpse of the truth came to him—the truth that a fellow picking here and there at the things he thinks look pleasant is going to fail of the best expression of himself.

He threw back his head and smiled. "I'll take the job, Uncle Dan," he said.

To have put up one life fight that had made him the stronger for a harder task was to have won indeed.

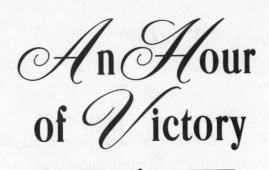

An Hour of Victory

Earl Reed Silvers

Neil knew with a certainty that he would fail that engineering exam tomorrow . . . unless he cheated. Downstairs his father was facing the same temptation, with even more daunting odds. The son listened . . . two decisions hanging on one answer.

The windows of Professor Gladstone's room on the top floor of the engineering building were three squares of yellow light; otherwise the building was just a dark blot against the blue dome of the sky. Sitting on the porch of his house directly across the street from the campus, Neil Douglas regarded the windows with open antagonism.

I'll be taking my exam in surveying up there tomorrow, he thought miserably. The door behind him opened, and his father joined him on the porch.

"What about studying a bit, Neil?" he suggested.

"I'm going upstairs in a few minutes. But it won't do me any good, Dad. I'm afraid that I'm not cut out to be an engineer." Neil could feel, rather than see, his father wince.

191

"It's a little too early in your course to decide that, isn't it?"

"I suppose so," Neil answered; but he knew, in his heart of hearts, that he had no aptitude for engineering. Mathematics did not appeal to him, and now, in his sophomore year, he found the more technical subjects increasingly difficult. He was, in fact, in imminent danger of flunking his course in surveying. Only a miracle would give him a passing grade in the final examination.

Neil knew that his father was worried. For the past two years, the contracting business had been at a standstill, had brought in no revenue. Gradually his surplus had been exhausted until now he was facing a crisis. Unless he received the contract for the new Municipal Hall that was about to be erected with the aid of federal funds, he would be compelled to close his offices and dismiss his force.

"Do you think you've got any chance for the big job, Dad?" Neil asked impulsively.

"I don't know. We've estimated as closely as possible, but other firms have done the same thing. I'm not especially optimistic."

"When will the bids be opened?"

"Tomorrow morning at nine o'clock."

"The same time as my surveying exam starts," Neil said, and he smiled wryly. "A rather important hour for both of us, Dad."

"Yes."

They lapsed into silence. The sound of men's voices came to them from one of the dormitories down the street. A group was singing on the steps of the porch, something about pledging to Alma Mater their loyalty and faith.

Neil stirred uneasily. As long as he could remember, he had lived on the border of the campus. As a small boy, he had heard seniors singing in the early summer evenings, and he had looked forward confidently to the time when he, too, would graduate from his father's college.

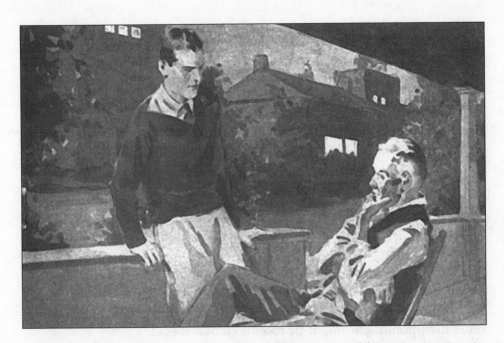

He could not graduate, however, unless he passed his examination in surveying. Failing, he would shatter a dream that his father had cherished for years. That he would win his engineering degree and take his place as a member of the firm of Douglas & Company had always been understood. Especially since his mother's death four years ago, it had been a tangible objective toward which he had striven. His failure would break his father's heart. Recognizing his own inadequacy, he resolved to do his best.

"I guess I'll go upstairs and do some studying," he announced. "I'll give it a battle, Dad."

"Good luck!" his father said.

Neil climbed the stairs to his den on the third floor and seated himself at his desk near the window. On the wall in front of him hung a picture of the freshman football team, with himself in the center, holding the ball. He had been captain of that team and had made his letter as a sophomore. Two glorious years of football lay before him, unless failure in examination placed him on probation. He shut his lips grimly.

"I'm not going to fail," he said aloud.

The text of the book that he opened served only to confuse him, however. He was woefully ignorant of the fundamentals of the subject, and after a minute he pushed it aside hopelessly. Leaning back in his swivel chair, he clasped his hands behind his head and took honest stock of himself.

The thing for him to do, he reflected, was to take his failure in surveying and transfer to another course. He could make up his deficiency in summer school and qualify for the arts college in September. That was where he belonged. He could major in psychology or English and receive his bachelor of arts degree. All would be clear sailing then.

This change would mean, however, the shattering of his father's dream. The gray-haired man downstairs had experienced trouble enough during the past two years. That was as much as his father could bear just now. One other disappointment might be too much of a shock.

Neil reached for the textbook and forced himself to study, but after a time he leaned back again and glanced idly out of the window. The engineering building was directly across the street. Through the lit windows on the top floor, he could see Professor Gladstone writing at his desk. As Neil watched, the professor walked over to the blackboard facing the windows, picked up a piece of chalk, and began writing sentences on the board. Neil's heart missed a beat. They were, he decided, the questions for the examination in surveying the next day.

I wish I could read them from here, he thought wistfully. He remembered that the transit he used in his field practice was on the table in one corner of his room. He had brought it home late in the afternoon, intending to take it back to the laboratory the next morning.

Impulsively he went over to the table and picked up the transit, examining it with impersonal curiosity. The transit, of course, magnified objects at a distance. By making use of it, he could read the questions that Professor Gladstone was writing on the blackboard across the street.

His hands trembled slightly as he carried the instrument to his desk and focused it on one of the open windows in the engineering building. He found the writing on the board as clearly distinguishable as if he had been standing beside the professor. His face lit in a relieved smile as he drew pencil and paper from a drawer in his desk and deliberately copied the questions.

When Neil had finished, Professor Gladstone was sitting at his own desk in the classroom. Neil watched with varied emotions as the professor stood up, picked a straw hat from a hook on the wall, switched out the lights, and departed.

I was just in time, Neil thought happily. Resting his elbows upon the desk, he read the questions critically. Without advance information, he could never have passed the examination, he admitted. Now, with less than an hour's work, he could pass with an honor mark. It was almost too good to be true.

He heard a car drive up and stop in front of the house, and he looked down curiously. A man whom he recognized as the city clerk got out of the automobile and joined his father on the porch. Neil frowned, forgetting for the moment his own concerns. The city clerk was the person who would open the sealed bids for Municipal Hall the next morning. What business could he have with his father at this time of night?

Neil had heard rumors of illicit practices in city affairs. According to reports, the party that controlled the common council was not above accepting remuneration for favors received. The city clerk was a member of the controlling party. Could it be that he was going to make it possible for Douglas & Company to secure the big contract? If so, his father's worries would be ended. Municipal Hall would give work to the firm for the next two years.

An hour ago they had both faced probable failure; now by a stroke of good fortune, the prospect had changed. Had it, though? Neil looked down at the examination questions that he had written in his own hand.

He knew when he copied them that he was being dishonest, but he had shut the thought from his mind. Now he faced it squarely. Was he willing to brand himself as a cheat simply to pass an examination in surveying?

He answered the question defiantly. As far as he was concerned, he would never consider such a deception, but he was doing it, not for himself, but for his dad. He was stooping to dishonor in order that his father might continue to cherish a dream.

I owe that much, at least, to him, Neil concluded. He was not satisfied, however. Unwillingly he remembered the slogan on the wall of the locker room: "Fair Play Is More To Be Desired Than Victory." He had subscribed to that sentiment as a freshman on the gridiron, and as a sophomore. He had discussed it with his father.

"After all, Dad," he had said, "victory doesn't mean anything unless it's fairly won."

"In life as well as in football," his father had added.

Neil remembered these incidents. Against his will, that slogan forced itself into his thoughts. All his former arguments seemed feeble by comparison. He told himself grimly that this was not so much a question of ethics as of loyalty. Cheating or no cheating, he decided, he was going to stand foursquare behind his dad.

With sudden resolution, he turned to the examination paper and read the first question. He wet dry lips with his tongue and opened the textbook. The answer was clear before him, but he pushed the book aside and stood up. His face was lined as if in pain, and a feeling of nausea gripped him. He had never cheated before. He decided that he would go downstairs for a pitcher of ice water.

I'll be needing it if I'm going to stay up here a couple of hours, he reasoned.

He descended quietly, not wishing to disturb his father; but at the bottom of the stairway he halted as the voice of Callahan, the city clerk, cut through the darkness.

"I'd be the last man to urge you to do something unethical, Mr. Douglas. But if you don't do it, someone else will. It's common practice at city hall."

Neil thrilled at his father's answer. "I've never condoned such practices, Callahan."

"But this is as easy as falling off a log, Mr. Douglas. The bids are supposed to be sealed, but I've seen them. You're only a couple of hundred dollars higher than the lowest bidder. You can peel $2,000 off your estimates and still make money; we won't hold you too close to specifications. I get the $2,000 as a . . . as a campaign contribution, and you'll make ten times that amount on the contract. That's a fair deal, isn't it?"

"It's a deal, but not fair," Mr. Douglas said.

"I'm only making this offer because I know you're up against it," Callahan argued. "And I'm thinking some of that boy of yours. If you go broke, he can't stay in college; and if he isn't in college, he can't play football. It will break his heart if he has to quit now; in another year he'll be an All-American halfback. Have you thought of that?"

"No," Mr. Douglas said.

"All you have to do is to change a couple of figures on your bid, and I can attend to that for you. It means that you'll be sitting on easy street for the next two years and that Neil can stay in college and play football. Just one word to me means the difference between success—and failure."

Neil heard his father push back his chair.

I shouldn't be standing here eavesdropping, Neil thought, but he seemed incapable of movement. His left hand gripped the banister of the stairway, and his right hand groped for support against the wall. He realized that his father was facing a situation practically parallel to his own. Before each of them lay the opportunity of solving a problem through the simple expedient of cheating. He himself had practically made his decision, but his father had not yet decided. The city clerk spoke again.

"After all, Mr. Douglas, what does a little irregularity matter when compared with your own future and that of your son? And nobody will ever know about this except you and me. You don't need to worry about getting caught."

"I'm not worrying about that," Mr. Douglas said.

"What's holding you back, then?"

"My son," Neil's father answered. "Do you think I could sit opposite him at the breakfast table tomorrow morning and look into his eyes if I knew in my own heart that I was a liar and a cheat? Do you think—"

Suddenly he stopped, as if realizing that the man to whom he was speaking could never understand. Some glimmer of comprehension must have penetrated into Callahan's mind, for Neil heard the man push back his own chair and climb to his feet. When he spoke, there was a new note in his voice, something that the younger man in the house recognized vaguely as respect.

"I don't think it will do me any good to talk to you any longer, Mr. Douglas. You're doing an unwise thing, and yet I can't help handing it to you. I guess you're the reason Neil's known all over town as a square shooter on the football field." He hesitated a moment, then cleared his throat. "You won't be saying anything about this?"

"I'm considering it a confidential matter between ourselves."

"Thank you, sir!" Neil noticed the "sir." "I'll be going now. I'll be sorry if the boy has to quit college."

"We can make a go of it, I think, Callahan."

"I hope so." A brief period of silence followed. "Good-night, Mr. Douglas."

Neil waited until the city clerk had driven off in his car. He was strongly tempted to walk out to the porch and tell his father that he had overheard, and to try to express to him some of his own affection and admiration. But first he had a job to finish.

Turning, he tiptoed noiselessly up the stairs. His den was just as he had left it: the textbook face down upon the desk, and beside it, the copied examination questions. Neil walked over to the window and looked out. The campus was deserted, but the group of men at the dormitory had resumed their singing. They sang of faith, loyalty, and honor, while Neil thought of the man downstairs, his father, who had risked failure so that he might leave those qualities as a heritage to his son.

Neil knew now that loyalty could never be expressed through a dishonest act. Reaching down, he picked up the examination questions and tore the sheet of paper into bits.

Thrusting his hands into the pockets of his flannel trousers, he turned to the window again. He would not take his test in surveying the next morning. It was probable, he reflected, that he would have to leave college, but he had just a chance by transferring to the arts course to carry on. It would mean hard work and sacrifice, but what did that matter?

He had learned a more vital truth in the past hour than any he could hope to learn in the coming years. Now, whatever lay in store for them, he and his father would stick together in perfect understanding. Smiling, he turned off the light, and with shoulders back and head held high, he made his way down to the porch, where his father was waiting.

Summer to Autumn

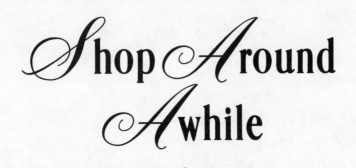

Shop Around Awhile

Mae Foster Jay

Because of a "small" thing, Priscilla Lee wanted nothing more to do with debonair Jack DeVore, for she was convinced that "small" things add up to "big" things. On the other hand, undistinguished Barry Stuart, down on his knees at four o'clock in the morning, doing a "small" thing, inexplicably moved her deeply.

"I suppose, Priscilla," speculated Bess Stuart as she rummaged in the chaos of her dresser drawer for a hairbrush, "that you have your love all wrapped in tissue paper, too, and tucked away in that cedar chest with the other 'hope' things. Has it occurred to you that the paper might turn yellow while you're waiting for a paragon?"

Priscilla tried to laugh at the warning as she continued the careful folding of a lovely scarf purchased that afternoon; but she sighed wistfully instead. "A virtuous, bossy, commonsense self keeps hounding me: 'You have reached the antiquity of twenty-five, Priscilla Lee. Your life is full and interesting. Your little gift shop is generously patronized, thanks to your having learned values, human

203

and material, during your mother's life. You know very well that, in business, it pays to shop around. So why not in—'"

"There's no oversupply of husband material on the market, Cilla. If you refuse to see Jack DeVore when he telephones—as he will, and for the third time—that means, practically, that you've thrown into the discard two men most any girl would think she was lucky to get. What do you want, anyhow?"

"I wish I knew," Priscilla said tightly. "Maybe I'd know if I saw him. I seem to know well enough what I don't want. I don't want a husband like Ronny Blair, who is the life of the party abroad and the world's worst grouch at home; nor one like Steve, who calls his wife 'the little woman' in public and I don't know what in private; nor one who lets a shopkeeper remember his wife's birthday for him, as Tommy West does me; nor—"

"Cilla!" Bess's fascinated eyes were upon the order in that chest, the meticulous arrangement of Priscilla's lovely dark hair, the prim neatness of her blue suit. "You know you . . . you do have certain earmarks of . . . of an old maid, Cilla. Did you ever misplace anything in your life?"

"You wouldn't"—wide, deep-set blue eyes twinkled—"have me begin with misplaced affections, would you?"

"And did you ever do anything impulsively in your life?"

"I bought this batik right now. Who knows—I might pick a husband that way."

"You? You'll stand back and look him over through a lorgnette. 'Is he marked sterling? Will he wear well?' As you shop, you know, Cilla!"

The sudden ringing of the telephone brought Priscilla quickly to her feet. She started to dash eagerly across the room, but checked herself and sauntered. Presently she was saying into the instrument, coolly enough, "I'm sorry, Jack, but I have another engagement for tonight."

A merry, intriguing voice answered, "You don't mean it, Priscilla! You're not angry with me, really, and you know it! Let me come out a minute, and I'll convince you—"

Somehow Priscilla summoned the stamina to be, again, "So sorry," and turned away from the telephone.

"Any girl," said Bess, "who'd—"

"I'm not sure"—Priscilla's voice was not quite steady—"that I ever want to accept an invitation from him again."

"You want to, but you won't let yourself. Because of a mere trifle!"

"Trifles are so illuminating!"

"You can't expect perfection in any man! Jack has money, personality, brains. He's wild about you. What if he didn't come that once?"

"There are women," Priscilla said, staring into the mirror at her too-flushed cheeks, "who spend their lives waiting for a man who doesn't come. Wouldn't it be better to take a little hurt now . . . "

Her voice trailed off. She was thinking of a recent Saturday afternoon when she had accepted an invitation to drive upstate with Jack DeVore to see the flaming autumn woods and to have dinner at an old-fashioned inn. She had dressed early. At seven she had made herself a sandwich in the kitchenette of the apartment she shared with Bess Stuart. Of course Jack had finally called and given an explanation. He had been called out of town—to a house party, Priscilla had learned accidentally.

Bess, watching Priscilla with a certain anxiety in her merry eyes, said suddenly, "You can't blind me, Cilla. You're low. It isn't so easy to be sensible as you make out. Come home with me for the weekend." Bess, a teacher in the suburbs, spent her weekends on the home farm. "You've always promised to come."

Priscilla turned. "I believe I will. I'd like to . . . get away."

"We're remodeling the house," said Bess, smiling. "The chaos will be a nice change for you. You are so neat, Cilla."

Priscilla laughed gratefully. At least it would be good—and safe—to have an engagement that took her out of town.

* * *

The train pulled into the little town at midnight. "What an unholy hour!" commented Priscilla. "However do we get out to the farm?"

"Oh, I wired Barry to meet us."

"He'll like that!"

"Oh, Barry won't mind."

No, probably he would not, Priscilla reflected as he came toward them, a slight, wiry figure, deliberate of movement, deliberate of speech, an equability about him suggesting that he was not the sort to mind things.

During the ride to the farm, Priscilla listened in some amusement while Bess pried the family news out of her brother. She was conscious, meanwhile, of keen dark eyes glancing down at her appraisingly as she sat between brother and sister on the roadster seat—eloquent, penetrating eyes that were not routed when she discovered them boring into her.

"How's the remodeling coming?" demanded Bess as they entered the house.

"Practically finished. And it has all but finished Mother, too. She had to go to bed early after a hectic day."

Priscilla followed Bess about the splendid old home with its high ceilings, its airy rooms, its genuine walnut woodwork—a thoroughbred of a past generation that had been modernized without losing its sterling old character.

At the kitchen door, Barry halted them with a dramatic gesture. "Only over my dead body. Mother's orders. Don't look farther—unless you want nightmares!"

Laughing, Bess passed her arm about Priscilla and led her upstairs, turning to call back, "How are all your little pigs and chickens and all that stuff, Barry?"

"As well as could be expected."

Priscilla wondered at the grimness of the grin until Bess said, as they reached the upper hall, "Poor old Barry! How he despises farming!"

"Engineer or something, isn't he?"

"Mechanical. Graduated from Boston Tech two years ago and to date has never had a chance to design anything more heroic than a chicken coop. Looked after the farm all during Dad's illness last year and has kept on since his death while Herbert finishes school. Herb's the farmer of the family. When he's ready to take hold here, Barry'll have a chance to show the world what he's made of."

Priscilla went to bed in a four-poster in a charming room finished in maple and mahogany. Sleepily she thought about Barry Stuart and the calm, inoffensive way he had studied her. He was a quiet individual, not the sort to attract most girls.

The wind, soughing through the great maples outside, swayed the ruffled curtains gently. Priscilla quickly fell asleep.

Hours later she was awakened by a peculiar, insistent noise—a low, regular *scratch-scratch* with an occasional thud. Was someone trying to break in somewhere?

She lit the candle in the old brass stick on the table by her bed and stole out into the hall. The noise came from the rear of the house. The other bedrooms were forward. No use disturbing the rest of the family until she had investigated. It probably was no more than the swish of a blind in the wind.

She followed the hall to the backstairs at the end of it. At the foot of the stairs, a ray of light showed through the door, which was slightly ajar. Priscilla crept down cautiously and peeped through the crack.

She was looking into the kitchen, a spick-and-span, orderly kitchen, shining with new white paint. The noise went on with gusto, but the field of her vision was so narrow that she could not determine its source. She pushed the door open a trifle wider. A very odd sight met her eyes.

Two well-shod feet protruded from under the kitchen table, their soles toward her; so she increased her field of vision. They protruded, she discovered, from a pair of old blue overalls. Their owner was down on hands and knees. The *scratch-scratch* was the friction between a new hardwood floor and a viciously wielded scrubbing brush. With widening eyes, Priscilla then watched the unusual spectacle of a conqueror doggedly retreating, bringing his weapons and the line of victory with him.

When Barry Stuart backed completely out from under the table, pail and brush in hand, Priscilla fled silently back up the stairs. She looked at her watch. Four o'clock! Now, what did one make of a performance like that?

* * *

Bess and her mother came into the room in the morning as Priscilla finished dressing.

"I'm sorry to have seemed so inhospitable last night," Mrs. Stuart greeted Priscilla. "Barry said I was at my nerves' end and needed sleep—

and he was right." She was a rather large woman with an uptilting mouth, jolly blue eyes, and capable hands. "The world's a different hue this morning. Last night, I'm ashamed to say, I was quite undone at the thought of a guest, with the kitchen in such a mess. I went to pieces. And this morning, I don't mind a bit."

Mrs. Stuart led the way down the backstairs. She opened the door at the foot of them and stepped gingerly forward, only to halt with an amazed, almost an alarmed cry. "Whatever—why, who in the world—?"

Priscilla could have told her that she was to step into a room so immaculate that the most fastidious could not pick a flaw. It was completely settled, even to the blue-dotted white curtains at the windows and the tea towels precisely placed upon the hanger.

"Bess!" Mrs. Stuart managed. "Did you—?"

"*I!*" Bess's astonishment matched her mother's.

"Then—it was Barry! That boy!" There was a catch in the mother's voice. "He . . . he must have stayed up all night to do it! Why, there were shavings and plaster and grime all over this floor; there were cupboards unfinished, woodwork unwashed! He has worked like a slave all week anyway, doing things the contractor left undone, and now *this!* Just because it was getting on my nerves!"

She pulled out a cabinet drawer. "That boy! He even has put all the utensils in their places, the dishes on the shelves. I've done nothing but fuss for days! Oh, I'm so . . . so ashamed!" She dropped into a chair, and her hands went over her face.

"That boy" appeared in the dining room doorway, grinning. "That's right, Mother! Cry over your little Cinderella! Probably I've ruined my health, to say nothing of my manicure—"

At this juncture, Priscilla Lee made her escape to the broad veranda. When she had rounded a corner or two, she ducked her head into her handkerchief and gave vent to a grand and gorgeous eruption of scalding tears and convulsive sobs. It was a prolonged session, not entirely ended when she heard a step behind her and a quiet, if astounded, "They sent me to tell you that breakfast is ready, Priscilla."

Priscilla turned. Barry Stuart stood there, looking at her miserably. "But . . . why, Priscilla?"

The eruption quieted as she caught her lip between her teeth and smiled up at him. "I . . . I have a silly way of crying at lovely things. And you . . . you—"

"Say," he said mischievously, "nobody ever told me before that I was lovely."

Priscilla laughed but studied him, fleetingly, and saw loveliness—not physical, perhaps, but still loveliness. It was made of steadfastness, self-control, unselfishness, dependability, something gentle and tender in the eyes that were boring into hers eloquently.

"You're a dear little silly, as bad as Mother, Priscilla, if you're moved by that come-into-the-kitchen stuff. You'd think I'd really done something to be given a hand for!"

"Trifles," Priscilla interrupted him, "are so . . . illuminating!" She then added mischievously in turn, "You're a bargain, Barry! Some girl ought to nab you!"

"I've been wishing since last night that some girl would. You don't happen to be interested in bargains, Priscilla?"

She kept her tone light, despite alarming undercurrents. "Oh, of course—" He might take it just for flirty nonsense, repartee, or again for something more serious. "Of course, like all girls, I'm shopping around for something that just suits."

"Good! Now I'll put this sample away on the shelf for you, madam, while you make up your mind. No obligation whatever, understand."

"Why don't you two come to breakfast?" Bess came around the bend in the veranda.

"Sorry, Bess!" Priscilla's eyes twinkled roguishly. "I was explaining to Barry that it pays to shop around."

Bess held her back and motioned Barry on—held her back to tilt up her face. Did she see something new there? "Priscilla Lee!" she cried incredulously, excitedly. "Do you . . . ? Can you mean . . . ? Priscilla Lee, you didn't use a lorgnette after all!"

"Oh, yes, I did! A honey of a lorgnette! It made everything so clear! I never dreamed," she said cryptically, "that you could see so much, Bess, through a crack in the kitchen door!"

A Case of Need

Author Unknown

*"For Sale: A dear dolly named Betsey
Amelia for One Dollar. A case of need."
That was little Sara's newspaper ad.
If only someone would read it and
buy Betsey. But, oh, what if someone did!*

Edward Newton had his fork halfway to his mouth with a morsel of food on it. As Nan spoke, he laid it down and looked across the table at her. "It seems as if I ought to save it," he said.

Nan laughed. "Oh, no," she answered. "Eat it. There isn't enough of it to save."

"It's enough to choke a fellow," said Edward gloomily.

Nan laughed again. "I shouldn't think it was big enough for that," she said. "You needn't look at me as if I had no feelings. I might as well laugh as cry, but I'm just as troubled as you are. Mama seems very weak today, and it's no wonder. There is nothing to tempt her to eat. She's been crying, too. She turned her head away quickly when I went to ask her how to make that miserable, sloppy gruel that she couldn't eat after all. I almost told Dr. Colton this morning, when he talked about all those delicacies, that he might as well order gold dust."

"Did he say she must have them?"

"Not exactly. He only spoke of it as a matter of course. 'Give her nourishing food,' he said. 'Broths and fruits, oranges and pineapples, anything that she fancies.' It all sounds so easy when he says it! I almost giggled. It seemed so funny to think of our being able to buy them. Mama shook her head at me. I suppose she was afraid I was going to disgrace her by saying some such thing."

"Mama ought to have what the doctor orders. We can't expect her to get strong if she doesn't."

"I know it," said Nan. "But what can we do? I should be willing to beg if Mama would let me. I thought of it last night when I stopped at Benham's and saw them unpacking a great box filled with fruit. I know I could have said, 'Oh, do please give me one orange and a little piece of pineapple for Mama!' If it hadn't been for Mama's asking me questions, I believe I would have done it."

"Something has *got* to be done," said Edward as he pushed his empty plate away and rose up.

His sister did not look encouraged. They had both said that before and meant it; yet nothing had been done. Edward was nearly fifteen, and his sister Nan, a year and a half younger, thought him almost a man. But he felt it bitterly that he could not earn a man's wages.

Both of these young people, however, seemed older than they were, for the reason that almost from babyhood they had shared their mother's cares and troubles and tried to help her plan.

Little Sara, their eight-year-old sister, was just beginning to talk plainly when their father died and trouble began. The pale little mother, who had never been strong, did her best. She gave up the front room of their small house for a store and moved into it whatever things were given to her after the auction sale at her husband's store. A strange, tumbled mass of things were there. Many of them nobody wanted, and the little mother did not know how to arrange those that might have been sold. She had never learned how to keep a store. But she managed to get enough to feed and clothe them and to keep the children in school, until she fell ill.

Then the two older ones tried to shoulder her burdens. After long hunting, Edward found a place as an errand boy in a downtown grocery; and Nan was housekeeper, nurse, and saleswoman at home. Customers did not hinder her much. Sometimes for days together the little bell over the front door did not ring.

It rang that day just as Edward pushed back his chair. Nan answered it and came back smiling.

"Ten whole cents!" she said, holding up the dime. "The first sale I have had today."

It was very still in the little kitchen after Edward had gone back to work and Nan to her mother. Little Sara was alone with Betsey Amelia, her one dear dolly. If you had been watching her, you would have noticed that the little girl hugged Betsey Amelia often; and sometimes, after she had put her face down to the doll's, there would be tears on Betsey Amelia's painted cheeks.

A great thought that meant a great sacrifice had come to little Sara. In order to understand it, you will have to know about Philip.

Philip was a boy who went to the school where little Sara went and who had been for some weeks trying to raise $25 to buy a pony. All the children in school had heard about it. When Philip had $20, he was in despair for the other $5. The owner of the pony would agree to wait for him but one more day. Then Philip had a bright thought: his bicycle. What should a boy with a pony want of a bicycle? He tried to find a purchaser among the boys and failed. Then he advertised in the morning papers: "For Sale: A first-class bicycle in good order. For Five Dollars. A case of necessity."

Within twenty-four hours, Philip's bicycle had changed hands and he was the owner of a pony. It is true that Philip's father said the bicycle was worth more than the pony; but Philip did not think so, and little Sara did not know it. Advertising was the way to sell things. That was what little Sara had learned.

She had but one thing of her "very truly own" that she thought anybody would care to buy, and that was her dear and dearly loved Betsey Amelia. *Could* she part with her? Yes, for Mama's sake she could. A doll not so pretty as she, and not quite so large, stood in a show window that little Sara passed on her way to school, and it was marked, "Only One Dollar." Little Sara was not stupid; she knew that one dollar would buy several oranges, a pineapple, berries, and even cream. What if she had a whole dollar to spend for Mama? Wouldn't anybody who cared at all for dolls be glad to give a dollar for Betsey Amelia? Little Sara felt sure of it. Left to herself that afternoon, she worked hard and printed her advertisement: "For Sale: A dear dolly named Betsey Amelia for One Dollar. A case of need."

When she went to school the next morning, she took her advertisement along and stopped at the office of the *Daily Bulletin,* the editor of which was a good friend of hers. He always said, "Good morning, Mouse," when she met him and often gave her an orange or a red-cheeked apple. He had told her that his girls were all boys, and he wished he had a little daughter like her.

He took her advertisement with a grave face and was very businesslike indeed; only he asked her one strange question.

"Isn't 'Betsey-Amelia-for-One-Dollar' a rather unusual name for a doll?"

"Why, why! Mr. Patten, what *can* you mean?" said little Sara. "That isn't her name. It is just Betsey Amelia."

"Oh," said the editor meekly, "I didn't understand."

As little Sara closed the door, she thought she heard him laugh; but she might have been mistaken.

The next day was a school holiday, and little Sara arose early, dressed Betsey Amelia in her best, and set her in the store window. She never had a chance to see the *Daily Bulletin;* but of course the editor put in her advertisement and told where the doll was to be found. He had promised, and little Sara believed that people would begin to come early to look at the doll. She had not yet told Nan or Edward. Indeed, she would have liked to make the dollar a surprise for both of them if she could. At the breakfast table, a plan came up that she saw might help her do this.

"Do you suppose, Edward, I could leave little Sara to look after the store for two hours this morning? There is hardly ever a customer, especially in the morning; and Mama wants me to go with that work she finished last week, and explain why it was so late, and show her about the bad place in the lace."

"I should think she might be clerk as well as not," said Edward, smiling at little Sara's eager face. "She knows the prices of things and can count all the money she will get, I am sure."

Was anything ever better planned? What if she should have a whole dollar to give to Nan as soon as she got home! Then Mama could have all she needed for a day at least, and there was no money coming in from anywhere else. When Edward asked whether money was to be paid for the work that was to be taken home, Nan shook her head and said soberly that it was to be charged on their coal bill. The thought of what she might do made little Sara feel almost happy in spite of the fact that she was to part with Betsey Amelia.

Never was there a neater-looking little saleswoman than the one who took her place in due time behind the counter, charged with watching two bells: the one on the door, and the one that her mother was to ring if she needed anything.

The doorbell rang first; but before it rang, an automobile stopped at the gate, and a lady stepped out of it.

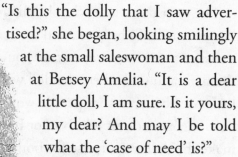

"Is this the dolly that I saw advertised?" she began, looking smilingly at the small saleswoman and then at Betsey Amelia. "It is a dear little doll, I am sure. Is it yours, my dear? And may I be told what the 'case of need' is?"

Little Sara had not meant to tell, but the lady was so sweet that before she knew it, she was explaining the whole plan and the reason for it. The lady was pleased with it, too, and told little Sara that it was a very kind, unselfish thought and that she would be glad to take the dolly, and considered $2 not a cent too much to pay for one so neatly dressed. More than that, she looked at pins and thread and buttons and needles and liked them so much that when she went away, she left five whole dollars in the cash drawer, which had been empty for weeks. Little Sara was so excited that she forgot to feel bad about Betsey Amelia.

What a morning that was! No sooner had the first automobile rolled out of sight, than another stopped, and three ladies made their way to the door. The small clerk met them eagerly.

"Oh!" she said. "I'm sorry. I mean I'm glad—" Then she stopped in confusion and began again. "If you came to see the dolly, she has been sold."

Of course they were sorry. Each lady had meant to have her. But they came in, and looked about them, and wanted tape and soap and pins and lace. While they were still there, others came, and little Sara began to think that something must have happened the night before to all the pins and needles in the city. How else could it be accounted for that so many ladies wanted them at once? Before Nan came back, every pin was sold; then they began on the buttons and thread. Never in its history had the little store had such a wonderful morning. The ladies kept coming, and every one of them asked about the "case of need," and every one of them bought what cost more than the price of the doll.

"Isn't this the little girl who used to bring such nice cookies to school with her luncheon?" one lady asked. "My children used to have bites of them and tell how good they were. I wish you had some of those for sale. But if your mama is ill, she cannot make any, I suppose."

"My sister, Nan, knows how to make them," said little Sara eagerly. "Mama said hers tasted every bit as good, and I know she would like to make you some."

Then every lady there wanted two dozen cookies as soon as she could get them.

When Nan reached home, she found a little saleswoman with cheeks so red that they almost seemed to blaze, and $23.30 in the cash drawer, and nine dozen cookies ordered.

But the strangest thing in that strange day happened at night, just as little Sara had laid her tired head on her pillow and was trying to keep back the tears because for the first time in Betsey Amelia's life she was sleeping somewhere else than by her side. The little bell over the store door rang once more, and Edward answered it, to receive a box and a note for "Miss Sara Newton." The note read:

Dear little Sara:

My Lillian has been very happy today with Betsey Amelia; but tonight she thinks the dolly is homesick for her own dear mama and wants her sent back to you, with

Lillian's love. I am sure you will keep her for my little lame Lillian's sake, for she truly wants to make you a present of her "to keep," she says.

And there, in the box, smiling her own sweet smile, was dear Betsey Amelia!

"I'm glad she's got back," said Edward, looking down on her and speaking with a strange tremble in his voice. "I didn't know I loved dolls, but this one has cured Mama and made our fortune."

Tiny Tim

Sharon A. Dunsmore

*This true story has become almost a legend
since 1995, the year it was written.
I predict it will be gathered to the heart
by all those who cherish the gift of life.
This is not a story for small children.*

It was a relatively calm day in the NICU (Neonatal Intensive Care Unit). I was on duty with two other nurses, and we were trying to have a conversation amid the customary sounds of ventilators and heart monitors. Occasionally an alarm would go off, and one of us would attend to the needs of a tiny patient. In this arena of life and death, we often exuded an ambivalent calm while executing our split-second decisions.

I was in midsentence when the shrill ring of the phone halted all conversation. It was the *red* phone, and I was leaning against it. The red phone was the emergency line between us and the labor and delivery room—very unobtrusive, unless it rings.

I fought the desire to walk away and let someone else answer it as I picked up the receiver. "Come fast," the voice said urgently. "We need a neonatal nurse *stat!*"

The other nurses looked at me and said, "You're on. We'll watch your patients here and set up for another admission."

Fear gripped my heart as I ran through the back entrance toward the delivery room. The labor and delivery nurses were ready when I arrived. Holding gown, gloves, and mask, they helped me into uniform and almost pushed me into the delivery room. When I didn't even get to "scrub in," I knew the situation was critical.

My adrenaline was up as I heard the sound of screaming and crying. Physicians and other staff members were giving orders.

Lord, I prayed, *give me wisdom and help the life or lives that are being threatened.* I made eye contact with the circulating nurse and asked, "What's happening here?"

She responded with little emotion. "It's an OOPS abortion [not a commonly used term], and now, well, it's your problem!"

The pediatrician ran by me with the fetus (now called a baby) in his hand. He swore and then yelled in my direction, indicating he wanted me to follow him into the resuscitation room adjoining the delivery room.

I looked into the bed of the warmer as I grabbed equipment. Before my eyes was a baby boy. A very, very tiny baby boy. The doctor and I immediately made an attempt at intubation (inserting a tube down the trachea from the mouth or nose of the infant to the tip of the lungs to ventilate, expand, and oxygenate the lungs). This procedure was unsuccessful and put the baby in much greater trauma.

I glanced at the doctor and hesitantly asked, "Will you attempt intubation again?"

"You've got to be kidding," he replied. "It would be inhumane to attempt to intubate this poor little thing again. This infant will never survive."

"No, Doctor, I'm not kidding," I said, "and it's my job to ask."

The doctor softened for a moment. "I'm sorry, Sharon. I'm just angry. The mother doesn't want the inconvenience of a baby, so she can pay somebody to get rid of it—all neat and tidy. Then the whole thing gets screwed up when the fetus has the audacity to survive." His words tumbled out. "Then everybody takes it seriously and calls the pediatrician, who's supposed to fix it or get rid of it. Then it's all on my shoulders, including the liability of this new unwanted little person!"

With anger in his voice, he went on. "The lawyers will fight for the right to do whatever we want to, to our bodies, but watch out for what they will do when these abortions aren't so neat and tidy! A failed 'homicide'—an OOPS! Then all of a sudden everybody cares, and it's turned from a 'right' into a 'liability' that someone gets the blame for."

As the doctor's emotions surged, he continued. "It's the last guy with his hands on this 'pro-choice entity' who now gets to be responsible for the OOPS." With sarcasm in his voice, he said, "Well, Sharon, today that's you and me. We are the lucky shift, and I answered my phone and you answered your phone. Lucky us, huh?"

I spoke quietly. "This is pretty upsetting, isn't it?"

As our eyes met, the doctor and I shared an unspoken anguish. We worked feverishly over the infant, doing everything that could be done according to the policy and standards of practice in our hospital—but we both knew we were losing the battle for the life of this baby.

We looked at our pathetic little patient. He was lying in the fetal position in the wrong environment, trying to get air into underdeveloped lungs that couldn't do the job.

In a calmer voice, the doctor said, "Okay, Nurse, I'm going back to the office. Keep him comfortable and let me know when it's over. I'm sorry about this. Call me if you need me for anything. I know this is a hard one. We've done all we can. If it helps, please know it's tough for me, too."

I watched the doctor retreat and then glanced back at the infant before me. He was struggling for oxygen. *Lord, help!* I prayed.

Almost instinctively, I took the baby's vitals. His temperature was dangerously low. I pushed the warmer settings as high as they could go. His heart rate was about 180 to 200 beats per minute. I could count the beats by watching his little chest pulsate.

Following the doctor's orders, I notified the intensive care unit that we wouldn't be coming and that we would be waiting it out right where we were. All of the same life-saving equipment available to me in the NICU was right here—and I knew the baby's time was short.

I settled down a bit and began to focus on this tiny little person who had no name. Suddenly, I found myself speaking to the baby. "Tiny Tim, who are you? I am very sorry you weren't wanted. It's not your fault. You didn't ask for this, and neither did I."

I placed my little finger in his hand, and *he grasped it!* As I watched him closely, I marveled that all the microscopic parts of a beautiful baby were present and functioning in spite of the onslaught.

I touched his toes and discovered he was ticklish! He had a long torso and long legs. I wondered if he would have become a basketball player. Perhaps he would have been a teacher or a doctor.

Emotions swept over me as I thought of my friends who had been waiting and praying for years for a baby to adopt. I spoke aloud once again to the miniature baby. "They would have given you a loving and happy home. Why would people destroy you before ever considering adoption? That goes beyond selfishness and turns into something sinister. Ignorance is *not* bliss, is it, Tiny Tim?"

He put his thumb into his mouth and sucked. I hoped it gave him comfort.

My dialogue with the baby continued. "I'm sorry, Tim. I don't know how we got to be such a screwed-up society. There are people who would risk their lives for a whale or an owl before they'd even blink about what just happened to you. Perhaps they just don't know."

Tiny Tim was gasping, and his little chest was heaving as if a truck were sitting on it. I took my stethoscope and listened to his tiny, pounding heart. I heard the swishing sound of a heart murmur. At the moment it seemed easier to focus on physiology rather than be with this baby as a dying human being.

The baby wet. And with that action, my mind took off again. Here was Tiny Tim with a whole set of kidneys, a bladder, and connecting tubes that functioned with a very complex system of chemistry. It was all working! He was an amazing little person! I turned the overhead light up, and Tim turned from it, in spite of eyelids that were fused together to protect his two precious little eyes. I thought about his eyes. They would never see the sunset, the trees, a mother's smile, or the wagging tail of a dog.

I took his temperature again. It was dropping. He was gasping for air and continued to fight for life. I stroked him gently and began to sing, "Jesus loves the little children, all the children of the world. Red and yellow, black and white, they are precious in His sight. Jesus loves the little children of the world." My spirit was still troubled. Again I prayed.

A nurse walked in. "The doctor is on the phone, and he wants to know what's happening."

I looked up and simply said, "Tiny Tim is dying. I will call when it's over, and it's not over. Tell him thanks for calling."

The nurse responded, "It's so hot in here! How can you stand it?" I looked at the clock. One hour had gone by.

She continued. "Can you stay over with this one? It's almost shift change."

"Sure. I'll stay," I replied. "He's been breathing like he's run a marathon, and he keeps on struggling." I paused. "How's the mother doing?"

"Oh, she's fine. She's back in her room, resting. The family said they don't want to see or hear about anything. They said, 'Just take care of it!'" The nurse retreated with one last glance at the tiny patient. "For such a little person, he's sure putting up a big fight!"

I looked at Tiny Tim and wondered if I should have turned the alarm up as a signal to the world that all was *not* well. I wanted to stand on a soapbox and yell at the top of my lungs, "Something serious is happening! Does anybody care? A baby is dying here, and this shouldn't be happening!"

Tiny Tim moved and caught hold of my baby finger again, and I just let him hang on. I didn't want him to die without being touched and cared for. As I saw him struggling for air, I said, "It's okay, Tim. You can let go. You can go back to God."

His gasping started slowing down, along with his other vitals, but he still clung to my finger. Nurses stopped in to check on his progress, and another call came from the doctor. He too found it upsetting that this whole thing was taking so long. I knew the doctor was living with the same agony I was experiencing. I tried to remember why I chose this profession, and couldn't.

I stroked the baby ever so slowly, and he gently curled around my finger in the fetal position. I watched him take his last breath and then said softly, "Good-bye, Tiny Tim. You *did* matter to someone."

Shortly after, I left the Neonatal Intensive Care Unit and accepted a new position as the manager of a psychiatric unit.

My story continues. . . .

One day a young woman was to be admitted into the unit. She was severely depressed and had made one unsuccessful suicide attempt. As I interviewed her, the patient kept her head down and she was almost nonverbal. Her appearance was haggard and her demeanor sad, yet she was beyond crying. Her clothes didn't match and smelled, indicating a total neglect of hygiene. She rocked back and forth slowly. Despite her wasted appearance, I saw a hint of beauty and intelligence.

I could tell the admission process was going to take a long time. After a while, Kathy began to speak. She had gone through an abortion several years before, and she had been looking for "something" for a long time, but didn't know what it was. She was having recurring nightmares. A baby was crying for help and kept calling her name. In her dreams Kathy searched for the baby, but could never find it.

She began to fill her days with workaholism and perfectionism. She was obsessed by a need for extreme cleanliness and excessive organization. Her efforts exhausted her.

Every time she saw a baby, she searched the tiny face for some kind of recognition. If she was near a crying infant, she would soon be shaking and in tears. In an attempt to cover her pain, she shopped and spent money she didn't have. Creditors and bill collectors followed her everywhere.

Kathy confessed, "I began using sleeping pills to chase away the insomnia and the dreams. The pills didn't work, but I'd wake up the following day in a stupor that kept me in a confused and irritable state of mind. I lost my friends. Then I lost my job. Then I began to drink alcohol with a different group. They said, 'Come on, just a few drinks. Let's party and you'll feel better.' I didn't. Nothing could get rid of the pain and the searching. And things got worse."

As she confided in me, Kathy became like a volcano, erupting with fiery emotions. She couldn't speak fast enough. She continued. "One day, when I thought I couldn't go any further physically or mentally, I decided to kill myself. I didn't know how to do it, but I took a bunch of pills and just went to sleep." Her deep, dark eyes softened. Looking up, she said, "Do you know what it feels like to decide to die and have no one in your life who really cares? No one should have to die alone. I tried to, but I couldn't even do *that* right!"

She began to cry, and I thought she would never stop. Kathy fell into my arms and curled up like a baby. She continued sobbing uncontrollably until she was consumed with exhaustion. I held her for a long time and rubbed her back, as I had done with my own children.

As she calmed down, I said, "Kathy, I care about you and you *are* important. God doesn't make mistakes, and I think you're a beautiful person."

She stared up at me with a look of wonder. Perhaps she felt accepted by another human being for the first time—I don't know. But her eyes changed to a look of total openness and honesty. I could tell she was no longer afraid of me.

Pausing momentarily, I said, "Are you ready to talk about the abortion tonight, or do you need more time?"

"No, please!" she responded. "I've got to tell *somebody.* I've never told anyone the whole story before. I'm tired of running from it." And Kathy began her story.

She had gotten pregnant at a very "inconvenient" time. Her fiancé was in the middle of a career change. Her parents had always used guilt to control her. Since the doors of parental communication were closed, she went to an abortion clinic on the advice of her boyfriend and coworkers. All the voices of influence around her said, "Just take care of it. It's no big deal."

At the clinic the doctor said the gestation was early and there would be no problem. She was scheduled for a D&C (dilation and curettage) on an outpatient basis. But soon after getting into surgery, things were *not* as easy as had been promised. The gestation age of the fetus had been inaccurately figured, and Kathy went into labor. Chaos ensued, and she was transferred to the delivery room.

Kathy thought she remembered hearing a baby cry, doctors and nurses racing around. She had screamed, "What's wrong?"

One of the nurses responded, "You're having a baby!"

Kathy recoiled and screamed, "No!"

A nurse came into her room much later to tell her and her family that

the baby had died. The nurse quietly asked if she would like to hold her baby and say good-bye. Kathy said the word *baby* shocked her. In all of her talks with the people at the clinic, the fetus was never referred to as a *baby*. She didn't want to hear the word and mentally shut it out of her mind.

Family members told the nurse, "No, just take care of it, and don't come back."

Kathy said, "I remember the eyes of the nurse as she looked at me and said, 'Is that what *you* want?' In my heart I wanted to see the baby, but my family assured me it was best to say no. I was confused and just wanted to have it all over with." Her voice was filled with emotion: "I never got to see my baby." Kathy put her head in her hands and cried softly again. Through tears, she continued, "I don't even know if it was a boy or a girl. No one told me."

After several weeks of intensive therapy and high doses of antidepressants, Kathy was making progress. She was a pretty woman and had an interesting personality. As time went on, she cried less often, but it was very painful for Kathy to deal with so much unresolved conflict. After keeping her story bottled up for years, she began verbalizing more of the details connected with her unexpected pregnancy and the ensuing failed abortion.

I agonized with her. This was a fragile time for Kathy. As time passed, she began putting in specific names and places. She used the name of the hospital and medical personnel. As I continued working with Kathy, a disturbing realization dawned on me. It couldn't be! But it was.

I compared her dates and events with my own three-year-old calendar and came to an amazing realization: *Kathy was Tiny Tim's mother!*

Because of hospital regulations, I couldn't tell her what I knew at that time, but I wanted to shout, "You had a beautiful baby. He was a little boy, and he *did* have a name: Tiny Tim! He had blond hair and long legs. He didn't die alone. He was loved and cared for and prayed over."

In my heart, as one mother to another, I knew I could give some semblance of peace to this young woman, who so desperately needed the missing pieces of a major puzzle in her life. If and when the time was right, I knew I could tell her about Tiny Tim.

Time passed. I was no longer a nurse therapist. Kathy was no longer a psychiatric patient. We met in a restaurant. Two human beings with a small segment of history in common. The meeting was at first awkward. Uncomfortable. Emotional. Painful. No last names, addresses, or phone numbers were exchanged.

I gently unfolded the story that had been hidden for so long. Tears flowed as I gave Kathy the gift of answers. Her baby had been touched and loved by another. He had been given a name. He didn't die alone. He was sent back to a loving God.

As the visit neared an end, we held each other and wept. I silently prayed for her with love, not judgment. I looked into Kathy's eyes and saw a new strength and calm. There were scars, but she was beginning to heal. The nightmares were put to rest. We hugged and parted, knowing we would probably never meet again in this lifetime.

I still live with the haunting impact of this experience. Sometimes I wonder why God allowed me to care for these two special human beings. Tiny Tim's pain didn't last long, but it was fatal. Kathy's pain almost cost her her life and is a wound that will take years to fully heal. The scar will last forever. A "choice" that was intended to be "no big deal" turned out to be a *very big* deal for all of us.

Editor's Note: The names and references to time periods have all been changed for purposes of confidentiality.

The Boy Who Couldn't Be Saved

Author Unknown

Buck Torres had set the school on fire—no ifs, ands, or buts. He was through in the town; perhaps reform school would straighten him out. Buck had but one defender: Miss Christie. One against the entire town—tough odds indeed!

They told Miss Christie, "You can't do anything with riffraff like that." Why did she keep trying?

Now the school day was over. Five minutes ago the last footfall had echoed down the hall, and the last harried teacher had turned in reports; but for Miss Christie Emerson, principal of Latimer Grammar School, the hardest job was still ahead. She was face-to-face with it this very moment, and she hadn't any idea how it was to be handled.

The boy sitting across the room was the school's problem boy. Miss Christie had taught for forty-three years, and this was the one pupil from whom she had failed to get some response. Although

233

she was working on reports and not looking at him, she knew he was not looking at her, either. He seldom met anyone's eye. He would be gazing straight ahead, that sneer on his face—almost a smile of satisfaction. Last night he had tried to set the schoolhouse on fire. Arson. A criminal offense. The evidence was nailed.

Miss Christie sighed. She had tried so hard to reach him, but now it was out of her hands. She could do nothing. They would turn him over to juvenile authorities for prosecution, and that meant the state reformatory.

Still without glancing up, Miss Christie spoke. "Buck, bring me the card index on that filing case, please." Her voice was detached, as if she were engrossed in her work. It was a trick she had used before. It eased the tension, and it gave Miss Christie a little more time to think.

There was no movement in the room. She could picture the sneering response to her simple request, meaning *I'm not in your custody now. I'm big time. Don't have to go to sissy school any longer. I'm a real character.* Then a foot scraped on the floor. Two feet. He shuffled across the room, slouched back, and dumped the box on the desk.

"Thank you. I'll be finished here in a few moments," she said conversationally.

It wasn't that she handled them with gloves—when Miss Christie pitched into a kid, he remembered it—but she tried to treat a boy as if he were a responsible human being. She often said, "This is a grown-up world. The children can't understand our laws and attitudes, having had no adult experience, but they've got to abide by them, and I'd like them to know why, if possible, and to feel that they can depend on grown-ups for a square deal."

The door opened cautiously, and the old janitor stuck his head in. Then, not scenting too much brimstone, he retrieved the wastebasket and trotted hastily away. Miss Christie's pen scratched on. *I'd give my prize possession to escape this next half hour.*

Last night the town had been aroused by fire sirens, and Superintendent

Clint had phoned Miss Christie after midnight. "We've had arson at your school."

"No!" There had been cases of vandalism, but arson—! "A fire? Do any damage?"

"Not much. The night watchman discovered it almost at once."

"But who would set the school on fire?"

Miss Christie hadn't slept a wink.

This morning Superintendent Clint came into her office early. "Well," he said, "we've got the culprit spotted. The night watchman had a good look at him as he ran. But we want conclusive evidence before we crack down."

"It wasn't one of our boys, was it?"

"Yes. Buck Torres."

"Oh, no, not Buck!"

The superintendent said impatiently, "Who else? He's the troublemaker here, a chip off the old block. You can't do anything with riffraff like that."

Miss Christie said, "Was Kerbs sure?"

"Absolutely. The boy has even boasted about it."

"To whom?"

"Jimmy King. Mr. King came in this morning to tell us."

Miss Christie pressed her lips together. The Kings were well-to-do, prominent people, and Jimmy was a little snob and a smart aleck. "Have you spoken to Buck?" she asked.

"They had a dozen boys up for questioning; he was one of them. He clammed up, of course."

Miss Christie thought fast. "Let me talk with him, Mr. Clint."

He frowned. "This is a serious matter. The town is panicked. They've stood enough from that Torres gang. People don't want their children in school with such as him, and they're right. Well, this will end it. I'm relieved to have enough on the boy to send him up."

"Give me one day, Mr. Clint," pleaded Miss Christie.

"It won't change matters. Why put it off?"

"I only want to hear Buck's version, not Jimmy King's."

He stood scowling, remembering that she always begged a second chance for the boys. "Well, all right, all right. One day, no longer. And I'll have to explain this to the chief."

All day Miss Christie had racked her brain. She had prayed. There was nothing one could say for Torres. His father had been killed in a police raid on a hideout. His father's brothers were doing time for burglary. His stepmother, with whom he lived, was a drug addict. What chance had a fourteen-year-old boy who had reached the fourth grade by staying in each class two years and then being moved up via a social pass?

You couldn't make him study or cooperate. Pass his desk and you saw behind the arithmetic or geography a paperback or a sport sheet. Miss Christie always claimed that if a boy took an interest in one thing of merit, he was redeemable, and the hidden books were all on baseball. Once he had organized the little fellows into two teams. Every player had been named for a big-league star. Sauntering near, Miss Christie could hear him giving instructions.

"You there, Nelson Fox, you're covering second. You've caught the ball, get your right foot on the base to put that man out; then whirl and throw to first to get that runner. See—this way." And to her surprise, the slouchy figure moved in a lightning-swift exhibition of skill that was pure grace and sureness. "It's as much the windup as the throw—you're Maglie. . . . Run in, Willie Mays; catch it backhanded. . . . Come on, Duke Snider. Put that ball over the fence. . . . You can't be a pitcher because you're left-handed? So is Joe Nuxhall."

Miss Christie was a little excited. Once, when a boy slid home safely, she clapped. Buck turned to discover her standing there and flashed her a grin, another face shining through the sullen lines of his habitual face. But the parents soon discovered what was going on and snatched their children away from the "bad influence." Buck had withdrawn into himself, reverting to the old don't-care slouch and the sneering responses. He walked to and from school alone, occasionally tangling with some tormentor. She had tried to talk with him about baseball, but had received only muttered replies. He was suspicious of everyone, defiant and distrustful. But that one glimpse of a different look kept haunting her.

"Buck, come here."

He came and stood by the desk, looking straight ahead at the wall.

"Do you know anything about the fire?" Direct as a knife cut.

His eyes flickered. His feet shifted a little, and his shoulders moved. Then, "Naw."

Miss Christie pressed her lips together. "You haven't anything to tell me?"

The feet shifted again. She waited. Her face was stern, but her eyes held compassion. Buck's head came up. For a split second she thought he was going to talk. Then the curtain fell over the pinched features.

"Naw." Defiantly.

Miss Christie sat back in her chair. "Very well, Buck. You may go now."

He was taken by surprise. He had braced himself for a third degree. He must know that she was his one chance. Turning, he slouched across the room to the door. His shoulders sagged, and Miss Christie felt the sting of tears back of her eyes. Buck reached the door and put a hand out to swing it.

Miss Christie spoke more to herself than to him. "I'm sorry," she said, and her voice was weary. "You can't know how sorry. I've believed in you. You did things that troubled me. But there were other things—like helping the little fellows with their baseball team—I liked that. Well . . . ," she said, dismissing him.

He stood with his hand on the half-opened door, and Miss Christie went back to her reports.

He turned. She could scarcely believe it. He was coming back! Miss Christie didn't look up until he had been standing by her desk a little while. Then she raised her head and spoke gently: "Just the truth, Buck."

His voice was low and halting. "Jimmy King is always riding me about my old man and bragging about his dad's war medals and bravery. He'd tell me who all his ancestors were and what they did. He says George Washington was his great-great-great-granduncle, and who was mine, and I said Paul Revere. He said, 'Oh, yeah? Let's see you prove it. I bet you won't put a lantern in that tower at midnight.' We were on the bridge they're fixing near the school, and we both looked at the lanterns that would be lit at night, and I said, 'Okay. You come back at midnight, and I'll show you.' So he came. I picked up one of those lanterns and went in through a basement window and ran up to the tower. I'd meant to wave it at him and bring it back, but he's slippery. He'd say he didn't see it. So I looked around for something to set it on, and there wasn't anything up there but stacks of old papers as high as a man's head. I put the lantern up on a stack of papers and ran down right quick, and I said, 'You see it, don't you?' And he said, 'Ha, I got you! Paul Revere didn't put a lantern in a tower; he watched for it. You didn't even know. That proves you're a liar.' I was going to paste him one when he began jumping up and down and saying, 'Now you've set the schoolhouse afire!' And I looked, and the lantern must have turned over. The papers were blazing up. I started running back, and here come old Kerbs. So I scampered. I never meant to set anything on fire, Miss Christie. I was gonna put the lantern back where I found it. But won't anybody believe that."

"I believe it, Buck," she said. "I don't know just what I can do, but I'm going to work mighty hard. You see, it will be your word against the way you've been acting. Not what your father did. What he did can't really hurt you. Only you can hurt yourself. But I'm staying with you, and you've got to stay with me—not let me down."

He had no graces of expression, and he could only stand there, head bent, fighting for control.

She said, "You go along home now."

"Yes, ma'am," he said humbly.

With the closing of the door, her sense of relief vanished into a gray fog of hopelessness. Buck might think that because she was principal here, her word would carry weight, but Miss Christie knew better. It might even go against him. They called it Miss Christie's weakness. She always took up for the bad boys. Superintendent Clint had said she mothered them; a stern hand was what they needed. He had been emphasizing this recently. Miss Christie knew what he meant. She was getting old. Was he right? Did she handle them too hastily? Easily? She thought not. Make too much of a child's fault, and you implant that fault in his character.

Sitting here in the empty, silent building, her thoughts went back, in an effort to gain from the past some course of action for the present. The years seemed to file through Miss Christie's heart in a troubled line of boys, of smoldering glances, sullen lips, shuffling feet, going out from here through this very door. To what? She had worked hard over them, but had it helped? Had it given them the chances they needed?

One case came back. She had been young then. Among her third-graders was an incorrigible Teddy Reynolds. When he got completely out of hand one day, she sent him to the principal with a note.

At recess she went down the hall to the principal's office. Opening the door, she stood shocked and horrified. Teddy cowered in a corner, a small bundle of quivering flesh. Above him, with a ruler in his hand, stood the principal, his face almost beyond recognition. He had lost complete control of himself.

"Miss Emerson," he said in a voice shaken with rage, "he fought me like a tiger, cursed me. He's a little devil, and I tried to kill him."

Oh, heavens, you almost have! The child has had a terrible beating!

"If he ever lifts a finger, bats an eye, send him back," the principal continued angrily. "The next time, I'll finish him." He scarcely knew what he was saying.

She was as sorry for the principal as she was for the boy, because normally he was an even-tempered man. Teddy must have given him a rough time. She left the room, sick at heart. Teddy was back in his place that afternoon, trying to hide his swollen face.

When the closing gong sounded, Miss Christie said, "Now, I've written something in this little book, and I want you to read it and think about it. Don't sign it unless you feel you can keep it."

She handed him a small black notebook in which she had written: "I, Teddy Reynolds, on my word of honor as a gentleman, do promise Miss Emerson that I will try to obey the rules of the school."

After a time, the little book was shoved across the desk. Teddy Reynolds had signed his word of honor.

Afterward, if ever he got obstreperous, she had only to show him the little black book and catch his eye and smile. He stuck to his agreement, finished school, worked his way through college, and graduated with honors. And he had built a career in this town on his word of honor. It wasn't that Miss Christie had given it to him. She had only pointed out to him what he already had. You can bring out the devil in a child or his word of honor.

But what chance had this one misguided boy when the whole world is against him?

Again the door opened, and the old janitor, troubled, said, "Miss Emerson, you goin' to sit here all night?"

She looked up, surprised that the room was growing shadowy. "No, John, I'm going now."

The eight-block walk home seemed extra long tonight. Every footfall was heavy. Fireflies filled the soft April dusk, and somebody was broiling a steak. Miss Christie wished she had a steak, but she was too tired to fix more than a pot of tea and a sandwich. When she had finished her second cup, she went to the phone and called Jerry Fisher, young editor of the Latimer *Clarion.* Jerry had a crusading spot somewhere in his makeup, but he was down-to-earth, too.

"Jerry, can you drive out here tonight?"

"Funny thing is, I was practically on my way there. I want to talk to you."

Half an hour later, she heard his car on the drive. "Well," said Jerry from the stoop, "there you sit brooding." He had been a handsome boy when she taught him, and he still was.

"Jerry, I've got trouble."

He shot his finger at her. "It's no good, Miss Christie. We're better off without any embryo hoodlum. This town has really suffered from the Torres family, and personally I dread having another one grow up here. Already turning into a firebug. We're not safe."

"I've heard that a good many times in the past forty-three years about one boy or another. The town's still here."

"What I'm concerned with is you." He picked up a chair, turned it backward, straddled it, and eyed her solemnly. She wasn't a woman to quibble with. "They're gunning for you."

"Don't I know—"

"Well, then drop it. Let the authorities take over."

Miss Christie sat and considered. She was sixty-four—almost at retirement age, unless she chose to go on. During the next few years, there would be other boys who would need her, if she stayed. Why throw away the needs of many for the need of one? But this boy . . . She looked at Jerry and shook her head. "Are you siding with them, Jerry?"

"I'm just thinking of you. You'd feel pretty bad if they fired you."

"I'd feel worse if they sent Buck to Gatesville. Look, Jerry, are there records in your office or in the police files about the Torres clan? I don't mean their criminal life, but family history."

"I can find out tomorrow."

"Do it tonight. I only have until tomorrow. One thing more: I want you to take me down where Buck lives."

"That's no part of town for a lady."

"I've got you with me."

He stood up and paced the floor. "Have they phoned you tonight, the school board?"

"No."

"They're having a called meeting tomorrow morning. They say you're too easy on incorrigibles. They've got their eye on a man."

"Oh, no." Latimer Grammar was her school. She'd helped build the big, new brick building in place of the old wooden one. Campaigned to get it sodded and equipped with an ice-water fountain, gymnasium, and playground apparatus. Fought every year for something new and needed.

Jerry was waiting, hands in pockets, troubled eyes on her. He'd hated to be the one to bring her this piece of news.

She looked up. "I can't drop it, Jerry."

"All right. Come on."

Step out under the stars. Sounds of distant music, lit windows, couples strolling, the happy shouts of children. Ordered, safe, and beautiful. God's world. A mile or so farther, a narrow dark alley, a stench from uncollected garbage, wooden shacks flush with the walk. Where are the stars now? This, too, is God's world.

"Do you know the house, Jerry?"

"Yes." And soon: "This is it."

They stopped. The place was totally dark.

"What d'you want?" a voice said almost at their elbow—a woman's voice, thick-tongued, drugged.

"Looking for Buck," said Jerry.

"He ain't here. Never here nights. Stays in that pool hall." The voice grew whiney. "Now, don't you take Buck away. He's all I got to do for me."

They turned and walked back to the car.

Miss Christie said, "Go into every pool hall till you find him. See what he's up to."

"And leave you in the car alone?"

"I'll be all right."

Jerry was back in ten minutes. "Found him. He's glued to the radio, listening to the Giants-Dodgers game."

Miss Christie had what she wanted.

"Now, you phone me later tonight, Jerry; no matter when," she admonished at parting.

"I'll do it."

* * *

For years, life may go along with scarcely a ripple of change in the ordered routine of duties, work, and pleasure. Then there comes a corner. Miss Christie had reached that corner today. She tried to pretend to herself that it was no more than many other crises in her forty-three years of teaching, but she knew better. She was old now. New methods had been established in other schools, and mostly she had stuck to the old ways. The world moves on. She drank her coffee, ate a little breakfast, and put on her best navy silk suit and a soft white blouse. She fluffed her hair about her temples. People are more likely to agree with you if you are not unpleasing to look at. Good of Jerry to tip her off about this called meeting.

The school secretary was already in the office when Miss Christie arrived. "Oh, hello, Miss Christie. You look spruce. They're having a meeting at nine-thirty in the superintendent's office. They want you."

"Thanks, Jenny."

At nine-thirty Miss Christie rose and walked down the hall to the super-intendent's office, her heart pounding a little. She paused, her hand on the doorknob, feeling abruptly alone. Then she got the smile back on her face and went in.

The door opening startled a discussion that hushed away into almost embarrassed silence at her entrance. Seven men sat about the big table—six board members and Superintendent Clint. The chairman of the board was the town's banker. He sat at the head of the table, a serious middle-aged man with a poker face. To either side of him were Superintendent Clint and the owner of the big textile mills, Richard Martin. Then Sid Seymore, a merchant; Olen Merriweather, president of the city council; Jake Bevins, a lawyer; and the board's newest member, young Dr. Henderson.

Miss Christie mentally reviewed them. The banker would be difficult; he stood for the right as he saw it. Rich Martin headed the Rotary Club— a go-getter, genial and friendly. Sid Seymore would be with the banker. Olen Merriweather was a hard nut to crack, and Jake Bevins could be stubborn as an old field mule. Dr. Henderson, young and malleable, was her one hope. You have to be pretty old or else pretty young to understand life.

There was a chorus of good mornings, and Miss Christie sat down. The seven looked at her with a sort of helpless chagrin, the way men look at a woman when they know she's going to disagree with them.

The superintendent said, "This is an emergency meeting, Miss Christie, because this problem can't wait. If the boy is guilty—and I think we're all pretty well satisfied on that score—we want to turn him over to the juvenile authorities this morning. The town is seething with uneasiness, and they don't want him loose tonight. I suppose you didn't get anything out of him?"

"Yes," said Miss Christie, "I did. He told me the whole thing."

"Admitted it?" asked the banker, leaning forward.

"Well, yes."

Everyone sat back. Superintendent Clint sighed with relief. "A confession simplifies everything."

Miss Christie said, "That depends on what you call a confession, Mr. Clint. He told me what happened. Did it ever occur to you that Mr. King, who came to you with the tale, might be covering up for his own son?"

A smile went around the table. The Kings against this Torres brat? Superintendent Clint said, "The night watchman saw him."

"Yes, Buck put the lantern in the tower, but he didn't mean to set the school on fire." Leaning forward, she told them Buck's story. Then she said, "If one boy is culpable, why aren't both of them?"

The lawyer, Bevins, raised a skeptical eyebrow; Richard Martin smiled amusedly; the banker looked at her from behind his business face; Dr. Henderson sat back in his chair, eyes narrowed thoughtfully. Not one of them believed Buck's story.

Then Superintendent Clint said, "Of course, he'd make up something like that—trying to shift the blame. He isn't noted for veracity, is he? The boys know you're too softhearted and you'll always take their part. It's got to where they can pull off anything in your school, Miss Christie, and hide behind your skirts."

Sid Seymore spoke up. "We've talked with him—talked at him, and there's nothing there. The boy comes from low stock, steeped in crime from the cradle. Actually, all of us here are to blame for what occurred and what it might have grown into, because we've already overlooked so much other vandalism. We couldn't pin it on him before, but now we have something he can't squirm out of. I really don't see how you can say one word in his defense, Miss Christie. He set this building on fire!" His fist came down.

Miss Christie had the disadvantage of always seeing both sides. She saw her side now, and she knew they were thinking, *We're always making concessions to Miss Christie, and it simply can't go on.*

"Ever look in his face?" asked Olen Merriweather. "At that sneer?"

"He's defending himself the only way he knows how. What any boy needs is someone on his side. Do a wrong to a boy and he grows bitter, resentful; you make a criminal out of him. He's confessed his part, and we ought to give him a second chance."

"A chance to burn up another school?" Superintendent Clint exploded. "I want to go to sleep tonight knowing that the town is safe. Safe from that Torres gang."

"Yes, I agree we ought to do something about it," said Miss Christie with spirit. "We ought to have a playground in this town with equipment, baseball teams, swimming pool, tennis courts. How much does it cost to keep a boy in the reformatory for a year? Fifteen hundred dollars. How much better if that money could be spent to keep the boys busy and occupied; develop their natural faculties. This boy is not a bad boy. I've had considerable experience, and I know good material when I see it. Buck Torres is good material. He could be valuable. I've watched him for two years, and I like what I've seen. He fights because the boys tease him. He takes care of that old woman out there, and he spends his evenings in the pool hall, where he can listen to the baseball games. You say he's a Torres. Well, Jerry Fisher looked the Torreses up last night. Torres was not Buck's father."

She saw Dr. Henderson nod slightly, but her words glanced off the rest of them without even a dent. They had come there with their minds made up, agreed among themselves that they had let Miss Christie bulldoze them too long.

The bank president spoke. "Miss Christie, we appreciate your kind heart and your unfailing interest in the boys. But none of us is right all the time. And you aren't. It's taking chances not to lock this boy up—put him in a place where he'll learn respect for the property and rights of others. When he comes out—and if he goes straight—he can live a normal, useful life and get a good job."

"In your bank?" asked Miss Christie. "Will you give him a job in your bank?"

The banker smiled. "Not by a long shot!" But he sobered quickly. "We've got a hard year ahead. The railroad is moving in twenty-five new families. Mixed nationalities. Some look pretty tough. Their kids will go to Latimer School. They'll be too much for you. Too much for any woman." He spoke kindly, but it had to be said. "You've carried the burden long enough. You've done wonderfully. All of us appreciate that. But now we need a man."

The room was very still—a rather uncomfortable stillness, touched with relief. This was out in the open. Miss Christie was fired.

For just a moment she seemed to grow smaller, sitting there in the navy silk worn to impress them. After all her years of effort and labor, she wished the end might have been otherwise. Not eulogies, but honest regret and appreciation. "I'm sorry you're going. Good luck, Miss Christie." She had brought it on herself, of course. Miss Christie stood up. She had entered the room as employed by the city fathers. But now everything was changed. She was no longer beholden to anybody. She was free. And her freedom gave her a long perspective—a sense of distance. She looked down the table at them, and abruptly they were not the town's leading citizens, but boys in school at various ages and in different years. She lifted her shoulders and held her head high. That old glint of steel came into her eyes. It made Miss Christie look taller.

"You don't need me at this meeting any longer, but before I go I want to ask you a question. Did any of you ever do anything when you were boys that might have turned into tragedy if someone hadn't taken your part? Think back. Every one of you." She pointed a finger at Richard Martin. "Rich," said Miss Christie sternly in her well-remembered schoolteacher voice, "what about those broken windowpanes? Was that a high-spirited prank or vandalism?" The finger moved to Lawyer Bevins. "Jake, who was it climbed the flagpole and took down the town's expensive new silk flag and hid it?"

His face turned red, but no one saw. Miss Christie had moved on to Merriweather. "Olen, a stolen car is something to laugh about now, but it might have been called plain theft. . . . Sid, who was it picked up a stone and threw it, and hit the principal on the arm? Just a small-boy dare, and the principal knew it was and tossed the little pebble back. But it could have been called assault." She looked at the bank president. "Reynolds, was there a time when you needed—not a strong arm, you had that—but somebody to understand, to believe in you?"

He sat transfixed.

"Just remember," said Miss Christie, "that what you do here in the next hour will save a boy or make a criminal."

She turned and started toward the door. But before she reached it, there was a hurried step, then a hand was on her arm. "Wait, Miss Christie." It was the bank president. "You're right. We forget. There's something that is ageless. You've got it, and we need it here in this school. We need you," he said gruffly. "That recreation center—I'll make it a personal gift to the town."

Chairs scraped and through a blur she saw them surge toward her, but the young doctor got there first.

* * *

Miss Christie was at her desk, working on reports. The building was quiet. The last boy had gone. The last but one. He sat on a chair against the wall, awaiting the verdict.

Miss Christie looked up. "Buck, come here." She was smiling.

He shuffled over, stood dejectedly; his pale face a degree whiter, the dingy cap twirling between unsteady hands.

"It's all right, Buck. They're going to take your word—to trust you. Jimmy King was sorry he got you into all this trouble. He came in with his father, and they talked to the school board about it. I think he'll be your friend now, Buck."

Too astonished to comprehend, he widened his eyes as they met hers. And back of the astonishment she saw a wonderful thing bloom on a scared boy's face: hope.

Miss Christie fought a battle with a stubborn lump in her throat and won. "I have something else to tell you. I've been investigating, and we found that Jacques Torres was not your father. He took you when you were a baby. Well, that relieves you from any responsibility to his wife. Buck," she said briskly, "do you think you could build a shed—a room on the back of my house? I want to get a power mower and other garden tools so you can keep the yard pretty. We can enclose the screen porch for a room for you."

His face underwent a series of changes as each surprising sentence opened a new facet of life.

"You mean—?" He swallowed. "You mean I'm to live at your place?"

"At *our* place. You're to be my boy," said Miss Christie proudly. "I've had it in mind a long time, Buck. I need somebody. I'm not so young as I was."

She could see the muscles along his jaw jerk. His eyes were swimming, but they met hers squarely. And something passed between them so bright, so dazzling, that for a moment it seemed to light the room, and the town, and the whole world.

Then Buck spoke. His voice was gruff, but this time it had a ring: "Yes, ma'am!"

Old Mount Gilead

Harry Harrison Kroll

Old Mount Gilead was just a cluster of old logs. Famous preachers had sat on its benches and preached to its congregations. And now it would become a service station?

Joshua Kleve picked his way among the debris of the gleaming white concrete bridge, thence for a short distance along the paving of the new Nashville-Knoxville Highway, and turned up the rise. In the glow of twilight, he entered the grounds of the old Mount Gilead Church.

His approach sent a nocturnal bird out of the wild tangle of undergrowth, the creature winging across the dim opening into the dense beech timber. The burial ground was a disordered array of undisciplined vines and briars, all forming a black mass in the decline of day. The church itself loomed black and square against the Cumberland Mountains. Stars came out; to the right Joshua could see the faint glow of Sparta, Tennessee.

He stood motionless—a powerful, gentle young man, with dark hair and thoughtful eyes—until night fell completely. He loved the spot with quiet intensity. It was here he had found God at the last revival some years ago to be held at Mount Gilead. To him had come the solemn pride and honor of being the last of thirty preachers this clambering hulk of logs had sent into the world.

Moved by something deeper than mere sentiment, he came to swift resolution: *I'm going to see Eli Taylor and try to get together with him on doing something about saving the old building.*

He returned to the highway, not yet open to traffic, walked through the cut, and emerged a short distance onward at young Taylor's gate. The Taylor lands and Kleve tract cornered at Mount Gilead. With modernity coming in the shape of a highway, the Taylors were remodeling their log house, having weatherboarded and painted it. Joshua called at the gate after the manner of mountain tradition: "Halloooo!"

Someone came out on the porch. "Hello yourself!" It was Eli.

Joshua entered somewhat hesitantly, for since he and Eli Taylor had had some words about the church several weeks ago, a definite coolness existed between them. He was cordial, nevertheless, when he said, mounting the steps, "Howdy, Eli."

"Ah, it's you," said Eli. His voice was flat. "Come—come in."

"I've just come by old Mount Gilead," said Joshua, after shaking Eli's unresponsive hand. He took the chair Eli pushed at him, while Eli dropped onto the porch swing. "I . . . I just can't see that old building torn down, Eli. It means too much to me. Isn't there some way you and I can get together—"

"What do you mean, get together?" asked Eli. "You mean you'll buy my right in the corner? Well enough you know the ground was given years ago by my father—"

"My daddy also gave part of the land, Eli," Joshua reminded him.

"Have you," asked Eli Taylor evenly, "found any evidence of that in writing? Any paper, or legal document—anything like that?"

"N-no." Joshua shook his head. "I thought there was one. I know there should be something of the sort; but I've not been able to find it since we had our . . . our talk—"

"Well," stated Eli determinedly, his voice carrying an overtone of anger, "I have such a paper, written in my father's hand, and the paper clearly reads that the land was granted for the use of religious purposes. When the land was no longer used for church grounds, it was to revert to our property. I'm a practical person, Joshua. The land is mine. I propose to put up a filling station and lunch stand, now that the new highway is about to be opened, and that's the end of the matter. I'm going to rip that old trap down and sell the cedar logs to a cedar mill at Murfreesboro, just as soon as crops are laid by." His voice at the end was hard.

For a moment, Joshua breathed heavily. He felt anger welling up inside of him. He wanted to ask how it happened that his own land lines, properly recorded in the county records, cut the Mount Gilead plot in half. He controlled himself, well aware any further argument would only end in open enmity. "Would . . . would you let me see that paper, Eli?" he asked quietly.

"Certainly not! I have it; in due time I shall see that it is entered on the records at the recorder's office. Plenty of time for you to read it there. That's all I've got to say on the subject!"

Thus dismissed, Joshua rose, saying in a restrained voice, "W-well, Eli, I'm sorry. Of course, I can't go without saying that I firmly believe I have an equal right to that property with you, and I shall try to establish that right."

"Go ahead!" Young Taylor laughed harshly. "I'm not preventing you!"

Joshua departed, walking fast under the stars. Once or twice he passed a slow, groping hand across his face. He had never felt exactly like this before, and he did not like his emotional revulsion against a neighbor. He mused, walking more slowly as he passed the old church, that Eli Taylor evidently felt sure of his ground; he seemed convinced Joshua's father had reserved no written evidence of the gift. Whether a lawsuit would do any good was a question. At any rate, a lawing row was the last thing Joshua desired. The best such a thing would accomplish would be a division of the land and logs; to Joshua it would be a sacrilege.

Reaching home again, he went in at the old double dwelling where he lived and entered the dark hallway. In the living room, he lit a lamp. The house had been wired for electricity from the new power line across the mountains, but the meter had not as yet been installed. In the far corner of the wide, low room, he searched through his father's papers in an ancient walnut secretary, but it was the old story: In the deeds, letters, faded receipts, and other crumbling bits, he found no paper that read somewhat as Eli said his did.

For a time he stood in the dim light, absently drumming with his fingers. Thirty men of God had gone from old Mount Gilead to labor according to their lights in the vineyard. Some were sorry preachers, to be sure; most were good; a few had become great. Perhaps Joshua himself was the least among them. The thought of seeing the inanimate stack of logs that had made this contribution being turned into a filling station and lunch stand filled him with a kind of dumb horror.

Impulsively grasping the lamp, Joshua went up into the attic, where plunder had accumulated over the years. He began a systematic search through ancient hair trunks and bales of yellowed papers and magazines; he looked high and low, not only in the attic, but from floor to gable of the entire big house. If he overlooked so much as a crack or cranny, he could not find his oversight. He found no written evidence that his father had given a foot of land to Mount Gilead. It was well after midnight when he at last, weary and dejected, gave up his search. Only the most vague plans suggested themselves to his mind.

Looks like the only thing is a lawsuit. That would be a sorry kind of soft answer to turn away wrath. Abruptly he squared his strong shoulders, and his habitually mild face assumed a stern determination.

After all, he told himself, *the law is man's tool for securing right and justice. If it were for myself, I'd let it go. But somehow there is a beautiful principle involved. One thing is certain: There can be no virtue in letting Eli Taylor, because he has the nerve to do it, get away with a thing like this.* That was as far as his resolution formed itself at this juncture. He went to bed, alone in the dwelling of his fathers.

At dawn Joshua was up, and after cooking his breakfast, he went through the sunrise to the barn to harness the mules for cultivating. As he worked slowly, it came to him why old rural churches like Mount Gilead made the greatest contributions to the ministry.

It was because he had the feeling the earth teaches a person intimate knowledge of God; and the rise and fall of the seasons, the going and coming of the birds, the patience one learns between the plow handles, and the high faith that breaking and seeding and cultivating give one against an uncertain harvest yield tolerance and understanding of life and its uncertainties.

He finished working about eleven o'clock, took out the team, and went to the house. He ate dinner, took a bath, and put on fresh overalls and a jumper. Afterward he walked down the highway to Squire Leathers'. He entered the dingy office next to the general store at the crossroads.

"Howdy, Joshua," the magistrate said with a nod.

"Howdy, Squire." Joshua dropped onto a hide-bottomed chair. "I came for a little talk about the Mount Gilead Church plot. Eli Taylor says he has a paper, in his father's hand, that the land was given for religious purposes, and as soon as the plot is no longer used, it will revert to the Taylor place."

The old man nodded his shaggy head. "Yes; in lots of cases that was the custom."

"I should have such a paper from my father, but I can't find it."

"You trying to head in with Eli to get the land and them there logs to sell to the cedar mill?"

"No, I'm not, Squire. What I'm after is, if I can, to preserve the old church as a kind of shrine and not let it be torn down to become a filling station and lunch stand. Not that there is anything wrong about filling stations and stands. But to rip down the old church—" He shook his head. "I just can't abide the idea!"

"I see," said Squire Leathers. "Well, what you aim to do?"

"What *can* I do, Squire? I came here to talk it over with you. I don't want any trouble over it. But half that land was my dad's. That can be established from the records."

"Yes; I know in reason the land lines split the church tract. But all you could do in law would be to get half the plot and half the logs and knock Eli out of his project."

"I don't want a lawsuit. I don't want to knock Eli out of anything." Joshua laughed briefly. "I reckon I'm sentimental, but I want to establish a shrine. Let me tell you what I have in mind, and see if you think it would be legal and according to the law books." He began to talk, and after an hour old Squire Leathers laughed and nodded.

"If you haven't waited too long, according to this paper Eli claims to have—and which would stand in a court of law, I take it—you maybe, Joshua, could do it."

During the swiftly passing summer days, while Joshua perfected his plans, young Eli Taylor was not sitting still. He took his paper to a lawyer in Sparta, and the lawyer gave it as his opinion that it was conclusive evidence in Eli's favor. The land would revert to the original Taylor land. Meanwhile the highway was opened to traffic, and gleaming cars shot both ways along the smooth concrete. Houses up and down the new road that had known only candles and oil lamps were now brilliant by night with electric lights.

Finally dawned the Sabbath day that Joshua had set for a time of meeting at Mount Gilead. Mostly with his own hands he had chopped and burned the brush and briars so people could get into the building without tearing their clothes. He swept and dusted the brown room and old benches. He made the whole place as comfortable and inviting as possible. Since there was no way of keeping his method secret, even had he desired to, Eli was well aware of what was going on. He came once and glowered. With the coming of Sunday morning, he was one of the first to arrive on the grounds.

Though a young preacher, and a trifle embarrassed by his duties, Joshua Kleve was on hand to welcome those who might come, and he shook hands with Eli. It was only a few minutes before nearby people began appearing. Soon cars began arriving. A few were small, but many were big cars. Groups strolled about or stood talking and laughing. Joshua watched with a vague tightening at his heart. He saw people walk slowly to the burial grounds, and though he could not remember them, he was aware they looked again on the graves of loved ones. They were folks who had gone out of the mountains to Nashville, Knoxville, Sparta, Murfreesboro, and other towns and taken up their abode and who had not for years made a visit back here. That was the chief part of his scheme: to have a big homecoming to old Mount Gilead.

The cars thickened. A few big, costly cars drove up. Out of one of these a well-dressed, handsome man of perhaps fifty stepped, and with him came his family: an equally handsome wife; a slim, beautiful girl; and a young man, evidently the son. They came up to the church steps. The gentleman shook Joshua's hand cordially when Joshua made himself known to him.

"Well, well, so you are old Mark Kleve's boy!"

"Yes, sir," Joshua said, nodding.

"This is my wife, Sarah Hardison; my daughter, Ruth; my son, Edward. And I am Tolliver Hardison himself, your pa's old boyhood friend. Well, Joshua, we are happy indeed to come here today. I got religion here, did you know that?" He turned with a smile to his wife. "Sarah and I both did, one camp meeting a long time back. And, I might confess, we got each other here. The place has changed a lot in some ways." He looked about. "Yet it's oddly the same. It's like a very old and beloved friend."

Joshua ushered Tolliver Hardison and his family to chairs he had arranged up front for them, and also to accommodate the ministers that Mount Gilead had sent forth into the world. That is, those who yet lived and were within reach. Seven or eight old men were already seated, and Joshua introduced them all around. He seated himself beside Mr. Hardison, who was one of the state's most important lawyers, now living in Nashville.

Tolliver Hardison said in a low voice, "Your letter only partly informed me of your exact situation here. You wish to preserve the old church as a shrine, that was clear. You said this young Taylor has a paper of some sort—duplicate, I assume—but you have not. Nevertheless, your land lines, from recorded deeds, would undoubtedly hold half the property to you. If the Taylors can take their share back, you can recover yours."

"That's not what I wish," said Joshua.

"I understand that. You want to establish a shrine; your neighbor would put up a filling station and lunch stand. Legally, you could fight it out, and the end would be simply that neither of you could carry out your purpose. That's all a fight would do for you."

"That's all fights ever do—" began Joshua Kleve. He was interrupted by the appearance of a gray-haired, bent man walking with a crutch. He rose to welcome the newcomer.

"You don't know me, young feller!" said the old preacher. "Well, I'm one of the thirty that God has spared in the land. I'm right glad to come back to where I first knew my Lord and Jesus. Are these the other old-timers?"

More handshaking followed. Joshua, mingling with the folks that now quickly filled the church, was forced to postpone further talk with Tolliver Hardison.

It was only a short while before the hour of service. The old organ that had served for forty years pealed forth a mellow note. Back of the pulpit Joshua had seated the sixteen ministers Mount Gilead had contributed to the world, who were living and could come here. The room was crowded when the young preacher rose to read the Scriptures. The old cedar logs seemed still to echo with the singing of the hymn, in which cultured voices mingled with the vigorous if crude singing of the hill folk. Perhaps Eli Taylor, standing near the window, was the only one who did not sing, a curious look on his motionless features.

Then began the preaching services. Joshua had it carefully planned. One by one the preachers rose. Three minutes had been assigned to each for his brief word. Some took perhaps a moment longer, but many of the very aged could only stand and say some choking word while tears filled their old eyes. Altogether it was a unique service, such as no dilapidated church had ever known. At the end, the organ pealed its melody; the people sang and, after the benediction, moved slowly out for the dinner to be spread under the trees.

Joshua rejoined the Hardison family, and he felt the soft eyes of Ruth Hardison. Ruth filled paper plates and brought food to her family. Tolliver Hardison nodded to her: "Bring another plate." To Joshua, he said, "Can you look up this young man Eli Taylor and fetch him here?"

Joshua found Eli and brought him back, though Eli came reluctantly. They all sat in the shade under the beech trees, Ruth near the young men.

As they ate, Mr. Hardison said quietly, "If I were you young men, I'd get together without further word on this matter. Mr. Taylor, I doubt if you can carry out your project. The land was given for religious purposes. Well, technically, Joshua Kleve here could hold services the day before you had a lawsuit and, by keeping that up, satisfy the legal requirements, and you could never possess the grounds, assuming *all* the land was granted by your father, which Joshua denies. Now, the spot is beautiful. It may be 100 years, or 200, or 500, before a pioneer church like this would come to its full historic value. But it is worth preserving, and filling-station sites are so numerous that 1,000 of them could be found in ten miles. Now, I've been thinking: I'd like to establish a small fund that would yield sufficient income to keep the building and grounds up. I have a streak of sentiment in me, too. Such a fund would prevent any reversion of the property, I take it, especially if occasional services, at regular intervals, were established. Now, you young men reach over there and shake hands on this, and get the matter settled."

For a moment Eli Taylor seemed torn in his soul. Joshua said, pointing across the road at a level spot, "That is part of my dad's land, now mine. I'll turn that over to you for your filling station. You give me, in return, your equity in old Mount Gilead."

"That's a fair exchange," said Mr. Hardison.

Joshua waited. Ruth smiled softly at him. Her eyes were very blue and tender. Abruptly Eli Taylor's hand went forth. There, in the summer shade, the two young fellows shook hands, and Mount Gilead was returned permanently to its memories, a workman that need not be ashamed of its contribution.

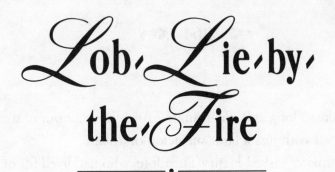

Lob·Lie·by· the·Fire

Elizabeth Goudge

Though forbidden to buy anything animate with their fifteen shillings, Oliver and Jane felt they had no choice. But then, before they could take him home to face the music, Lob took them on a journey to they knew not where.

"You can buy what you like," said their mother, "but it must *not* be another dog."

"A canary?" asked Jane.

"No," said their mother.

"Rabbits are decent little beggars, don't you think?" suggested Oliver tentatively.

"Running wild in the woods, yes," said their mother. "As domestic pets, no."

"Pussycat?" whispered Henry Theodore.

"Nothing alive," said Mrs. Murray. "Nothing that can run up a bill at the vet or have kittens in my wardrobe. Nothing that has fleas or lays eggs. Get a croquet set, darlings, or an Indian outfit. Get anything you like so long as it's inanimate." And she went out of the room and shut the door with just a faint suspicion of a slam.

"What's inanimate?" asked Henry Theodore, who had lived for only five years in this world and knew only the really important words in the English language, words such as "dog," "pussycat," "bunny," "bird," "dinner," "bath," and "mother." With these, shouted loudly, he had hitherto been able to satisfy his wants. But now, for the first time, his simple request for a pussycat was denied him. It might be that presently "food" and "drink" would fail him. The foundations of his world shook. He wept.

"Something that doesn't move," shouted Oliver above the din of Henry Theodore's grief. "And who wants that? Uncle George wouldn't have given us fifteen shillings to buy something that won't move. He buys hunters and terriers. All sensible people do. And look at Father. When he was in India, he spent his last penny on polo ponies."

Jane heaved a little sigh. "Mother says that's why we had to sell Whiteways and come here. So you can't blame her if she's tired of animals."

"Here" was a very ugly little modern villa in a very ugly south-coast town. They had taken it for the summer holidays while they looked about them and faced the situation. Whiteways was in Scotland, and it had belonged to the children's grandfather and to his father before him. The Murrays, father and children, loved it so deeply that when they had to leave it, they fled right down to the south of England to find another home. They wanted the break between the old and the new life to be utter and complete. Mrs. Murray, who was not Highland-born, was secretly influenced by an unworthy hankering for a modern house, complete with every modern convenience, in a modern town. For at Whiteways, Mrs. Murray had had enough of servant problems and lack of modern conveniences to last a lifetime.

It was all very difficult. "If only we *had* to live somewhere," Mrs. Murray had cried, "it would be so much easier. If we could be as restricted geographically as we are financially, then it would be quite easy."

She had spoken a little bitterly. Major Murray, the children's father, who had expected a life endlessly full of shooting and fishing when he left the army, had gone out to the backyard to smoke his pipe. The children had chosen this unfortunate moment to suggest to their mother that they should buy a dog with their fifteen shillings.

"I suppose we must spend this fifteen shillings on something," said Oliver gloomily. "But what?"

"Let's go look at the shop windows," said Jane. "Call out to Mother and ask her if we may."

Mrs. Murray said yes, but to take great care of Henry Theodore and to be back for tea; and they started out.

They were nice children, brown and lean, with the unmistakable stamp upon them of a country upbringing. Oliver and Jane walked easily, with long strides, as though there were turf beneath their feet and a wind behind their backs. Henry Theodore, being only five, had not learned to stride yet; he trotted, holding Jane's hand and playing a game with the paving stones, trying to step twice in each and never putting a foot on the cracks. It was with difficulty that he was recalled from it by Jane and Oliver to look in a toy shop window.

"What'll you buy with your five shillings, darling?" Jane was asking him. "Do you like anything there?"

He laid a pudgy finger upon Jane's reflection. It was the only thing in the window he cared for, for it moved and laughed, while all the other things were as dead as dead. He withdrew his gaze from the window and bent it once more upon the pavement. "Doggie!" he shouted suddenly.

"Where?" cried Oliver and Jane.

"Here!" shouted Henry Theodore and pointed at the pavement. And sure enough, there upon the pavement were the faint footprints of a dog's wet paws.

The hunting instinct of all three was immediately aroused. "He must have got wet down on the shore," said Jane. "Look, he crossed the road here. Where's he gone to?"

"Come on," said Oliver.

They tracked the padding paws, the mark of them growing fainter and fainter, down the street and around the corner to a big restaurant where travelers often went in the afternoons to have their teas, and here, outside the door, they found him.

Jane called him Lob on the instant, without knowing why.

He was attached to the person of a seemingly blind man with dark glasses who was selling matches, and he was sitting up on his hind legs in a begging position with a can for pennies hanging around his neck and his forepaws crossed on his chest below it. He was a black spaniel and very old. The coat that must once have been shiny and glossy was dulled and rusty. His long ears drooped wearily, and his eyes were unutterably sad. Yet he never shifted his stiff, uncomfortable position. He did not dare.

The children came to a dead standstill, staring first at him and then at the blind man. They instinctively knew two things about that blind man: first, that he wasn't blind at all, and then, that he mistreated his dog.

"How much is that dog?" Jane asked the blind man.

"Eh?" he cried in astonishment, peering over his glasses to get a better view of her.

"How much is that dog?" repeated Oliver. "We don't want matches, but we want a dog."

"This 'ere dog," said the blind man, "ain't for sale. Why, 'e's my means of livelihood. 'Ow can a blind man get about without a dog?"

The children looked at Lob, and Lob looked at them. His eyes made no complaint and asked for no redress, for hope was dead in him.

"It's surely worth your while," said Jane to the blind man, "to sell an old, sick dog."

Now, the blind man had that very morning been offered a young and amusing mongrel for a mere song and was considering the offer very seriously, but he was a good man of business and he knew how to drive a bargain.

"We will give you five shillings for that dog," said Jane.

The blind man spat contemptuously. "Likely!" he averred. "I'd not part with my old pal for all the money in the world." And he began shouting out, "Matches! Matches, sir! Help the poor blind man!" in a perfect fury of wounded pride and affection.

"Ten shillings!" shouted Oliver above the row he was making.

The blind man shook his head.

"Twelve shillings," said Jane.

"You're wasting my time, you are," said the blind man.

"Fourteen shillings," said Oliver.

The blind man did not even deign to answer.

It was then that Jane showed her feminine guile. "We can't go further than fourteen shillings for that poor, sick old dog," she said, and she marched her brothers off down the street.

"'Ere!" shouted the blind man.

"Yes?" they queried, stopping and looking back over their shoulders.

"I've a good 'eart," said the blind man. "You shall 'ave this beautiful young dog for fifteen shillings. 'Erbert Barker was never one to disappoint kids."

"Done!" said Jane promptly, and coming back, she handed over the whole of their worldly wealth.

"You did that well, Jane," conceded Oliver. "You did that jolly well."

"You backed me up well. It was a good business. Let's get down to the sea and have a good look at him."

It took them some while to get there, for like most spaniels in their old age Lob had, in spite of a starvation diet, become extremely stout, with a back as broad and flat as a table, and he could only waddle along very slowly. But at last they were all four sitting together on a seat on the esplanade.

"What do you suppose," said Oliver, "Mother will say?"

"I don't care what she says," said Jane, blinking savagely. "Lob is ours!"

"Mine!" said Henry Theodore. "I saw his paws."

"Ours!" said Oliver. "We all paid for him."

And at this moment, a bus drew up at the curb beside them and Lob heaved himself up, lunged off the seat, waddled across the esplanade, and scrambled into the bus. And as though it had drawn up there especially for him, the bus immediately moved off.

"Hi, stop!" yelled Oliver.

"After it!" shouted Jane. "Quick! Run!"

Their long limbs and their agility stood them in good stead now. With Henry Theodore gripped between them, Oliver and Jane raced after the bus, which was fast gathering speed, flung their young brother in like a sack of coals, and scrambled in on top of him. Lob, wagging his tail, was sitting very comfortably upon a well-cushioned seat.

"He knows where he's going, I think," said Oliver. "There seems to be a sort of purpose about him."

"What I want to know, if you'll excuse me mentioning it," said the conductor, "is where you kids are going? And where's your money?"

"We don't know where we're going," said Jane sweetly. "Only our dog knows. And we've no money. But I'll give you my father's name and address and you can have my watch as a hostage."

The bus was a small country bus, so perhaps regulations were not very strictly enforced. Perhaps it was just because the conductor had a sense of humor as well as children of his own, but after some consultation between himself and the driver, the four were allowed to stay on the bus, the address having been duly noted down and the watch accepted as hostage.

And they went on into the green country, along quiet roads and through villages of thatched cottages with gardens blazing with asters and golden-rod. The children, throwing all conscientious scruples to the winds, gave themselves up to exquisite enjoyment. They sniffed the cool scents that blew in through the windows and feasted their eyes on the gardens. And Lob dozed, waking up only at the bus stops to signify that no, they hadn't got there yet.

"Seems like it's the terminus he's taking you to," chuckled the conductor.

* * *

"Here we are," said the conductor. "Out you get. And the last bus back is at five; and that's in another half hour, so look lively."

Lob was out already and rolling ecstatically in the short, sweet grass beside the road. Chamomile daisies were growing in the grass, and Lob stretched and wriggled his scarred body upon them with the delight of a returned traveler.

The children's first impression was of a wide, rainbow-colored plain, a vast curve of blue sky, and white wings that soared through depths of clear, unsullied air. There came to them that sense of space and freedom that they had known in the mountains around their home.

This was a little hamlet set among sea marshes. The gold of rice grass lay like a veil over the amethyst of sea asters and sea lavender. Blue channels of seawater meandered through patches of green meadow, where cows sat companionably with resting gulls and plovers. In the distance was a harbor where yachts and fishing boats rode quietly at anchor. From the harbor, a meandering little lane led to a cluster of weathered gray houses, behind them a quiet stretch of green fields and haystacks.

"Why haven't we been here before?" demanded Jane. "One can breathe here."

"Think of the sailing and fishing there'd be," said Oliver.

"Bunnies," announced Henry Theodore and pointed.

It was true. There were rabbits in the marsh—real live rabbits that scuttered their tails in the sunshine. There would be shooting here, too. And it would be a paradise for dogs.

Suddenly, Lob began to pant and choke against his collar, pulling eagerly in the direction of the gray house behind the oak trees.

"He's going somewhere again!" cried Jane. "Come along! Quick!"

Lob was transformed. He who a short while ago had scarcely been able to waddle was now pounding along like a young dog. He led them through a broken iron gate in a beautiful rose-red wall, into a riotous wilderness that might once have been a garden. Roses and honeysuckle had run wild over the stunted oaks, and the paths were moss-grown. But there were still flowers in the beds, starred with butterflies.

Lob was through the garden in a flash and leaping upon the shut front door of a gray, old house. It was the typical eighteenth-century house of a country gentleman with small means. Built of gray weatherworn stone half hidden beneath creepers, it had tall chimneys and casement windows, and the eaves were full of swallows. There was an old horse block beside the door and stables on the right of the house. To the left was a walled kitchen garden with the tops of fruit trees visible. But the door was locked and the windows closed, and when they parted the curtains of Virginia creeper that hung over them, they saw that the rooms inside were empty and desolate.

Meanwhile Lob was continually attacking the door. He leaped upon it, whining pitifully and giving short, sharp, anguished barks; he scratched at it with his paws and snorted beneath it.

"If we don't get the door open, he'll have hydrophobia," stated Jane.

Oliver took off his shoe, smashed a pane of glass in the hall window, unlatched it, and climbed in. In a moment he had the front door open, and Lob shot in as though discharged from a catapult.

The children accompanied him in a wild stampede all over the house.

In spite of the dust and dirt and emptiness, they were vaguely aware of a suggestion of graciousness and dignity about the house, and of that sense of space and freedom they had felt on the marshes outside. The people who had lived here had been people with whom Lob and the children would have been at home.

The children realized that Lob was looking for these people. He went all over the house again, waddling very slowly this time, sniffing and whining softly, his cry a pitiful thread of sound compared with the ecstatic yelps of half an hour ago. The children followed him silently and at a little distance, not liking to intrude upon his grief. Lob had come home, but his home was empty.

But Lob was a dog of sense who through long years of life had learned to accept the inevitable. After a final tour of the upstairs bedrooms, he descended the stairs heavily, sat himself down before the wide, empty grate in the drawing room, and woofed softly and imperatively. It was obvious what he wanted. The autumn evening was growing chilly, and he wanted a fire. He was old and he was bereaved, and these evils he accepted with resignation; but warmth and a cozy fire Lob demanded.

The children flew to obey him. There was wood in plenty in the garden, torn from the trees by storms, baked dry by the sun. Oliver had a box of matches in his pocket, and soon they had a glorious fire with a delicious scent that recalled familiar and comforting things: potatoes baking in the cinders, chestnuts roasting on winter evenings, and the yule log flaming upon the fire at Christmas—smells that one could know only in one's home, the sort of home that has a large garden without and wide hearths within. As this house had.

Suddenly, the children looked at one another. The fire, with the old dog asleep now before it, had made this house home.

"This," said Oliver, "is it."

"There's no question about it," said Jane. "We've got to live here because of

Lob. He likes it here. Mother wanted us to be obliged to live somewhere and now we are." She paused to stroke Lob's silky ears. "And now I know why I called him Lob . . . Lob-Lie-by-the-Fire."

"Who was he?" asked Oliver.

"He was in a fairy story Mother read us once," said Jane. "Don't you remember? He was a fairy person, a 'rough black fellow' who did all the work of the house when its owners weren't looking. He asked no reward except a bowl of cream placed for him on the kitchen floor at sunset and that he might come in from the cold and lie by the fire all night."

Oliver was skeptical. "Our Lob won't do all the work of the house," he assured Jane. "And if Mother feels that she can't get servants in the country, will she be keen on taking this house?"

"She may not be keen," said Jane, "but she'll see that she has to. There's no question about it."

"Absolutely none," agreed Oliver.

"Supper," requested Henry Theodore very suddenly.

He was right. It was time for supper; they had had no tea, and their insides were aching voids.

"The last bus must have gone ages ago," said Jane, and there was a certain urgency in her tone.

"It doesn't matter," said Oliver. "We'll catch the morning one. I'll go out and buy some bread and milk with my wristwatch, and then we'll spend the night here."

"I was just wondering," said Jane, "if Mother and Father will be anxious."

"We can't help it if they are," said Oliver, already at the door. "And anyhow, they've learned by this time that whatever we do, we're always all right." And he went off through the glimmering garden, whistling like a blackbird. He was not really a heartless child, but he was unimaginative and knew nothing of the pains of parenthood.

* * *

It was an exceedingly comfortable party that Major and Mrs. Murray discovered an hour later. From Rosie Bains at the post office, Oliver had purchased with his wristwatch bread and milk, apples, and the rear portion of a cooked fish; and when their irate parents entered upon them they were munching bread and fish, roasting the apples over the fire, and sharing a bowl of milk with a large, very old, and exceedingly dirty black spaniel.

"And what," demanded their father thunderously, "is the meaning of this?"

"Hullo, Father," they said with cheerful imperturbability. "How did you get here?"

"The conductor of that bus," stormed their father, "had the good sense to bring back Jane's wristwatch to the address she gave him. A father himself, he tells me, who knows the meaning of parental anxiety. Which is more than you do, you young—" He stopped, thinking better of it.

"Devils," finished Jane sweetly.

Her father fell heavily onto one of the window seats. Mrs. Murray, with Henry Theodore clasped in her arms, had already fallen onto the other.

"I shall thrash the lot of you," said Major Murray, "in the morning."

His children were unperturbed. This was a threat that was often made but had never, within living memory, been carried out. "Have some fish," they said.

He had some. It was extraordinarily good. "Hullo!" he said. "Caught in these parts?"

"Of course," said Oliver. "The fishing around here is jolly good. Shooting, too. There are no end of rabbits in the marshes. They also told me at the post office that the man who used to live in this house was out shooting every day with his dog. And then he died suddenly, and everything he had was sold by auction, even his dog. Wasn't it a beastly thing to sell a dog by auction?"

"But they couldn't sell the house," chimed in Jane. "It's been empty for years."

"I can quite believe it," said their mother. "Exactly the sort of house that no one in his senses would buy. The whole place is out of repair."

"We bought Lob with Uncle George's fifteen shillings," Jane went on quickly, "and he brought us straight here to his old home. So of course we must live here. It's nice to have the house question settled at last, isn't it? You look awfully white, Mother. Would you like an apple?"

Mrs. Murray tottered over to the fire, dumped Henry Theodore beside it, sank upon the floor beside him, and meekly accepted an apple. Over her weary head there was a steady flow of question and answer between her husband and children. They were telling him how they had come to buy this disreputable dog, who was now lying with his dirty chin propped upon her crossed silken ankles, just as though he and she had always been intimately acquainted.

He was fairly well bred, Major Murray thought. *He had evidently been a good shooting dog and might be again.*

Shooting, fishing. The words occurred again and again. Her husband, Mrs. Murray noted, was growing excited, eager, boyish, and quite unmanageable. He wanted to buy this house, apparently. The children, too, not only wanted it, but for some reason or other were convinced that they simply *had* to buy it. She heard herself feebly trying to protest. But it was no good. She was too tired to argue. She was being submerged. She heard herself saying meekly, "Very well, then, have it your own way," and she closed her eyes in weary submission.

* * *

Giving herself a little shake, Mrs. Murray opened them again and looked about her. The sun had sunk and the sky was a cool, quiet green, with a star caught in the branches of the ilex tree. She caught the white flash of a seagull's wings and remembered that gulls always sleep within sound of the sea. She heard the faint sound of the full tide lapping against the harbor wall; and suddenly she understood how that sound might become utterly necessary to happiness.

She looked back at the room, lit now only by the twilight and the leaping flames of the fire. *The mixture of twilight and firelight is the perfect light,* she thought, *and the one that suits children to perfection, matching their mystery with its own.* Her own were changelings, moving away from her into this new world of wind and water that they had themselves discovered. Her husband too, sitting there in the flickering shadows, looked curiously as if he belonged. They had all four found their home, and if she did not want to lose them, she must follow.

The dog stirred, lifted his chin off her ankles and stretched himself to sleep again with his head pushed against her knee. He seemed, strangely enough, to have taken to her more than he had taken to the children. She stretched out a hand and caressed his wise, domed forehead. She knew that this dog she had not wanted was going to be her ally and her friend in this home to which he had brought her children. When the winter storms raged outside, when the burden of living in so lonely a place weighed heavily upon her, his familiar form lying before the fire would yet make the place her inevitable home.

The Lady with the Lamp

Mary Brownley

The cream of England's fighting men were dying needlessly, due to lack of nursing care and food. It had created a national crisis. But who would take on such an impossible job?

"What can have happened! Look at old Roger! His sheep are scattered all over the hillside, and he seems to be having trouble."

The speaker, a little girl about ten years old mounted on a shaggy pony, pointed to where a flock of sheep were running hither and thither, ignoring the voice of an old shepherd who, with his tall crook in hand, was vainly striving to keep them together.

"Yes, something does seem to be the matter," said the child's companion, an elderly gentleman, evidently a clergyman.

"Shall we ride across and speak with him?"

"Oh, yes! Do let us," was the ready answer.

In a few seconds, the two had ascended the hillside and were within hail of the shepherd, who, worn out, had sunk down on the soft green

277

grass, grumbling aloud, "It is of no use. They must take their own way!"

"Well, Roger, what's wrong with you?" shouted the clergyman.

The old man lifted himself up and, seeing who it was addressing him, rose, touched his cap, and went over to where the riders had stopped their horses.

"Please, sir," he said, "there's no doing anything with them sheep, they be so skittish, the old as well as the young. Just look at 'em!"

"But where's Cap?" asked the little girl.

"Ah! That's just all the mischief, missy. Cap's done for! An' them cunning things, they knows it."

"Cap done for! Do you mean to say he's dead?" exclaimed the clergyman.

"It be pretty much as if he were," answered the old man sadly. "I'd rather he were; then I shouldn't have to do it!"

"Do what, Roger?" asked the child.

"Why, put him out of his misery, missy," he answered sadly.

"Kill Cap? Your dear, good Cap? There's not a better sheep dog on the downs, Roger!" exclaimed the vicar.

"I know it, sir, but he ain't of no more use to me, and we poor folks can't keep useless mouths to feed. I must get another dog. Cap can't work no more."

"Why, a week ago I saw him running after the sheep. What has happened since?"

"Some boys got to throwing stones, and one hit Cap on the leg and smashed it up. He just crawled into the hut, and there he have lain ever since, a-moaning, not able to move, till it makes my heart ache. It would be a kindness to put him out of his pain, and I've made up my mind to do it tonight."

"Oh, Roger, how can you! He may get well still," exclaimed the little girl, her eyes full of tears.

"If he'd been for getting better, he'd have shown signs of mending before now, Miss Florence; and he's worser. Why, his leg were as big well-nigh as my head this morning when I left him."

"I'm sorry for your trouble, Roger. Cap was a good dog, and I'm afraid you'll have some trouble in replacing him," said the vicar.

"I'm afraid so, too, sir. Thank you kindly!" And the old shepherd pulled his forelock. "Good day, missy," he continued, "an' don't you be for vexing yourself over Cap," and he patted the neck of the pony.

"Good-bye, Roger. I'm very sorry," was the gentle answer, and her brown eyes looked sad as she followed her companion down the hillside to regain the high road.

The shepherd watched her for a minute or two; then, as he turned back to his scattered flock, he muttered, "She have a good heart, have Miss Florence, let it be for man or beast."

The little girl and the vicar rode on for some time in silence. At last the latter said, "I wonder whether the dog is as bad as Roger thinks? These country people know so little about doctoring themselves, much less their animals. A stone may have injured the leg, but hardly to the extent of smashing it up, as he seems to say."

"Let's go and see!" cried Florence eagerly. "Roger's cottage is only out yonder." And she pointed to a group of low buildings nestling under the hills.

"We may as well," answered the vicar. "The dog is a valuable animal and very intelligent. I often notice him. It would be a pity to kill him if there were a chance of his recovery."

Once more they turned their horses' heads and rode the lane leading to the cottages.

Florence sprang lightly off her pony and tried the latch to the last cottage in the row. To her dismay, the door was locked. From within came a low, angry bark, followed by a moan of pain.

"Roger's locked him in!" she said as the vicar joined her.

"I'm sorry for that," he answered. "Of course he's taken the key with him. Well, Florence, I'm afraid we must leave poor Cap to his fate!"

At that moment the next cottage door opened, and a woman, with a small boy of about seven half hidden behind her, stepped out. "Roger is out, sir," she said, "but he's after his sheep, and a precious sight of trouble he'll have with Cap's a'dying!"

"He makes noise enough still," said the vicar as the dog continued to bark at intervals. "It's to see Cap we've come, Mrs. Norton, but the door is locked, so our visit was useless."

"Oh," she said, "if it's Cap you want to see, my Jim knows where the key is hid, and he'll take you into the place. Cap won't let no stranger go in, not though he's dying; but he knows Jimmy."

"That's well! Come, Jimmy, my lad; find the key and let us in," said the vicar.

The little chap, who needed no second bidding, opened the door and called out softly, "Cap, Cap, it's all right. They're friends!"

The dog growled and tried to lift himself. The little girl went fearlessly up to where he lay, talking in a soft, caressing tone: "Poor Cap, poor Cap!" It was enough, and he looked up into her face with his plain-speaking brown eyes, now bloodshot and full of pain, but did not resent it when, kneeling down beside him, she stroked with her hand the large, intelligent head.

To the vicar he was less friendly, but after much coaxing he at last allowed him to touch the wounded leg.

"As far as I can tell, there are no broken bones," he said at last, "but the leg is badly bruised. It ought to be fomented, to take the inflammation and swelling down."

"How do you foment?" asked Florence.

"With hot cloths dipped into boiling water," answered the vicar.

"Then that's quite easy. I'll stay here and do it. Now, Jimmy, let's get sticks and make the kettle boil."

There was no hesitation in the child's manner—she was told what ought to be done and set about doing it as a simple matter of course.

"They will be expecting you at home," said the vicar.

"Not if you tell them I am here," answered Florence. "My sister and one of the maids can come and fetch me home in time for tea, and—" She hesitated. "They had better bring some old flannel and cloths; there does not seem to be much here. But you will wait and show me how to foment, won't you?"

"Well, yes," said the vicar, carried away by the quick energy of the little girl.

And soon the fire was lit and the water boiling; an old smock frock of the shepherd's had been discovered in a corner, and Florence had deliberately torn it into pieces. And to the vicar's remark, "What will Roger say?" she answered, "We'll give him another."

And so Florence Nightingale made her first compress and spent the whole of that bright spring day nursing her first patient: a shepherd's dog.

The simple villagers who watched her labor of love little realized that here was one of earth's greatest women in the embryo, and they would not have believed, had some prophet told them, that in years to come men, wounded and dying, far away from home and loved ones, would kiss her shadow as she passed their cots at night.

She was born in Florence, Italy, May 15, 1820, but the Nightingale home was in Derbyshire, England. There she grew to young womanhood, surrounded by all the luxuries that their wealth could provide. But society and a life of ease and pleasure made no appeal to her. There was just one thing in all this world that she wanted to do, and that was to help the sick and suffering. In this course she became even more determined after a visit to the London hospital, where she found dirt and misery and needless suffering among the patients, and drunkenness and ignorance among the nurses. And so she went to Kaiserwerth, a Protestant institution in Germany, for training, there becoming "familiar with all diseases and their treatment."

Returning to London, Miss Nightingale began work in a Home for Sick Governesses and succeeded in transforming the place completely before failing health compelled her return to the family home in Derbyshire.

For forty years England had been at peace with its neighbors, but now war clouds began to gather on the horizon, and in the spring of 1854, the storm of the Crimean War broke over Europe. "For Queen and Country," Great Britain's brave sons went forth to dare, and do, and die, as duty called.

Presently, from the battlefront across the water came a cry for help. Thousands of England's sick and wounded soldiers were dying for want of care. Through mismanagement, supplies had been delayed. Even the commonest necessities—bedding, stretchers, medicines, clothing, soap, towels, suitable food—were lacking or tied up securely in official red tape and "unavailable." There was not a single operating table supplied to the army. Think of it! Doctors worked like Trojans, but they could not care for one-tenth of the sufferers. Nurses were needed—needed desperately!

Florence Nightingale, not quite recovered from her illness, read of these conditions, and her heart was stirred. The letter that she wrote the minister of war, volunteering her services, passed on its way to delivery one from this same official asking her to go to Scutari as leader of a band of nurses.

Six days later she was ready to start, with thirty-eight carefully chosen women and a boatload of supplies. They slipped away from England quietly one October night. Four days later, the great Battle of Balaklava was fought; and as you read Tennyson's "Charge of the Light Brigade," remember that he pictures only one incident of this terrible battle.

Miss Nightingale and her companions arrived at the barracks hospital, which was to be her headquarters, to find conditions even worse than had been described. The hospital itself was a great barnlike place built by the Turks as quarters for soldiers and large enough to take in whole regiments. It lay in the form of a hollow square, each side more than a quarter of a mile in length, and arranged in long corridors, story upon story. At each corner was a tower, and one of these was assigned to the nurses—"The Sisters' Tower," the soldiers christened it.

Everywhere was dirt and filth unspeakable. There was no kitchen worthy of the name, where proper food could be prepared for the sick—if such food were to be had. No laundry! The patients lay in dirt and grime, wrapped for the most part in their army blankets. And the wounded were coming in by the hundreds across the rough, restless waters of the Black Sea, which separated the field of battle from even this poor refuge.

No woman in history has ever been called to face such a test as that before Florence Nightingale. But she met it bravely, calmly. Her orders were given quietly, but with an authority that none dared dispute. Supplies appeared as if by magic, but these were the necessities that this wonderful woman with a genius for leadership had realized would be needed when she selected her cargo before she sailed from England. At once the men had proper food. Within a week, a respectable kitchen was in running order, a laundry was functioning, and so strenuous a "cleanup" campaign had been undertaken that vermin departed posthaste for safer quarters.

But the lady-in-chief knew that the supplies she had brought would not last long, so she proceeded to shock the official dignity of the army by ignoring "regular channels" and had signed orders for the warehouses and the goods on the way to the hospital before the startled "red-tape holders" had recovered from their surprise at her audacity. While grumbling that she did not understand "service rules," they were compelled to admit that she knew how to run a hospital—not only the great Barracks, but the seven other hospitals over which she had charge.

During those first terrible days, Miss Nightingale was known to stand for twenty hours at a time receiving the soldiers, directing where they should be placed, overseeing her nurses, and assisting personally at the most serious operations. Sometimes she begged for a case that the doctors in their haste considered hopeless, and all night long she bent over the pain-racked sufferer with the same tender, pitying care she had shown in her first case long ago on the downs of England. Many lives were saved by this means. Small wonder that the soldiers came to call her the "Angel of the Crimea." At night, with a tiny hand lamp to guide the way, she went here and there through the long wards of suffering men, "stooping beside each cot, listening to the breathing of the sleepers, whispering a word of encouragement to those who woke. And as she passed, many a poor fellow turned and kissed her shadow upon his pillow, then fell happily asleep."

Worn out by months of this strenuous effort, the dreaded typhus finally laid Miss Nightingale low, and as the news went abroad, all England wept with sorrow; and in the wards at Scutari there was not a man who did not long to give his life for hers, if only that might be. But devoted care saved her, and she took up her duties once more, laboring untiringly, refusing to give up and go home for a rest when urged to do so.

Then came the fall of Sebastopol, and at last peace in 1856, when the English army was withdrawn from the Crimea. But Miss Nightingale would not leave until the last patient was aboard the transport. Then she set up a great cross of white marble on the heights above Balaklava, as a tribute to the brave men and devoted nurses who had died there, and turned her face homeward, traveling under an assumed name to avoid public demonstrations.

She was entertained by the queen and honored by dukes and lords and nobles, but the common people loved Florence Nightingale too, and as a token of their appreciation, they raised "fifty thousand pounds, which were presented to her with the grateful thanks of the nation for her services." She was deeply touched, but while ever treasuring their kind thoughts in her heart, she asked that the money be given to the St. Thomas Hospital in London, for the purpose of forming a training school for nurses. So the Nightingale Home was founded and stands today, with a reputation worthy of its noble founder.

The strain in Scutari had been too much for Miss Nightingale's delicate health, and long before she realized her own condition, her friends knew that her active service was over. But during the years of semi-invalidism that followed, her mind was as active as in the old days, and "her sickroom became the busiest place in all England." Here plans were laid for the building and organizing of the Nightingale Home, for army reforms, for improved care of the sick poor, and for pensions for war sufferers. Several valuable books on nursing stand to her credit.

Florence Nightingale died in London on August 13, 1910, having spent most of the ninety years of her life in loving, unselfish service to humanity.

Pavane for a Princess

Arthur A. Milward

More than three centuries ago, a brokenhearted princess had gazed across the English Channel from the castle where she was a prisoner. Now another little girl gazed out to sea, and tears were in her eyes. Tightly, almost painfully, did she clench her father's hand.

It was a perfect summer day. The sky was blue, with a few fluffy, high clouds moving over the scintillating waters of the English Channel, blown by the cool, refreshing breeze. This same breeze stirred the long grasses of the sea meadows, and a slight movement was perceptible even among the stiff, wiry stems of the heather on the exposed cliff tops.

The battlement of the castle in the distance across the headland added enchantment to the scene, and my daughter and I, sighting the gray stones ahead of us, pressed on through the grasses and wildflowers, pausing occasionally to sniff the salt-laden air.

Except for my young daughter, in her brief sundress and open-toed sandals, her long auburn hair waving down her suntanned back, it looked just as it must have looked 300 years ago when another little girl, some six years older than my seven-year-old Victoria, looked across at the same meadows, the same cliffs, the same ocean.

Thirteen-year-old Elizabeth, however, was looking out toward the ocean from within the castle walls, the walls that constituted the limits of her world. Elizabeth was a prisoner, imprisoned for the "crime" of being the daughter of Charles Stuart, lately King Charles I of England, recently beheaded by the Puritans, the infamous Roundhead riffraff who constituted the supporters of Oliver Cromwell, self-styled "Lord Protector" of the Commonwealth of England, now a kingdom without a king.

* * *

Elizabeth, a fragile child in indifferent health, hardly knew her father. Having spent most of her brief life in exile in France with her French mother and two younger brothers, her English was imperfect and accented, and her memories of her royal father were hazy and colored by imagination.

How is it possible, thought the impressionable, introspective young girl, more than a child, not yet a woman, *to love someone so much and yet to know so little of him? I wonder if he will remember me. I wonder if he will like me. I know that I am not beautiful. I have heard the ladies of the court express their regret that I have not inherited my mother's beauty. I know I am not very wise. But perhaps, because I am his own little girl, he will like me just a little.*

It suddenly seemed desperately important to the lonely little princess that her almost unknown father would be happy to see her, would want her. No one else had seemed to care very much about her for what seemed a very long time. She barely remembered when she had not lived in France. And now, for reasons not made clear to her, she and her brothers were to join their father in England.

The Lord Protector had seen fit, for reasons best known to his Puritan conscience, to concede to the condemned king's urgent request that he be permitted one last interview with his children before his impending execution.

Chroniclers of the times record that the meeting between Charles Stuart and his children—in particular the exchange between His Majesty and the young Princess Elizabeth—was emotional in the extreme. Even the Puritan guards, it is recorded, were moved to tears.

Having made clear to the barely comprehending children that this was the last time they would see him in this world—that before another sunset he was to be beheaded by his, and England's, enemies—Charles Stuart, on signal from his captors, prepared to bid farewell to the three he loved best.

He assured his daughter, the oldest and best able to comprehend the situation, that her father was no criminal. "I am no traitor," he assured the weeping child. "I love England and have done no wrong.

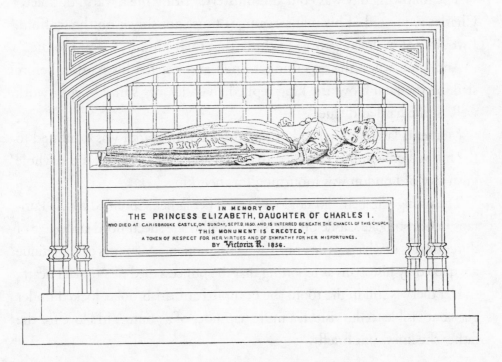

IN MEMORY OF
THE PRINCESS ELIZABETH, DAUGHTER OF CHARLES I.
WHO DIED AT CARISBROOKE CASTLE, ON SUNDAY, SEPT. 8. 1650. AND IS INTERRED BENEATH THE CHANCEL OF THIS CHURCH.
THIS MONUMENT IS ERECTED,
A TOKEN OF RESPECT FOR HER VIRTUES AND OF SYMPATHY FOR HER MISFORTUNES.
BY Victoria R. 1856.

"Darling, you will forget what I have said," he admonished the now almost hysterical girl, to which she vehemently replied, "I will *never* forget."

Torn from their father's arms, the three weeping children were ushered from the room by the waiting guards; but the princess, crying hysterically, broke away from the soldiers and ran back into her father's arms for one last embrace.

True to her promise, the brokenhearted child, as soon as she had regained her composure, seated herself at the desk in her quarters and asked the lady-in-waiting to bring her diary.

"He told me he was glad I was come," she wrote in her childish hand. "He took me in his arms and kissed me. I do believe he truly loves me."

* * *

The following day was cold and blustery. "Bring me a warm doublet," Charles requested of his manservant. "I must not shiver on the scaffold. I would not wish my people to think that their king was afraid to die."

And later, when the executioner knelt and begged his pardon before striking the fatal blow, the king replied, "Gladly, my son. Do your work well. Strike hard and true."

Moments later, as the head of the murdered monarch was exhibited to the hushed crowd, it is recorded that a great moan arose, "as if the whole great city of London was mourning for their king."

The young Elizabeth did not long outlive her father. Confined by the Puritans in Carisbrooke Castle on the Isle of Wight, she succumbed at the age of thirteen years to what was described as "consumption." Members of her retinue are quoted by historians as reporting that the princess died of a broken heart.

Her diary is still in the room she occupied at Carisbrooke, locked under glass but visible to the visitor, a mute reminder of a young girl's love for the father she knew but briefly.

The princess herself sleeps in a grave on the grounds of Carisbrooke, overlooking the restless waters of the Channel, facing the coast of France, visible on a clear day, where she spent most of the years of her brief life.

* * *

Victoria looked for a long time at the yellowed pages of the other child's diary, suspended in time under the plate glass. "She was a sad little girl," is all she said.

On the way back we paused for a few moments at the resting place of the young princess. Victoria knelt in the lank grass surrounding the grave and read the inscription barely visible on the tombstone: "Elizabeth Stuart, Elizabeth I, Princess of England, Aged 13 Years." That was all.

She took the flowers we had brought and laid them gently on the small grave. When she rose from her knees, she had tears in her eyes.

We walked away together. Neither of us looked back. Victoria grasped my hand tightly.

"Oh, Daddy," she exclaimed, "I'm glad I'm not a princess."

"Sweetheart," I replied, "so am I."

"I'm glad, though," Victoria continued, "I'm glad her daddy really liked her. That must have made her happy."

"I know it did, darling," I assured her. "Every little girl needs someone who thinks she's perfect. Even a princess."

Woodcut depiction of Charles I and family

Autumn to Winter

Number Nine Schoolhouse

R. Lovewell

Malvina was nostalgic that particular September morning. More and more, her thoughts had to do with the past, the years when she was making a difference in people's lives as schoolmistress in Number Nine Schoolhouse. Now the old schoolhouse was empty—only memories remained within. She must go there to be with them.

Wonder why the doctors haven't ever been smart enough to think up some way to cut out whatever 'tis women cry with, Malvina Marean considered as she listened to the sound of spasmodic sobs in the room behind her.

She had come out on the piazza and was prepared to rock patiently until Mary dried her tears. *'Twould certainly save a sight of trouble in the world if women weren't able to cry. Crying always riles men up. Wonder what they would do if they couldn't bawl once in so often. Men take it out in hollering their heads off or having dumb spells or something else. But women cry. All that started Mary off was Sam's never saying a word about that lemon pie she took such pains with. 'Twouldn't have hurt him a mite, either, to have said it was good, but that's the man of it. They don't see the*

need of praising a woman's cooking—think they ought to be satisfied if what they bake is eaten. Oh, well, they'll get over it. First year after young folks get married there's bound to be some spats—always are, I guess.

Malvina lived in two upstairs rooms in the house with Mary and Sam, who were her next of kin. And her last of kin. Part of the place was hers; the rest Sam had inherited.

She squinted nearsightedly up the yellow dirt road toward the village. In a moment the school truck rattled into sight packed with noisy youngsters swinging schoolbooks and dinner pails. She waved her hand as the truck flew by, watching it go down the hill past the white schoolhouse, Number Nine. Before the town voted to transport all the children to the Center, Malvina had taught there many years. Now that she taught no more, the sturdy, deserted old structure seemed to her like a friend, a companion. The key to Number Nine was inside the clock in her kitchen, and every few weeks she went down the hill and sat for a while at the desk that had so long been hers. The one skeleton in the closet of her peaceful life was the fear that the town would tear it down or move it away.

A consuming longing to go back across the years possessed her. She wanted torturingly to teach school again just for a day. She had little to do now—only to make her bed in the morning, to putter with the family mending, to sit in the sun and dream.

Mary came out to feed the hens. Watching, Malvina saw Sam slip from the barn and join her, saw his arm go around her shoulders, Mary's yellow head drawn close under his chin. She was glad they had made up; but, in some way, the pretty thing she had seen only made her more lonely, shutting her out completely from their united lives. She pulled herself from the rocking chair, went indoors, put on her hat and cape, took the schoolhouse key from the clock, and started down the road.

* * *

Malvina was so deep in her dreams in the old schoolhouse that she did not hear the purring of the car that had halted outside. But footsteps in the entry startled her, and she looked up to find a man standing on the threshold.

"Miss Marean!" he cried. "Well, what do you know about this? I didn't expect to find you still on the job." His twinkling dark eyes awakened vague, faraway memories: a little boy with a freckled nose.

"I was driving up this way on a trip to the White Mountains, and I thought I'd swing off through the old town. I was going to hunt you up, but I saw the door open and had to stop and take a look. Say," he went on, stretching his hand out to her, "it's great to see you. But I don't believe you know who I am."

"You're little Joe Becker. And you used to have to sit out in front, where I could watch all your cutting up."

"'Little' Joe is good!" he said, laughing. "Weighed myself this morning— 225 pounds." The visitor sat down on the platform at the old woman's feet. "You kept me after school pretty often, Miss Marean," he accused.

"And made you spat the erasers to get the chalk out. That wasn't much of a punishment, though, after the way you used to cut up—throwing spit-balls and such mischief. I never once supposed you'd ever grow to be such a whopping big man. You were such a skinny fellow. I'd lost all track of you, too. Where do you make your home, and what business are you in?"

"I live in New York, and, well, I don't have to work much now. My business has prospered, and I've made quite a lot of money. . . . Say, I can see old Bill French up in the back seat wrestling with cube root, anyway. Wonder where he lives now."

"I don't know as I know myself. But it was fun teaching cube root— getting the answers to come out right."

Becker gazed for a moment out over the desks in the schoolroom. "Do you know what ever became of Sadie Davis?" he asked slowly.

"I've lost track of her, too, Joe. She went off to work someplace and never came back. Seems as if I've heard she was married. But it was so long ago, I've almost forgotten. I suppose you're married and have a family?"

"Yes, two boys and a girl. My, but I wish I had sent them out here for you to teach. They've been to the most expensive schools in the country, and they can't add a column of figures straight to save their necks."

"But I'm not teaching anymore, Joe. I'm only just sitting here. This school's been closed going on five years. Let's see. I'm almost seventy. I taught up until I was sixty-five—that makes it longer than I thought. The school committee doesn't dare to put me out. Had to shut up the school-house in order to get rid of me." She chuckled, and a twinkle came into her blue Yankee eyes.

"I can't seem to remember the year we moved to Boston," Joe said reminiscently. "I was only a little shaver then."

Malvina bent over the desk. "I shouldn't wonder if the register is down in the bottom drawer. Maybe it's the one you're in." Hunting, she found it. "In September 1885 there was entered the name of Joseph T. Becker, aged thirteen. Look at all the tardy marks after your name. You gave me considerable trouble, as I recollect it. Here's the Davis girl's name. She was eleven years old. I kind of suspected you were sweet on her, weren't you?"

The big man grinned, rose, and went down the aisle. He flung up a desk cover and studied it for a moment. Cut deep in the wood were the initials "J.B." and "S.D."

"Funny how I remember whittling them out with a jackknife. Just popped into my head like a flash."

* * *

For weeks Malvina Marean talked and dreamed of Joe Becker's visit. On the afternoon of Labor Day, she heard a knocking at the front door and a man's voice speaking her name. The voice had a familiar sound. In a moment Mary came tearing up the stairs and rushed, bright-eyed, into the room.

"Aunt Malvina, you're wanted. Do you feel well enough to get up and take a little ride? Wear your new dress. That Mr. Becker who was here awhile ago has come back."

Malvina was so flustered that she didn't even notice which way they were going, until the car stopped right in front of the schoolhouse. She looked out then and saw long rows of cars parked beside the roadway.

"What's going on? Must be they've sold the schoolhouse."

"Just you come and see what's going on," Becker told her as he helped her out.

Keeping his arm about her, he led her into the entry. And there, crowding the aisles and seats, were fifty or sixty men and women. On her desk were piled letters and telegrams. A great bunch of American Beauty roses greeted her misting eyes.

"Why, what—?" She recognized a woman with gray hair. "You haven't changed a particle. You look just the same as you did when you were a little girl, Lucy Mann."

"It's you who haven't changed," said Lucy Mann. "There never was a teacher like you in the world, and I don't believe there ever will be again!"

They pressed forward to shake hands, her old pupils of the years that were gone. One by one they reported: Sadie Davis; Lewis Hallock from Chicago; Jessie Joslin, who had never married; Mary Briggs, who had six children. Mary's brother, Sam, had died—he had been a great surgeon. *Always was doctoring animals*, Malvina remembered. The Harwell boys were out in California; they had sent their telegrams.

"I don't see for the life of me how you ever found them all, Joe. They have scattered to so many places and live so far off."

"That was easy enough. I took along the register when I was here in June." He did not add that he had put three men to work tracing down every name—and that no one but himself knew the money it had cost to stage that reunion.

It was he who presented the loving cup her pupils had bought, a shining thing from a famous Fifth Avenue shop. "Malvina Marean" was engraved upon its side, with an inscription beneath, which cut itself deep into her heart.

When they called upon her for a speech, and she stood up behind the battered desk—her thin hands grasping the silver cup, their blue veins puffed and swollen with the years; her gaunt old figure trembling—the crowded room became suddenly very still. The roughened face of Sadie Davis softened to tenderness, and Joe Becker's eyes were full of tears.

Malvina could not speak. Words would not come. A moment or two she stood, looking down at the men and women seated upon the school benches. Then she bowed her silvery head and shut her eyes. As she had "opened school" times without number, so now she would close it—for the last time.

"Our Father, who art in heaven—" Her voice came tremulously. "Hallowed be Thy name—"

* * *

When the shortening September day had ended, the depot bus took its load away in time for the downtown train. The other cars started one by one. Miss Marean would not let anyone take her up the hill.

"I'm just going to sit here a spell," she told them. "I want to think it all over by myself."

Mary and Sam came back, after a while, and looked in at the window. But when they saw Malvina sitting happily at the old desk piled high with telegrams and letters that it would take a day to read, they went softly away without disturbing her.

No longer did Malvina feel alone in the world. These strange men and women had by no means forgotten her. What did it matter now if she could not teach anymore, if there were nothing left to do but sit in the sun and dream? Her arm brushed against the great loving cup, tipping it over, and she saw that there was a piece of paper inside it. She pulled out a long legal document. Unfolding the paper, her astonished eyes saw that it was a deed: the deed to the schoolhouse, Number Nine, made out to her—and then she was weeping.

"I guess the dear Lord knew what He was doin' when He made folks so they could cry. 'Twould be a terrible pity if they couldn't when they feel the way I do."

The Show Must Go On

Author Unknown

Today was an exciting day for the children in Ward C, because the circus was coming! Most excited of all was Eddie, the tiny crippled boy with periwinkle eyes and daffodil hair, for he would be seeing his father, Koko the clown. But today the painted smile on Koko's face would not be matched with a real one underneath.

As Miss Beamish came down the long corridor, her blue-and-white uniform rustled cheerfully and the early morning sunlight lingered intimately in the hair that glinted under her pert white cap. Because Miss Beamish was young and merry of spirit, the children in the hospital had shortened her name to "Beamy"; and because of her gentle kindness, they loved her.

As she came toward Ward C, the tinkle of little voices reached her ears. Miss Beamish always listened for the voices of the children, for their tone was her forecast of the many little moods inside the ward. Sometimes the voices were fretful and cross. That meant that Miss Beamish must summon all the sternness she possessed and put away the smiles until the voices changed.

Sometimes, too many times, the voices were anguished. Then Miss Beamish's bright eyes softened with sadness, for the voices told her that the dark hours of the night had been marked by pain. But today the voices were happy, so Miss Beamish smiled her brightest smile, and as she opened the ward door, some of the morning sunshine seemed to hurry through with her.

For a moment, the children did not see her. During the night, a new child had been brought into the hospital, and all the excited talk was directed toward him. He lay there, his body making a miniature mountain in the whiteness of his little bed, his eyes starry, as he listened.

The spokesman was Eddie. Miss Beamish and Eddie were very old and tried friends, for Eddie had spent almost half his brief life in Ward C. He had come there as sad a little specimen of humanity as anyone ever saw. It was not neglect that had made Eddie that way; rather, he had been loved too well, but not wisely. His mother had loved him so much that she had given her life for him without even seeing him; and his father had given his baby love enough for two.

But a father who is Koko, the most famous of circus clowns, living the kaleidoscope life of a big circus, hasn't very much time to give to a little son. The circus, which was the breath of life to Koko, had been too much for Eddie. Some obscure and terrible thing had stricken Eddie's little spine, and his two little feet, meant to carry a sturdy little boy around, hung limp and useless.

For over three years now, from his crib, Eddie had watched the world of the hospital go on before his eyes. It was a world as changing as the circus world—but different. Eddie had seen dozens of other little boys come— and go. He had grown from a wan baby to a very small little boy whose white face was dominated by blue eyes several sizes too large for it. Everything possible had been done for him, but the little legs had never moved. All the doctors said that only a miracle-working operation would ever make them move now. And not one of the doctors dared attempt it.

Miss Beamish loved Eddie, as did everyone else. He was always so good. He never whimpered or complained, as the other children did. He was a pensive little boy who sat propped up in the small domain of his bed, looking reflectively at life with big, questioning eyes. He was not very talkative.

There were just two topics that excited him and made the words tumble out—two topics so closely related that they were one: the circus and Koko, his famous father. And as Miss Beamish stood listening in the doorway, Eddie was talking of these, his heart's dearest, and enthralling the new child with glamorous details.

"And my father has let me sit on the effalunt's back, and when he brings the circus to the hospital today, maybe he'll let you do it, too! Honest!"

But the new child was slow to believe. "Aw, say," he answered, his words contrasting pitiably with the angelic innocence of his face. "Listen to the kid! Whetcha givin' us? Nobody ain't ever heard of no hospital where they have any free circuses!"

An expression of hurt dignity settled on Eddie's face. He looked away from the unbeliever, blinking his eyes rapidly and swallowing hard. Then he saw Miss Beamish and turned toward her eyes that held panic in their wide blueness. There was anxiety and supplication in his frail voice.

"O-o-oh, Beamy!" he faltered, pointing a bud of a finger at the newcomer. "He says there won't be a circus today. I'm right, aren't I? There will be the circus, won't there? And isn't my pop coming to see us this morning? You tell him!"

Miss Beamish smiled from one to the other of the tiny combatants. "Of course it is too good to believe," she said, "but the circus *is* coming to see us today. You see," she went on, crossing the floor and twinkling down at the new little boy as she stood by his bed, "it's like this:

"Once upon a time, there was a very good man who loved children a great deal, so he knew how much they liked circuses. And he thought to himself that boys and girls who were sick were so good, and had to be so patient, that they deserved to see the circus even more than well ones. So he asked Dr. Bruch, who is in charge of all the big hospital full of boys and girls, if he could bring the circus to the hospital every year when it comes to town. And now the circus comes every year.

"They parade all the way out through the streets, with bands and steam pianos and everything. Then they come right into our backyard, and we take all of you outside there"—she pointed toward the courtyard, which lay in the pool of sunlight outside the window—"and you can see the whole show!"

The child's face was ecstatic as he peered up at her. "And elephants?" he whispered, his voice tempered with awe.

"Well, I should say so!" Miss Beamish assured him. "And clowns!" She pointed to the bit of a boy whose minute chest expanded at the mention of the word. "Eddie's father is the head of all the clowns. They call him Koko, and he's the funniest man in the whole world!"

Doubt was erased from the boy's face, and he glowed with a transfiguring belief. "Boy!" he said.

Then the excited patter of voices rose in a twittering chorus, and the convert was showered with more details than even his eager mind could absorb. Eddie still led the talk, but the others were not far behind him. They all spoke with assurance, for they had talked of nothing else but the circus for days—talked of it, dreamed of it.

They had played menagerie, too, with Eddie as the baby lion behind the bars of his white crib. He had done his best, but even to the soaring imaginations of the other children, there was something lacking in a baby lion whose roar was so tiny and who had to lie so very still in his cage.

Now that the day of days was here, the children were more excited than ever. In every ward, in every little white bed, there was an exclamation point of a child who looked forward with an intensity of eagerness that marked no other day in the year as it did this one. And of all the children,

Eddie was the most excited, the most eager. For Eddie's excitement was not born of a week's expectation; it was the cumulative result of a whole long year. While the other children talked and dreamed of the circus for a week or so, Eddie thought of it all the time.

To the others it was a dream come true, a spectacle to be regarded breathlessly from a distance. But Eddie was part of it. He belonged to the circus. To him it was so very much more than one crowded, glittering little while, to be forgotten in a surprisingly short time after the last elephant had flicked its ridiculous tail through the straight gate of the hospital.

The circus meant to Eddie the only real joy he had ever known. It meant the only home he had ever had, and more than all these, it meant his father, his wonderful father, who could make a little boy forget that there was such a thing in the world as pain. And today his father was coming! Even the sacred routine of the hospital had been set aside so that he might spend the whole morning with his little son, instead of coming with the other visitors for one short hour in the afternoon.

The breakfast trays with their round blue bowls of cereal were brought in and taken away. The hour for baths was much more placid than usual, for what is the mere inconvenience of a bath when the circus is coming? At last all the little beds in the even rows along the walls stood as fresh and smooth and white as the petals of a big flower; and in each bed a tense bit of humanity waited, bright-eyed, for the coming of the great moment.

In his crib in the far corner of the ward, his hair against his pillow like a bit of pale gold, Eddie lay as still as a doll in its cradle, his eyes squeezed shut so tightly that his little parody of a nose wrinkled.

He was playing a game with himself. He was going to keep his eyes closed until he heard footsteps coming toward his bed. Not just any foot-steps would do. There was only one step that would make him open his eyes, like the princess in the fairy tale whose eyes could be opened by the kiss of one who really loved her.

At the sound of the ward door opening, Eddie's eyelids squinched tighter than ever. But the footstep was not the one he was waiting for. It was only Miss Preble, the fat probationer, going around hanging the temperature charts on the little hooks on the foot of the beds. She passed him; he heard her footsteps going around the ward and back to the door, and then the slap of the door as it closed behind her.

Then there was a time that seemed very long to Eddie in his self-imposed darkness. Several times his little eyelids fluttered uncertainly, as though they would defy him and let in the light in spite of all the strength of his baby will. But at last the door opened, very slowly, to be sure, and the plod of big footsteps came toward him.

Oh, how the eyelids wanted to flick open just for one reassuring second! Nearer! Nearer! Now Eddie could distinguish that there were two pairs of footsteps, instead of one. One or the other would be nice young Dr. Curtis, who had special charge of Ward C and who always grinned so happily at Miss Beamish whenever he saw her. And there could be no mistake about the quick, vibrant pad of the other feet.

He couldn't wait any longer! Like the wings of a white butterfly, the fragile lids flashed open, and the periwinkle eyes beneath them were excited almost to the brightness of tears.

Yes, there, smiling down at him with his round brown eyes, was Dr. Curtis. Eddie's blue gaze did not linger on him. He could see "Doc" every day. His look flashed joyfully to the owner of the other footsteps, then grew blank, and the miniature face drooped with trouble. For with Doc was someone Eddie had never seen before, a great big someone who towered over his bed just as Goliath, the circus giant, loomed over Sir Toby, the smallest midget.

This was a shaggy mountain of a man, who looked intently at Eddie with eyes like steel buttons and whose face was almost hidden from view behind a gray beard that rushed away from the middle of his chin as though he were facing a high wind.

He snapped his sharp eyes from the baby, cowering back against his pillows, to Dr. Curtis, and he spoke in a voice as unexpectedly gentle as the hum of a great bass viol. "You did not tell me, monsieur doctor, that he was so tiny, this little one. Nevertheless, we shall see."

Eddie regarded him with bewildered eyes. *See what?* he wondered. Were they going to see if he was too little to go to the circus? If only his father would come, everything would be all right, he knew!

The doctor came to him and patted his bit of a shoulder with a kind hand. "Eddie," he said, "this is Dr. Ronesoy. He came all the way across the ocean from a place called France. He knows all about boys and girls, and he wants to have a look at the old feet. He's not going to hurt you. All right?"

That was what the whiskery man wanted, was it? This was nothing new to Eddie. There had been so many who had wanted the same thing. Eddie knew the routine by heart. Someone would turn back the covers of his crib. Then the inquisitive one would wiggle his toes and hit him gently on his knees with a funny little rubber hammer. Then he'd be turned over so that his face was fully buried in the pillow. He kind of liked that, because he could stretch out his shoulders while the hum of conversation went on over his head and soft fingers gently prodded his misbehaving spine.

Then he'd be turned back again, and for a few minutes the doctors would stand by his bedside holding up to the light strange black and white shadowy pictures that Eddie thought Doc called "Eddie's extra-plates." Then there would be a shaking of heads, and the doctors would go away, leaving the smoothness of the bed so tumbled that Miss Beamish would have to come back and straighten it all out again. It was always the same.

So Eddie met the comradely grin on Doc's face with a wisp of a smile. "Sure," he said in his piping voice. "It's all right, Doc. Only, say, listen, Doc," and he lowered his voice to a shrill whisper, "don't let him wrinkle me all up! My pop's coming, and I want to look nice for him."

"Not a wrinkle!" Dr. Curtis promised as he turned the pocket-edition blanketing back in a neat fold. "Will you begin your examination, sir?" he said, turning to the shaggy one, who stood looking down at the offending baby legs for a minute, his great fingers straying thoughtfully through his beard.

"Ah, yes," he said, "ah, yes." And bending closer he engulfed one of the tiny feet in a hand as gentle as a woman's and as big and soft as a down pillow. Then with a series of "Humphs," he did as all the others had done. Each tiny toe was wiggled; the little rubber hammer was produced from the straw basket filled with funny, shiny things that Doc carried on his arm. *Tap, tap*. It came against his knee. *Tap, tap*. Would it never stop? There; that was all of that.

Eddie heaved a pygmy sigh and waited for Doc to turn him over so that his befringed visitor could run expert fingers up and down the lazy spine. But Dr. Ronesoy did not ask to have Eddie turned over. Instead, he stood looking hard at the too-quiet little toes and pulling at his ambush of beard.

"Yes," he rumbled finally, "yes, monsieur doctor, it could be done. But the risk is of a greatness that—" He stopped suddenly and turned kind, keen eyes toward the atom of a boy. "Well, you can judge. It would be either a success the most perfect, or—"

Eddie lay gazing up at the two men, his eyes blue pools of bewilderment. What were they talking about? It couldn't be about the circus. That was always a success, no matter what happened. *What was it?* Eddie was thinking so hard, and watching the two faces above him so raptly, that he did not hear the ward door open and close again behind the figure he had waited so long to see.

Even in the unobtrusive gray suit he wore there was something remarkable, arresting, about the man who stood in the doorway, something that made people smile happily and a bit wistfully when they looked at him. For Koko did not doff his personality with his clown's ruff and peaked hat. The appeal that made children laugh, and men and women forget for a moment that they were no longer children, was always with him.

It was there in the curve of the wide mouth that needed no grease-paint smile to make it turn up rakishly at the corner. It was there in the funny way he cocked his head on one side. And it was there in the grown-up edition of Eddie's blue eyes, which danced like bright spots of concentrated joy in Koko's face.

Then suddenly Eddie saw him, and in his one word of greeting he voiced all the yearning of his year of lonely waiting. "Pop!" he called.

And as Koko came and gathered his little son in his arms, loneliness was forgotten and remembrance of pain was erased.

Doc's voice broke in on the moment of ecstasy. "Dr. Ronesoy, this is the boy's father."

Dr. Ronesoy smiled behind his beard and nodded his head. "It is well," he said to Koko, "that you have come. It would be happiness to me if I might say a few words to you." He turned to Dr. Curtis. "There is, perhaps, somewhere we could talk? I would not excite the little one, and how is it you say it? Little pitchers hear much."

"Would you come with us a minute, sir?" Dr. Curtis said to Koko, and with a lingering pat on his little son's bright head, Koko followed the doctors out of the ward.

This was almost too much! A microscopic fury of resentment burned in Eddie's eyes as he watched the three figures go away from him. He felt sure that there was nothing important enough to take his pop away from him at that moment.

But in the spare brightness of the waiting room outside the ward, Koko was listening to the deep-voiced words of Dr. Ronesoy, and the expression in his intent eyes said that the words were too important to miss even one of them.

"Yes," Dr. Ronesoy was saying, "as I said, it is well you came this day. I would have your consent before I attempt this operation. It is of such a delicacy, and there is so very much danger in it, that I should hesitate otherwise."

Koko's blue eyes searched the doctor's face with a look of anguished absorption. "And you say," he said hesitantly, "that . . . afterward . . . my boy will walk?"

"If the operation be a success, monsieur. Otherwise—" Dr. Ronesoy shrugged massive shoulders. He hesitated and then went on in his big, slow voice. "I think it only just, monsieur, that you should know all there is one can know about the chances. It may be he will walk again. It is with frankness I say that it is in the hands of God as well as in these hands." And he held out his great hands with their delicate fingers. "It may be—"

He stopped abruptly and walked away from Koko, who watched him in an agony of anxiety as he turned his vast back on the room and stood a moment looking out of the window. Suddenly, he wheeled about.

"Monsieur," he said, "it would be a great pain for you to lose your little child. I have seen that, I know. Therefore, I tell you now that this may happen. There is but one chance in ten that he will . . . that he will survive the operation."

"And if you don't operate? I'd rather have him always as he is"—Koko's voice was almost a whisper—"than . . . than to let him go!"

"Ah, but, monsieur, you could not keep your boy as he is now. There might be, at most, three, four years. Who can say? During those years, the pain would not grow less. And the child's spirit, now so hopeful, so bright . . . Can you not see? Too much suffering darkens the mind, monsieur.

"Therefore, I say to you, your boy might live for a few short years; but, ah no, he would not be the same, either in mind or in body." He came toward Koko and laid a great, gentle hand on his arm. "Monsieur, I too have a son. I love him more than my life. Were this my son, I should know no hesitation."

All the thousands who knew the Koko of the circus ring would not have recognized him now. His eyes no longer laughed, but in their depths was only remembered pain. "One chance in ten, you said?" he faltered.

"Monsieur is right."

Koko's hands trembled, then gripped each other in an iron clasp. "Give him his chance!" he said, and this time his voice did not falter.

In the quiet corridor Miss Beamish sat at her desk, folding immaculate bits of gauze into perfect little squares. As Koko came from the waiting room, she saw him and came toward him, her hand extended in a gesture of sympathy.

"Dr. Curtis has just told me about Eddie," she said. "No one has told him about it yet, and I wondered if you wouldn't like to be the one to do it. He'll be so disappointed to miss the circus!"

Koko looked at her with grateful eyes. "Bless you!" he said softly. "I would like to tell him. We've both got to help him, Miss Beamish. It's pretty hard for such a little tike to buck this all by himself."

Miss Beamish's eyes were bright as she answered. "I'll do all I can. You know that."

"I do, I do, indeed," he replied and went from her into the ward, where Eddie awaited him with unwhetted eagerness and greeted him with a joy-laden shout.

"Pop! The fellows want you to tell 'em about the circus. Pop, say, tell 'em about the time the baby effalunt ran away, will you?"

"Aren't you going to let your pop talk to you for a little while first?" Koko said as he sat down in the stiff chair by the side of Eddie's crib. "Let's have a good old visit first. Then I'll tell 'em all the stories I know."

Eddie smiled proudly up at his father. "Sure!" he agreed in what he thought was a most manly tone of voice.

Koko took Eddie's hand, which lay like a wee wax model on the counterpane.

"I've got a story to tell you about the circus," he said. "It's a story I've often told you; but I want you to listen harder than you ever have before, because you must understand what I'm going to say. When you grow to be a big man"—Eddie felt his father's hand tighten on his, and his voice seemed to come all soft and husky—"you're going to be with the circus, too, and I hope you're going to be a much better clown than your pop ever was. But before you can be a clown, or anything else, there's one thing you must learn, and learn it so well you will never forget it. It is this: 'No matter what happens, the show must go on!'"

Koko stroked the baby hand that lay happily in his big brown one, and he smiled into Eddie's rapt eyes. "See, Ed, it's like this! Sometimes, maybe, I don't feel like going out and bumbling around in the sawdust. Lots of times, I'd much rather run away and see you. But every day, in every place I go, there are all the people waiting to see me, and no matter how much I want to run away, I mustn't. No matter what I want, no matter what happens, the show must go on. So I stay and act just as if I want to.

"Then again, perhaps I feel sick, just like you do—sometimes. Or, often I'm sad because my boy's not with me. Then it's hard to act happy; but I do, because everybody expects me to. In show business, we call it 'foolin' 'em'! And everybody—every single person in the whole circus—knows just what I've been telling you. That no matter what happens, the show must go on! That's the tradition. So, you understand what your pop's telling you?"

Eddie grinned at him. "S-s-sure!" he said in his baby voice. "When I get to be a man, even if I got a stomachache or pains in my back, I've gotta grin, because all the boys and girls are waitin' to see me act."

"That's right. But you don't have to wait to be a man. This afternoon"—Koko looked suddenly away from Eddie's eager eyes—"the circus is coming here. But something much more important is coming for you. It's going to mean that you can't see the circus this time; but it's going to mean that next year, maybe you'll be with the circus and with your old pop again."

Eddie's eyes and voice were full of anguished protest. "Miss the circus," he quavered. "Me?"

"Steady, now. Wait until Pop tells you all about it. That big doctor with the beard that came to see you this morning said he thinks he can make you able to walk again; and he's going to try this afternoon, because tomorrow he has to go away, back to France. To do that, he's got to take you out of the ward and do what they call an operation. Do you know what that is?"

"Yes, I know. Like Mike, that used to be in that bed." He indicated the spot with his tiny finger. "They didn't give him any lunch, and they put a white hat on his head and took him for a ride in a funny long cart with rubber wheels. He never came back, and I guess he must have got well, because Miss Beamish told us he wasn't ever going to have any more pains in his legs or anywhere else. Why, Pop, what's the matter? You're not smiling, Pop! What you thinking about?"

"I was thinking of a promise I want you to make. Will you promise me something?"

Eddie nodded solemnly. "S-s-sure!"

"Will you promise Pop that when they put the funny white hat on you this afternoon and take you away in the buggy cart, you'll remember what I told you just now? That no matter what happens, the show must go on! You can help the whiskery doctor and me, and yourself, if you will. If you do, you'll be foolin' 'em! Promise now that you're going to remember that no matter what happens to you, my old man, the show must go on."

"I promise!" Eddie said with deliberation and wondered why his father's eyes were brighter than usual.

"And now which story shall it be first?" Koko called, and a spell as of sudden enchantment settled on the sunny ward while he talked, for Koko talked as he had never talked before, talked until the whole world of the circus seemed to come alive in the quiet of that place.

But even the best stories must come to an end sometime. At last Koko stood again in the doorway, waving a comic farewell to the ecstatic children.

"See you all this afternoon!" he grinned at them, his eyes resting long on the bed in the corner of the ward where a boy with daffodil-colored hair watched him with mute adoration. Then suddenly Koko crossed the sunny space between them and lifted the child in his arms, holding him against his heart as though he would never let him go.

"Ed, my son," he said, his lips against the bright hair, "you won't forget what I told you, will you?"

Eddie snuggled his head into the curve of his father's neck. "I remember," he said.

"Let Pop hear you say it!"

Eddie's little voice repeated the words like a familiar lesson well learned. "No matter what happens, the show must go on. That's foolin' 'em!"

They were silent for a brief moment, the man with the wee boy in his arms. Then Koko tucked Eddie into his bed again, turned swiftly, and hurried away. This time he did not look back.

* * *

The green lawn of the hospital blossomed like a bright garden with children. They were everywhere, their heads nodding and bobbing like beds of flowers. The balconies around the court were full of children—little ones, middle-sized ones, big ones—clapping excited hands and voicing their approval in a pelting of happy sounds.

The great hour had come and partly gone. Oh, what an hour to remember! First of all, there had been the rush of getting into the court-yard, a great adventure after the four walls of a ward. Never before had the sunshine been so bright! From a distance had come the wavering melody of the steam piano; then the courtyard gates had opened, and there was the circus, all ready and waiting to come in: the calliope, festooned with gilded mermaids and bunches of grapes; white horses mincing along, guided by beautiful pink-cheeked ladies with shiny dresses on; little ponies, just the right size for a boy, ridden by funny little men in high silk hats; elephants, lazily rolling, their big trunks swaying, holding each other's tails.

And seated on the first elephant's head, laughing and chuckling and waving his hands in their big white cotton gloves, was Koko! Koko, Eddie's father, the man they had seen that very morning, only so different now, so glorious! Oh, to have a father like that!

There never was anything funnier than the chalk-white face with its perpendicular slits of eyes, its pink nose, and its grinning mouth. And when Koko in his ruff and red-and-white-spotted domino, slipped like a rag doll from his perch on the biggest elephant and fell in a laughing heap right in the middle of the courtyard, the shouts of the children proclaimed that the circus had really begun.

Everything was wonderful—glorious and wonderful! The horses pranced and the spangled ladies jumped through paper hoops. The elephants knelt down just like great big clumsy boys and said their prayers. The funny little men made pyramids and triangles and squares of themselves. Oh, it was grand!

But Koko was best of all! No matter what anybody else was doing, he was doing something funnier. He just didn't let you forget him for a minute. He was everywhere and into everything. The children gurgled and laughed and shouted, and called him by name, and loved him. Even the circus people laughed, as though he had never been so funny before.

They wouldn't have believed it if someone had told them that under the wide grin on the white face, Koko's mouth was set in a hard line; and under the painted, silly lids, his look was one of anguish, of despair. They would have laughed at you if you had told them that the ears that seemed to respond so eagerly to each approving shout were deaf to all the tumult, because one little voice was missing.

They had no way of knowing that in the brain that originated so many laughs for them, tortured thoughts were pounding over and over: *We've got to fool them. One chance in ten! Oh, Eddie, Eddie!*

And in a silent, shining white room within the walls of the hospital, two other people were tense with an emotion that gripped them as the joy of the circus gripped all the little spectators outside—the emotion of suspense.

In that silent white room, a big, bearded man sat humped up in a chair by the side of a little white bed. On the other side of it, a nurse in a crisp blue-and-white uniform with shiny hair under a pert white cap gripped tense hands in her aproned lap and looked on with stricken eyes at the little form so quiet under the white counterpane.

Dr. Ronesoy raised weary eyes and looked across Eddie's crib to Miss Beamish, then rose heavily from his chair. "If he had been a bit stronger, mademoiselle!" he sighed. "I have made it so that he can walk if he lives. But what can I do against such frailty?"

Miss Beamish nodded. "I know!" she whispered.

"If I am needed, I shall be nearby. If there is anything I can do—" The shaggy man paused a minute in the doorway. "I fear, mademoiselle, it is, however, beyond our power now."

Miss Beamish did not answer, but reached beneath the smooth counterpane and held Eddie's little hand, which lay in her clasp as quiet as the hand of a doll.

As the door closed without a sound behind the doctor's big, drooping back, she leaned over the crib, gazing intently at the white flower of a face on the pillow, as though she would breathe into the tiny boy her own warm vitality. Bending close to the little figure, she whispered to him in a breaking voice, "Oh, Eddie, you must . . . you *must* get well! Eddie, it's Beamy talking. Eddie, Eddie dear, don't you hear me? Open your eyes and look at me! Eddie, Eddie!"

But the petals of eyelids did not move, and the pulse in the little hand that she held fluttered and wavered as though each uncertain beat would be its last.

Outside, the courtyard grew quiet. The sunlight shifted and dimmed in the silent white room.

Miss Beamish still watched the quiet baby and whispered to him. So intent was she that she did not hear the soft opening of the door. She started when a gentle hand was laid on her shoulder.

"Any change, Miss Beamish?" Dr. Curtis asked. "His father's here."

There was Koko, his silly clown's hat twisted between anguished fingers, the painted-on eyes strangely smudged in his white face. Miss Beamish looked at him and shook a reluctant hand.

The drooping figure in its gala red and white knelt by the bed and

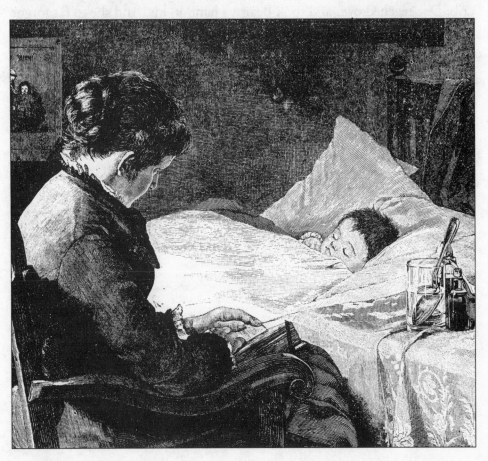

buried his head in his arms. Had the children seen him there, they might have thought he was laughing, for his shoulders shook.

"Eddie," he was murmuring, "you didn't fool 'em after all, did you? Oh, Eddie, come back to your pop! Come back, I tell you, Eddie!"

As if in answer to an imperative summons, a shadow of a tremor passed over the tender little face on the pillow, and the tousled gold head moved the faintest fraction of an inch. Then slowly, slowly, the eyelids fluttered open. In a voice smaller than the smallest whisper, Eddie's mouth framed the words of the lesson he had learned that morning. "I'm foolin' 'em!" he said.

In the dimness of the shadows that had crept gently around the white crib, Doc reached over and took Beamy's hand in his. And she so far forgot her professional dignity that she didn't seem to mind a bit!

The Bet

Anton Pavlovich Chekhov

*What value can we put on freedom?
Could a great deal of money compensate
for it? Or accumulation of vast wisdom?
What are the effects posed by voluntary
self-confinement? These are questions
raised by Chekhov, one of Russia's greatest
writers, in this powerful story.*

It was a dark autumn night. The old banker was pacing from corner to corner of his study, recalling to his mind the party he gave in the autumn fifteen years before. There were many clever people at the party and much interesting conversation. They talked, among other things, of capital punishment. The guests—among them not a few scholars and journalists—for the most part disapproved of capital punishment. They found it obsolete as a means of punishment, unfitted to a Christian state, and immoral. Some of them thought that capital punishment should be replaced universally by life imprisonment.

"I don't agree with you," said the host. "I myself have experienced neither capital punishment nor life imprisonment, but if one may judge a priori, then in my opinion capital punishment is more moral and more humane than imprisonment. Execution kills instantly, life imprisonment kills by degrees. Who is the more humane executioner: one who kills you in a few seconds or one who draws the life out of you incessantly, for years?"

"They're both equally immoral," remarked one of the guests, "because their purpose is the same: to take away life. The state is not God. It has no right to take away that which it cannot give back, if it should so desire."

Among the company was a lawyer, a young man of about twenty-five. On being asked his opinion, he said, "Capital punishment and life imprisonment are equally immoral; but if I were offered the choice between them, I would certainly choose the second. It's better to live somehow than not to live at all."

There ensued a lively discussion. The banker, who was then younger and more nervous, suddenly lost his temper, banged his fist on the table, and turning to the young lawyer, cried out, "It's a lie! I bet you $2 million you wouldn't stick in a cell even for five years."

"If you mean it seriously," replied the lawyer, "then I bet I'll stay not five but fifteen."

"Fifteen! Done!" cried the banker. "Gentlemen, I stake $2 million."

"Agreed. You stake $2 million, I my freedom," said the lawyer.

So this wild, ridiculous bet came to pass. The banker, who at that time had too many millions to count, spoiled and capricious, was beside himself with rapture. During supper he said to the lawyer jokingly, "Come to your senses, young man, before it's too late. Two million is nothing to me, but you stand to lose three or four of the best years of your life. I say three or four, because you'll never stick it out any longer. Don't forget either, you unhappy man, that voluntary imprisonment is much heavier than enforced imprisonment. The idea that you have the right to free yourself at any moment will poison the whole of your life in the cell. I pity you."

And now the banker, pacing from corner to corner, recalled all this and asked himself, "Why did I make this bet? What's the good? The lawyer loses fifteen years of his life, and I throw away $2 million. Will it convince people that capital punishment is worse or better than imprisonment for life? No, no! All stuff and rubbish. On my part, it was the caprice of a well-fed man; on the lawyer's, pure greed of gold."

He recollected further what happened after the evening party. It was decided that the lawyer must undergo his imprisonment under the strictest observation, in a garden wing of the banker's house. It was agreed that during this period he would be deprived of the right to cross the threshold, to see living people, to hear human voices, and to receive letters and newspapers. He was permitted to have a musical instrument, to read books, to write letters, to drink wine and smoke tobacco. By the agreement, he could communicate, but only in silence, with the outside world through a little window specially constructed for this purpose. Everything necessary—books, music, wine—he could receive in any quantity by sending a note through the window. The agreement provided for all the minutest details, which made the confinement strictly solitary, and it obliged the lawyer to remain exactly fifteen years from twelve o'clock on November 14, 1870, to twelve o'clock on November 14, 1885. The least attempt on his part to violate the conditions, to escape if only for two minutes before the time, freed the banker from the obligation to pay him the $2 million.

* * *

During the first year of imprisonment, the lawyer, as far as it was possible to judge from his short notes, suffered terribly from loneliness and boredom. From his wing day and night came the sound of the piano. He rejected wine and tobacco. "Wine," he wrote, "excites desires, and desires are the chief foes of a prisoner. Besides, nothing is more boring than to drink good wine alone, and tobacco spoils the air in this room." During the first year the lawyer was sent books of a light character: novels with a complicated love interest, stories of crime and fantasy, comedies, and so on.

In the second year, the piano was heard no longer, and the lawyer asked only for classics. In the fifth year, music was heard again, and the prisoner asked for wine. Those who watched him said that during the whole of that year he was only eating, drinking, and lying on his bed. He yawned often and talked angrily to himself. Books he did not read. Sometimes at night he would sit down to write. He would write for a long time and tear it all up in the morning. More than once he was heard to weep.

In the second half of the sixth year, the prisoner began zealously to study languages, philosophy, and history. He fell on these subjects so hungrily that the banker hardly had time to get books enough for him. In the space of four years, about 600 volumes were bought at his request. It was while that passion lasted that the banker received the following letter from the prisoner: "My dear jailer, I am writing these lines in six languages. Show them to experts. Let them read them. If they do not find one single mistake, I beg you to give orders to have a gun fired off in the garden. By that noise I shall know that my efforts have not been in vain. The geniuses of all ages and countries speak in different languages; but in them all burns the same flame. Oh, if you only knew my heavenly happiness now that I can understand them!" The prisoner's desire was fulfilled. Two shots were fired in the garden at the banker's order.

Later on, after the tenth year, the lawyer sat immovable before his table and read only the New Testament. The banker found it strange that a man who in four years had mastered 600 erudite volumes should have spent nearly a year in reading one book, easy to understand and by no means thick. The New Testament was then replaced by the history of religions and theology.

During the last two years of his confinement the prisoner read an extraordinary amount, quite haphazardly. Now he would apply himself to the natural sciences, then he would read Byron or Shakespeare. Notes used to come from him in which he asked to be sent at the same time a book on chemistry, a textbook of medicine, a novel, and some treatise on philosophy or theology. He read as though he were swimming in the sea among broken pieces of wreckage and, in his desire to save his life, was eagerly grasping one piece after another.

*　*　*

The banker recalled all this, and thought, *Tomorrow at twelve o'clock he receives his freedom. Under the agreement, I shall have to pay him $2 million. If I pay, it's all over with me. I am ruined forever. . . .*

Fifteen years before he had too many millions to count, but now he was afraid to ask himself which he had more of: money or debts. Gambling on the Stock Exchange, risky speculation, and the recklessness of which he could not rid himself even in old age had gradually brought his business to decay; and the fearless, self-confident, proud man of business had become an ordinary banker, trembling at every rise and fall in the market.

"That cursed bet," murmured the old man, clutching his head in despair. "Why didn't the man die? He's only forty years old. He will take away my last farthing, marry, enjoy life, gamble on the Exchange, and I will look on like an envious beggar and hear the same words from him every day: 'I'm obliged to you for the happiness of my life. Let me help you.' No, it's too much! The only escape from bankruptcy and disgrace is that the man should die."

The clock had just struck three. The banker was listening. In the house everyone was asleep, and one could hear only the frozen trees whining outside the windows. Trying to make no sound, he took out of his safe the key of the door that had not been opened for fifteen years, put on his overcoat, and went out of the house. The garden was dark and cold. It was raining. A damp, penetrating wind howled in the garden and gave the trees no rest. Though he strained his eyes, the banker could see neither the ground, nor the white statues, nor the garden wing, nor the trees. Approaching the garden wing, he called the watchman twice. There was no answer. Evidently the watchman had taken shelter from the bad weather and was now asleep somewhere in the kitchen or the greenhouse.

If I have the courage to fulfill my intention, thought the old man, *the suspicion will fall on the watchman first of all.*

In the darkness he groped for the steps and the door and entered the hall of the garden wing, then poked his way into a narrow passage and struck a match. Not a soul was there. Someone's bed, with no bedclothes on it, stood there, and an iron stove loomed dark in the corner. The seals on the door that led into the prisoner's room were unbroken.

When the match went out, the old man, trembling from agitation, peeped into the little window.

In the prisoner's room, a candle was burning dimly. The prisoner himself sat by the table. Only his back, the hair on his head, and his hands were visible. Open books were strewn about on the table, on the two chairs, and on the carpet near the table.

Five minutes passed, and the prisoner never once stirred. Fifteen years' confinement had taught him to sit motionless. The banker tapped on the window with his finger, but the prisoner made no movement in reply.

Then the banker cautiously tore the seals from the door and put the key into the lock. The rusty lock gave a hoarse groan and the door creaked. The banker expected instantly to hear a cry of surprise and the sound of steps. Three minutes passed, and it was as quiet inside as it had been before. He made up his mind to enter.

Before the table sat a man totally unlike an ordinary human being. It was a skeleton, with tight-drawn skin, with long, curly hair like a woman's and a shaggy beard. The color of his face was yellow, of an earthy shade; the cheeks were sunken, the back long and narrow, and the hand upon which he leaned his hairy head was so lean and skinny that it was painful to look upon. His hair was already silvering with gray, and no one who glanced at the senile emaciation of the face would have believed that he was only forty years old. On the table, before his bent head, lay a sheet of paper on which something was written in a tiny hand.

Poor devil, thought the banker. *He's asleep and probably seeing millions in his dreams. I have only to take and throw this half-dead thing onto the bed, smother him a moment with the pillow, and the most careful examination will find no trace of unnatural death. But, first, let us read what he has written here.*

The banker took the sheet from the table and read:

> Tomorrow at twelve o'clock midnight, I shall obtain my freedom and the right to mix with people. But before I leave this room and see the sun, I think it necessary to say a few words to you. On my own clear conscience and before God who sees me I declare to you that I despise freedom, life, health, and all that your books call the blessings of the world.
>
> For fifteen years I have diligently studied earthly life. True, I saw neither the earth nor the people; but in your books, I drank fragrant wine, sang songs, hunted deer and

wild boar in the forests, loved women. . . . And beautiful women, like clouds ethereal, created by the magic of your poets' genius, visited me by night and whispered to me wonderful tales, which made my head drunken. In your books, I climbed the summits of Elburz and Mont Blanc and saw from there how the sun rose in the morning, and in the evening, suffused the sky, the ocean, and the mountain ridges with a purple gold. I saw from there how above me lightning glimmered, cleaving the clouds; I saw green forests, fields, rivers, lakes, cities; I heard sirens singing and the playing of the pipes of Pan; I touched the wings of beautiful devils who came flying to me to speak of God. . . . In your books, I cast myself into bottomless abysses, worked miracles, burned cities to the ground, preached new religions, conquered whole countries. . . .

Your books gave me wisdom. All that unwearying human thought created in the centuries is compressed to a little lump in my skull. I know that I am cleverer than you all.

And I despise your books, despise all worldly blessings and wisdom. Everything is void, frail, visionary, and delusive as a mirage. Though you be proud and wise and beautiful, yet will death wipe you from the face of the earth like the mice underground; and your posterity, your history, and the immortality of your men of genius will be as frozen slag, burned down together with the terrestrial globe.

You are mad and gone the wrong way. You take falsehood for truth and ugliness for beauty. You would marvel if suddenly apple and orange trees should bear frogs and lizards instead of fruit and if roses should begin to breathe the odor of a sweating horse. So do I marvel at you, who have bartered heaven for earth. I do not want to understand you.

That I may show you in deed my contempt for that by which you live, I waive the $2 million of which I once dreamed as a paradise and which I now despise. That I may deprive myself of my right to them, I shall come out from here five minutes before the stipulated term and thus shall violate the agreement.

When he had read, the banker put the sheet on the table, kissed the head of the strange man, and began to weep. He went out of the wing. Never at any other time, not even after his terrible losses on the Exchange, had he felt such utter contempt for himself as now. Coming home, he lay down on his bed, but agitation and tears kept him a long time from sleeping. . . .

The next morning the poor watchman came running to him and told him that they had seen the man who lived in the wing climb through the window into the garden. He had gone to the gate and disappeared. The banker instantly went with his servants to the wing and established the escape of his prisoner. To avoid unnecessary rumors, he took the paper with the renunciation from the table and, on his return, locked it in his safe.

Lawrence Thorne, Junior

Grace S. Richmond

The boy was leaving home, for his father was disappointed in him, ashamed of him, and distrusted him. His father asked for twenty-four hours. What could the boy possibly learn in twenty-four hours that would change his mind? If he could just start over again somewhere else!

He closed the door of his father's library with a hand that trembled on the knob. He stole swiftly through the hall and up the stairs into his room, the door of which he instantly locked. Crossing the floor, he flung himself, full length, face downward, upon the bed.

The attitude of the figure, with its boyish outlines of rumpled hair, square young shoulders, and strong legs beneath the colorful golf stockings, suggested both grief and despair. At eighteen, these forms of suffering are sometimes intense, but seldom prolonged. Yet it was a full hour before the shoulders stirred, except with an occasional long-drawn breath.

An onlooker might have fancied Larry Thorne asleep, but when he slowly drew himself erect, it was not sleepiness that made his eyelids droop so heavily. His handsome face was angry, and the lines about the mouth were straight and hard.

He began packing a leather traveling bag, moving softly about from closet to chiffonier, selecting and rejecting with care. He glanced down at the modish bicycle clothes he wore, and after some hesitation decided to make no change in them, except to replace the bright stockings with a more quiet pair. In the bag, he put one lightweight summer suit and a store of shirts, collars, and neckties that he chose from a lavish stock. He took a handsome topcoat from its yoke in the closet, but shook his head and replaced it with a sigh.

The packing accomplished, he glanced about the attractive room. His eye lingered upon a fine rifle that stood in one corner with a collection of oars, golf clubs, tennis rackets, and the like, then turned to the photographs on the top of the low bookcase. He walked slowly over to these.

His lips curled into something very like a quiver for a moment as he took down one photograph. The sweet face of his mother looked into his with eyes that spoke to him of a very tender relation sundered all too soon. Her son, standing motionless for a long minute, suddenly kissed the picture with a smothered cry of pain and put it carefully into a pocket of the bag; then he drew himself up with his habitual proud air. Setting his lips again, he picked up his cap and the bag and strode downstairs to the library door. There, after an instant's hesitation, he knocked. A voice bade him enter, and setting down his bag outside, he went in and closed the door.

He advanced to the desk, where sat a keen-eyed man of features like his own. The father—smooth shaven, clear cut, and fresh colored of face—was Larry grown older. Mr. Thorne, turning in his revolving chair and looking sternly at the boy, waited for him to speak.

"I came to tell you, sir," began Larry respectfully, "that I will leave home tonight. I am ready to go."

His father looked at him steadily for a moment, then said quietly, "You will leave home? You mean—without my permission?"

"I don't think you can refuse to let me go, sir."

"Why not?"

The boy's eyes dropped, but he answered firmly, "You have told me why not today."

"In what words?"

"You have said you were disappointed in me . . . ashamed of me, that you—" Larry's voice nearly broke, but he controlled it, although the words came in a lower tone. "—couldn't trust me. I think, since you feel that way, there is no reason why I should stay."

There was silence again for a minute. Then Mr. Thorne asked in a dry voice, "Do you think that I spoke more harshly than you deserved?"

The father waited for a reply, but receiving none, went on: "My son chooses to defy my commands, to break his promises to me, to disgrace my name at the college where I have placed him, and to choose for himself evil associates. His misconduct happens not once, but many times. When I tell him that I am disappointed in him, ashamed of him, that I cannot trust him, he feels that I have been unduly hard upon him. But is all this sufficient reason for his determining to leave my roof—for his threatening to do so without my consent?"

The boy looked up quickly.

"No," said Mr. Thorne, "you did not say so, but I think I am to infer, am I not, that if I refuse, you will go, notwithstanding?"

"I could have gone," said Larry proudly, "without saying a word."

"I appreciate that. At the same time, you intend to go. Are you willing to tell me where you are going?"

"I meant to do that, sir," said Larry. "I shall go to my cousin, Barrett Warner, in Montana."

"Have you enough money?"

"I have my last month's allowance, sir."

Mr. Thorne turned back to his desk and resumed the writing that Larry's entrance had interrupted. The boy watched the pen travel steadily over line after line until the firm handwriting had covered half a page. Then Mr. Thorne rose and spoke slowly and decidedly, holding himself in his usual erect fashion and looking into the eyes of his son—on a level with his own, for the two were of the same athletic build.

"Lawrence," he said, not harshly, but so gravely that the words sounded very stern to the listening ears, "for twenty-four hours I forbid you to start on your journey. If you care to preserve any tie whatsoever between us, you will not disregard this command. At the end of that time, if you still feel that the best thing you can do in the circumstances is to take yourself off, I shall not say or do anything to restrain you. But you must understand that from the time you go, your allowance ceases. If you remain, it will be cut down one-half."

The boy's eyes met his father's in one long, steady gaze. A strong will looked out of both pairs, the inflexible determination in the elder matched by the full-grown purpose in the younger. Then Lawrence Thorne, junior, turned and went quickly from the room, saying bitterly to himself, *He doesn't love me—he can't! Why, he may never see me again in this world—the only son he has left! He doesn't understand me a bit. He's as hard as flint. He wouldn't even say he wanted me to stay. Stay! I couldn't stay now!*

Lawrence Thorne, senior, dropped into his chair with a breath that was almost a groan and sat leaning his head upon his hand.

Am I taking the right course, he asked himself, *or am I carrying it too far? I have tried every other method with him and failed to arouse what I am sure is in him. His careless, reckless ways will ruin him as surely as he is a Thorne. Perhaps a year with Barrett would bring him to his senses—yet he is only eighteen. I cannot see him leave me for that rough life with a man who is none too trustworthy. My only son, my little lad—how short a time it seems since he was*

that! His mother could have managed him, but somehow I have failed to hold his heart; and he thinks I don't care!

Larry, roaming moodily about his room while the sounds and odors of the early May afternoon came alluringly in at the open window, was conscious of a very heavy heart. Somehow it was far harder for him to wait the required twenty-four hours than it would have been to go at once from the house. He had thought when he came to the room that he would not leave it until the time of his permitted departure, but after an hour of intolerable boredom, he found himself unable to abide by this decision. He went hastily downstairs, flung himself upon his bicycle, and in a moment more was speeding toward the nearest avenue that led out into the open country.

Action was such a relief that he wheeled on and on without the pause of an instant, until the suburbs were far behind and he was flying over the smooth cycle path to a neighboring summer resort. Many others were riding on this path, and to avoid some too-exuberant friends whom he saw coming, he turned aside onto a quiet road. Not long afterward, as he approached a fine old country house, he saw a girlish figure upon a bicycle come out from the gateway and turn in his direction. He recognized her with surprise.

Why, it's Juliet! he thought. *How does she come out here? This must be her grandfather's place. Of course it is—I remember now. Well, I didn't mean to say good-bye to anybody, least of all to Juliet; but I can't get out of it now, and I suppose she'd feel it if I didn't. So here goes—but I'd rather be shot!*

"Why, Larry Thorne!" cried the girl as he dismounted and pulled off his cap. "What are you doing here? I didn't know you had a vacation now."

"This is luck to meet you, Juliet," he said as the two looked smilingly at one another in the middle of the quiet road. "No, there's no vacation. This is one of those enforced leaves of absence, you know. Yes," in answer to the astonished expression on her face, "I'm suspended again. Fine record, isn't it, for a fellow's first year?"

He tried to speak lightly, but the quick change in her look from one of happy surprise was painful to see. He went on rapidly, feeling that he must make his explanations as soon as possible and be gone. He realized, as he faced her, that it would not be easy work to explain to Juliet.

"You see," he began, finding himself unable to meet her clear gray eyes and shifting his own as he talked to the meadows, the sky, the ground, to anything but that sober girl face, "the faculty had warned me that a second offense would mean suspension to the end of the year. I fully intended not to displease them again, but—of course I can't make you understand—our crowd had reasons for wanting to get even with a certain set in '99, and the fun of it tempted me—as usual. Well, the result is, here I am; but I won't be . . . for long. I—I'm glad to have met you, for I sha'n't see you again very soon. I'm going west—to Montana—tomorrow."

A rapidly approaching carriage saved Juliet an immediate reply, and the two retreated to a fence at the side of the road. Here Larry disposed of the bicycle and leaned against the fence, feeling that while he dreaded what Juliet might say, it would be rather a relief to talk things over with her a bit. He had talked over so many things with Juliet! Since the days when they made mud pies and snow forts together, she had been his neighbor and friend, and until the last year, she had shared nearly all his plans and secrets. He could trust Juliet; and it was better that he should not go away leaving her to think what she would of him.

She did not speak but stood with her face turned aside, while he wondered if she would lecture, scold, or snub him. It was not Juliet's way to do any of these things. At the same time, she never left him in any doubt as to her position in matters of right and wrong.

"Do you mean," she asked him slowly at last, "that you are going away on account of that?"

"What—suspension? Oh no, that's only part of it! The truth is—" He hesitated. "You know well enough I hate to study worse than, well, than a girl like you who adores books could possibly understand. There's something in me like a steam engine under tremendous pressure; and after I've plugged away about so long with a steadily mounting steam gauge, I've got to break bounds or burst. That's what gets me into scrapes. Why, if I had been old enough when the Spanish War broke out, I'd have been the happiest fellow on earth. Yet I couldn't stand the discipline of a military school, so it's no use going in for that. If I can get off on Barrett Warner's ranch, where I can live the life of a wild Indian pony—"

"You?" she interrupted skeptically, with a glance at the handsome bicycle suit, at his well-kept hands, at the fine lines of his face. "You going in for the rough life of a Western ranchman?"

"I don't suppose I look it now," he acknowledged with a flush, "and I'll admit that it's not my ideal. But . . . I'll tell you, Juliet. The greatest of all my reasons is one I can't say much about. Perhaps I oughtn't even to hint at it, but I must, or you'll misjudge me. You see, Father has come to the end of his patience with me. I don't know that I can blame him, for I have disappointed him in every way. But"—his face darkened—"he has said things to me I can't stand. I don't have to stand them. He told me—"

"Larry," interposed the girl, "I don't think you ought to tell me."

"I will," cried the young fellow fiercely, "whether it's dishonorable or not, because I must make you understand, and you can't do it unless I tell you! He said—no, I won't stop—that he was ashamed of me, that he couldn't trust me.

"There! That's what cuts worst. He never said anything like that before. I suppose I'm a miserable good-for-nothing, but I don't think I . . . I could stand it to be with him and know he didn't care for me better than to say he couldn't trust me. He might as well have said—"

Larry's voice broke; he turned away to hide the angry tears that were welling into his eyes, but Juliet did not seem to be observing him. She was breaking little splinters from the rough mill fence. Below the downcast gray eyes, a pair of very pink cheeks testified to her interest in her old comrade's fortunes.

When Larry had waited what seemed to him an interminable length of time for Juliet to speak, he broke the silence gruffly. "You may as well tell me what you're thinking. It can't be any worse than I'm imagining all this while."

The girl looked up. "I'm sorry for you, Larry," she said in a low tone, "because I can see you are very unhappy. I don't suppose it's any use to beg you not to go, and I'm not wise enough to say the right thing; perhaps I ought not to say anything. But what I can't help thinking is that it seems a pity for you to . . . to run away from your record."

"To run away from my record?" repeated Larry slowly while a singular gleam came into his eyes. "Is that what you think I'm doing?"

"I don't see what else it is," she answered gently. "You've made this record, and now when things are at their worst, you go off and leave them so. Even if you do well in the West, you'll always have to remember what you left behind you here."

"But you don't understand," Larry told her hurriedly. "What else can I do? I've failed in every way to please everybody—you included. What's the use of my trying to do what I'm not adapted to, and be what it's not in me to be? And now that Lawrence Thorne, senior, has shown what he thinks of me—"

"I don't believe he thinks it!" cried Juliet eagerly. "I think you misunderstood him. Even if he really doesn't trust you anymore, why don't you *make* him do it? You can earn his confidence all over again. As for your not being fitted for study, what difference does that make? You wouldn't take a dare in the gymnasium. I've known about that other fellow of a different build doing a thing it was twice as hard for you to do, but you wouldn't be outclassed, and you kept at it till you could do it—and better than he could, too. Why don't you go at your books in the same way, whether you like them or not? Even on a Western ranch, you'd find use for your knowledge, and even if you didn't, your mind would have had the training just the same. Think of your father. Such a splendid mind he has, and what a disappointment it would be to him to have his son an—"

"Ignoramus," finished Larry grimly.

"You know I didn't mean that," she said with a deepening of the excited color in her cheeks. "And, Larry—I don't mean to preach, but I'm afraid when you get out there, you'll find it, perhaps, still harder to . . . do right."

The boy turned away abruptly at the low-spoken words. He was not sure how much Juliet knew of the fast set of his class, leader of which he had come to be. But a vision of one of the evenings spent among them flashed before his eyes, and it occurred to him that if he were not strong enough to influence for the better his own mates, he might easily be dragged downward by the association with a far wilder, rougher sort.

The sun was sinking rapidly toward the west. Juliet looked back at the house from which she had come and consulted a tiny chatelaine watch at her belt. "Grandma expects me in time for tea," she said, "and I must go."

Larry retrieved his bicycle and began the slow walk by Juliet's side to the gate, saying not a word. She glanced at him shyly once or twice, but he had pulled his cap visor far over his eyes, and his lips were firmly compressed. The girl waited anxiously, and getting no word as they reached the gateway, she turned and laid her hand softly on Larry's arm.

"Chum," she whispered (it was their old name for each other), "you won't forget how this would make *her* feel?"

It had needed only that to break up the depths in the boy's softening heart. He desperately tried to cover his emotion with a muttered, "Ah, that's different! She cared."

"Larry," breathed Juliet, her heart beating painfully fast, "you may think I don't know, but I do. She did care, but so does he. I know you misunderstand him. Dignified as he is, one has only to look at him when you are by and it shows, although you may not see it. Go back to him. Tell him you will do your best to make up for your mistakes. Tell him—oh, tell him what you like, but do it! I know you can make him tremendously proud of you, if you only will. Show him what you really are. I believe in you, Larry. Don't run away from your record. *Change it!*"

The boy's eyes came slowly back to her face from the ground where they had been steadily fixed. He drew a long breath, pulled himself erect, looked squarely into the pleading gray eyes in which his little "chum's" confidence in him was plainly written, and as he gave her her bicycle and prepared to leap upon his own, he made this brief speech—a far more eloquent one could not have pleased her half so much: "Juliet, you're true blue if a girl ever was. Thanks to you, I will."

Then he was off like the wind down the road toward home.

An hour later, Mr. Lawrence Thorne was surprised by the sudden entrance of his son. The young fellow no longer looked either angry, proud, or sullen, and his step was light. He came up to the desk and stood looking straight into the eyes of the elder man.

"Father," he said quietly, "I've made up my mind. I want to tell you that I beg your forgiveness for all I've done to make you disappointed in me.

I'm ashamed of myself clear through. If you'll let me, I'm going to stay and try to earn your trust again."

Was that his father's face, with that glad smile breaking up all the cold, hard lines? Perhaps neither could see the other's face quite distinctly, for there was a very perceptible huskiness in the voice of the senior Lawrence Thorne as, grasping the hand Larry had not dared hold out to him, he said heartily, "My son, you have it now!"

Answers at Nightfall

Arthur Gordon

It was only an ungainly pelican, there on the beach at dusk. Yet in that one bird lay most of the questions a fourteen-year-old girl would ask about life and death and the eternal scheme of things.

Sometimes I think, a bit wryly, that a parent can't really teach children anything of importance; all you can do is expose them to living. That way the lessons come so quietly and unobtrusively that often you aren't aware of them, until you begin to think back.

Yesterday, for example . . .

* * *

We were returning, the four of us, from an hour of late-afternoon fishing. Our little skiff took the rollers easily, gold-flecked in the burnished light. To our left, the low dunes of the Georgia coast. To our right, nothing but birds and sea and sky, and now and then the quicksilver flash of a leaping mackerel. Ordinarily we would have been five in the boat. But Dana, our fourteen-year-old lover of all living things, had elected to stay at home with a baby raccoon she had somehow acquired.

"I have to fix his formula," she had said happily. "Besides, if I leave him, he squeaks."

I decided to land my crew—one wife, two children—and let them walk home while I took the boat to its anchorage up an inlet. As we eased in to the beach, I noticed a pelican on the sand near the water's edge, huddled and motionless. He watched us as we approached, but made no attempt to fly.

"That bird doesn't seem very happy," I said and thought no more about it until I arrived home after mooring the boat.

At the foot of our steps, head drooping, great wings half-spread, was the pelican. Around him, silhouettes of concern, were the members of my family—now including Dana, who crouched close, blond hair falling across her face, sunburned arms protectively around the bird's neck. She looked up, her gray eyes misty.

"Oh, Daddy," she said, "what's wrong with him? He can't fly, and he can hardly walk, and he's shivering."

I resisted an impulse to say that, no matter what was wrong with him, a family with eight cats and a poodle and a baby raccoon hardly needed any more animal problems.

My wife, as usual, read my mind. "We couldn't just walk away and leave him," she said quietly.

"We carried him all the way," our youngest said proudly. "I carried his head and part of his neck, and he didn't even try to bite!"

I looked at the great bill with a hook at the end, so light yet so strong, and thought—not for the first time—how strange and marvelous it was that a creature so grotesque could know one moment of flashing beauty: At the last split-second of his dive, a fishing pelican folds his clumsy wings and cleaves the water like a hurled javelin, all grace and power and precision. But I had a feeling that this bird would know such moments no more.

I ran my hand along the silky throat feathers. I could feel no obstruction. The bird flinched a little, took a few floundering steps, and then grew still, yellow eyes watching us remotely.

"Maybe," I said, "we should call the vet."

"We did," my wife told me. "He said that about all we could do for tonight was give him some water and watch him."

"He doesn't want water," Dana said sadly. "He doesn't want bread, either. I offered him some."

"We can cut up some fish," I said. "But I doubt if he'll eat any."

We offered the fish; it was ignored. We poured a little water into the corners of the unresisting bill. He did not seem afraid of us, but now and then convulsive tremors ran through him.

"Oh, he's cold," wailed Dana, and she pinned a beach towel tenderly around him.

The sun went down in a smear of crimson. The others finally went inside to supper, leaving Dana and me alone with the bird. Out over the ocean, seeking their night resting places, long lines of pelicans were arching across the sky, and I wondered if the earthbound one was aware of them.

"Let's take him back down to the water," I said at last to Dana. "When he sees all his friends going home, maybe he'll try to go with them."

With Dana carrying the huge, passive bird, we walked down to the seawall, through the dunes, across the deserted beach. The tide was ebbing; the waves were steel-colored in the fading light. Almost above us now, from south to north, the silent wings swept past. Dana waded out ankle-deep. I watched as she unpinned the towel and put her burden down. And it was very strange: As if on signal, at the instant the broad webbed feet touched

the water, something was released, something ended. Without a sound, the great, ungainly head fell forward into the waves.

"Bring him back, baby," I said gently. "He's dead."

She brought him back and laid him on the sand, somehow smaller, very quiet, very still. She knelt beside him, tears streaming down her face. "Oh," she said to him in an anguished voice, "why did you do that? Why did you have to die?"

The wind blew, the waves moved in, and the question hung in the air as it has since the beginning of time.

"Don't be sad," I said at last. "He's not sick or unhappy anymore."

She drew a long breath and wiped her eyes with the back of her hand. She looked up at the great procession overhead. "Do you think any of his children are up there?"

"Probably. Children and grandchildren and great-grandchildren."

She nodded slowly, eyes shadowed with the mystery and miracle of death and life. She reached out once and smoothed the damp feathers gently. Then she stood up and shook back her hair. "Can we bury him now?"

We buried him at the foot of the dunes, where the melancholy sea oats could watch over him. I shaped a mound and put some broken pieces of concrete on top. The tides would never reach this far.

At the seawall we looked back to where the concrete glimmered. Then Dana spoke softly. To me or to herself? "He *was* back where he wanted to be, wasn't he? And he *is* still part of it, isn't he?"

The stars were beginning to show through; the sea was dark; the birds were gone in the gathering night. My daughter took my hand with a grown-up firmness.

"Let's go in now," she said, "and see about feeding that hungry raccoon."

Between Strokes

Walter R. Schmidt

Dexter had no friends—he was a self-admitted coward. But one day a young freshman sat down next to the uncommunicative senior and began to talk. Later on, Dexter asked why. Later yet, he did something about it.

Dexter Parker entered the University Express. All around him were boisterous laughter, friendly slaps on the back, and loud greetings. None of them were for him, however.

As the train pulled out, a short, slim fellow came down the aisle, threw his suitcase on the rack above Dexter's head, and nonchalantly took the empty place next to the tall, blond youth. Dexter kept reading his magazine, but out of the corner of his eye he observed the lad quizzically.

"On your way to Pomfret?" asked the stranger finally.

Dexter nodded.

The smaller youth said, looking around, "Funny—the train's packed, there's a mob standing, and yet this seat was unoccupied."

Dexter shrugged. "I have no friends," he said simply.

"Then you're a freshman, too?"

"No, a senior."

The other appeared puzzled and repeated: "A senior!"

Dexter laughed grimly and nodded his head.

* * *

Two weeks later Dexter saw Lee Morrison again. Lee stopped him and invited him to see the bicycle races. As tactfully as possible, Dexter declined.

"Is it just because I'm a freshman that you don't want to go with me?" demanded Lee.

Dexter shook his head vigorously. "No, it's not that at all."

"Well," argued the younger boy, "I'm new here, you know. You're the only friend I have. Come along, won't you?" He smiled and looked up from his five feet five to the top of Dexter's six feet one.

Dexter could refuse no longer. "Maybe I could arrange—"

"Great!" said Lee eagerly. "I'll pick you up in front of the library at seven."

That evening the two young men made their way by bus to the wooden saucer ten miles from Pomfret. The main race was a motor-paced affair. The machines droned around the track like speeding, darting bees. They watched in silence for some time; then Lee, turning sideways toward Dexter, asked, "Why doesn't anyone at college ever talk to you or pal with you, Dexter?"

"Because I'm a coward."

"A *coward?*" The younger boy's voice was incredulous.

"Yes," Dexter went on. "I'm the best oarsman in school—so the coach and a lot of others insist—but I'm yellow. I've never learned to swim. I pretended I could during my frosh year, but one day the shell tipped over and I was found out.

"What made me afraid of water happened long ago," he continued after a pause. "A little pal of mine drowned, and I was too small myself to help him. I've never gotten over it. Lots of people have tried to teach me to swim, but it's no use. Maybe I am yellow, I don't know."

Lee sat very quietly beside Dexter and waited for him to continue.

"I suppose," said the latter finally, "you're wondering how I ever took to rowing. At prep school there was an indoor machine fixed up like a shell. I enjoyed it, and you know how it is with anything you like. When we took to the water, I found myself stroking the first boat.

"In the zest and excitement of shelling, I forgot all about my fear of the water over which the boat glided. I was captain for two years. There, you see, we didn't have to know how to swim. I had a great time.

"Then I came to Pomfret. The crew I stroked the first year at Pomfret ran away with every race. Then the others learned about my not being able to swim. It broke up everything. We've lost every big race the past two years. They think I'm yellow because I won't learn. It's not that I won't; I *can't*. Why, I've tried millions of times, but—" His voice cracked and his hands gripped hard on the arms of the wooden seat. He sat staring straight ahead of him, seeing nothing.

He heard Lee say, "But you're not a coward, Parker. Anyone ought to be able to see that. Can't the idiots see that if you really were yellow, you wouldn't have stuck it out here at Pomfret as you've done? Can't they see that? I can."

Dexter said nothing.

"When is the regatta?"

"The fifteenth of May."

"And the crew that wins goes north to meet Navy?"

"Yes."

Lee leaned toward his friend. "You may not believe it, Dexter," he said, "but I have a roomful of cups that I've won at swimming meets. Could you, I wonder, find an hour's spare time every day from now until the big race?"

Dexter nodded again, unthinkingly.

"And would you be game enough to let me try to teach you to swim?"

Thoughts whirled through Dexter's mind, but they were so jumbled they hardly made sense. The one fact that stood out clearly was that this slip of a freshman was offering to teach him, a giant of a senior—a fellow strong enough to pull an oar for four miles—to swim. Instinctively he knew that if he refused Lee, he would hurt him. The smaller youth was offering to help him win back the place that belonged to him, Dexter Parker, in the school, in the world. Lee had said he was not a coward, not yellow; what would he think if Dexter refused?

"When do we start?" he asked quietly.

"Tomorrow!" There was unrestrained happiness in Lee's voice.

"What time?"

"I think during lunch hour. We won't be doing any cutting then, and too many nosey bodies won't be prowling around at that hour."

Neither of them said anything more. They merely looked at each other. So is friendship born in the hearts of men, young or old.

At one o'clock the next day, Lee and Dexter met at the beach around the cove. They trudged out to the float, where the water reached Dexter's chest. He shivered, but Lee pretended not to notice.

"You feel safe with your feet on the bottom the way you're standing now?"

"Ye-es," replied Dexter.

"That's fine. Now the next thing for you to do is to convince yourself that nothing can happen to you if you hold your breath when you're under water. Inhale now."

Dexter inhaled.

"Hold it."

Dexter held it.

"Now put your head under water."

Dexter hesitated.

"Just for a second," urged Lee.

Dexter ducked quickly and came up sputtering.

"Try it again," ordered his instructor.

Dexter looked at Lee a moment and hesitated. He could not let this slim youngster, who was so much smaller than himself, think he was afraid. He took a long breath and ducked again. The time after that he found he could stay under twice as long as the first time.

When the next day's lesson was over, Dexter had learned something else: that it was possible for him to hold on to the float with his hands and kick his legs and thereby make the float move.

Two days later, he learned that if he let go of the float occasionally, he faltered and went under; but he always remembered about holding his breath.

* * *

One day as Dexter turned away from the stationary shell in the boathouse, having just finished pulling the mechanical oar, he found Anderson, the crew coach, watching him. Dexter was so surprised that it was seconds before he could find his voice. Even then all he could manage was a rather weak "Hello."

"Hello, Parker," said Anderson. "I hear you're trying to learn to swim so you can get in the regatta." The coach tossed him a folded piece of writing paper on which was written:

> Coach Anderson:
> Dexter Parker wants his place back in the varsity boat. He is learning to swim, and by the fifteenth I know he will be able to pass the necessary swimming test.

The note was unsigned, but Dexter knew who had written it. A lump surged up into his throat and almost choked him. Dexter received the impression, as Anderson walked off, that a grim yet hopeful smile lurked at the corners of the coach's mouth.

While Dexter was by no means a water bug, his old fear of the water had practically vanished. Under young Lee's coaching and encouragement, he had reached the point where he actually looked forward to his daily swim.

Then, one day, about a week before the big race, Lee said, "You're going to swim from the float to the ropes for today's lesson."

Dexter looked at his friend quizzically; then he measured the distance with his eyes. It was all of fifty yards. "If I could do that—" He did not finish.

When it was time for them to leave, Dexter had not been able to cover more than half the distance from the float to the ropes. Lee looked disappointed but said nothing. He got into his clothes silently and was all ready to go. Dexter remained in his bathing suit.

"What's the idea?" asked Lee. "Aren't you coming up?"

Dexter shook his head doggedly, determinedly. "No, I'm going to stay until I can swim from that float to that rope."

"You'll do it too, Dexter," said Lee quietly. "I know you will." Then he was gone. When he reached a point around the cove where he was out of Dexter's sight, however, he carefully retraced his steps and hid behind a huge boulder. He had crouched there only a few minutes when he heard the crunching sound of footsteps behind him. Another person knelt beside him. It was Coach Anderson. Together they observed Pomfret's former stroke make the greatest fight he had ever made.

Dexter turned to the water. A fierce determination seemed to have taken possession of him. He walked out into the deeper water and shoved off from the float. There were one or two periods during his various attempts to cover the distance when the two watchers were frightened. Once it looked as though Dexter might go under, and Lee was on the verge of dashing out of his hiding place and diving in after him. By some super-human strength and courage, however, Dexter somehow fought his way back into the clumsy stroke and awkward kick that kept him afloat and moving. This was the young man who was called yellow, a coward!

Finally, after at least a dozen attempts, with much thrashing, wallowing, and swallowing of water, Dexter grasped the heavy rope. *He had won!* He was not a coward. He was not yellow. It had taken a little slip of a fellow, a freshman, a true friend, to prove this to him.

Dexter was not sure whether it was five minutes or five hours after he had returned to his room that he heard a knock at his door. It was the first time anyone had knocked at his door for a long, long time.

Whoever it was knocked again. Dexter sat up and called, "Come in."

Coach Anderson entered. "I saw you this afternoon, Parker," he said. "Young Morrison and I watched you from behind a big rock down there at the beach. Right now Doc Healy is filling out your swimming certificate."

Dexter gulped hard. "Why, why that's great! Now I can—"

Anderson cut in. "I guess you know I've not been satisfied with the eight all year. Pete's a good number six, but he's not a stroke. I have a hunch that beginning tomorrow that crew'll begin looking like a winner. We're getting out early tomorrow, Parker."

"I'll be there, Coach," said Dexter.

* * *

When the three crews took to the water the evening of the fifteenth, the smooth, glassy surface of the lake had changed to a choppy, white-capped series of slapping waves. Every so often the sun was blotted out by threatening, blue-black clouds.

Ramsey reached the starting line first and jockeyed around until Houston pulled up. Right behind the blue-and-white shell came Pomfret. In the first seat of the Pomfret boat sat Dexter Parker, Coach Anderson's last words still ringing in his ears.

"Listen, gang," he had said, "keep the beat low for the first mile and a half. Conserve your strength because when you get down around the bend, you'll find the water calmer. Then hit it up. Hit it up hard!"

Dexter did not see the thousands lined up along the lakeshore, nor did he hear their frenzied roar as the gun went off and his big red blade bit into the choppy water, the seven men behind him dipping simultaneously. All he could see was Lee Morrison's face before him.

They had covered the first mile. The going was terribly rough. Dexter did not see either Ramsey or Houston. He knew they must be ahead, but he did not care where they were, or which was leading. When Grant called on him for more, he would give it.

Just as the coach had said, when they swept around the bend, the water was calmer. Immediately Grant raised the count. The eight red sweeps struck the water in quickened tempo, the seats slid back and forth in faster rhythm. Someone swung into Dexter's sight. It was the Ramsey coxswain. Grant asked for more, and Dexter hit it up another beat.

Inch by inch, the entire Ramsey crew came into Dexter's view. Then, another heave, another, and another, and there was open water between the two shells. At the two-mile mark, the big red boat caught the blue-and-white Houston oarsmen.

Smith barked for more speed, and Dexter gave it. Grimly and determinedly he dipped, pulled, and slid in time with the bark of the little coxswain's voice.

"Houston's three-quarters of a length behind," screeched Grant, "and there's only a half mile more. We got it, men, we got it. This race is ours."

Dame Fate then, swift and sudden, took a hand in the matter. What it was his blade struck, Dexter never knew; but as he followed through a particularly vicious thrust, the oar went lifeless in his hands. He knew without looking that the blade was gone. He saw Grant's face go white.

For just a second Dexter sat there still as death. In that second it flashed through his brain that it would be impossible for Pomfret to hold that lead the next half mile carrying "dead" cargo. Without him . . .

As the seven seats slid forward as one on the next stroke, Dexter jumped. He felt the water close over his head as he slipped down into the cold depths. *I can swim for at least fifty yards,* he thought confidently.

When he came to the choppy surface, his hopes dropped. The only place of safety was the shore and that was far away. But then he heard the *putt-putt* of a motorboat behind him, and he began swimming, awkwardly but confidently.

As Dexter was being helped into the motorboat, a gun went off. The roar of the crowd along the banks boomed across the lake. Above it sounded clear and strong the Pomfret victory cheer.

"Looks like you boys'll be goin' north to race Navy," someone said.

"We won?" Dexter asked hopefully.

"By a quarter of a length," said the man. "Houston couldn't quite catch you. Now, if you hadn't jumped out of your shell, it would have been a different story."

* * *

No doubt it was just like any other college party, but to Dexter Parker everything was different. The coach shook hands with him and told him he was proud of him. Little Grant Smith laughed with him. Big Pete Campbell slapped him on the back and told him he was "the goods." Arthur Meyers smiled quietly and said that they would beat Navy sure as anything. Other students, too, drifted over singly and in couples to talk with Dexter.

The greatest joy of all, however, lay in the wide smile on Lee Morrison's face and the happy glint in his eyes. When, later in the evening, he and Lee were alone together for a few minutes, Dexter said nothing at all. He merely gripped the younger fellow's hands, and Lee silently returned the pressure. They both knew that there had been welded between them a friendship that would last as long as they lived.

The Hanging Lamp

Melcena Burns Denny

When the clothesline post broke and all her washing fell onto the dusty ground, it was the last straw for Elizabeth Day. Reluctantly, John agreed to sell the family farm and move back to the city. But first they had to fix up the place.

And then the clothesline broke! No, not the clothesline. That was new. The ancestral clothes post! It had simply fainted. Down went the united garments of the family, into the dust.

After all I had endured that morning, the accident was too horrible. I wept aloud. Presently, I felt my husband's hand pat my shoulder.

"I won't!" I raged. "I won't go on living here in Tillicum Valley forever! I hate the farm! The wash bench wobbles! The tubs are preposterous! The pump creaks! My skirts swish! My shoes ooze! Every Monday of my life forever—and I'm only thirty-two!"

"Go in and rest, darling. I'll rinse the clothes," said John.

I swished in, but not to rest. It was time to set the table in the dining room—500 extra steps. I squeaked about in weary haste. A

fly sought sanctuary on the hanging lamp. I swatted the lamp with peculiar satisfaction, for I hated it. Its glass pendants jingled with an absurdly
merry sound. I began to laugh.

I laughed more when I looked out and saw John hanging the clothes at
strange angles between two apple trees. A shining car passed with a flut-
ter of hands. John flapped a towel gaily. What would the Henleys think of
me? Another neighbor approached: Life Smith, a pleased but not pleasant spectator. His whole name was Life Liberty Pursuit Smith—or so we
judged from his initials. Certainly he was always in pursuit of us with
advice and commiseration.

"Dinner!" I called.

John waved the last towel. Junior and Betty came running, happy with
hunger. To my despair, Mr. Smith stopped his fat horses, descended, and
ambled toward the house as if I had called him, too. He slapped John on
the back with a loud guffaw.

"How-de-do, Mrs. Day. I wouldn't of missed seein' John hang out the
Monday wash fer a farm. Clo's post broke smack off, eh? Rotten at the
roots like the rest of this old place! Them I-talian tenants did more harm
in two years than John can fix in three. That Tony was a born loafer. Fences
down, alfalfa pastured to death! Even when John's folks was alive, this place
was no better'n mine, an' I'd jump at $5,000 fer my place any day!"

"Dinner is ready. Won't you join us, Mr. Smith?" I was trying to stand
so he couldn't see my shoes.

"No, I jest come in to ask if you've found your freezer yet. You ain't?
What did them I-talians do with it? We always used to borrow from John's
folks, but I guess I'll have to buy a freezer!" He looked at me piercingly.
"Ain't you about tired of farm life, Mrs. Day?"

"'Deed I am!"

"Pity you ever tried it, an' John gettin' good money in the city. Next
you'll be tryin' to sell, like I am."

"I am planning to sell in the spring," said John.

At these incredible words, I gasped. Never before had John uttered one syllable about selling. My joyful glance flew to Mr. Smith. A strange gleam of triumph seemed to retreat into his cold, pale eyes.

"You'll be lucky if you can get $4,000. Tony's wife was always naggin' at him to save up an' make you an offer. But the ghost scared 'em out. Whether you believe in 'em or not, a ghost lowers the value of your farm."

"What's a ghost, Mother?" asked little Betty.

"A ghost, precious, is a limb rubbing against the roof in a wind. Junior is almost sure which limb it is. Must you go, Mr. Smith?" Then, when he was gone: "Oh, John! Do you really mean you are willing to sell and move back to the city?"

John put both hands on my shoulders in his kind, elderly way—he is two months my senior—and said, "We are going to be happy, Elizabeth. If our happiness lies in the city, there we will live."

"Near the Whitneys again!" I knew John missed the Whitneys. He and Howard Whitney had been pals from boyhood, and Belle had gone to the same school, too—the little one-room district school with the tall oak tree and the pump, where my own children were actually eager to enroll.

"Can we take Rover to the city?" demanded Betty, close to tears.

I had a daunting vision of the big dog occupying our tiny apartment to the exclusion of ourselves. "We'll see, dear."

"We can't take my pony." Junior spoke with low-voiced reasonableness, as if to himself.

"John, I don't want to influence you too much," I quavered. "I'm worn out. Four months trying to get settled! I work and work, and my hair strings down, and to cap all, when the clothes post fell—"

"I'm going to get you iron posts and set them in cement."

"Don't," I protested. "We're going to sell!"

"Every little improvement helps a sale." He smiled whimsically. "I don't know but that two strong posts of chaste design might sell the place."

"Then get them!" I cried. "And watch what I do to this house! I can make it fool anybody."

"Fool anybody?"

"It's all so ugly—like that hanging lamp! But I can cheer it up."

"I always thought the lamp was pretty," confessed John. "But I read so many good books under its light when I was a boy . . . " Then, changing his tone, he said heartily, "Go to it! Spend $100."

One hundred dollars! We could not afford it. But it would come back quadruple in a sale, I felt sure. I fell to figuring.

* * *

John installed the new clothes posts. It was gratifying to have plenty of line, immovably supported by those neat, slim posts. But I was all for hastening through my daily work and not lingering to enjoy clothes posts. Clothes worn unseen went unironed. I planned every step to save myself time. Without robbing the children of play, I turned their energies into helpful channels. And the children were such good sports about it, I put some money into their purses every week.

"It's yours, children. Part may have to go for things you need, part for pleasure. But it's yours."

"I think that's a good plan," John remarked. "Fine man as my father was, I had to ask him for every dollar I needed till I was grown. I left the farm really because I wanted to handle my earnings like a man. When we came back, I planned to make the children partners with you and me—to let them raise a calf or pig apiece every year and enjoy the profits. It isn't merely a back-to-the-farm movement our country needs; it's a stay-on-the-farm plan that will keep the young people interested."

"But the wives! Are farms forever going to have worked-to-death wives?"

"Why, hardly!" John, with twinkling eyes, read from a clipping his pocket yielded. "Here is the pronouncement of some intelligent Nebraska women: 'A power washing machine for every tractor; a bathtub for every binder; running water for every riding plow; a kerosene cookstove for every automobile truck; a fireless cooker for every mowing machine; and their share in the farm income.'"

"Fine!" I approved. "I hope my successor can work that out."

At that moment, the children came in with a squash from our garden. I enthroned it on a black enameled tray, where it shone like a futurist sun.

"There!" said Junior admiringly. "I guess if any buyers come now, that summer squash would sell the place."

"What a lovely yellow! Betty, I'm going to make your walls mellow sunshine. Peter Pease is coming tomorrow to do the ceilings, but I'm going to do the walls myself."

"I want pink. I love pink," said Betty wistfully.

"I want my walls the color of that squash," declared Junior.

After all, why not? I might as well please the children, even if I was painting for buyers.

* * *

Next day Peter Pease, who had already cleaned the flues and gutters and pronounced the old house firm as a rock, washed the mud-colored tint from the children's rooms and did the ceilings in ivory. I had decided to paint the walls so they would stand soap. First I sized them—a process easy but essential. Then I mixed buff and ivory for Junior's room, using a flat-tone paint that looked velvety. I curtained his windows in yellow, and together Junior and I mended and rubbed the old walnut furniture that had belonged to John's mother. Junior undertook to make shelves. It was astonishing what skill he showed with tools.

Finally, he assembled all his boyish treasures: books, Indian implements and arrowheads, and his strange new collection of agricultural pests, from the earwig that imperiled Betty's garden to our ancient enemy, the codling moth. I didn't care for this collection, but Junior beamed and embraced me.

"Say, it's great to have some space all your own! Remember how I had to keep my boxes of beetles under the dining room couch in the city?"

Yes, and I remembered how he had to sleep on that same couch.

Betty's room had been furnished in what we called our museum pieces: relics of maid's room furniture. We changed them to ivory enamel. The room developed into an ethereal pink, between shell pink and ivory. I put bluebird and apple-blossom cretonne at the windows and copied the blue-bird and apple-blossom motif onto her bed and dresser and rocking chair; and every place there was a knob, I made it blue. Betty expanded and glowed and kissed the walls every time she entered her room.

"Pink is so beautiful, Mother! Oh, did that kiss make it dirty?"

"Never mind. Kiss it again. It will wash."

"How the children love your work!" John said with shining eyes. "Junior's room used to have trunks in it. I remember the *drip-drip-drip* on the porch outside. How did you brighten the room so?"

"I made it yellow!" I boasted. "Junior demanded it. If our buyers come in a storm, this room will sell the house."

"It's bully! But no more stepladder art, Elizabeth. You may be brittle. I'll paint for you when it's pouring."

But I couldn't resist climbing. Besides, John was working like two men, mending fences, harvesting crops, and getting the farm shipshape.

The children entered school and adored the long walk across the fields. Betty loaded herself with weeds and wildflowers indiscriminately and presented them daily to her teacher, in the solemn belief that they were all beautiful. And her teacher did make them beautiful! How Mary Henley, with her college education, could be content to teach the little home school was a puzzle to me. But of course the Henleys were unusual people. The children drew inspiration from even the weeds on her desk.

"The very same desk I used to put red apples on!" John said with a grin.

In October John had to go to the city for a week. When he returned, I flung the whole house, as it were, before him. The kitchen was deep cream, with green and gray linoleum. It had green checked gingham curtains at the windows that seemed to invite the whole outdoors to come a little closer. The living room, guest room, and our bedroom were fresh with new paper. The dining room was smart in new paint, too.

"Can't we take down the hanging lamp?" I urged.

"Why, yes," John agreed, with that look in his eyes I'd seen before—a secret, boyish, ashamed look of loyalty.

"Oh, Mother, the roses and the bee on it are so pretty!"

"It isn't a bee," objected Junior painstakingly. "It isn't a horsefly, either."

"Well, I'm glad of that!" I gasped. "Maybe our buyers will be mid-Victorian," I reconsidered. "Really, the lamp is so ugly, it's almost beautiful. Now let our buyers come!"

"Elizabeth, the Whitneys may buy from us. They have inherited a little money."

"The Whitneys!" I was dumbfounded.

"They know this farm. I told them Mr. Smith wants to sell, too."

"Oh, why did you do that? Let's sell them ours! I'll write and invite them for Thanksgiving. My kitchen will sell the house!"

The Whitneys promptly accepted our invitation. Then the Henleys invited us. It was so neighborly, it made my heart warm, even though we were obliged to decline.

It was wonderful to be expecting dear friends as guests. Of course it meant work—but there was little to do to the house now except polish the doorknobs. I made mincemeat and arranged my jelly for display.

John was as boyish as Junior. For, happy culmination of our thrift, our

THE END

OF A

SUMMER DAY.

crops were marketed, and we had money in the bank. The wood was in. The smell of apples in the cellar was like carnations.

"That smell will sell the house!" cried my little echo, Betty, drawing an intoxicated breath. "I wish I had a bottle of apple perfume."

* * *

Neighbor Smith had watched our undertakings with amazement, not to say disfavor.

Early one morning, when the wind was in an unusual quarter, Junior found the ghost. John climbed up to saw it off. Mr. Smith chanced to be passing.

"What are you doin' up in the elm tree, John?" he shouted.

"Sawing off the ghost!" John roared back.

"Pursuit's coming in," I giggled, wobbling the ladder.

"Steady there! I'm the only husband you've got, woman!"

"Land sakes, wasn't it anything but that limb rubbin' an' groanin'?"

"Apparently not. We caught it in the act."

Mr. Smith hung around. "Still calculate to sell, now you've nabbed the ghost?" Pursuit, with a cold, thoughtful eye, was seemingly in the throes of some thrifty scheme. "Times ain't favorable fer sales!"

"Can't you sell?"

"No! Buyers ain't to be found! Farmlands have let down—prices have dropped so the crops ain't worth a nickel. I'd like to sell and clean out. But if I've got to stay, I need more alfalfa land fer my critters. I'll offer you $4,500 spot cash fer your whole place, complete."

I trembled, but John threw down a limb of the ghost with great coolness. "I think I have a buyer, Mr. Smith. I'll consider your offer, however, if my friend doesn't buy."

"Has he seen it?" pried Pursuit.

"He's coming on Thanksgiving Day."

Pursuit's pale blue eyes turned on me. "You're sick of the place, ain't you, Mrs. Day?"

"Oh, I don't know!" I said airily. I let him look at me as sharply as he wished, and I didn't try to hide my feet. Since my house was in order, my hair was usually in order, too; and my dress.

"Spot cash!"

"His will be spot cash, too."

"I'll make it $5,000, since I want my answer now. By heck, that's a lot of money, John! I'd jump at it if anybody offered me that fer mine."

John came down out of his tree. "If you'll give me an option on your place for thirty days for $5,000, I'll write to a number of my city friends about it."

"Well, now, he-he-he! I was speakin' figurative!"

"Well, what is your price, then? You've always said $5,000."

"Seven thousand five hundred—not a cent less!" said our neighbor with a rasping noise in his bony throat, like a pan being scoured.

John made a memorandum.

"Will you sign that?"

"Sign it?" grated Pursuit, trying to look offended. "Ain't my word good?"

"Yes, but my city friends don't know you as I do. They might not bother to answer unless I can write them definitely that I have an option."

Poor Pursuit seemed torn in two. Finally, he signed. We went in to breakfast.

"We've had a real offer!" I hurrahed, hugging the family.

Strangely enough, my elation did not last. We were so comfortable in our clean kitchen, we four. John looked so healthy and fine, the children were so calm and rosy, and I felt pretty fit myself. The toast was golden; the eggs were buff shells of a delicate roughness, unslickened by age; and when I broke them in the sputtering pan, they stood up. And the jelly quivered in its glass bowl, and the cream chugged when you tried to pour it—

"Let's hold out for $10,000!" I cried suddenly.

"The place is worth it," said John. "I mean in income. When we sell, rent begins, you know."

Though Pursuit pushed us for a decision and in anguish of spirit raised his bid to $7,500, we told him we were in honor bound to let our friends see the place before we sold.

The Whitneys arrived Thanksgiving morning. The house was radiant with welcome. The logs blazed, the windows glistened; the aroma of the twelve-pound turkey, which the Henleys had given us, made the kitchen eloquent. The guest room was sweet with order. Little Helen Whitney was to sleep with Betty; Dean with Junior. The ecstasy of the children as Betty and Junior displayed their treasures was music to our older ears.

Howard and Belle were all appreciation. They looked out past the orchard to the hills. They had come a long way, but Tillicum Valley was their birthplace.

"How can you bear to leave Meadowlark Farm?" asked Belle. "That view! It rests my eyes. And the winter silence! Actually, Elizabeth, I draw my feet up in my sleep sometimes. I have a nightmare that the trains will run over them!"

The table, with a centerpiece of our own fruit, looked opulent. At intervals through our Thanksgiving feast there were punctuations like this:

Belle: "What delicious turkey, Elizabeth!"

I: "The Henleys sent it over when they learned you were coming. They warm the cockles of my heart, those people!"

John: "Wonderful neighbors. In the city they'd be, well, hard to know. Here their neighborliness touches everyone. They were neighborly even with our Italian tenants. Tony, I guess, was the scum of the earth—not at all like the Italian farmers down in the valley. They fled this house because of the ghost." (A long story of the ghost, which was even then crackling cheerfully in the fireplace.)

Howard (smacking): "What's this racy jelly?"

John (eagerly): "Wild crabapple! Don't you remember the little tree by the schoolhouse? The one Belle broke her arm falling out of?"

Howard: "We gave her our two apples and begged her not to cry. Wasn't she plucky? Well, the jelly has a good sporting flavor!"

John: "It's a big tree now. It's getting along, like us."

Helen: "Just look at the teeny-weeny pickles! Can I eat one?"

Belle (to Howard, appealingly): "I don't think one will hurt her."

Betty (gobbling): "I eat 'em. They grew on my own pickle vine."

Junior (scathingly): "Cucumber vine!"

Betty: "They're not cucumbers now. They're pickles. And mine has clothes."

Junior: "Cloves, silly!"

Dean (who till now had not wasted time on a single word): "Pumpkin pie!"

Junior: "You may thank me for that pie. I killed a thousand squash bugs. Next year I know how to kill a million! Only, [crestfallen] I don't suppose the old city has any squash bugs."

I: "You have probably noticed that you each have an extra glass."

All: "Yes!" and Howard: "Not one of us has asked why!"

I: "You have behaved beautifully. Now for the treat!"

John (pouring proudly): "Spitz cider!"

Howard: "Whoop!"

Belle: "How clear it is! How it sparkles!"

John: "I filtered it through Crystal Ravine sand, the way Father used to."

Howard: "Pretty good, what? For a city chap! This is great! Well, here's to our happiness, wherever we all are on next Thanksgiving Day!"

When our feast was finished and the dishes were washed, the children played Authors under the hanging lamp.

"The same lamp!" remembered Howard Whitney. "By Jove, we played Authors in that very spot!"

We sat down by the fire and talked intimately, as dear friends of the same age and station in life are likely to do. John and Howard discussed the hard work on the farm, in contrast with the exhausting efforts a city man must put forth. Belle and I gossiped about high rents and close quarters, the strife to keep in fashion, movies, dancing classes, homework, and children's parties.

"Really, my children have every hour taken. Their obligations are as exacting as mine. Where is the time for the long thoughts of childhood? We can't save. The children have no idea of thrift. And soon they'll be in their teens, and then . . . gone!"

"What I miss most is friends. But fine people live here, of course, like the Henleys. Mary Henley is the children's teacher."

"What? Little Mary? She entered the year I graduated. I suppose she was six. Well, well, well! Who teaches our children, Belle?"

"Oh, they have a number of teachers," said Belle vaguely. "They are all very fine, I think. Dean, isn't your teacher Miss Case?"

"Miss Williams. I had Miss Case last spring." Dean returned to his Authors. "Under 'C' I want—"

"Well, well, well!" mused Howard again.

"I should visit school more. What I miss most"—Belle turned to me—"is friends. People make friends, but they lose them on moving day. I love the city, love what it gives you—music, art, lectures; but I think I love the peace and permanence of the country more."

"How lovely it would be," I exclaimed suddenly, "if you would buy the Smith farm and be our neighbors!"

"Why, Elizabeth! Do you really mean you could make yourself contented to live here? On this farm? Do you?"

I think I flushed. "Contented?" I mused. "That's just it! There's something so real and satisfying about sitting here by our own fire, with our land stretching about. Only since my house has been in order have I felt it. I believe I have found contentment."

"If Life Smith's farm can be bought for less than $8,000 . . . ," considered Howard Whitney. "You see, I know that farm like a book. Uncle Ben used to own it."

"It can be bought for $7,500!" said John.

"Then, Belle, why don't we buy it?"

"And we could build our new house on the hill!" said Belle in a hushed, ardent voice.

A wonderful silence fell upon us four old friends. We sat—Belle's hand in Howard's, my hand in John's—and our eyes rested upon our children playing Authors under the hanging lamp.

Harvest Home Harmony

Margaret E. Sangster, Jr.

She had invited two dozen guests to her home for a Thanksgiving party, only to be told there was no money for it. How would she be able to entertain them now? It was her father's love of gingerbread that solved the problem.

Mildred Hazen said, "It must be the nicest party that anybody's ever given in this town. You see, it will be my coming-out party, and I want people to feel"—she laughed—"that I'll be an addition to the community. For refreshments there'll be creamed chicken in pâté shells and a fruit salad and three or four kinds of cake and ice cream in shapes. And I'll decorate the house with all sorts of Thanksgiving favors—papier-mâché turkeys and pumpkins filled with fresh fruit." She paused, perhaps for breath.

Mrs. Hazen looked up sadly from the book that she was reading. "I'd like you to have a lovely party, dear," she said, "but I think you're forgetting that we've just had terrifically heavy expenses. Moving from one town to another is a big item. Also, your dad's starting in a new place. In other words, the kind of party you're planning would cost dollars and dollars, and we haven't got them. Why must you give a party, honey?"

"Because I've invited my entire Sunday school class to come to one. The members were wonderful to me the first day I joined the class; that was two Sundays ago. Ever so many of them have called me up, and two of the young men have asked to take me places; and I thought it would be fun if I entertained them at the beginning instead of waiting until they'd entertained me. And so last Sunday, after class, I up and invited the whole crowd! It didn't occur to me that you'd worry about the expense of a party. You never did before."

Mrs. Hazen sighed. "No," she said, "I know I never did before. There's always been a little extra money set by that I could use for this and that. That extra money is gone now, Mildred. The living room and dining room curtains didn't fit, and I had to buy new ones, and there were other things, too. I haven't a penny left, and I can't bear to ask your father for more this month. Why don't you put off your party for a while?"

Mildred was not pouting, but her face was set in lines of disappointment. "Oh, Mother," she said, "I've asked everybody to come to a Thanksgiving party! I made that the reason for my invitation. I said I was a Pilgrim in a strange country and they were the good Indians, and I wanted them to come in and share my harvest. It'll be a pretty poor harvest, won't it?"

Mrs. Hazen sighed again. "Well, we'll manage somehow—we always do manage—and the house is pretty and fresh and gay. Only there won't be creamed chicken in pâté shells or fruit salad or three or four kinds of cakes, and certainly there won't be ice cream in fancy shapes. I happened to be passing the caterer's the other day, and I saw what those shapes cost. Why, they're four dollars a dozen. How many are there in your Sunday school class?"

"Just exactly two dozen," sighed Mildred. "Oh, yes," she added, "I can see that it's out of the question. Eight dollars for ice cream alone, and that wouldn't be the half of it. But what shall we do?"

Mrs. Hazen, in her sweetest voice, answered, "We'll make the best of it, even though we have the simplest kind of party. Our decorations will be autumn leaves and late flowers from the garden, and our refreshments will be plain, though ample. If the young people in your Sunday school class don't like the party and don't like you for what you are, it will be too bad!"

If Mildred Hazen was not happy about the course her plans had taken, it was not because she was the sort of girl that liked to show off; but you know how things are! On the spur of the moment she had given an invitation and had made it sound exciting. Now she felt that she could not quite live up to her invitation.

The twenty-four young people in her Sunday school class, when judged by their clothes and their conversation, were well-to-do. The young men were mostly starting in business; one or two of them attended the state university and were home only for weekends. The girls were divided: some in college, some in business, and some helping out at home. One or two of them were engaged and were busily planning for homes of their own. They were a nice group, representative of a comfortable, easygoing town in which nobody was terrifically rich and nobody was very poor. Mildred had come from just that kind of town. She had felt comfortable immediately when she entered the church and became a member of the young people's group. The young men and women had taken her to their hearts and had showered her with invitations.

Entertaining, she explained to herself in justification, *is one of the first ways that a new girl can give a picture of her background. When the young folks meet Daddy and Mother and see my home, they'll know I belong. But,* she sighed, *what will I do about refreshments?*

The party was a week off, not too much time in which to plan. The evening after her conversation with her mother, Mildred tentatively brought up the subject at the dinner table. Her father, a kindly, gray-haired man with tired eyes, looked up in interest as she told of her plans.

"My goodness," he said, "you're getting ambitious, having twenty-four at the house so soon. It's lucky your mother is straightened out. Maybe I can manage extra money for things, a couple of dollars or so. Will that help?"

A couple of dollars or so would not help with the elaborate plans that Mildred had made, but she did not say so. She smiled at her father and answered, "You're sweet, Daddy, but we won't need money. Mother and I will manage."

* * *

The next Sunday Mildred walked home from church with a girl who lived in one of the largest houses on the block, a big white affair with a portico and a wide veranda. As they came down the quiet street together, Mildred asked a question.

"I'm new to this town," she said frankly, "and I'm entirely at sea about your customs. What do you usually do when you have parties? Play games?"

The other girl laughed. "Oh," she said, "we just play games and serve refreshments, and we go home fairly early. We girls have taken to vying with one another, though, in the matter of refreshments. Each girl tried to be different and smart."

"What do you mean by different and smart?" asked Mildred.

The neighbor girl explained. "Well," she said, "one girl will have a hot dish cooked in a chafing dish: chicken à la king or lobster wiggle (that's lobster meat and green peas and creamed gravy). Another girl will have something special made up at the caterer's: a mousse or a frozen pudding. The last party"—the girl chuckled—"was one that Mazie Holliday gave.

She's that tall girl with the naturally curly blond hair. Know what she had? A spun-sugar nest with an ice cream chicken and ice cream eggs in it! That was the most amusing stunt yet."

"I should think it would be amusing," agreed Mildred. When she reached home she went up to her room, threw herself across her bed, and dissolved into a flood of quiet tears. Frozen puddings and creamed lobster meat and spun-sugar nests, that was too much!

Mildred cried until the dinner gong sounded downstairs. Her mother had been quietly going about the preparations of the midday meal, and Mildred, realizing that nearly an hour had passed since she arrived home, got up, dashed cold water on her face, and repaired the ravages that the tears had made. She went downstairs with apparent calm and seated herself at the table with her father and mother.

When Mr. Hazen asked the usual questions about Sunday school, and while she and her mother and father discussed the church services, her mind was far away. Only when her mother was bringing in the dessert did inspiration come. For at the sight of the dessert, her father's face brightened magically, and he said, "Yum-yum! Here's my favorite!"

Mildred was being a trifle food conscious. At the delighted expression on her father's face, she turned to look at the dish her mother was bearing. "What's your favorite food, Daddy?" she asked, smiling. "Seems to me you like everything that Mother cooks."

"He *does* like everything I cook," her mother said with a laugh. "But you must know that his favorite is gingerbread, Mildred. We haven't had it for months, either. I'd forgotten it until I came on the recipe in my book yesterday."

"There's nothing better," he said, "in November, or any other month for that matter, than good, hot, spicy gingerbread. Some people"—he elaborated the thought—"make it so it's light tan colored and dry, but your mother's way is unique. I never tasted the like of it anywhere."

"Well . . . " Mrs. Hazen was flushed with pride, for the man she loved was praising her skill. "My gingerbread isn't really gingerbread. I suppose you'd call it molasses cake. Also"—she chuckled like a child—"I have a trick. When it's rising, I open the oven door and peek in, and I always make my peek so long that the cake drops a trifle. So when I take it out, it's black and gooey and—"

"Utterly grand," finished her husband. "I feel right now that I could eat eighteen pieces. Why didn't you tell me we were going to have it, Mary? I wouldn't have taken the second helping of roast."

"Oh," exclaimed Mildred, "Daddy's given me the most superb idea! We'll have gingerbread for my party, lots and lots of it. And we'll call Dad on his offer of an extra dollar or two, and we'll spend it on cream. We'll have the gingerbread with big dabs of whipped cream, and I know it will be different from anything anybody ever served in this town."

"What an idea, Mildred!" replied Mrs. Hazen. "And gingerbread's as cheap as cheap. Tell you what—let's have an old-fashioned party, from beginning to end. We'll have gingham runners on the table, and we'll have some corn husks and autumn leaves in the center, and we'll serve nice fresh, warm applesauce with the gingerbread, and old-fashioned cheese sandwiches on homemade Graham bread, and some of those spiced peaches with the sandwiches. Maybe I'll put a bit of bacon with the cheese—that'll be tasty."

Mildred was thrilled. "I'll say it will be tasty!" she exclaimed. "And when they get through with my party, they'll at least say we're original. What price spun-sugar nests and ice cream chickens?"

* * *

The day came for the party, and Mildred was not the woebegone girl who had planned the party and found that her plans had come to naught. She was radiant and excited. As she put the finishing touches to the dining room, where the refreshments would be served, she felt that she had never seen a cheerier room. It was bleak November out of doors, but the dining room was as colorful as an autumn garden. It happened that the dining room curtains, new since the Hazens had moved, were fashioned of cretonne in autumn tints. Those autumn tints blended with the great cluster of red and gold leaves that filled the pewter bowl in the center of the table. The pewter bowl was an antique (it had belonged to Mildred's great-grandmother), and the dining room table upon which it stood was fashioned of aged, gleaming mahogany. The mahogany shone with a warm luster between the runners of red-and-white-checkered gingham.

As Mildred thought of the food, her mouth actually watered. Her mother had gone further than she had planned: She had baked a Virginia ham the day before, and that ham, sliced in thin, rosy fragments, was going to be served between disks of beaten biscuit. Homemade pickles and homemade preserves were brought out. Black walnuts from the old home-town had been shelled and salted.

For their drink they were serving sweet-smelling coffee in tall pewter pitchers. The coffee went well with the ham and beaten biscuit and with the Graham bread sandwiches, which showed a golden glimmer of store cheese.

Of course, the pièce de résistance of the meal was black, spicy ginger-bread. It was not yet baked. Mrs. Hazen would pop that into the oven before it was time for refreshments, but after everything else was done. Even the cream was whipped and standing in the icebox—a great bowl of it.

"It looks lovely, darling," declared Mrs. Hazen as she surveyed the table, "and I think you're the best girl in the world not to be disappointed because we can't have an elaborate spread."

"Disappointed!" exclaimed Mildred. "Why should I be? I'm giving a real party, a harvest home harmony."

"What are you going to wear, dear?"

Again Mildred laughed. "I'm going to wear a red-and-white gingham dress," she said, "left over from last summer. I'm going to match my table, believe it or not."

"Then," said her mother, "I'll wear a gingham sunbonnet when I serve the gingerbread."

When the guests arrived, twenty-four of them, they found Mildred looking her prettiest in the red-and-white gingham dress.

"Don't stare at me that way," she cried, dimpling as she welcomed them. "You see you've been invited to an honest-to-goodness harvest home, the kind of Thanksgiving party people might give on farms rather than in towns like this one. As you can see, I'm dressed"—she took the skirts of her gingham dress in the tips of her rosy fingers and made a deep curtsy—"to fit the occasion."

One of the boys spoke up. He was David Herring, the son of the town's most influential man and the most popular young man in the Sunday school class. "If you're any sample of the party, it's going to be an occasion. And when I say occasion," he added, "I mean occasion!"

* * *

Well, David was right. The party was an occasion. From the beginning, the Sunday school class entered into the spirit of the party with a zest that was as wholehearted as it was spontaneous. They played old-fashioned games: Going to Jerusalem, Blind Man's Bluff, even London Bridge Is Falling Down. Mildred, darting here and there like an autumn leaf, was the spirit of the party.

David Herring whispered to Elliott Bailey, his roommate, "It looks as if we're going to have a new social leader!"

At last the time came for the refreshments, and the merry party trooped into the dining room. The "Ohs!" and "Ahs!" of the girls, and the lip-smacking sounds that the young men made, justified Mildred's faith in her mother's cooking.

Oh, the party progressed like a dream, no doubt of it! When at last the gingerbread was served, Mildred's happiness was complete.

"You know," said Mazie, the tall blonde who had electrified the group with her spun-sugar nest and the ice cream chickens, "you've made every party we've ever given look sick, Mildred. Here we've been trying to make things fancy and frivolous, and you've taken the cake"—she laughed—"with gingerbread. You've set a new vogue in parties, my dear. We'll be copycats for the rest of the winter, I can see that. And if your mother will give me her recipe for gingerbread, I'll earn my family's undying gratitude."

Mildred thought that her cup of happiness was full to overflowing, but it was not quite. The crowning delight of the evening came when David Herring, the last of the group to go, lingered for a moment in the doorway and pressed her hand tightly in his strong brown fingers.

"Speaking of gingerbread," he said, "I'm going to ask you if you won't come down to our midwinter house party at college. My mother will be the chaperone. She'll drive you down in the car, and if—" He hesitated, a trifle embarrassed. "If you'd bring a box of that gingerbread with you—a big box—we'd have it at dinner the first night."

Mildred spoke softly. "You're sure," she said, "that you want me to come down to the house party? The party isn't for a couple of months, and you may change your mind."

David Herring chuckled. "I can see that you're the sort of girl," he said, "who's got to be dated up a couple of months ahead if a fellow wants a chance!"

Pandora's Books

Joseph Leininger Wheeler

It was just another bookstore—well, another used-book store. And what could possibly happen in a bookstore that would be worth remembering?

Prologue

Later it would be remembered as "the year with no spring." All the more surprising because it had been a bitterly cold winter, complete with record snowfall, frequent ice storms, traffic gridlock on the Washington, D.C., beltway, closed airports, and snow days—longed for by children and teachers alike.

At first, people assumed it to be a fluke: Surely the geese couldn't possibly be flying north already! Why, the iced-over Potomac and Severn rivers were only now beginning to break up. But the honking geese kept coming, attuned to their planet's moods in ways human beings will never understand.

Surely the cherry blossoms down on the Tidal Basin couldn't possibly be blooming this early! And the daffodils, too? But they were—and those who delayed but a day missed Jefferson's lagoon at its loveliest, for unseasonably warm air, coupled with sudden wind, stripped the blossoms from the unbelieving trees.

Azaleas and dogwoods were next—way too early, as well. Usually, the multihued azaleas, along with dogwoods of pink and white, ravish the senses for weeks every spring. Not so this year: They came and went in only days. By early April, the thermometer had already climbed to 100, and now schools began to close because of the heat instead of the cold.

Once entrenched, the heat dug in. And the mercury kept climbing. Even the spring rains failed to come; farmers shook their heads, trembling in their mortgages. Plants dried up, lawns turned brown in spite of frequent watering—and centuries-old trees dropped their already yellowish leaves in abject defeat.

Tourists stayed home, making sizzling Washington a veritable ghost town. For the first time in recent memory, one could park anywhere one went—no waiting, no endless circling.

And for those Washingtonians who did not have air-conditioning—in home, office, and cars—it was unbearable. One couldn't even escape by boat, for prolonged calms, interspersed by blasting gales of fierce, tinder-dry winds, plagued the Chesapeake.

On TV weather maps, the entire eastern seaboard turned brown in early April—and stayed brown, altering only to a deeper hue of brown. There was a morbid fascination in watching as heat record after heat record fell before that immovable front, seemingly set in concrete.

So, when the weather reporters trumpeted the glad news that, come Memorial Day weekend, the siege would at last be lifted and blessed coolness from Canada would flow in, most people greeted it as a second Armistice Day, as a time to climb out of their bunkers and celebrate.

Traffic jams clogged roads everywhere, and Highway 50 became a parking lot from Washington to Ocean City. Strangely enough, the euphoria ran so high, people didn't seem to mind. They got out of their cars and vans, set up their lawn chairs on the median, threw Frisbees back and forth, and ate picnic lunches. One enterprising caravan of college students found enough room between their cars to play a screwy sort of volleyball in the middle of the Chesapeake Bay Bridge.

But some people find happiness in places other than the beach: places like bookstores, used-book stores—Pandora's bookstore.

* * *

Oh, it feels so great to have a cool day again! mused Jennifer O'Riley as she drove out onto Highway 50 with the top down for the first time in, well, it *seemed* like a year. It felt good to just let her hair fly loose in the wind. As Annapolis loomed ahead of her, she veered off on Riva Road and then headed south on Highway 2. Stick-um'd to her checkbook were Amy's directions.

"Oh, Jen, you'll just *love* it," her closest friend had raved. "It's unlike any other bookstore you have ever seen!"

Jennifer, a veteran of hundreds of used-book stores, strongly doubted that, but not wanting to flatly contradict her friend, she merely mumbled, "Oh?"

Amy, noting the doubt written on her face—Jennifer never *had* been able to keep a secret, for her expressive face gave it away every time— merely grinned and looked wise. "Jus' you wyte, 'Enry 'Iggins, jus' you wyte!" she caroled.

In the intervening weeks and months since that challenge, several other friends had rhapsodized about this one-of-a-kind bookstore, each report torquing up Jennifer's curiosity another notch.

Now, on this absolutely perfect late May day, she saw no reason to delay further: She would see this hyped-way-beyond-its-worth place herself. After all, there were no other claims on her day. *More's the pity,* she told herself. And her truant memory wafted her backward without asking permission—backward to a time when she *had* been needed, *had* been wanted, *had* been loved. *Or,* she qualified to herself, *at least I* thought *he loved me!*

It had been one of those childhood romances adults so often chuckle about. The proverbial boy next door. They had played together day by day—inside one of their homes in bad weather, outside the rest of the time. When school started, they entered first grade together. He carried her books and fought anyone who mistreated her, and at home they studied together.

He had been the first boy to hold her hand, the first she had kissed. Their parents had merely laughed, in that condescending way adults have about young love, and prophesied: "Puppy love *never* lasts. . . . Just watch! They'll find someone else."

But they didn't find "someone else." Not even when puberty messed them up inside, recontoured their bodies, redirected their thoughts. Each remained the other's all.

They even chose the same college—and studied together still, went to concerts and art galleries together, hiked the mountains together, walked barefoot on the beaches together, haunted bookstores together, went to parties together, even attended church together.

So it had come as no surprise that spring break of their senior year, when walking among the dunes near Cape Hatteras, he asked her to marry him. And there was no hesitation in her joyous, "Yes, Bill."

That it somehow lacked passion, that there was little yearning for the other physically, didn't seem to matter. Hadn't their relationship stood the test of time? How much longer than twenty years would it take to *know,* for goodness' sake!

So the date had been set, the wedding party chosen, the bridal and attendants' dresses made, the flowers ordered, the tuxes measured, the minister and chapel secured, the honeymoon destination booked, the apartment they would live in arranged for, the wedding invitations sent out.

And then, thirty-six hours before the wedding, her world had caved in on her. He had come over and asked if they could talk. "Of course!" she had smiled, chalking up the tense look on his face to groom jitters.

They sat down in their favorite swing on the back porch and looked out at the yard, already festive for the reception to be held there. Her smile faded quickly as she took in his haggard face, his eyes with dark circles under them. Premonition froze her into glacial immobility. Surely it couldn't be what she, deep down, sensed it would be. Not after all these years!

But it was. He could only stammer brokenly the chopped-up words and phrases that would amputate two dreams that over a twenty-year period had grown within hours of becoming one. He had found someone whose presence—or absence—raised him to the skies or plunged him to the depths, someone who ignited his hormones to such an extent that life without her was unthinkable. Bill hadn't gone far before his face turned scarlet and he began to sputter.

In mercy, Jennifer broke in. "Don't say anything more, Bill," she cried in a strangely ragged voice. "You can't force love—not the real lifetime kind. . . . I . . . I'd far rather know this now than later." She paused for control.

Bill could only sit there miserably, his head in his hands.

So it was up to her to finish this thing. She knew she would always love him; after all, he had been her best friend for almost as far back as she could remember. And there is no trapdoor to open and dump such things—for the memories remain always and cannot be so easily disposed of.

He couldn't bring himself to face her parents, so after a few more minutes they stood up; there was one last hug—and he walked away.

She salvaged a bit of her battered pride by calling off the wedding herself. That was the hardest thing she had ever done. Numbly, she phoned them all, but gave no reasons. They would know why soon enough, if they didn't know already.

And so her marital dreams had died.

A year passed, and another, and another . . . until six years separated her from that fateful parting that, like "no man's land," separated the girl from the woman—on one side, trust and unconditional acceptance; on the other, suspicion and reserve.

During the first two years, she turned down all the men who asked her out. But gradually, as her bludgeoned self-esteem began to get up off the floor, she realized that life must go on, that she must not wall herself off from living. So she began to date again, but not very often. Nine months of the year the children in her third-grade classroom were her world. During the other three, she took graduate work, traveled, wrote, visited art galleries, and attended plays, concerts, and operas—often alone, but frequently with dear friends such as Amy or with her brother, James.

She sometimes wondered if she would ever find the kind of mate Bill had found: the kind of magnetism that would call her even across the proverbial crowded room. Would there ever be someone who would set her heart singing? Who would be the friend Bill had been, but who would also arouse a passionate yearning to be his physical, mental, social, and spiritual mate? Every once in a while she would wonder, *Why is it so difficult to find* The One? *Is there something wrong with me?*

So the long hours, days, weeks, months, and years passed. She completed her master's at Johns Hopkins, and always she was doing *something*, anything, to avoid admitting to herself that she was unutterably lonely.

None of her diversions worked. Not one.

* * *

Oh, she had almost missed her road! She slammed on the brakes, nearly getting rear-ended in the process, and turned left. "Three and seven-tenths miles," Amy had said. Sure enough, there loomed the sign: PANDORA'S BOOKS.

Gotta be a story here somewhere, she thought with a smile.

Now she slowed and turned into an ancient-looking brick gateway. About 200 feet past the entrance was another sign announcing that this was a wildlife sanctuary. *Some bookstore!*

The road snaked its way through first-growth trees (according to reports, one of the only such stands of timber left on this part of the Chesapeake). Here and there azalea, rhododendron, and wild laurel bushes banked the road.

She slowed the Camaro to a crawl to give some deer time to get off the road. Birds seemed to be everywhere: cardinals, goldfinches, sparrows, even a couple of bluebirds and, high overhead, hawks and gulls. It seemed incongruous, this close to the Washington metroplex of 6 million people, to discover such solitude.

At last the road straightened and dropped into the strangest parking lot she had ever seen. Following directions from a sign, she drove into another grove of trees until she came to a pull-in spot without a vehicle in it. After putting the top up and locking the car, she found a path to the beach.

She sensed the water's edge before she could see it, and now she could plainly hear the *ca-ca-ca*-ing of the gulls. Suddenly, there it was: a blinding white clapboard framed by the silver-flecked blue of the Chesapeake. No clouds overhead today, only seagulls; and on the water, like swans taking flight, sailboats as far as the eye could see. She stopped, transfixed, and inwardly spoke these words to her best Friend. *Lord, thank You for this day—this almost-too-beautiful-to-be-true day.* She had always been more intense than any of her friends, and more deeply affected by beauty. Before going in, she added a rather strange postscript: *Lord, please let only good things happen to me today.* Then she opened the door and walked in.

Inside, classical music was playing softly, meshing wondrously with the lapping of the waves on the shore, the cawing of the gulls, and the occasional raucous croak that could come only from the long throat of a great blue heron.

And ah, that one-of-a-kind fragrance of old books . . . which to book lovers is the true wine of life! And not marred, as is sadly true of so many used-book stores, with disorganization, overstocking, clutter, and grime. This one was blessedly different—she set out to analyze it and find out why.

First of all, it was clean—not antiseptically so . . . but just close enough. No grime besmirched the shelves, books, walls, windows, or floor. Second, although the store contained tens of thousands of books, there was no perception of clutter or of being engulfed by the sheer mass of it all. Why that was so was easy to see: Masses of books were broken up by old prints, paintings, sculpture, bric-a-brac, and flowers—*real* flowers. She could tell that by their fragrance! The windows—which today were open—let in the outside world. Or just enough of it. And there were benches and soft chairs everywhere, graced by lamps of great beauty.

Quickly, she discovered that the artwork tied in perfectly with the genre displayed on the shelves. For instance, Remingtons and Russells dominated the walls of the Western room, supplemented by dust-jacket originals, magazine art, movie posters, lobby cards, and old photographs. The adolescent/youth section had as its focal center a wondrous display of Maxfield Parrish, with its pièce de résistance: the largest print she'd ever seen of his "Ecstasy." Blowups of dust jackets, paperback covers, and magazine art graced the walls in just the right places.

And amazingly, different music played in every room—softly. In the Western room could be heard most of the old standard country western artists, from the Sons of the Pioneers to Eddy Arnold. In the religion and philosophy room, she heard the great music of the church. Lilting, happy music that children love flowed from the children's room.

But best of all was the literature and general fiction room. For one thing, it dominated the seaward side of the second story. And on walls where no direct sunlight would fade them hung faithfully reproduced copies of old masters: Zurbarán, Titian, Da Vinci, Ribera, Caravaggio, La Tour, and Rembrandt.

A massive stone fireplace anchored the southeastern corner. Just to its right stood a nine-foot grand piano, and on its shiny surface was flopped in abandoned feline comfort as beautiful a Himalayan as Jennifer had ever seen. Without even thinking, she crossed the room toward it and reached out her hand, allowing it to be sniffed before she ventured to scratch the cat's head and massage its ears. A loud purring told her that she had been accepted into the narrow circle that could induce purring.

Jennifer crossed to one of the open windows, leaned against the sill, and gazed out across the silver-flecked blue. Then—ever so softly, floating out of the very walls it seemed—she heard those haunting first bars of Chopin's *Étude in E.* It was just too much. Her intensely passionate nature could handle only so much circuit overload. She lost all track of time and reality.

* * *

Coming up the stairs with a load of books for restocking, Arthur Bond sighed. On this seemingly perfect day, he longed to be outside. But so did his employees, so he had let most of them go—reluctantly. As he heard *Étude in E,* he slowed his pace. No matter how often he heard it, that étude got him every time. Something in its melody brought an ache, reminded him that he was alone—incomplete. Thus his normal defenses melted like wax when he stepped into the room that housed his classics. When he saw the figure staring out the window, he stopped, rooted to the floor. The woman's sapphire blue dress draped long, loose, and Maxfield Parrish classical; her complexion cameo ivory; her long hair a copperish flame; her ankles and Teva-sandaled feet slim and graceful. A pre-Raphaelite painting suddenly come to life there in the room. Arthur hardly dared breathe, lest he break her trance.

Subconsciously, he weighed the external pieces that added up to the totality. *No*, he concluded, *she is not beautiful, though she has classical features and a classical form. But she's alive—as alive as any woman I have ever seen.* He watched as the strains of *Étude in E* internalized in her heart and soul and overflowed into her face (that face which always mirrored her inner self in spite of all efforts to control it). A tear glistened in an eye, the color of which he could not from that angle see, and slowly made a pathway down her cheek. But in her reverie she did not even notice it. Strangely enough, even though he'd never seen her before, he yearned to wipe that tear away and find out what had caused it—if it was the étude . . . or if it was something more.

* * *

Something woke her, told her she was no longer alone. She turned slightly and saw him standing there, photographing her with his blue-gray eyes. (Hers, he now discovered, were an amazing burnished emerald green.) Gradually, as the mists of her trance dissipated, he came into full focus. He stood six feet two, dark brown hair salted with premature gray; trim, physically fit. Dressed well in a button-up chambray shirt, khaki pants, and loafers, he was probably in his mid- to late thirties.

But his face . . . Jennifer felt instinctively that this man standing there knew pain, for it etched his face. Especially did she note it in the ever-so-slight droop of a mouth that seemed made for smiling. His eyes, she concluded, were wonderfully kind. He was not photographing her with pin-up intentions, but with tenderness and concern; and for such ammunition, she had no defense. Until that moment, she had never needed any.

Arthur, feeling a familiar softness rubbing against his leg, looked down and smiled. She liked that smile and wished to prolong its stay. Clearing her throat, she spoke just one word: "Yours?"

His smile grew broader as he tenderly picked up the purring cat, cradled it in his muscular arms, and announced, "Pandora."

She laughed, a delightfully throaty laugh, and retorted, "So here is the *real* owner of all these books!"

He laughed, too. "Yes, well, it's a long story. If you're not in a hurry, I'll tell you."

I'm not in a hurry, she decided. *Never in less of one—in all my life.*

So they sat down on opposite ends of a sofa, and he told her the saga of a Himalayan kitten into *everything!* (hence her name), and how she had wrapped her tiny little soul around his when things weren't going very well for him. (Jennifer sensed that admittance to be a major understatement.) So when certain developments made possible this bookstore, in gratitude, he had named it in her honor.

And he smiled again. "It *is* her bookstore. I'm sure she feels it is hers, perhaps more so than a human being ever could. And our customers— well, the people who come here—feel she is boss. Everyone asks about her, and no one ever wants to leave without paying his or her respects." He chuckled again. "I'm not so important. Not many feel shortchanged if they leave without seeing me."

She thought but did not say, *I'm afraid . . . I'm very afraid . . . that I would.*

So interested did she become in the story of this wonderfully different bookstore that she kept at him until the entire story spilled out. Even— or perhaps *especially* even—a brief account of the motivation for it: the failure of a relationship central in his life. He did not elaborate.

Other book lovers came and went; some eyed the man, woman, and dozing cat on the couch, attempted to listen in, and reluctantly moved on. Three times they suffered interruptions: once for a customer downstairs, once for a phone call, and once by refreshments brought up by the assistant manager. Noticing Jennifer's raised eyebrows, Arthur explained that fresh-brewed coffee, regular and decaf, and herbal tea were always ready on both floors, as were bagels and cookies, cold sodas, and bottles of fruit juice.

"Yeah," Arthur admitted, "coffee's one of my besetting sins . . . the jump-start that gets me going. Maybe it isn't very smart to mix coffee and snacks with books . . . but real book lovers rarely mistreat books. No one's wrecked a book yet because of it! But no smoking! I can't stand it, and"— he looked down at the sleeping cat on his lap—"neither can Pandora."

Suddenly, Jennifer looked at her watch and jumped to her feet. "I can't believe it. Where has the day gone? So sorry . . . but I gotta run. Thanks ever so much for everything, but I'm late for an appointment. But I'll be back! Bye-bye, Pandora." And she stopped to give the cat one last scratch under the chin. Then she was gone, without so much as revealing her name.

But then, he mused, *neither did I!*

With her departure, although there remained not a cloud in the sky, a partial eclipse darkened the sun. To Arthur, the day had lost its brightness. The droop came back to his lip—but not quite so pronounced as before.

* * *

Jennifer stayed away for almost two weeks, but each day she felt the magnetic pull; then she'd recoil from her inner yearning to return: *How silly! How ridiculous to blow out of proportion a simple little conversation. He'd probably talk like that to anyone who came by and asked the same questions. After all, he's in the business to make customers and sell books!*

Finally, thoroughly confused by her inner turbulence, she went back—and he wasn't there! But books are books, and she soon lost herself among them. She wanted to ask about him but could find no reason that didn't seem transparently obvious.

She did find the books in the vicinity of the checkout stands to be abnormally interesting: She kept taking them off the shelves one at a time, studying them intently, then returning them to the shelves—all without remembering anything about them! She blushed crimson when it suddenly came to her what she was doing.

Scolding herself: *You foolish, foolish schoolgirl, you!* she sheepishly put the last book back on the shelf and moved toward the next room.

She had not waited in vain, however. While she was passing the first cash register, she heard someone ask the clerk where the boss was. She slowed her pace. The clerk's voice was low and pleasing to listen to: "Mr. Bond?"

"Yes, of course! Mr. Bond!"

"Oh . . . uh . . . he didn't tell me where he was going."

Jennifer's sharp ears then picked up a whispered jab from the clerk at the next register: "But you surely wish he had, huh?"

Jennifer sneaked a look. The face of the first speaker flamed scarlet, her blush speaking volumes. *So that's the way the wind blows!* Jennifer thought. She appraised the girl carefully: young, at most in her mid-twenties; statuesque, with midnight black hair (undoubtedly Spanish), and strikingly beautiful. . . .

Even more confused than when she came in, Jennifer hurried out of the bookstore without even looking for Pandora. She was disturbed, angry, and more than a little jealous of this girl who got to work there all the time.

* * *

The three-digit heat returned after the Memorial Day reprieve, and the steamy humidity slowed life to a gasping crawl. Since it was too hot to do anything but wilt like an unwatered impatiens outside, Jennifer returned again to Pandora's Books.

Looking for him, but not looking for him, she reconnoitered her way through the various rooms, restless as a child the last afternoon of school. Suddenly, she saw him, sitting in an easy chair by the empty fireplace, a portable phone at his ear. And curled around the back of his neck like a fur stole—and just as limp—was Pandora.

Her eyes twinkling, Jennifer surreptitiously edged her way out of the room, assuming he had not seen her. Eventually, she gravitated back to the children's room, in the center of which was a sunken playground; apparently, there were always children playing there. After browsing awhile, she found a book she had always wanted to read but could never find: Alcott's *Flower Fables*. Sinking into a soft chair with a seraphic sigh of pure joy, she opened its covers.

But she was not to sink into another world so easily. Across from her, a sandy-haired little boy of about five was vainly trying to capture his mother's attention: "Mama, Mama . . . please, Mama, will you . . . ?"

"Oh, don't bother me!" she snapped.

Undeterred, the little boy persisted. "But, Mama, I found this pretty book, and uh . . . I wonder if you'd . . . "

"Oh, for goodness' sake! Will you leave me alone!" she snarled.

At this, the boy recoiled as if struck, and lips quivering, he backed away. After one last look at the unyielding face of his mother, engrossed in an Agatha Christie thriller, he turned and headed toward a raven-haired woman who was restocking books across the room. But his courage wavered as he approached the clerk. Would she rebuff him, too?

By now, Jennifer had forgotten her book completely. *How will the Spanish beauty respond to a child's need?* she asked herself.

She didn't have to wait long to find out, for the woman, on being tapped on the leg by little fingers, whirled around in surprise—but she did not smile. She had been enduring a raging migraine that afternoon. Seconds later, her dark eyes scanned the room to see if anyone had seen. Satisfied that no one had—Jennifer was watching her through veiled eyes (a trick women have and men do not)—she brusquely turned her back to the child and continued restocking the shelf.

The little boy didn't cry. He didn't say anything at all. He merely turned around and just stood there, the book still in his hand, lips trembling, and a tear finding its way down his cheek.

It was just too much! Mother or no mother, clerk or no clerk, Jennifer swiftly left her seat and swooped down like a protective hen; then slowed, knelt down, and spoke words kind and gentle: "Can *I* help, dear?" And she tenderly wiped away the tear.

But he had been hurt that afternoon—hurt terribly!—and was no longer as trusting as he had been only minutes before. He just looked at her, eyes still puddling. She, respecting his space and his selfhood, didn't touch him again—only waited, with tenderness in her eyes. It was no contest. An instant later, vanquished by those soft eyes, he was in her arms, his eyes wet, his little shoulders heaving, but making not a sound.

Across the room, his mother continued reading.

When the little body had stopped shaking, and the tears had ceased to flow, Jennifer led him to a nearby couch, sat down, and drew him to her. Then she asked him about the book. As he slowly turned the pages and read some of the words, she helped him with the others and explained the illustrations. The look of joy transfigured his face, and excited comprehension filled his voice . . . if one had been there to hear it.

Arthur—who had entered the room just in time to catch the entire tableau—*had* seen it. But Jennifer did not see *him*—neither then nor when she took the boy across the room to find another book, his hand held trustingly in hers.

Withdrawing quietly from the scene, Arthur returned to his office, asked his secretary to field all his calls and inquiries, and shut the door. He walked over to the window and looked unseeingly out on the iron-gray bay.

* * *

The next time, Jennifer came on a rainy afternoon. Evidently a lot of other people agreed with her that a bookstore was the best place to be on such a day. Long lines piled up behind the cash registers, and many people waited with questions. The clerks, she noticed, tried to be helpful and answered all questions politely and with obvious willingness to go the second mile. They knew many customers by name.

Even the Spanish girl. From time to time, Jennifer saw the girl turn to see if a certain gentleman remained in his office. Then, when Mr. Bond finally did come out, the girl's cheeks flamed as she looked everywhere but in his direction. A number of people clustered around him, asking questions, and each one received that same warm smile and attitude of eager helpfulness.

Then the Spanish girl went up to her boss to ask a question. Jennifer didn't fail to notice both the smile he gave his lovely clerk and the rapt expression in the girl's eyes. *Hmm.*

She moved on to the American writers section, looking for some of her favorite authors. *Oh! What a selection of Harold Bell Wright! I've never seen so many of his books in one place before!* She took down a dust-jacketed *Exit.* No sooner had she done so than she felt a presence behind her.

"Are you into Wright?" a familiar voice asked.

She turned, smiled (*I like her dimples,* Arthur observed to himself), and said, "Well, sort of. I've read five or six, but I've never seen this one—or, for that matter, a number of the others here. Rarely do I see more than a few of his books in any one place."

"Well, there's a reason for that . . . uh . . . Miss—it *is* Miss . . . ?"

"Yes." She found his steady gaze, kindly though it was, more than a bit disconcerting. "My last name is O'Riley."

"Mine," he grinned a little wickedly, "is Bond. Not James—" (*Obviously he's used this line many times before,* she concluded.) "—but Arthur."

"And I answer to Jennifer," she said, blushing.

Ignoring the opening, he returned to Wright. "Well, Miss O'Riley, Wright books are hard to get, and harder to keep in stock. . . . Might I ask which ones you've read?"

"Well, the first of his books that I read was when I was only seventeen. Read it one beautiful day on California's Feather River Canyon. I was visiting a favorite aunt and uncle at the time—will never forget it, for it changed my life."

"I'd guess it was one of his Social Gospel Trilogy," he broke in.

"Trilogy?" she said. "There's a trilogy? The one I read was *The Calling of Dan Matthews.*"

"Oh?" he asked quizzically.

She stumbled a bit for words, finally stammering out, "I just don't know how to go on . . . and I don't know yet if . . . if . . . uh . . . "

"If I am a Christian?" he finished for her.

"Yes."

"Well, I am. Why do you ask?"

"Oh, it's just that *The Calling of Dan Matthews* gave me a new vision of God, of His all-inclusiveness. I'm afraid I had been rather elitist before I read that book."

He laughed (conspiratorially, she thought). "I agree, Miss O'Riley. It hit me that way, too. Only, I had read *That Printer of Udels* first—it anchors the trilogy—so I was somewhat prepared for his contention that Christ's entire earthly ministry was not about doctrine at all . . . but about— "

"Service," she broke in softly.

"Yes, service to others," he agreed.

They talked a long time about Wright that day, and after that, about other authors of mutual interest as well. Some they loved in common; others they did their best to convert the other to.

Arthur had always felt he could more than hold his own in any battle of wits, but he discovered that in Jennifer he had met his match. One day, as they sparred back and forth on the historical romances of Rafael Sabatini (while each had favorites, both agreed on the one that stood out above all others, *Scaramouche,* that great tale of the French Revolution), he grimaced, thinking, *She never misses a trick. . . . Not a nuance escapes her!*

Not long after, during another visit, she found a copy of a book she'd searched for for years: Gene Stratton Porter's *The Fire Bird.* She quickly found a quiet niche, settled down in an easy chair, turned up the lamp, and began leafing through the book. She held no illusions about buying it, though. Beautiful and rare, true—but the price was far too high for *her* budget.

Then she heard voices, one of which sounded very familiar. She pulled in her feet so as to be as inconspicuous as possible. When the voices drew nearer, she drew her legs under her, yoga style. Since the speakers sat down in the alcove just before hers, she couldn't help but overhear.

"I just don't know what I'm going to do, Mr. Bond!" quavered a woman's voice. "I really don't. Lately . . . I . . . I . . . just feel even the good Lord has forsaken me."

"*That,* Mrs. Henry, I can assure you is not true. The Lord *never* forsakes His children," he responded.

"Oh, but Mr. Bond, you just don't *know,* or you wouldn't be so sure. My oldest son—you remember Chris! . . . Well, he's on drugs. Worse than that: He's become a pusher. . . ." Her voice broke. "And Dana—I . . . I . . . I just found out she's pregnant. I just can't believe it. She grew up so faithful at attending church every week. . . . And the man, the man who . . . uh . . . uh . . . "

"The father of the unborn baby?"

"Yes. He attends our church, too."

"Oh? Are they planning to marry?"

"That's the worst part. He says it's all her fault for not taking precautions. Won't have anything more to do with her. And Dana's near desperate. I'm afraid she'll, she'll . . . " And again her voice broke.

Arthur broke in firmly and kindly. "Mrs. Henry, there is no time to lose. Is Dana home this afternoon?"

Answered in the affirmative, Arthur led Mrs. Henry out, and after explaining to the clerks that an emergency had come up, he and Mrs. Henry hurried through the heavy rain to their cars.

For a long time Jennifer sat there, thinking, *Just what kind of bookstore— what kind of man—is this?*

She came back within the week and shamelessly stayed within listening range of where he worked. She simply *had* to know, for sure, what manner of man this was. So many times before, she'd been disappointed, disillusioned—so why should this one prove to be any different?

She was, by turns, amazed, then moved, by what she overheard. Apparently, he possessed endless patience, for she never heard him lose his temper, no matter what the provocation—even with bores, who insisted on talking on and on about themselves. She discovered that while most asked book-related questions, a surprisingly large number of these people felt overwhelmed by life and its problems. In Arthur, they found, perhaps not always solutions, but at least a listening, sympathetic ear. In used-book stores, she had discovered, there appears to be an implied assumption: one finds an ear, no matter how stupid, inane, or ridiculous the topic may be. In that respect, used-book stores function as courts of last resort: the last chance to be heard before outright despair sets in. But in Arthur's case, it went far beyond mere listening—for he genuinely *cared!*

* * *

At last came August, and with it school pre-session. Vacation was over, for school would begin in a few weeks. So busy was she that it was almost Labor Day before she got back to Pandora's Books. She browsed for about an hour, and as she was leaving, he came out of his office and smiled at her. On the confidence of that smile, she walked over to him and asked if he could spare a moment.

"Of course!" he replied. He steered her into a quieter room and seated her by an open window, for the heat had finally broken and the cool bay breeze felt heavenly.

During the small talk that followed, she became increasingly aware of how strongly she was affected by this man, this tangible synthesis of strength, wisdom, and kindness. She was more aware of being near him than she had ever been with any other man. Stumbling a bit over her words, she asked him if he ever spoke to students about books—not just singly but in the schoolroom itself.

"Often, Miss O'Riley."

For some unaccountable reason, she blushed.

Pandora chose this moment to demand attention, and he lifted her up into his arms, where she ecstatically began to purr and knead her claws into him.

"You see, Miss O'Riley," he continued, "they represent our future. There can be no higher priority than children."

She found herself inviting him to speak to her class, and he gladly accepted.

As she drove home, and her Camaro left a trail of greenish-yellow leaves dancing in her wake, she acknowledged to herself that she'd just, by that act, set forces in motion—forces that might breach almost any wall she'd built up through the years.

Apprehensive she was, a little. But she sang an old love song over and over all the way home—not realizing until her garage door opened on command just what she'd been singing.

* * *

He came! And the children loved him. He came with a big box of books and sat down on the floor with the children, holding them enthralled by stories that came from those books . . . and the men and women who illustrated them. And he answered each of the many questions they asked; the ones he couldn't, he promised to answer the day their teacher brought them on a field trip to his wildlife sanctuary/bookstore, where they could meet Pandora.

Jennifer pulled back from her usual focal center to give him the opportunity to be in control. She needn't have bothered. She knew now that when he walked into a room, it was as if he were iridescent, for he attracted all eyes just as if he shone like the sun. Just as was true—though she didn't realize it—of herself.

She watched his every move, listened to his every word, and watched the quicksilver moods as they cavorted on his face and danced in his blue-gray eyes—eyes with the impishness of the eternal child in them. Like the legendary Pied Piper of Hamlin, he so enthralled the children that they would have followed him *anywhere*.

And he, though apparently he saw nothing but the children, never missed a nuance of her. The vision she made, leaning against the window, would hang in the galleries of his mind for all time: a Dante Gabriel Rossetti dream woman. Her long bronze hair, ignited by the late morning sun, her emerald green dress, and her seize-the-day face added up to far more than mere beauty.

Before he left, he let each child choose a favorite book—and left the rest for the room library. Then, after reminding them to come see Pandora soon, he was gone . . . and the halcyon day clouded over. But the sun came out again when one curious little boy sneaked to the window and caught sight of Mr. Bond getting into his '57 Thunderbird. His awestruck "Wow!" brought the entire class to the window in seconds, and they all waved—and he, catching the motion at the window, waved back as the coral-sand convertible sped out of sight.

But not out of memory.

Just to make sure, that afternoon a florist delivered a large autumn floral display to the class, crowned by a couple of book-topped spears, and at the very top, a goldish-brown cat.

That night, he called: Did she want to go with him to the Kennedy Center to hear the Vienna Boys' Choir? . . . *Is the pope Catholic?*

Not long after, his second call came, asking her to attend church service with him. After that, the telephone worked both ways. Concerts, the many galleries and exhibits of the Smithsonian, operas; rides to the seashore, to quaint restaurants in old inns; and hikes along mountain trails—all these brought roses to her cheeks and put a glow in her eyes.

After Thanksgiving dinner at her folks', he told her to bundle up for a rather chilly ride. Always, it seemed with him, the top stayed firmly down—he reveled in the 360-degree view. On and on the Bird sped. And as she nestled down, the excitement brimming over in her eyes and her sapphire-blue paisley scarf setting off her flaming mane of hair—well, it made it mighty difficult to keep his eyes on the road.

The population thinned out as the Bird's deep throat rumbled into old St. Mary's City. Here, they stopped by the river for a while, ostensibly to watch the geese, but in reality because he felt reflective.

"You know, Jennifer, I think it's time I told you a little more about my failed marriage."

"That's up to you, Arthur."

"Let's see, how do I start? . . . Well, I had known Marilyn for a number of years; we attended the same parochial high school, same college—even same church. My folks were good friends with her folks—had been for many years. We liked the same things, shared many of the same dreams."

She listened, gazing out at the river.

"Actually," Arthur laughed, a strangely undefinable laugh, "I don't think I ever actually proposed; we just drifted into it. All our friends, our families, our folks, took it for granted. So we married. We loved each other. *That*, I'm sure of. It was to be for life—at least it was for *me*."

There was a long pause as he searched for the right words.

"We were married about eighteen months. Then one never-to-be-forgotten spring morning, after breakfast, she announced that marriage was 'a bore,' 'a drag,' and that she wanted to regain her freedom."

A pause; he continued in a flat voice. "So she divorced me and found someone else—several someone elses. That was about twelve years ago, but it seems like yesterday. . . . Oh, I floundered for a time. My self-esteem was at its all-time low. But God saw me through," he said, visibly brightening. "I escaped to the New England coast—stayed there a long time, healing. It was there that the epiphany came to me: 'Pandora's Books.'"

"Oh!" she breathed, half a sigh, half a paean.

"Yes, a dream bookstore—unlike any I had ever seen or heard about. . . . But the Lord showed me that mere business success would not be enough: I must also care for His sheep. *That* would be my ministry. And the frosting on the cake—"

"Was Pandora," she finished.

"Yes, Pandora." He smiled as he started the engine, and they were again out on the highway, heading south.

I'm so glad he told me! she thought happily as the Bird gathered speed. *He didn't walk out on her! That's what I was afraid of. . . . He had to have been hurt more than I was, yet he didn't let it destroy him. There was closure—a long time ago. And joyously, there's a clear road ahead! O Lord, thank You!* And her heart began to sing.

Then she lost all track of time as the Bird raced down the peninsula, churning up waves of gold, brown, orange, crimson, and green leaves in its wake. Suddenly, there ahead was only a narrow, gray strip of land, banked by white-capped blue waves below and white-winged gulls in the blue sky above. The Bird nosed into a parking space at the end of the road: Route 5, dead-end. Since it was both cold and blustery, they had it all to themselves.

For a few minutes they just sat there, watching and listening to the gulls. She wondered what he was thinking.

Leaning back, his hands behind his head, he finally broke into her reverie. "You know, Jennifer, this is what I miss most. Solitude. The solitude you can still find out west and up north. So many people live here that, after a while, one gets claustrophobic. At least I do. If anything ever moves me away from this bay, it will be that. Well, that and my beloved mountains. I miss them."

Suddenly, he shifted in his seat and laughed. "Am I ever the gabby one today! Enough about me. What about *you?* What is *your* story? Hasn't some armor-clad knight tried to gallop away with you?"

Shyly, she answered, "Y-e-e-s."

"Well, what happened?" he demanded, an impish look in his eyes. "'Fess up! I did my stint, now it's your turn."

So she told him . . . and took awhile doing it.

When she finally finished, he sat in silence awhile, then smiled. "I'm glad. Someday I may tell you why."

"Someday you may, huh?" She laughed, her eyes narrowing.

"You know, Jennifer, your voice has bells in it . . . your laugh, most of all. Even on the phone, I hear bells ringing when you speak. You radiate happiness."

She blushed, started to say something, then stopped.

"Go on," he chuckled. "Might as well get it out."

"Oh!" she said, trying to slow her racing heart. "It's just that I've been happy a lot lately . . . and . . . and"—refusing to meet his eyes—"*you're* to blame."

There! It was out, and her eyes fell, unable to meet his.

Silence thundered in her ears, and when at last she looked up, he was looking out to sea with an enigmatic look on his face. His body had tensed, his face was now rigid. She felt utterly humiliated by her admission.

Then he turned, placed his hand on hers butterfly-briefly, and said, "Well, it's getting late. What do you say to heading back?"

All the way back, she wallowed in misery. *Why did I wreck what had been so perfect? Why change gears when just beginning to gain momentum in the lower one?* Once she caught him eyeing her pensively.

When he walked her to her door, they didn't banter as usual. He didn't ask her for another date, just said in a flat voice, "Thank you, Jennifer, for a perfect Thanksgiving!"

* * *

That was a long, long night for Jennifer. To herself, she wailed, *Stupid me! I've blown it! I took a wonderful friendship, just beginning to bud, and destroyed it. Might just as well have demanded the full-blown rose! But that's just it: I'm in love with him. Been in love with him for a long time—just refused to admit it. He storms me in his quiet, gentle way. I . . . I . . . I've never met anyone before who lights up every room he's in—at least for me. I know it's shameless. But here am I—in my thirties—having never known passion (wondering if I even have it in me!), and now, with this man, I yearn for him, long for him, desire him, with every inch of my body, heart, and soul!*

Her thoughts raced on. *Friendship alone is no longer enough, even if—as is all too obvious!—it is for him. My passionate heart cries for far more. I cannot be merely another in a long line of friendships—perhaps even romances—with him.*

If only, if only, though, I had waited, perhaps it would have come.

Oh why, O Lord, did I do it? O God . . . to find my soul's other half—after all these long years—and then to lose him because of my big mouth!

And she wept through that endless night.

When he called, as usual, to ask her to attend church with him, she turned him down in an icy voice, then cut the conversation short by saying, "I'm sorry . . . but gotta run—I'm late!" and hung up. Then she *was* miserable, for in reality she had nothing else to do at all, and an entire evening to mope about it.

* * *

Jennifer loved the Christmas season, a time when being a child again became an accepted thing. With what joy she always greeted the wreaths and garlands, the multicolored lights on the neighborhood eaves and trees, the Advent candles, the Christmas trees seen through the windows, the Christmas carols played continuously by radio stations. This year, though, she just wished it would go away. Even in her schoolroom. True, she decorated it in the usual way, drilled the children for the big Christmas program, and helped them make personalized gifts for those dearest to them. But it all seemed hollow, all a sham. Even God, she felt, irrationally, had somehow let her down: *Lord, how could You do this to me? How could You let me make such a fool of myself?*

She no longer kidded herself about what Arthur meant to her. Or that he could be but a passing fancy that would go away. No, for better or for worse, he'd be a deep-rooted part of her as long as she lived.

He did not call again. Several times—nay, a hundred times!—she felt the urge to call him and apologize for her curtness on the phone, but her lacerated pride just would not let her.

Her last papers had been corrected and the scores added up, gifts had been accepted from each of her students, and the big program—to which she'd once planned to invite Arthur—had gone off without a hitch . . . yet none of it meant anything to her. Nothing at all.

Finally, it was over for another fall. On a certain exceedingly dismal winter evening, she sat in her undecorated townhouse, wallowing in misery and self-pity, wishing for him, *yearning* for him, and dreading Christmas week.

The phone rang.

She answered it, but no bells rang in her voice, just a subdued "Hello?" Almost she hung up when she heard his voice on the other end, inwardly raging because his voice still possessed this power over her, giving her goose bumps. It just didn't seem fair! But there *was* something different in his voice, almost a pleading note. He had a big favor to ask of her, he said.

"A favor?" she snapped, and then could have choked her misbehaving other self for that snippiness.

Silence swirled around her. Then he continued, more haltingly this time. He had a big favor to ask, yes, but with a qualifier or two thrown in. First of all, he wanted her to share *The Messiah* with him at Washington's National Cathedral, and second, he wanted to show her something of extreme importance.

When the silence on the other end of the line continued, he gulped and added, "If you'll accept just this once, I'll promise not to ever bother you again."

Seeing no graceful way out of it, she grudgingly parted with an under-nourished, "Yes."

There! Finished! That would end it. No comma, no dash, no exclamation mark. Period! Period! Period! But three periods would be an open-ended ellipsis! shouted an irrational thought from a far corner of her brain.

Her mind raced, her thoughts milling in chaotic confusion: *I shouldn't have said yes, that I'd go . . . but I'd hate to miss out on going! I don't think I can handle being close to him again—I'm so sure my face will give me away if my big mouth doesn't. Yet, how can I possibly give up this one last time—the last time we'll ever be together? Oh, it will tear my heart out to be close to him and not be able to touch him! Not to be able . . . Oh! Oh! Yet I don't want him to take anyone else there! Certainly—make that double certainly!—not that Spanish beauty! . . . Oh! What am I gonna wear?*

The big evening (the *last* evening! she promised herself) finally came. She dressed carefully in her favorite blue gown, a Diane Fries she had purchased, in a rare fit of recklessness, from Nordstrom. She'd make it a swan song to remember. Then she put on her heavy black cashmere coat, bought on sale just before I Magnin closed.

The doorbell rang, her pulse quickened. She forced herself to walk very slowly to the door, lest she appear too eager. *Oh, I'm a despicable vixen!* she reprimanded her misbehaving other self.

When she opened it and saw him standing there, in spite of her well-planned intentions, emerald stars sparkled in her eyes and her cheeks crimsoned. For he was so . . . so . . . so detestably dear.

At the curb, its motor purring, was a car she had not seen before, a Mercedes 560, in color a suspiciously emerald sort of green.

"Wouldn't dare park the Bird in D.C.," was his only explanation.

Outside the window, the white of the first snowfall of the year enveloped the world. Christmas CDs played softly through the sophisticated sound system, and she relaxed a little in spite of herself.

Neither said much during the ride to the cathedral.

They had a tough time finding a parking space, but finally did, then joined the well-dressed throng filling the streets. Excitement flooded Jennifer's cheeks, and once or twice she trembled as Arthur's hand brushed hers.

Inside the world's sixth-largest cathedral, all was Christmas, and Arthur moved, with Jennifer just behind him, toward the nave. He took her hand now to keep her close. Eventually, they arrived at the spot where he felt the acoustics to be nearly perfect, and they found a pillar on which to lean, for the seats were all taken.

Then the organ found its voice, shaking the near-century-in-the-making building. Chills went up Jennifer's spine. Pipe organs had that power over her. She sneaked a sideways glance at Arthur and felt satisfied by the look of awe on his face. Then the orchestra, then the soloists, then the choirs, and then she lost all track of time as Handel transported her through the drama of the ages.

Through it all, she remained aware of him, but in a sort of haze. He left once and brought back two chairs; she sank down with a sigh of relief. After a couple of hours, unconsciously declaring a temporary truce, she took advantage of his tall frame next to her and leaned her head against him. She felt him tremble when a draft of cold air blew a strand of her flame-colored hair across his face.

Soaring upward, her soul drank deeply of the majesty of the mighty columns and graceful arches that portrayed the architectural yearning for the Eternal. The words and music and organ and choirs and soloists and cathedral battered her sensibilities into a pulp. It was too much of a sensory overload for mere flesh and blood. During the "Hallelujah Chorus," as she stood at his side, she again felt him tremble; peeping sideways, she found him wiping away tears. Since she was crying too, she felt a renewed sense of kinship with him.

The crowd was unbelievably quiet as they found their way out—almost as if words seemed far too fragile to accommodate such divine freight.

On the slippery road again, neither spoke, and the sound system remained silent, as if anything else right now would be anticlimactic. For this she inwardly thanked him, for his sensitivity and empathy, for not shattering the mood.

So surreal was it all that she didn't even notice they had passed her highway exit until the Mercedes veered off Highway 50 onto Riva Road. To her raised eyebrows, he merely smiled and said, "Remember, there's more yet to this promised evening."

As the traffic thinned out south of Annapolis and the flocked evergreens flashed by, slowly, haltingly, he began to speak.

"Undoubtedly . . . you . . . you . . . uh . . . wondered about my strange response to your, uh, to what you said about yourself . . . the last time we were together."

She stiffened. *How dare he bring up that utterly humiliating afternoon when he rejected my stupid disclosure of my inner feelings. How* dare *he!*

But he plowed on, not looking at her. "You see, Jen"—he'd never called her by her family pet name before!—"I was so wounded, so scarred, by the rejection I told you about . . . that I determined that never again"—here he struggled for control, then continued—"never again would I let a woman get that close to me."

He paused, and she hardly dared breathe.

"But it's been hard, Jen, because I'm still young . . . and lonely. It's been very hard."

Inadvertently, her lesser self got in another lick. "The beautiful black-haired girl who works for you?"

He almost hit a tree, but when he turned toward her, his face had relaxed just a little. "How did you know?"

"I have eyes. Any woman could have told you."

There was a long silence as he searched for the right words. Finally, as if he had given up finding any better ones, the refrain again: "It's been hard." But he did not tell her that it was the Spanish beauty's lack of tenderness, her repulsing of the little crying boy, that had turned the tide of his life.

Neither did he tell her about the effect *she* had made on him that same day: a Raphael madonna tenderly holding a child.

After a time, he continued. "You see, Jen, I could not take such rejection twice in one lifetime. I'm afraid it would . . . uh . . . destroy me!" He paused again. "Marriage for me is for life—even if our society seems to disagree with me." Here his words seemed sadly bitter to the wondering woman at his side. "And marriage without God to cement it is a dead-end! I don't see how any marriage can last a lifetime without a Higher Power to anchor it. All around me I see marriage after marriage, live-in relationships galore, collapse, so few making it through. I have been afraid. I'm not ashamed to admit it, Jen. I've been terribly afraid to even consider marriage again!"

She remained silent, numb.

"As for children and what divorce or separation does to them . . . There are simply no words in the dictionary terrible enough to fully describe what it does to them, to their feelings of self-worth. I see it every day. And I don't yet know what to do, what to say, to their anguish—anguish so intense it's long since wrung out all the tears they can cry."

And she, remembering those lonely, deep-scarred wounded ones in her classes, could only nod her head.

"And then *you* came," he added, groping for the right words. "You scared me."

He caught her whispered, *"Scared?"*

"Yes . . . scared. For you were, well, what I never had, yet had always wanted. In a way, too good to be true. Jen, I never expected to find such a woman as you. So, when you told me last Thanksgiving that I . . . that I made you happy, like an absolute fool, I panicked! I had blocked such a future out of the realm of the possible for so many years that when it came, I just . . . just didn't know how—"

Suddenly, he slowed and turned down a familiar road, now a fairyland in snow. Her heart began to thud so loudly that she felt certain he must hear it. Then he turned down a road she had never noticed before and made a long, wide turn. Suddenly, directly ahead, in a blaze of holiday lights, stood Pandora's Books. It was so beautiful that her lips formed an O and her hands flew to her face. She didn't see his relieved smile.

Inside, festive music played in every room, only all the same track this time. Christmas decorations were everywhere, as were lights and trees of various sizes.

"I've always loved Christmas—kinda never grew up," he said simply.

Unconsciously, she groped for his hand.

He showed her each room, and her delighted response and the restored bells in her voice were all he could have hoped for. Finally, they came back to the office area and he stepped briefly behind the counter, where he must have flicked a switch, for suddenly silence shattered the mood, and she was alone with him in the big building.

He walked back to her, and she raised her emerald eyes to his, seeking something that had not been there before. Suddenly, she heard music again—froze for a moment—and whispered, *"Étude in E."*

"Yes."

"Why, Arthur? I don't understand what you're trying to—"

Softly placing his finger on her lips, he whispered, "Listen!"

She listened. And as she knew it would—it always had—it melted her. And as she knew she would—she always had—she cried.

Fire blazed through her tears, and she accused, "How could you! You *know* how that affects me. I saw you watching me that day."

Know? Yes, he knew. *She's right. It's come. . . . It's all come down to this question, this moment,* he thought. *I hurt her terribly by my inexcusable fear of commitment. And now I must answer. But one thing is certain: This is no time for halfhearted measures. Words . . . words can be such inadequate things! How can I make her know?*

Gathering her in his arms, he answered softly, "I just *had* to, dear . . . dearest."

Her wounded pride struggled to assert itself. *How dare he assume I'd forgive him this easily for the pain he's put me through—how dare he!*

In the end, her pride lost. Gentle he remained, but as immovable as Gibraltar. The étude was on his side, too—it was two against one. She felt

her resistance ebbing. Then she made the mistake of trying to read the expression on his face—not easy, considering the dim light in the room. But what she saw there closed forever all avenues of escape. It was love. Love undiluted, unqualified, undistilled, unreserved, undivided—he had cleared the deck of his heart of everything else but *her*.

Her struggles ceased, and all the lights of the world came on in her eyes as her arms stole up and closed behind his neck. Then it was, as the shackles of fear and regret fell clanging to the floor, that he started to tell her in mere words how much he loved her, but she, cutting his words off with her lips, showed him a better way. A far better way.

Some time later, Arthur sensed a familiar presence at his ankles. Looking down, but not releasing Jennifer from the prison of his arms by so much as one link, he smiled and said, "Sorry, Pandora, you jealous ol' thing. From now on, you're just gonna have to share!"

Afterword

Unbeknownst to me, I've been preparing to write this story all my life. Each of the thousands of used-book stores I've known—many that I've loved—represent the gestation period. Also part of the mix is Annapolis's Haunted Bookstore, with Mike the big tabby cat, who undisputedly ruled its premises. Occasionally, he could even be found sleeping in the streetside display window! Sadly, due to the escalation of the rent, Mike and that wonderful bookstore no longer grace Maryland's capital city. And there is some of Christopher Morley's wonderful book *The Haunted Bookshop* stirred in as well. Actually, the story represents a synthesis of my own dream bookstore, had I only the money and time to make it happen.

Étude in E has been called by many "the most beautiful étude ever composed." Chopin dedicated it to his dear friend Franz Liszt, and it remained Chopin's personal favorite of all his own études. Norman Luboff recorded it, in perhaps as romantic a recording as has ever been made, in his Norman Luboff Choir *Reverie*.

The deeply wounded Jennifer and Arthur—each of us knows them personally, for they represent a far too large part of our "love 'em, leave 'em, and never count the cost" society.

As for Pandora, in real life she *is* Pandora, the pampered Himalayan who has ruled our book-laden house for almost thirteen years now. Life without that furry presence, that constant companion, that flopper-against-me every time I sit or lie down—or try to write something worth reading!—is too unthinkable to even consider. But always, in this story, she will live on.

About the Contributors

Frank R. Adams wrote during the first quarter of the twentieth century. Nothing is known of him today.

Mary Brownley wrote biography shorts and works of fiction for family magazines during the first third of the twentieth century.

Anton Pavlovich Chekhov (1860–1904) is considered to be the greatest Russian writer after Tolstoy. His plays—such as *The Seagull* (1896), *Uncle Vanya* (1899), *The Three Sisters* (1901), and *The Cherry Orchard* (1904)—continue to be performed around the world. Many consider Chekhov to be the greatest short-story writer who ever lived, his only competitor for the title being the French writer Guy de Maupassant. Chekhov's stories are remarkable for their pathos and irony and for his ever-present theme: the loneliness of the human soul.

Melcena Burns Denny wrote for magazines such as *The Youth's Companion* during the first quarter of the twentieth century.

Annie Hamilton Donnell (1862–?), early in the twentieth century, was one of the most beloved writers in America. Besides writing prolifically for family and inspirational magazines, she also wrote numerous novels, including *Meeting Cousin Agatha* (1898), *Rebecca Mary* (1905), *The Very Small Person* (1906), *Glory and the Other Girl* (1907), and *Miss Theodosia's Heartstrings* (1916).

Sharon A. Dunsmore writes and lectures from her home in Smiths Creek, Michigan.

Edna Geister wrote numerous stories, editorials, and essays, which were published in family magazines during the first third of the twentieth century. Among her books are *Geister Games, Ice-Breakers and the Ice-Breaker Herself,* and *The Fun Book.*

Arthur Gordon (1912–) still lives and writes on his natal seacoast near Savannah, Georgia. During his long and memorable career, he edited such renowned magazines as *Good Housekeeping, Cosmopolitan,* and *Guideposts.* He is the author of a number of books, including *Reprisal* (1950), *Norman Vincent Peale: Minister to Millions* (1958), *A Touch of Wonder* (1974), *Through Many Windows* (1983), and *Return to Wonder* (1996), as well as several hundred short stories.

Elizabeth Goudge (1900–1984) is one of the most beloved inspirational writers of our time. Her writings sensitively evoke the English countryside, English history, and the world of children. She is among the most quotable of all modern writers, her phrases and sentences ringing out with power and beauty. Among her most popular novels are *City of Bells* (1936), *Towers in the Mist* (1938), *Green Dolphin Street* (1944), *Gentian Hill* (1949), *The Dean's Watch* (1960), and *A Scent of Water* (1963).

Mrs. **O. M. Hatch** wrote about a century ago. I have never been able to find out anything about her life.

Mae Foster Jay wrote for family magazines during the first third of the twentieth century.

Archie Joscelyn (1899–?), of Great Falls, Montana, was one of the most prolific Western writers of all time, writing also as A. A. Archer, Al Cody, Tex Holt, Evelyn McKenna, and Lynn Westland. His books continued to be published into the 1980s.

C. G. Kent wrote for family magazines during the early part of the twentieth century.

Rudyard Kipling (1865–1936), born in Bombay, India, became the most famous English writer of his age and was the first Englishman to receive the Nobel Prize for Literature. Besides writing some of the most memorable poetry of his time, he also wrote novels such as *The Jungle Book, Captains Courageous*, and *Kim*.

Indiana-born **Harry Harrison Kroll** (1888–?), besides being a linguist, was the author of several books, including *The Cabin in the Cotton* (1931), *Lost Homecoming* (1950), and *Riders in the Night* (1965). He also wrote many short stories.

R. Lovewell wrote stories for the family during the first quarter of the twentieth century.

Ruby Holmes Martyn wrote for family magazines around the turn of the twentieth century.

Mabel McKee, early in the twentieth century, was responsible for some of the most memorable inspirational literature in print. Sadly, little is known about her today.

Arthur A. Milward, printer and freelance writer, lived in England and California before moving to Pennsylvania, where he retired. Many of his stories have been carried by *Reader's Digest*.

P. J. Platz is a successful mother/daughter writing team who live in Chisago City, Minnesota. They are prolific writers of short stories as well as movie scripts, and their work shows up in many women's and family magazines.

Penny Porter, author of *Heartstrings and Tail-Tuggers* (Ravenhawk Books, 1999), has had many of her nature stories published by *Reader's Digest*. Mrs. Porter lives in Tucson, Arizona.

Grace S. Richmond (1866–1959) was born in Pawtucket, Rhode Island, and lived most of her life in Fredonia, New York. Not only were her many short stories and serializations published in the top women's magazines of her time, but she also was one of the most popular and highest paid novelists of the first half of the twentieth century. Among her best-selling books are *The Indifference of Juliet* (1905), *The Second Violin* (1906), *Red Pepper Burns* (1910), *The Twenty-fourth of June* (1914), *Foursquare* (1922), *The Listening Post* (1929), and *Bachelor's Bounty* (1932).

Margaret E. Sangster, Jr. (1894–1981), granddaughter of the equally illustrious Margaret E. Sangster, Sr. (1838–1912), was born in Brooklyn, New York. Editor, scriptwriter, journalist, short-story writer, and novelist, she was one of the best-known writers of the early part of the twentieth century. She served as correspondent and columnist for *Christian Herald Magazine* and was the author of *Cross Roads* (1919), *The Island of Faith* (1921), *The Stars Come Close* (1936), and *Singing on the Road* (1936).

Walter R. Schmidt wrote for family magazines during the first third of the twentieth century.

Earl Reed Silvers (1891–1948), besides being an English professor at Rutgers University, director of Rutgers University Press, and editor of the *Rutgers Alumni Monthly*, was a prolific writer of stories and books for young people, especially boys and young men.

Harriet Lummis Smith (?–1947), born in Auburndale, Massachusetts, was a prolific writer of inspirational and value-based stories early in the twentieth century. She is the author of several novels, including *Other People's Business* (1916), the three books in the Peggy Raymond series, and the last four books in the Pollyanna series (1924–1929); she also wrote numerous short stories.

Delia Morris Stephenson wrote for Christian magazines during the first third of the twentieth century.

Josephine DeFord Terrill wrote prolifically for Christian and family magazines early in the twentieth century. Today, virtually nothing is known about her.

G. E. Wallace's niche was unique: stories dealing with that intangible line between success and failure, in terms of both career and lifestyle. Little is known about him (or her) as a person or writer.

Mary Wells wrote for magazines such as *The Youth's Companion* around the turn of the twentieth century.

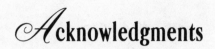 Acknowledgments

"Three Thousand Miles from Home," by Frank R. Adams. Published in *Redbook Magazine,* October 1918, and abridged by *Reader's Digest* in November 1942. The text used is that of the original of 1918.

"Nearest His Heart," by Josephine DeFord Terrill. Published in *The Youth's Instructor,* November 10, 1931. Reprinted by permission of Joe L. Wheeler, P.O. Box 1246, Conifer, CO 80433, and Review and Herald® Publishing Association, Hagerstown, MD 21740.

"Family Ties," by P. J. Platz. Reprinted by permission of Tracy and Patricia Lambrecht.

"The Leaf That Mother Turned," by Annie Hamilton Donnell. Published in *The Youth's Instructor,* January 8, 1924. Reprinted by permission of Joe L. Wheeler, P.O. Box 1246, Conifer, CO 80433, and Review and Herald® Publishing Association, Hagerstown, MD 21740.

"Love on the Wing," by Penny Porter. Condensed in *Reader's Digest,* September 1997; also appeared in Porter's book *Heartstrings and Tail-Tuggers* (n.c. [private printing]: Ravenhawk Books, 1999). Reprinted by permission of the author.

"Ransom's Papers," by Mary Wells. Published in *The Youth's Companion,* May 25, 1911.

"The Message of the Orchid," by Harriet Lummis Smith. Published in *The Young People's Weekly,* February 11, 1931. Reprinted by permission of Joe L. Wheeler, P.O. Box 1246, Conifer, CO 80433, and Cook Communications Ministries, Colorado Springs, CO 80918.

"A Promise and a Ski Run." Author unknown. If anyone can provide knowledge of the author and the earliest publication place and date of this story, please relay this information to Joe Wheeler, c/o Focus on the Family.

"Something of Father's," by C. G. Kent. If anyone can provide knowledge of the earliest publication place and date of this story, please relay this information to Joe Wheeler, c/o Focus on the Family.

"How We April-Fooled Aunt Patty," by Mrs. O. M. Hatch. Published in *The Youth's Instructor*, April 2, 1918. Reprinted by permission of Joe L. Wheeler, P.O. Box 1246, Conifer, CO 80433, and Review and Herald® Publishing Association, Hagerstown, MD 21740.

"The Song of Songs," by Mabel McKee. Published in *The Youth's Instructor*, April 28, 1931. Reprinted by permission of Fleming H. Revell, a division of Baker Book House, Grand Rapids, Michigan; and Review and Herald® Publishing Association, Hagerstown, Maryland.

"The Marshaling of the Maples," by G. E. Wallace. Published in Review and Herald's *The Youth's Instructor*, May 12, 1942, and in *The Red Letter Day*, 1942. Reprinted by permission of Joe L. Wheeler, P.O. Box 1246, Conifer, CO 80433, and Review and Herald® Publishing Association, Hagerstown, MD 21740.

"Dawn Comes to Dr. Faris," by Archie Joscelyn. Published in *The Young People's Weekly*, March 10, 1934. Reprinted by permission of Joe L. Wheeler, P.O. Box 1246, Conifer, CO 80433, and Cook Communications Ministries, Colorado Springs, CO 80918.

"Rikki-tikki-tavi," by Rudyard Kipling. Excerpted from Kipling's *The Jungle Book* (1894, 1895).

"That Frivolous Gold Digger," by Delia Morris Stephenson. Published in *The Young People's Weekly*, September 10, 1932. Reprinted by permission of Joe L. Wheeler, P.O. Box 1246, Conifer, CO 80433, and Cook Communications Ministries, Colorado Springs, CO 80918.

"The Unmousing of Jean," by Edna Geister. Published in *The Young People's Weekly*, February 4, 1933. Reprinted by permission of Joe L. Wheeler, P.O. Box 1246, Conifer, CO 80433, and Cook Communications Ministries, Colorado Springs, CO 80918.

"The Jonah Pie," by Ruby Holmes Martyn. Published in *The Youth's Instructor*, April 13, 1918. Reprinted by permission of Joe L. Wheeler, P.O. Box 1246, Conifer, CO 80433, and Review and Herald® Publishing Association, Hagerstown, MD 21740.

"An Hour of Victory," by Earl Reed Silvers. Published in *The Young People's Weekly*, June 17, 1934. Reprinted by permission of Joe L. Wheeler, P.O. Box 1246, Conifer, CO 80433, and Cook Communications Ministries, Colorado Springs, CO 80918.

"Shop Around Awhile," by Mae Foster Jay. Published in *The Young People's Weekly*, January 21, 1933. Reprinted by permission of Joe L. Wheeler, P.O. Box 1246, Conifer, CO 80433, and Cook Communications Ministries, Colorado Springs, CO 80918.

"A Case of Need." Author unknown. If anyone can provide knowledge of the author and the earliest publication place and date of this story, please relay this information to Joe Wheeler, c/o Focus on the Family.

"Tiny Tim," by Sharon A. Dunsmore. Published in *Focus on the Family Magazine*, April 1996. Winner of the Evangelical Press Association's First Place (First Person Article) Award in 1996. Reprinted by permission of the author.

"The Boy Who Couldn't Be Saved." Author unknown. If anyone can provide knowledge of the author and the earliest publication place and date of this story, please relay this information to Joe Wheeler, c/o Focus on the Family.

"Old Mount Gilead," by Harry Harrison Kroll. Published in *The Young People's Weekly*, July 15, 1933. Reprinted by permission of Joe L. Wheeler, P.O. Box 1246, Conifer, CO 80433, and Cook Communications Ministries, Colorado Springs, CO 80918.

"Lob-Lie-by-the-Fire," by Elizabeth Goudge. Published in *The Woman's Home Companion*, August 1940; the story was illustrated in color by Norman Rockwell. Reprinted by permission of Harold Ober Associates, Inc.

"The Lady with the Lamp," by Mary Brownley. Published in *The Youth's Instructor*, May 12, 1925. Reprinted by permission of Joe L. Wheeler, P.O. Box 1246, Conifer, CO 80433, and Review and Herald® Publishing Association, Hagerstown, MD 21740.

"Pavane for a Princess," by Arthur A. Milward. Reprinted by permission of the author.

"Number Nine Schoolhouse," by R. Lovewell. If anyone can provide knowledge of the earliest publication place and date of this story, please relay this information to Joe Wheeler, c/o Focus on the Family.

"The Show Must Go On." Author unknown. If anyone can provide knowledge of the author and the earliest publication place and date of this story, please relay this information to Joe Wheeler, c/o Focus on the Family.

"The Bet," by Anton Pavlovich Chekhov. This translation appears unacknowledged in H. C. Schweikert's *Short Stories* (New York: Harcourt, Brace, and Company, 1925); apparently, it was translated by Constance Garnett in London during the years 1916 to 1922. Referred to in Avrahm Yarmolinsky's *The Portable Chekhov* (New York: The Viking Press, 1947, 1975).

"Lawrence Thorne, Junior," by Grace S. Richmond. Published in *The Youth's Companion*, August 9, 1900.

"Answers at Nightfall," by Arthur Gordon. Published in Gordon's *A Touch of Wonder* (Old Tappan, N.J.: Fleming H. Revell, 1974). Reprinted by permission of the author.

"Between Strokes," by Walter R. Schmidt. Published in *The Young People's Weekly*, April 30, 1932. Reprinted by permission of Joe L. Wheeler, P.O. Box 1246, Conifer, CO 80433, and Cook Communications Ministries, Colorado Springs, CO 80918.

"The Hanging Lamp," by Melcena Burns Denny. Published in *The Youth's Companion*, December 30, 1926. The earliest publication of this story is not known.

"Harvest Home Harmony," by Margaret E. Sangster, Jr. Published in *The Young People's Weekly*, November 25, 1933. Reprinted by permission of Joe L. Wheeler, P.O. Box 1246, Conifer, CO 80433, and Cook Communications Ministries, Colorado Springs, CO 80918.

"Pandora's Books," by Joseph Leininger Wheeler. Copyright © 1997. Reprinted by permission of the author.

About the Editor

Joseph Leininger Wheeler's earliest memories have to do with books and stories—more specifically, of listening to his mother read aloud both in public and to him at home. Wheeler recalls that, as soon as he was able to read, he followed his mother around the house, relentlessly reading his storybooks to her.

Shortly after Wheeler turned eight, his parents moved from California to Latin America as missionaries. From the third through the tenth grade, he was home-schooled by his mother. Of those years, he says today, "I was incredibly lucky and blessed. My mother, a trained teacher and elocutionist, was a voracious reader of books worth reading and had memorized thousands of pages of readings, poetry, and stories. All of that she poured into me. Wherever we went, she encouraged me to devour entire libraries."

At 16, Wheeler returned to California to complete his high school years at Monterey Bay Academy near Santa Cruz. Because of his inherited love of the printed word, Wheeler majored in history at Pacific Union College in the Napa Valley, completing both bachelor's and master's degrees there. After completing a master's in English at California State University in Sacramento, Wheeler attended Vanderbilt University, where he obtained a Ph.D. in English.

Today, after 34 years of teaching at the adult education, college, high school, and junior high levels, Wheeler is Professor Emeritus at Columbia Union College in Takoma Park, Maryland. The world's foremost authority on frontier writer Zane Grey, Wheeler is also the founder and executive director of Zane Grey's West Society and Senior Fellow for Cultural Studies at the Center for the New West in Denver, Colorado. He is editor/compiler of the popular *Christmas in My Heart* series (Review & Herald, Focus on the Family, and Tyndale House), *Christmas in My Soul* series (Doubleday/Random House), *Great Stories* series (Focus on the Family and Tyndal House), *Heart to Heart* series (Tyndale House and Focus on the Family), *Stories of Angels* (Guideposts), and *Easter in My Heart* (WaterBrook/Random House.) Along the way, Wheeler has established nine libraries in schools and colleges, as well as building up his own collection (as large as some college libraries).

Joe Wheeler and his wife, Connie, are the parents of two grown children, Greg and Michelle, and now make their home in Conifer, Colorado.

Photo by Joel Springer

IF YOU LIKED *GREAT STORIES REMEMBERED III*, YOU'LL LOVE THE OTHER BOOKS FROM FOCUS ON THE FAMILY'S® "GREAT STORIES" COLLECTION!

The Best of Times

There was a time when stories were read aloud, remembered and passed on.
Now, discovered tales from the golden age of story writing have been
woven into one heartwarming collection: *The Best of Times*.
These beautifully crafted stories honor the virtues we all hold dear:
love, courage, loyalty and sacrifice.

Freckles

An orphaned young man called Freckles arrives at a logging camp looking for
work, though he has just one hand. While seeking answers to his
mysterious past, he soon falls in love with the forest—and a beautiful girl.

Ben-Hur

In an unforgettable account of betrayal, revenge, and rebellion,
a nobleman learns the grace of God when he falls from Roman
favor and is sentenced to life as a slave.

Little Women

Despite the Civil War, four sisters discover the importance of family
and manage to keep laughter and love in their hearts—even through
illness and poverty, disappointment and sacrifice.

Heart to Heart: Stories of Friendship

This engaging short story collection, *Heart to Heart: Stories of Friendship*,
celebrates the richness friendships bring to our lives. For anyone
who has known the special bond friends share, these moving stories
will bring back fond memories and remind us to treasure
the friends we hold close to our hearts.

Anne of Green Gables

When Matthew goes to the train station to pick up a boy sent from an orphanage, he discovers a *girl* has been sent instead! Not having the heart to disappoint her, he agrees to take her home, and their lives are changed forever.

A Christmas Carol

When the miserly Scrooge retires for the day on Christmas Eve, he is visited by the ghost of his long-dead partner who warns him of what surely will be if he doesn't change his stingy ways.

The Christmas Angel

After throwing all the reminders of her childhood away, Miss Terry decides to keep the Christmas Angel, after all. When the angel comes to life, it reminds the bitter, lonely woman of a family's value and the joy of reconciliation.

The Twenty-fourth of June

Grace Richmond's *The Twenty-fourth of June* is rich with romance, suspense and a deep love for the home. To prove himself worthy to Roberta, Richard Kendrick undertakes the greatest challenge of his life—one that makes this novel almost impossible to put down.

Quo Vadis

Vinicius was an unbeliever, Ligia was a Christian. Brought together during Emperor Nero's reign of terror, whose world would survive? *Quo Vadis* vividly captures the madness and suspense of an unforgettable era in history—and the faith of Christians that could not be denied.

• • •

Call 1-800-A-FAMILY or write to us at Focus on the Family, Colorado Springs, CO 80995. In Canada, call 1-800-661-9800 or write to Focus on the Family, P.O. Box 9800, Stn. Terminal, Vancouver, B.C. V6B 4G3. Or, visit your local Christian bookstore!

FOCUS ON THE FAMILY®

Welcome to the Family!

Whether you received this book as a gift, borrowed it from a friend, or purchased it yourself, we're glad you read it! It's just one of the many helpful, insightful, and encouraging resources produced by Focus on the Family.

In fact, that's what Focus on the Family is all about—providing inspiration, information, and biblically based advice to people in all stages of life.

It began in 1977 with the vision of one man, Dr. James Dobson, a licensed psychologist and author of 16 best-selling books on marriage, parenting, and family. Alarmed by the societal, political, and economic pressures that were threatening the existence of the American family, Dr. Dobson founded Focus on the Family with one employee—an assistant—and a once-a-week radio broadcast, aired on only 36 stations.

Now an international organization, Focus on the Family is dedicated to preserving Judeo-Christian values and strengthening the family through more than 70 different ministries, including eight separate daily radio broadcasts; television public service announcements; 11 publications; and a steady series of award-winning books, films, and videos for people of all ages and interests.

Recognizing the needs of, as well as the sacrifices and important contribution made by, such diverse groups as educators, physicians, attorneys, crisis pregnancy center staff, and single parents, Focus on the Family offers specific outreaches to uphold and minister to these individuals, too. And it's all done for one purpose, and one purpose only: to encourage and strengthen individuals and families through the life-changing message of Jesus Christ.

• • •

For more information about the ministry, or if we can be of help to your family, simply write to Focus on the Family, Colorado Springs, CO 80995 or call 1-800-A-FAMILY (1-800-232-6459). Friends in Canada may write Focus on the Family, P.O. Box 9800, Stn. Terminal, Vancouver, B.C. V6B 4G3 or call 1-800-661-9800. Visit our Web site—www.family.org— to learn more about the ministry or to find out if there is a Focus on the Family office in your country.

We'd love to hear from you!